Praise for Denzil Meyrick and t

'F... ... ...ates a ... ...
to conventional "tartan noir" thrillers. This is a crime
setting far from smoky pubs and the bookies' shops
of the average city'
The Times

'Universal truths . . . an unbuttoned sense
of humour . . . engaging and eventful'
The Wall Street Journal

'A compelling lead . . . satisfyingly twisted plot'
Publishers Weekly

'This new DCI Daley thriller brings the strongest elements
of Meyrick's storytelling together to make his latest novel
a page-turner with convincing plot, an atmospheric setting
and trademark dark humour'
Dundee Courier on *Well of the Winds*

'Striking characters and shifting plots vibrate with energy'
The Library Journal

'Compelling new Scottish crime'
The Strand Magazine

'If you like Rankin, MacBride and Oswald, you'll love Meyrick'
The Sunday Mail

'S.....d'. b... ... ...'

800 657 277

'Touches of dark humour, multi-layered and compelling'
Daily Record

'The right amount of authenticity . . .
gritty writing . . . most memorable'
The Herald

'Meyrick's portrayal of island – and rural – Scottish life
is well drawn'
The Scotsman

'All three books have a strong sense of place, of city cops
trying to fit in to a small, tightly-knit rural environment'
Russell Leadbetter, *Evening Times*

'Meyrick has the ability to give even the least important
person in the plot character and the skill to tell a good tale'
Scots Magazine

'Following in the tradition of great Scottish crime
writers, Denzil Meyrick has turned out a cracking,
tenacious thriller of a read. If you favour the
authentic and credible, you are in safe hands'
Lovereading

'DCI Daley is shaping up to be the West Coast's
answer to Edinburgh's Rebus'
Scottish Home and Country

A note on the author

Denzil Meyrick was born in Glasgow and brought up in Campbeltown. After studying politics, he pursued a varied career including time spent as a police officer, freelance journalist, and director of several companies in the leisure, engineering and marketing sectors. Previous novels in the best-selling DCI Daley thriller series are *Whisky from Small Glasses*, *The Last Witness*, *Dark Suits and Sad Songs*, *The Rat Stone Serenade* and *Well of the Winds*. Denzil lives on Loch Lomond side with his wife Fiona.

ONE LAST DRAM BEFORE MIDNIGHT

THE COMPLETE DCI DALEY SHORT STORIES

Denzil Meyrick

This anthology first published in Great Britain in 2017 by Polygon,
an imprint of Birlinn Ltd.

Birlinn Ltd
West Newington House
10 Newington Road
Edinburgh
EH9 1QS
www.polygonbooks.co.uk

ISBN 978 1 84697 378 9
eBook ISBN 978 0 85790 936 7

British Library Cataloguing-in-Publication Data
A catalogue record for this book is available on request from the British Library.

Typeset by 3btype.com

CONTENTS

To the other wee boys who caught the taxi to school in Dalintober, every day, long, long ago.

DALINTOBER MOON

A DCI Daley Short Story

Thankfully the rain had stopped, but the wind raged on as Daley and a handful of others gazed down at the hole in the sodden sand. Even though it was mid-morning, the dark sky seemed to hang low over the tiny beach, sucking the light from the day.

Once a separate village in its own right, Dalintober had been eaten up by Kinloch over the years, and now formed the town's northern shore. Its inhabitants, though, still thought of themselves as apart from the rest of the community; and many were descendents of the old fishing settlement's population. For them, Kinloch was the interloper.

'Yes, well, I think we can say that judging by the nature of the remains this isn't a recent burial, Chief Inspector,' said the young doctor McLaren. 'We'll have to get your forensic boys to get it out of there and send it up the road for more rigorous testing, but from this initial examination I'd say the body's been here for decades, if not longer.'

Daley stared down at the skeleton, the skull of which was angled forward, leaning on the bony knees. It appeared to be staring up at him. The remains were contained within a large black barrel, and in remarkable condition given the time they might have spent buried in the sand of Dalintober beach.

'The SOCO boys are on their way,' said Daley. 'Should be here within the hour. We'll need to get the body and the barrel out of the sand before the tide turns, but they're bringing the right kit they tell me, so all the better.'

'It's a sherry butt,' said council workman Anderson, the fluorescent orange of his jacket bright in the November gloom.

'What?' said Daley.

'Type of barrel, Mr Daley. I used to work in the distillery, and these are the big casks they buy from Spain tae fill with whisky. All the best stuff comes oot o' a fresh sherry cask. Aye, and you pay for it, tae. They'd never have fitted the poor bastard in a hoggy.'

It was clear that the body had been crammed into the cask then buried deep in the sand. Only the exceptional severity of the storms that had lashed Kinloch for the last four days had managed to strip away layers of sand and expose the white bones of the corpse. Remnants of blackened cloth lay at the feet of the skeleton, save for one piece attached to a buckle, which had rusted to the bones of the right shoulder. The top of the whisky cask had rotted away, exposing its gristly contents.

Daley contemplated the skull's rictus grin. Even if this unfortunate individual was indeed from an earlier time, this was obviously a crime; one side of the skull appeared to have been smashed by some blunt force. He watched as the doctor examined it further. As far as he was aware, there was no tradition of such burials in Kinloch, though, in the town he now called home, anything was possible.

As he ruminated on this most baffling problem, the shrill voice of a woman could be heard on the wind.

'Let me through!' she shouted at the uniformed cops who were trying to hold her back. 'Jeest get yer hands off me this meenit!' Her tone changed to one of pleading. 'I might be able tae help you here.'

As Daley stood up, his knees clicked and popped, and he grimaced in response. 'OK, lads, let her through.' Now unhindered, the elderly woman, dressed in a bulky waterproof jacket, made her way to the hole in the ground. Without a word to Daley or anybody else, she put her face in her hands and began to wail, 'Grampa Billy! Efter all this time, Grampa Billy!'

II

'Please take a seat, Mrs Hutchinson,' said Daley, glad to be out of the biting wind on Dalintober beach. Across from him sat the old lady who had cried when she saw the skeleton in the barrel. She was quiet now, with a look of great sadness on her face.

'I'm sorry I made such a fuss jeest there, Inspector.' She took a gulp of the warm tea Daley had given her. 'I just didna expect tae find oot the truth in my lifetime, that's all.'

'The truth?'

'Of whoot happened tae my grampa Billy, Mr Daley. I don't think any o' the family ever thought we'd find out what that brute McMunn did tae him.'

'McMunn? I'm afraid I'm a bit lost, Mrs Hutchinson. Can you tell me from the start, please?'

'Aye, jeest so, Mr Daley, jeest so,' she said, taking a sip of her tea and settling back in the chair. 'My faither was jeest a wee boy when it happened. Nineteen ten it was, before the Great War, ye understand.'

Daley nodded as the woman spoke. Her expression was blank, as though she was seeing pictures in her mind's eye.

'My grampa Billy worked at Wellside Distillery – long gone noo, mind, but a thriving business at the time. Och well, apparently he was a good-looking lad – curly hair, blue eyes – and folk often said that my faither was his spitting image. A nice young man, full of fun, and only twenty-three when it happened.'

'When what happened?'

'Him and Archie McMunn were on the nightshift. Archie was a wee bit older than my grampa, no' much, mebbees in his late twenties. He'd been in the army for a wee while, but it didna suit him – well, mair like he didna suit it, I wid say.'

'Why was that, do you know, Mrs Hutchinson?'

'Och, at the time everybody knew whoot Archie was like. A brutal man, Mr Daley, cruel, wid fight with his own shadow, or so they said. He had a lovely wee wife, gied her a hell o' a time, apparently. Didna stop there, neithers. He was jeest as cruel tae the folk he worked with. His uncle was the distillery manager, so he got the job as foreman. If you didna dae as you were telt, well, you suffered the consequences. He had a right spite at my grampa Billy for some reason, tae. Poor Grampa would come home black and blue from his work, regular, so my faither said.'

'Didn't he complain?'

'Whoot was the point? With McMunn's uncle the boss, who would have listened?'

'True, I suppose,' said Daley, trying to imagine the young man's plight at the hands of his vicious foreman.

'In those days, you jeest shut up an' got on wae it. There was no benefits or the like, so if you lost your job you and your family starved, so Grampa Billy wid likely have had tae jeest grin and bear it all.' She wiped away a tear.

'Take your time, no hurry.'

'Och, I'm jeest being stupid, Mr Daley. I didna even know my grampa, but I've heard so many tales aboot him, I feel as though I can picture him standing before me as plain as day. Do you know how it is?'

'I do,' Daley replied, remembering how real the stories his

6

mother had told him about her father had made the man, despite the fact he had been killed in World War II, long before Daley was born.

'At any rate, this night the two o' them was on nightshift,' continued Mrs Hutchinson with a sniff. Despite being in her eighties, she was clear-eyed and sharp-witted. 'Their job was tae load a coastal puffer wae barrels o' whisky so the captain could catch the tide first thing in the morning. They had a horse and cairt and used tae put the barrels on a pulley and lever them aboard the boat. I mind seeing it done when I was a wee lassie.'

'Wasn't it dark?'

'Aye, nae electric lights or anything like that in they days, Mr Daley. Normally, they wid work by the light o' the boat's big storm lanterns. But on this night – so the story goes – they didna need them. There was a Dalintober moon.'

'A what?'

'Jeest that, a Dalintober moon – big an' blue in the sky, lit up the whole scene. You don't see them very often.'

'Once in a blue moon?'

'Aye, well, a Dalintober moon's no' as regular as that,' she said dismissively, with another sniff.

'So where were the crew?'

'Och, sure you know, Mr Daley. Oot in the toon enjoying themselves. The whisky boats were dry, ye see. Wae all that booze on board, it widna do for the crew tae get drunk and start tapping intae barrels o' whisky to keep the sensation going. They were paid by how quick they were. The earlier they got intae port, the mair money they got. A well-oiled machine at sea, and well-oiled in port, if you know whoot I mean.'

'So your grandfather and this McMunn are loading the boat?'

'Aye, jeest so. The crew got back efter their carousing – in the early hours o' the morning, you understand – and there was no sign o' either o' them, neither my grandfaither nor McMunn. The horse jeest standing haltered tae the cairt, fair scunnered, but o' them nothing. The next day they found Grampa Billy's bunnet washed up on the shore at Dalintober beach.'

'Really?' remarked Daley, remembering the location of the skeleton.

'Aye. At first, everyone thought they'd had some accident – a fight mair like – tumbled intae the sea an' drooned. For years folk thought it, that my grandfaither had enough o' McMunn's bullying an' fought back. And then, twenty years later, the money started,' she said in a matter-of-fact way.

'What money?'

'McMunn's wife started tae get money from America. At first naebody knew where it came from, but her son, born jeest two months efter the pair o' them went missing, started poking about.' Mrs Hutchinson sat back in her seat and sighed. 'Turns oot that after killing my grandfaither, McMunn had made it tae America, where he'd made good. He was the mayor o' a wee toon in New Jersey. The boy wanted tae go over tae America tae see him, but McMunn didna want tae know. Kept sending the money, mind.'

'Surely there was some kind of official investigation? This was a murder, after all,' said Daley.

'Och, you know fine. He was interviewed by the police over there. They were happy with his story.'

'Which was?'

'Jeest that Grampa Billy had attacked him, would you believe? In the scuffle, my grandfaither fell overboard. McMunn said he panicked, made it tae Glesca an' worked a passage tae America, an' that was that.'

'So he basically got off with murder,' said Daley with a shake of his head.

'Aye, that he did, Inspector. Though today is the first time we've been able tae prove it. In them days if there wiz no body tae be found, the polis jeest weren't interested, an' that's a fact.'

'What was your grandfather's second name, Mrs Hutchinson?'

'Cardle, Willliam Cardle,' she replied as another tear slipped down her cheek.

'Cardle? There are still Cardles in Kinloch now, aren't there?' said Daley, recognising the name from somewhere.

'Aye, and McMunns tae. There's been a feud ever since. My ain great nephew was up in court recently for fighting with Hugh McMunn, I'm ashamed to say. Some things never change, Mr Daley.'

'Ian Cardle, am I right?'

'Yes, you are,' she replied ruefully. 'In wee places like this, Mr Daley, a slight is a slight and can last for generations. My grandmother struggled tae bring my faither and his brother up on a pittance, while the man who killed oor grandfaither made sure his family wanted for nothing.'

'I can see that would cause bad feeling, Mrs Hutchinson.'

'Mair than that, Mr Daley. Both families hate each other. All these years, me, my weans – theirs, tae – have been playing on that beach, no' knowing that poor Grampa Billy is right underneath us, horribly murdered. I'll tell you something for nothing, finding my Grampa Billy deid in a barrel will dae

9

nothing tae make this feud any better. Aye, no matter how many years have passed.'

III

DS Brian Scott had arrived with the forensic team, who set to work removing the barrel and its contents from the sand on Dalintober beach.

When Daley briefed Scott about the discovery of the body and its possible history, the detective sergeant was sceptical.

'Dae you no' think we've got enough on oor plate without having to investigate murders from over a hundred years ago? Is there no' a special department devoted to this now?'

'All very well, Brian, but I've been looking back at this little feud between the Cardles and the McMunns: assaults – lots of them, intimidation, fire-raising, fraud. You name it, it's been going on for years.'

'Aye, a hundred years,' replied Scott. 'You know fine by now what folk are like here. Best just tae leave them tae it.'

'What, and allow all this bollocks to go on for another century? Not likely.'

Scott gave up when he realised that Daley had the bit between his teeth, eyeing his superior doubtfully as he scribbled on a piece of paper. 'What's this, another memo? I could paper oor kitchen wae the amount o' paper that comes my way in the course o' a day.'

'Well, if you were part of the modern world, we'd give you a tablet and save the rain forests,' said Daley, handing Scott the note with a smile.

'And dae ye no' think I've got enough hassle working wae computers when I'm in the office, without carrying one o' them aboot? They gave me a new mobile phone the other day, no' a button tae be seen. My dear lady telt me it wiz like giving a chimp a Rolls-Royce.' He grimaced.

'The only difference being that the chimp would have the engine running and be off down the road before you managed to turn your phone on. You have a poke about and find out what they have at the local library, old newspapers and so on. I'm going to have a word with our colleagues in New Jersey, see if we can find out more about this McMunn's time in the States.'

'Aye, you're the boss, Jim, but I canna help thinking that this is one hell o' a waste o' time,' opined Scott, tucking the memo that Daley had given him into his jacket pocket. 'And I notice it's me that's got tae go oot in the elements, while you sit in your cosy office. It's blowing fit tae wake the deid oot there.'

'Off you go, Bubbles,' said Daley, smiling. 'At least it's dry now.'

With that, the wind blasted a flurry of rain against the windows of Kinloch Police Office that rattled the panes like grapeshot.

'Oh great, right again, Sherlock. What's this wae Bubbles, by the way?'

IV

Kinloch Library was housed within a modern building that overlooked the loch. As Scott waited for the librarian to print out what she had on the disappearance of Cardle and McMunn he looked out of the huge plate-glass window that gave him a view across the harbour: yachts and fishing boats strained

11

at their moorings as the cold grey sea sprayed up over the harbour wall in foaming white torrents, soaking anyone who got in its way. Scott watched as the sea propelled its flotsam onto the road, landing a large length of green seaweed onto the bonnet of a parked car. Of the island that guarded the head of the loch, there was no sign, shrouded as it was by rain pouring from a blackened sky. He shivered involuntarily.

'Here we are, Sergeant,' said the librarian as she padded up to Scott, a folder of papers under her arm. 'Sorry I took so long. The big printer is quite slow, but the station said you preferred hard copies for your files instead of a download to a flash drive.'

'If I understood what you just said, I'd be able tae give you an answer,' replied Scott, as a huge wave broke over the sea wall and onto the road. 'I might just have a sit doon and go over these, if that's all right? Wait for this to blow over.'

'No problem. Just take a seat over there,' she said, pointing to the reading area. 'There's a coffee machine, and if you need to go online, just give me a shout.'

'I widnae worry too much aboot that,' Scott said. He laid the folder on a table and fumbled about in his pocket in search of change for the coffee machine.

'If it's coin you're efter, I've plenty,' said a familiar voice from behind him.

'Hamish, how are you? I've only got notes. Do you mind?'

The old man handed Scott some coins and, as the policemen fed them into the machine and squinted at the instructions, took a seat at the table and looked at the folder Scott had left there.

'Aye, a terrible business altogether,' said Hamish, sucking on his unlit pipe. 'My grandfaither wiz one o' the last tae see them both alive.'

'Really?'

'Aye. He wiz only a boy, mark you, but he minded fine them clopping past him doon the Main Street on their way tae the quay. A fair stow o' whisky on the back o' the cairt, tae. He never got tired o' tellin' the story.'

'Why does that not surprise me?'

'Och, he wiz a bit o' a storyteller, my auld grandfaither. Could be a lot o' blethers sometimes, mind, but always worth listening tae.'

'Is that where you get it from?'

'You can still hear his screams, every time there's a Dalintober moon,' continued Hamish, pointedly ignoring the remark.

'Your grandfather's?'

'Nah, not at all. Poor Billy Cardle's cries, as that bastard Archie McMunn beat him tae death. Hellish noise, I've heard it myself,' he mused, sucking at his empty pipe again.

'Aye, right, and I've seen oor Jimmy knock back the offer of a sticky toffee pudding.'

'I'm telling you, Sergeant Scott. Enough tae chill the blood. There's naebody in the toon that's no heard it, hand on heart. Every night there's a Dalintober moon, poor Billy can be heard, fair screaming for mercy. There's one due any day, though you can never jeest predict when or if it'll come.'

'Well, I'll take your word for it, Hamish. Anyhow, thanks for the change. I'll get you a couple o' drams in the County tonight for your pains. Noo, you'll need tae gie me peace wae this bloody lot,' said Scott, patting the file of documents.

'Aye, not tae worry yersel'. I've the newspapers tae read. Whoot's the point shelling oot good money when ye can read them a' here for free, eh? Aye, an' a lovely cup o' tea wae it.'

'Better than the coffee, anyway.' Scott winced as he took his first sip.

'Och, I widna put that bilge in my mooth. No, wee Janet makes me as many cups o' tea as I want wae the kettle in her office. Here she is noo wae my first brew o' the morning.'

As the librarian left a large mug of steaming tea on the table and went back about her business, Hamish leaned into Scott's left ear conspiratorially. 'I'll tell ye somethin' ye'll no' get fae any paper clippings, or the like.'

'Oh aye, what's that, Hamish?'

'Billy Cardle wiz a good-looking lad, bit o' a ladies' man, so the story goes.'

Scott scowled. 'Poor bugger didn't get much time to practise his art.'

'Time enough, Sergeant, time enough. It wisna jeest the look o' him that Archie McMunn didna like.' He sucked on his pipe again and winked. 'Billy Cardle wiz mair than friendly wae McMunn's wife, if ye get my drift.'

V

Daley looked out of his office window as the phone at his ear played the hold music he so despised. Just as he was about to give up and disconnect the call, the music was interrupted by a voice on the other end of the line.

'Wantage Police Department. Go ahead, caller.'

Daley explained the reason for his call and waited to be put through to the sheriff. Wantage, he'd discovered, was the small town in New Jersey where Archie McMunn had fetched up after he and Cardle disappeared.

'Good day to you, sir,' said the voice on the line.

'Hello, Sheriff. It's Jim Daley, Detective Chief Inspector, from Kinloch in Scotland. I'm hoping you can help me.'

Daley gave his opposite number in Wantage the background to the case. The man on the other end, Sheriff Walter P. Engler, listened quietly until Daley had finished his tale.

'Intriguing, sir, most intriguing. However, there are parts of your story that do not tally with what I know of Archie McMunn, sir.'

'Meaning?'

'Mr McMunn was a pillar of our community, Chief Daley. Before he died, he owned just about anything worth owning in this town, yeah, and much of Sussex County besides. I'm pleased to say that I'm one of his successors in this job.'

Daley drew in his breath sharply. 'You mean he was the local sheriff?'

'He was that. Three terms in office, totalling twenty-three years in all, and a legend in the police department. A fine businessman, too. His family still have extensive business interests hereabouts.'

As Daley heard more about McMunn and his good works, love of liberty, fair play and the fortune he had apparently amassed, he began to understand why nothing had come of the investigation into the disappearance of William Cardle. McMunn had made himself an institution, in not just his adopted community but further afield. He was a prominent member of the Republican Party, and courted as such by the state governor, a number of senators, and at least one US president. The chances of his being arrested and brought back to Scotland to answer questions about an incident years before – where not even a body had been found – were negligible.

'So, as far as you know he was a popular man, Sheriff?'

'More than that, sir. He was literally the father of our community. From the top of his hat to the toes of his boots, he was Mr Wantage. He helped the poor, he kept the peace and he gave people jobs. In fact, I'm looking at a picture of him right now. It hangs in the sheriff's office here to remind us of our duty to our fellow citizens,' he said proudly. 'But don't just take my word for it. I'll have the archivist from the town hall email you what we have on Archie McMunn.'

'Thank you, Sheriff Engler, and for your time. It's been most illuminating. I look forward to reading more about your predecessor.'

'My pleasure, sir. Do you mind if I relate this story to our mayor? This is something he'll most certainly want to know about.'

'No, not at all, go ahead,' replied Daley. 'As this is a live investigation, despite the passage of time, I'd be grateful if he'd keep it to himself until we have some answers, though. What's your mayor's name?'

'You won't need to write it down to remember it, Chief Daley. He's called Archie McMunn. He's the grandson of the man we've just been talking about.'

Daley wound up the conversation and leaned back in his chair, deep in thought. Unless the stories about the brutal distillery foreman were all wrong, it appeared that whatever happened between Archie McMunn and William Cardle had transformed the former's personality. The man Daley had been told about was kind, industrious and compassionate, a model citizen. He was the very antithesis of the McMunn who disappeared from Kinloch so many years before.

Daley had seen many men change: some for the better, many the opposite. A few hardened criminals he'd known had turned their back on chaotic destructive lives and turned to religion and good works. Was Archie McMunn one of them? It certainly seemed so.

The office door swung open to reveal DS Scott, so thoroughly drenched that he could quite easily have been for a swim, fully clothed.

'Bugger me, but I've never seen rain like it. I hope you've got a towel.'

Daley looked at his colleague for a moment, then started to laugh.

VI

As Daley and Scott walked down Main Street towards the County Hotel, a plump full moon appeared from behind a cloud and illuminated the town in an icy blue light. Though the rain had once again ceased, the wind was relentless and as Daley looked up at the great orb in the sky, small clouds flitted past, their shadows reflecting on the slick wet slate roofs of the town's tenements.

They made the familiar left turn under the faux rampart and through the door of the hotel, which inside was warm, bright and welcoming. Behind the bar, Annie was busy serving a throng of customers, who were no doubt anxious to forget, in a fug of alcohol of their choice, the relentless wind and rain that had battered Kinloch for days.

'How ye doin', boys?' she shouted cheerfully. 'I'll be with yous in a meenit.'

Now used to the County Hotel's clientele, neither detective was surprised when a hush descended as they stood waiting to be served.

'Aye, a terrible crime, right enough,' said an old man with a pockmarked face and a bulbous nose tinged purple by regular boozing. 'Poor Billy Cardle didna stand a chance, beaten and dumped in a barrel. It's a bloody shame.'

'I wonder just whoot the McMunns will have tae say aboot this?' mused a middle-aged man in a thick fisherman's jumper. 'There can be nae doubt noo. They're a' off a murderer, and that's a fact.'

Normally, Daley would have ignored this kind of speculation, which was in the main designed to draw information from whichever policeman was present. However, on this occasion, he decided to make an exception.

'You should all know better than to assume that the body found earlier has anything to do with the persons you're talking about. You'll get nothing from me, or any other police officers in the town, come to that, until we know the facts. So, can we all just relax and have a dram or two and talk about something else? I'm sure I'm not the only one who needs his cockles warming.'

The comment elicited a few laughs, but served its purpose: a murmur of general conversation returned to the bar of the County Hotel.

'Jeest you boys take a seat,' shouted Annie. 'The usual?' She was already pouring Daley's favourite malt whisky into a small glass.

Daley and Scott did as they were bid, and soon Annie was weaving her way towards them through the other customers with their drinks on a tray.

'There ye are, get that doon yer necks. You'll be needin' it efter being oot in this weather, an' that's a fact. Especially exposed tae the elements doon on Dalintober beach. Have yous been there all day?'

'Now, Annie,' replied Daley with a smile, 'you should know better. You'll get no more out of us than anyone else. In fact, there's nothing to tell, apart from what you know already.'

'Aye, well, a girl's got tae try.' She smiled. 'Ye widna expect me tae neglect my duty tae my fellow toonsfolk here and no' try tae get something oot o' yous, would ye?'

'Naw,' said Scott. 'Par for the course for the Gossip Master-in-Chief.'

'Watch it, you,' she said, flicking her towel at Scott. 'Anyhow, I thought you'd be away listenin' tae Billy Cardle's screams, it being a Dalintober Moon and a'.'

'We're police officers, Annie,' said Scott. 'Nae time to listen tae all that rubbish, woman.'

'No, nor rubbish, neithers. I've heard his screams wae my ain ears. When we were kids we used tae go across tae the beach tae find oot if the story wiz true. I can tell you, Brian, every night there's a Dalintober moon you can hear poor Billy screaming, fair pleading fir his life. If you don't believe me, you should go an' have a listen tonight.'

'Aye, right,' said Scott, taking a gulp of his pint.

'Maybe we'll take you up on that, Annie,' replied Daley, much to his colleague's surprise. 'Fling another one in there, please, and we'll take a wander down.'

'Are you serious?' said Scott, an incredulous look spreading across his face.

'Yup, I am. We'll have another one to take the chill out of the bones and then head over. You never know what'll turn up.'

'Aye, double pneumonia and sand in oor shoes, Jim. Bugger me, I've just dried oot an' aw. I tell ye, this place is getting tae you,' concluded Scott with a sigh.

VII

Scott grumbled for the whole five minutes it took them to walk down the town's Main Street, across the arc of the esplanade at the head of the loch and towards Dalintober beach. The blue-tinged moon was now huge in the sky; its distorted reflection writhed in the choppy waters of the loch as the wind howled across the water and through trees and buildings. Though the rain had stayed away, the men were flecked by spray from the sea, which left a salty taste on their lips.

Ahead of them, under the acetylene glow of the streetlights, the policemen could see the old jetty, the short stretch of Dalintober beach at its side in shadow. The wind seemed to intensify, gusting past the old stone quay with a wail.

'Only the deid would come out on a night like this, Jimmy,' shouted Scott. Having turned a corner, the gale was now directly at their backs, pushing them onwards in staccato steps.

'You go onto the beach, Brian. I'll walk along the pier, see what's what,' Daley roared in response.

'Aye, whatever you say, boss,' Scott mumbled to himself, as he flipped up the collar of his jacket and shivered. He walked towards a slipway that led onto the small stretch of sand. As he made his way onto the beach, the darkness forced him to slow his pace; even the blue light from the huge moon seemed to be eaten up by the darkness here. To his right, he could see Daley silhouetted against the orange glow on the pier, now some hundred yards away. Even though the tide was out, flecks of the angry sea spattered his jacket as he looked around. He switched on his torch and shone it over the rocks and sand. Just ahead, the hole from which the barrel and its grisly contents had been removed was visible in the sand, though much less deep since it had again been under the waves and partially filled in by the tide. The loch looked black and restless, white tips of whipped-up waves racing towards him on the shore, and the stench of rotting seaweed was strong in the wet salty air.

Suddenly, just within the range of the torch beam, a movement on the sand caught his eye. Something large and black darted across his path.

'Fuck me! A rat, near the size o' a dug!' he exclaimed to himself, as the rodent disappeared into the night, coat glistening in the moonlight.

Cold, wet, unhappy and increasingly thirsty, he shone his torch down the length of the beach. Apart from a white plastic bag, blowing along in the wind, nothing was moving; even the rat had seen fit to remove itself from the elements. Swearing under his breath, Scott decided to do the same.

Just as he turned towards the slipway though, he heard it. Barely audible at first, then more intense, someone was screaming fit to chill the blood.

Scott flicked the torch beam left and right, but nothing was there. The cry was distinct now, despite the howling wind. It was high and shrill, desperate, like someone screaming for their life.

He scanned the length of the pier and could see no sign of Daley under the streetlamps, swaying on their thin metal posts in the wind. He ran across the beach, up the slipway, nearly falling on the greasy seaweed-slick surface, and along the road. He raced onto the pier and looked frantically around.

'Jim, Jim!' Scott bellowed, his calls lost on the wind and the screaming. He wrestled the phone from his pocket, cursing the fact that it wasn't the one he was used to. His hands were

21

numb with cold as he found the button on the side of the device, illuminated the screen, then tried to remember how to make a call. Before he could summon assistance, however, the screaming stopped.

Scott looked around frantically for any sign of his friend, the phone clamped to his ear. He walked to the edge of the pier and stared into the black waves that lashed the structure. How easy would it have been for Daley to lose his footing and be blown into the loch?

Just as his call to Kinloch Police Office was answered, a light flashed from somewhere beneath him. He spoke hurriedly on the phone as he looked over the sea wall. Two figures were struggling in the darkness, partially illuminated by the beam of a torch that lay on the sand beside them. Scott ran towards the sea wall, scaled it gingerly, then eased himself onto the rocky foreshore in time to see a large man subdue a smaller adversary with one punch to the jaw.

'Ye big bastard,' shouted the young man, now lying on the wet sand and pebbles of the foreshore. 'I think you've broken my jaw.'

'Lucky he didnae break your neck,' shouted Scott above the wind. 'What's a' this about?'

'Let's get out of this wind and I'll tell you,' gasped Daley, out of breath after his exertions. At that, they saw a police van with a flashing blue light speeding along the esplanade towards them.

'Brian, meet Hugh McMunn,' shouted Daley.

VIII

Daley and Scott sat opposite Hugh McMunn and the duty solicitor in the interview room at Kinloch Police Office. McMunn had refused a change of clothes, but sat with the large white towel he had been given around his shoulders. His lank hair was swept back off his forehead, and there was a sneer on his sharp-featured face.

'I'll ask you again: why were you on Dalintober beach with this?' said Daley, pointing to a large ghetto blaster on the table between them, the plastic facing and handle of which were cracked.

'I'm not sure that this is a crime, Mr Daley,' interrupted the solicitor.

'But assaulting a police officer most certainly is,' replied Daley testily. 'Answer the question, Mr McMunn.'

Hugh McMunn simply looked at Daley and smiled, revealing a row of gappy front teeth.

'Who's your dentist?' asked Scott. 'I'd gie him the bullet if I wiz you. You've got a mouth like a row of condemned hooses, son.'

This seemed to rile McMunn, whose sneer turned into a scowl. 'You know fine who did it – that bastard Ian Cardle. I jeest havena had a chance tae pay him back yet.'

'Is that a threat, Mr McMunn?' enquired Daley. 'I'll ask you again: what were you doing on the beach tonight with this? Good machine, mind you, quality stuff. Despite getting dropped and soaked, it still works.' He leaned forwards and pressed the play button. Immediately, the small room was filled with the same scream they'd heard on the beach, so loud that the solicitor was forced to cover his ears.

Daley switched it off, then sat back in his chair. 'Well, anything to say?'

McMunn stared at the detective for a moment and chewed his lip. 'It's an auld family tradition, if you must know,' he said

23

finally. 'Jeest a bit of fun. My faither did it, aye, and his before that. A wee reminder for the Cardles that they shouldna mess about wae us.'

'Fun? I'm assuming you don't care how this will make some people feel.' Daley shook his head.

'Ach, who cares?'

Hugh McMunn was left to cool his heels in the cells at Kinloch Police Office overnight, and in the morning he was charged with a breach of the peace and released, his ghetto blaster retained as evidence.

It appeared that the screams which the residents of Kinloch had heard at the time of a Dalintober moon over the years were all courtesy of the McMunn family, a tradition that had been passed down through the generations and recently brought into the modern era by the use of electronic sound effects.

It was one of the occasions since his arrival in Kinloch that Daley suspected most people of the town knew the truth, but were happy to keep strangers – policemen especially – in the dark. Like most legends, even though it could easily be explained away, more superstitious locals clung to a more macabre origin of the disembodied screams. This was one Kinloch tradition Daley was happy to consign to the past.

As he sat at his desk pondering the death of William Cardle, he stared out into the gloom. The new day had dawned and the weather hadn't changed. A strong wind was blowing from the north, and the relentless rain carried flurries of snow and hail to add to the tumult.

He picked up the receiver of his phone and dialled a number quickly. 'DCI Daley at Kinloch. I want you to check our DNA records for samples from Hugh McMunn and Ian

Cardle.' Since both men had been convicted of recent crimes, Daley knew that their DNA would be on file. He gave their details and waited.

'Yes, we have both profiles, sir,' answered the efficient-sounding woman on the other end of the phone.

'Good, I'd like you to do me a favour . . .'

IX

Daley looked at the black-and-white image of an elderly man on his computer screen. The email had arrived from the county archivist at Wantage Town Hall in New Jersey, as promised by Sheriff Engler.

The old man was dressed in a dark three-piece suit; the links of a watch chain stretched across his ample belly. He had a broad jowly face and a plump-cheeked grin under a drooping white moustache. He was bald, save for unruly tufts of hair that poked out from behind his ears. His expression was open, friendly, even, but there was a hint of steel in his eyes. Daley studied the face of Archie McMunn carefully as DS Scott peeked over his shoulder.

'Aye, It's amazing how folk change as they get older,' said the DS. 'Here's us looking for a brutal murderer and we're sent a picture o' the Santa auditions for the weans' Christmas grotto.'

Daley had to admit Scott had a point. The man's demeanour seemed to bear no connection to the brutal Archie McMunn he'd heard about. People did change, though. And the memories of those who had never met the man, coloured by prejudice and time, were hardly likely to have been as accurate as he could have wished for.

'Here,' said Scott, 'I meant tae show you this before.' He

handed Daley a photocopy of another old photograph, this one even grainier than the one flickering on Daley's screen. Two rows of men stood behind a stow of barrels. All of them were wearing flat caps, save the man in the middle of the bottom row who wore a bowler hat. All had moustaches, apart from one, whose head of thick curly hair poked out from under his bunnet.

'Yer man with the curly hair is oor Billy Cardle. The guy in the back row behind the bloke in the bowler is Archie McMunn.'

Daley studied both men. Cardle was as his granddaughter had described, with youthful good looks and a friendly face. In this image, Archie McMunn looked the part, too; his head was bowed and his dark moustache drooped at the corners of his mouth. Daley compared this man to the image of McMunn's older self on the computer screen; the facial hair was about the only common feature. Still, the group photo of the men from Wellside Distillery was a poor-quality reproduction.

'The plot thickens, Jim.'

Just as Scott finished his sentence, Sergeant Shaw burst into the room. 'Sir, there's been a commotion in the Douglas Arms – Ian Cardle and Hugh McMunn. Thought you'd like to know. The lads are off to sort it out now.'

'We'll tag along. C'mon, Brian.'

When Daley, Scott and two uniformed officers arrived at the Douglas Arms, Hugh McMunn was already being stretchered out to a waiting ambulance. Clutching bloodstained white wadding to a gash on his forehead, he began ranting at the policemen. 'Away and arrest some real criminals!'

'Another whack on the heid, son,' said Scott. 'Maybe better

just tae keep your mouth shut and your opinions to yoursel', if you're wanting tae stay as handsome, that is.'

As the police officers entered the Douglas Arms, the sounds of shouting and smashing glass could be heard. Ian Cardle was standing on the bar brandishing a stool, its metal legs thrust out like the spines of a porcupine. His jeans hung below his waist, displaying quite a paunch beneath a blood-soaked T-shirt. His eyes were wild and bulging as he challenged all-comers. 'C'mon, ye bastards! Does nane o' ye have the balls tae come and have a go? All mates wae McMunn, eh?'

A couple of customers shouted back, though they were hushed by an elderly bald man with a hooked nose, who was standing behind the bar, well away from Cardle. Daley recognised him as the proprietor.

'Now, there you are, Ian,' he shouted, his accent not of Kinloch but County Antrim. 'The bloody boys in blue are here now. The game's up, my friend.' He winked at Daley. 'The rozzers'll pile you into the Black Maria and you'll be behind bars before Jack can say how d'ye do. Be a good lad and come down, before the copper in the front there gets that Taser out of his pocket and zaps the hell out of you, like bloody Flash bloody Gordon.'

Despite the commotion and the broken glass everywhere, Daley could have sworn the landlord was enjoying this diversion.

'Can I get a pint of Sixty Shilling, Den?' asked a red-haired man in a distinctive welder's cap who was sitting at the other end of the long bar. 'I'm wile an' dry ower here.'

'You want me to risk life and bloody limb so you can have the tipple of your choice, Billy boy.' The landlord gesticulated wildly with his hands, adding dramatic emphasis to what he was saying. 'Normal service will be resumed in no time at all now that the constabulary are here.' He held a Paris Goblet under a beer tap. 'In the meantime, quench your thirst with a wee pony of good honest ale and try to think more on the plight of bloody others.' He smiled at Daley who was opening the hinged bar hatch. 'Be my guest, gentlemen. I'd offer you all a drink, but I've lost enough money during this little battle as it is, and your sergeant there has the look of a man that could drink a brewery dry.'

'Just you get doon here right now,' Scott shouted up at Cardle, ignoring the barb, 'before I come up there an' get you.'

'I'm wanting a lawyer!' roared Cardle. 'I know fine whoot will happen tae me up the hill if I don't have representation.'

'Right! That's enough!' said Scott, as he ran towards Ian Cardle and grabbed his right ankle, sending man and bar stool tumbling to the floor.

'Bravo, sir, bloody bravo,' said the landlord, clapping his hands triumphantly. 'Poor Ian.' He glanced at Cardle, who was lying in a heap on the floor. 'In the door at eleven like John bloody Wayne, and out again by two like Mickey bloody Rooney. Now, Billy boy, a pint of our best Sixty Shilling, if I'm not much mistaken.' He thrust a pint glass under a beer tap as the uniformed police officers handcuffed Ian Cardle and hauled him to his feet.

X

Hugh McMunn was patched up at Kinloch's hospital and returned to the cells at the police office, where he and Ian Cardle, already resident, proceeded to yell abuse at each other through the walls, despite the best efforts of Sergeant Shaw.

'A Skype call for you, sir,' said a harassed-looking Shaw, poking his head around the door.

'Don't worry, I'll send Brian in to see them in a minute,' replied Daley, as they walked down the corridor to the AV suite. 'That's bound to shut them up.'

Shaw pressed a few keys as Daley took his seat; soon, after a few flashes and numbers, an image appeared.

'Good morning, Chief Inspector Daley,' said the elderly man in a deep American drawl. 'I'm Mayor McMunn, Archie McMunn.' He hesitated. 'I suppose it's later in the day with you there in Kinloch. So, good afternoon, my apologies.'

The perfect pronunciation of the town's name struck Daley, as he studied the man on the large screen in front of him. In his sixties, he was tanned and healthy-looking with a long thin face and steel-grey hair shaved close to his head, military fashion. Wearing a dark blue suit, white shirt and red tie, he sat straight-backed in front of a sign which read 'Wantage Mayoral Department'. A furled stars and stripes was visible to his left.

'I intend to visit your lovely town before I die, Mr Daley. My grandfather told me so many stories about the place when I was a kid, I felt as though I could walk down any street and know where I was heading.'

'Good of you to get in touch, Mr McMunn. I take it Sheriff Engler has briefed you on our little discovery?'

'Oh yes, he did indeed. I don't really know what to say about that.'

'You remember your grandfather well?'

'Very well. Though he died in sixty-three, I spent a lot of time with him when I was a child. He was a kind funny man, and he told a hell of a good story, Mr Daley.'

'So he was a happy man?'

'Very. Do you know, I never saw him angry. He never

cursed or raised his voice, and even when we got outa line, he brought us back on course with a smile.'

'So he didn't hit you, or discipline you?'

'Hell no!' replied McMunn, looking shocked. 'My grand-mother was the one who would chase us, or give a quick cuff round the head. My, my, but she was a formidable woman, Mr Daley. But my grandfather, he wouldn't have hurt a fly. Well, not often,' he said, suddenly serious, looking at Daley from under his brow.

'Very different to the stories I've heard here, Mr McMunn.'

'Yeah, well, that's kind of why I'm talking to you, right now,' said McMunn, shifting in his seat. 'I guess we – my late father and I, that is – have been expecting to hear from someone like you in Kinloch for most of our lives.'

'I don't know what you mean,' replied Daley.

'I could sit here and tell you why, but I think that the man who started all of this will do it so much more justice than I could ever do. We – me, my family, this town – we owe him so much. He came here with nothing and built a fortune, not on the backs of others, but with good old hard work.' He picked up a piece of paper from his desk and waved it before the camera. 'I'm sending you a copy of this, Mr Daley.'

'What is it?'

'Well, let's just say it speaks for itself,' he said with a sad smile. 'When I took the reins of this business from my father when he was dying, he gave me this letter and told me never to breathe a word about its contents.'

'So why now, Mr McMunn?'

'Respecting my grandfather's instructions.' He smiled again, but Daley could see tears in his eyes. 'I don't know what you'll want to do after you read it, Mr Daley, but, please, try not to judge him too harshly. Those were very different days.'

'Thank you for your honesty, Mr McMunn. I'll be back in touch when I've read it.'

'Thank you, Mr Daley. It's in your in-box now. And I mean what I say – now that things have changed, I'm going to visit Kinloch.' He nodded solemnly as the screen went blank.

XI

Daley opened the email, the header bearing the title and logo of McMunn Inc. He clicked on the attachment and peered at the screen. The letter had been scanned, but the yellowing of the page revealed its age. Though the handwriting was old-fashioned, it was bold and clear:

Wantage
September 10th, 1963

To Whom It May Concern,
I fear that my days are running out, and I have more reason than most to shy away from Death's clammy embrace.

I have been a lucky man – a very lucky man – much more than I deserved to be. For instance, I have loved – truly loved – two beautiful women, though my heart ached for one of them for more years than I care to mention. I came to America with nothing, and America took me to its heart. Here I have wealth, family, respect, security – what more could any man wish for?

Despite this good fortune, I fall asleep with the same image on my mind every night: a face on a distant shore. For the first time since it happened, I will tell the tale.

31

It was still dark, but I could see the first light of day breaking over the hills as I looked down on that face for the last time. Those unseeing eyes stared up at me; they stare at me still, despite the passage of time. There was blood on his face and in his hair. When I hit him, I did so out of desperation, as he'd come at me with a length of timber. The only weapon I had to hand was a mallet used for hammering bungs into whisky barrels. I will never forget watching the life drain from him as he sank to his knees and then fell forward onto the deck of the little steam puffer. One blow was all it had taken; an act that changed every second of my life still to come, and ended his for good.

Of course, I panicked. I felt the hangman's noose; felt it tighten around my neck.

I found an empty butt on the deck. It was a cask that had leaked and was to be brought back to the distillery. Because it had been badly coopered – no doubt old Tommy had been drunk when he'd done it – I managed to force two metal hoops up and off, take out the end of the cask, then cram the man I had killed into it.

As I drove the cart to Dalintober beach, our old mare was restless and she whinnied, smelling blood and death. I calmed her, and soon we were at the pier. I rolled the cask down the little slipway and onto the sand, dreading the moment that the barrel I had hammered back together as best as I could would fall apart and its grim contents spill out onto the sand.

The butt remained intact, and as I rolled it along the beach I could feel the motion moving the dead man within. Rolling a barrel with a dead man in it is much easier than carrying his weight over your shoulder, and though the bright blue Dalintober moon helped me, by the same token it would have been my undoing had I not been able to hide the body and someone seen me at my dark deed.

As the last shovels of sand buried the dead man, I considered my next move. I took the horse and cart back to the pier in Kinloch and started walking.

It was light now, though early, and I was mindful lest a hardworking crofter already at their toil should witness me. I cut across fields away from the road, in the main. Luck was with me though and I wasn't spied.

After a long and fretful trek, I knocked on the cottage door of the Gentleman from Blaan, as we in the distillery used to call him. Simply put, he was a smuggler; I won't name him here, but he and I had done a handsome trade in illicit whisky, which he sailed off to Ireland under the very nose of the Excise men. I hope, like me, he had a long and prosperous life; he deserved it. He helped me – gave me a few coins to see me on my way – and never breathed a word.

I took to sea with him to Ireland, and once there made my way to Cork, where I sought to work my passage on a ship bound for America. At every moment I feared two things: the hand of a stout Bobby on my collar, and the thought that I would never see the woman I loved again.

Oh, Cathy McMunn, how I missed you.

For a long time, I hoped that I would be able to send for her, and that is why I did what I did. When the purser on the Winter Star asked me my name, I gave it: Archibald McMunn. I knew it was a risk, but in those days word spread more slowly than it does today. I was told that the name under which I travelled would be the one given to the authorities in America. Despite the risk of discovery, I had to do it. Soon, when the fuss had died down back in Kinloch I would send for Cathy and we would live as man and wife.

It was in that hope that I carried the name that took me to the

United States of America, and the name I have lived with all these years. It is a name that belongs to another. To a dead man buried on the beach at Dalintober, where I left him so long ago.

As the years passed, the fear of being caught lessened. I kept myself busy and tried to plan how to bring Cathy and the child she had carried in her belly when I left and that I knew to be mine, over to America to be with me. But the time was never right; mostly I couldn't raise the money, and when at last I could afford it, I had fallen in love with another – my beautiful wife Rebecca.

I found that America and Scotland were very different. People took to me and I was able to make my way, first as a salesman and then with my own small company. It didn't matter who you were here. You didn't need wealth or a title to succeed. If you worked, and worked hard, you could live the American dream. I did.

I made one mistake, though. Feeling guilty, I sent money to Cathy, to help her and her child, who by that time would be grown and perhaps in need of a start in life. You may ask me why I didn't offer this same financial support to my own wife and family; the answer is, I don't know. I suppose we were married very young – mere children – and anything I had found alluring about her I later found irritating. If it is any consolation, I will take the guilt of abandoning them to my grave. Along with everything else, that is.

I was the town sheriff, and when the questions came from Kinloch, it was easy for me to dismiss them as the ramblings of men in a distant land. How could Archie McMunn, Sherriff and doer of good, ever have been responsible for such a thing? The folks here in Wantage used to joke about it, while my blood ran cold.

I feel guilt, real guilt; not for the man, but for the crime. I had no love for the real Archie McMunn, and still don't. He was a *brute, and the world was better off without him; but as for murder, I feel it in my soul every waking minute.*

I am leaving strict instructions for those who come after me, so I suppose that now you are reading this, the body of Archie McMunn has been discovered on Dalintober beach. I have made financial provision for him to have a proper Christian burial with a headstone. I want it to bear his real name: Archibald McMunn. It is a small price to pay in return to the man whose very name – whose life, in truth – I stole.

For me, I await God's judgement. Ultimately, it is all that really matters. I seek forgiveness from no other.

The name I append to this letter seems entirely foreign to me now. It is as though it is the calumny, not the reverse.

Yours, most sincerely,

William Cardle

XII

The shouting from the cells of Cardle and McMunn was audible as DS Scott opened the door to Daley's office.

'Here, Jim, this has just come in from forensics. They tested that pair's DNA, and it turns out they're related in some way. Aye, an' neither have any connection to oor man in the barrel. How's that possible? They tell me you were the man who put them onto it.'

'It was just a hunch, Brian, but now there's no doubt. We're about to reunite long-lost cousins,' replied Daley, getting to his feet.

'Eh?'

35

As Daley bent down to close the email from Wantage he noticed the corporate logo of McMunn Inc. It was a whisky barrel.

EMPTY NETS AND PROMISES

A Kinloch Novella

1

I

1968

It was a warm, gin-clear July day. The wooden fishing boat bobbed gently on the low swell of an ocean that looked as thick as treacle. Under a blue sky unburdened by cloud, the dome of Ailsa Craig shimmered in the haze, framed by the dark line of the Ayrshire coast, which appeared to be distantly floating on the still air.

All was quiet, save for the gentle lap of the waves on the side of the clinker-built hull and the occasional plop as a seal surfaced before diving back into the torpid depths in search of fish. The creature would reappear every time with no sign of a wriggling silver herring clasped between its jaws and, if such a thing were possible, a rather disconsolate look on its face.

The stout old mariner surveyed the scene with dismay, his pipe clenched between his teeth. 'Och, even the creatures o' the deep canna get a bite,' he observed, addressing the spotty youth at his side. 'That beast is looking fair emaciated, and nae wonder.' A cloud of pungent blue smoke spiralled into the air.

'In fifty years o' this, I've never seen the like. Mid-July, and no' a catch worthy of the name. It's enough tae gaur ye greet.'

'Is that a nautical term?' asked the boy, anxious to impress.

'No, it's not, young Peter. It means it's enough tae make you burst intae tears.'

'Is it really that bad? I mean, will the fish no' jeest turn up when they're ready?'

'Och, aye.' Sandy Hoynes took the pipe from his mouth and fixed the ship's boy with a beady eye. 'The herring are probably away on one o' they new package holidays. A few weeks swimming in the warm waters o' the Mediterranean, before coming back here tae surprise the hell oot o' us by fair jumping intae the nets. We'll no' need tae bother putting tae sea at all. Likely, the silver darlings will jeest launch themselves intae the fish boxes on the quay, and tell auld Erchie Keacheran the fish buyer tae get on his bike and come up the hoose and let us know how big the catch is.'

'I canna work oot whoot's wrong,' said Peter, desperately trying to retrieve the situation.

'Noo, you're less than a year oot o' school. Jeest you tell me: whoot would we normally expect tae see when we're plying oor trade here?'

Peter bit his lip, deep in thought. 'Water, we always see plenty o' water, skipper.'

'My, but you're a bright spark, right enough. It's easy tae see how I spotted your fine intellect and offered you a half share aboard this fine vessel.'

'Dae you mean that?'

'No. The only reason you've been given the chance tae learn your trade aboard a state-o'-the-art craft like this, is that I owed your aunt Ina a wee favour.' Hoynes tapped his pipe on the hull and searched in the front pocket of his bib and braces for his pouch of tobacco. He wore an almost beatific expression as he stared out to sea.

'I didna know you knew my auntie Ina.'

'Clearly there are a multitude o' things you don't know aboot. Your auntie an' me have been freens for a long number o' years. A clever, bonnie lassie she was in the school. I'm mair than sad tae note that none o' that intelligence has managed tae fight its way through the family tae you. Have you ever heard the like, Hamish?'

A round face appeared through the wheelhouse window. 'The answer you were looking for was gulls, Peter. We'd be in a poor state right enough if we were oot here and there was nae water,' chided Hamish. He looked to be in his late thirties, though it was hard to tell under the olive tan of his skin. Certainly, there wasn't a fleck of grey to be seen in the dark quiff he'd constructed from what was left of his hair. It rose from his head like a small edifice. Had it not been for the bright blue of his slanted eyes, he would have had an almost oriental appearance. 'No' a gull tae be seen – I've never known it like this. They're usually fair mobbing the boat. I canna think it's anything less than the worst sign.' He craned his head further out of the window and looked heavenward. 'We'll have another seven hours o' light anyway. Maybe we'll hit a proud shoal yet, skipper.'

'You're like your faither, Hamish. Never saw him wae an attack o' the glums in all the years I knew him. Quick wae the premonitions, tae.'

'He looked pretty glum the last time I saw him,' remarked Hamish ruefully.

'Och, how so?'

41

'He was laid oot on auld Kennedy the undertaker's slab in his best Sunday suit.'

'Well, anybody can be forgiven for looking a wee bit glum under they circumstances. I wouldn't hold that against the man. A natural optimist, he was – right cheery when he'd a few drams on board, tae. But I tell you this, even he'd be crying in his whisky by now.'

'Nae herring, and you with your Maggie getting wed, tae,' said Hamish, leaning on the wheelhouse windowsill, lighting his own pipe.

'Me and the wife have been waiting thirty-five years for that – I'm buggered if the lack o' a fish or two will put paid tae the exercise. Aye, even if I've got tae dip intae my own nest egg.'

'She's been a while settling,' observed Hamish, a coy look on his face.

'Och, you know yoursel', the Good Lord didna see fit tae adorn her wae the keenest o' looks,' replied Hoynes. Beside him, young Peter raised his eyebrows, out of sight of his skipper. 'But she's got a big heart.'

'And a fair-sized arse, tae,' said Peter, thinking out loud then regretting it when his skipper caught him a clip behind the ear.

'That comes from her mother's side o' the family – nothing she can dae aboot it. The women canna all be as svelte as your auntie Ina . . .' His musings as to the feminine qualities of Ina Blackstock were cut short by a low rumble followed by a distinct boom.

'There it's again,' shouted Hamish. 'That's the sonic boom o' that jet they're testing.'

Hoynes relit his pipe, a look of distaste spreading across

his face. 'Noo, Hamish, you've been at the fishing since you were a boy.'

'You have the right o' it there, skipper,' he agreed.

'And in all that time, have you ever known a spell like this wae hardly a herring tae box?'

'No, I have not. I mind fifty-seven wisna such a good year, but it was nowhere near as bad as this.'

'Man, fifty-seven was like a bumper compared tae this, man. I'll tell you why I think it's happened, tae.'

'You mean you know?' asked Peter excitedly, keen to restore his skipper's faith in him after his ill-advised comment as to the size of his daughter's backside.

'It's that bloody plane. All this sonic boom stuff. When did they start they flight tests, Hamish?'

'Och, aboot the end of April – jeest as the nights were getting longer.'

'Aye, and jeest as oor wee silver freens were getting busy spawning. I'm telling you, that racket's fair frightening the fish. It's no' natural, and that's a fact. I'm no' the only man who thinks so, neither.'

'But whoot can we dae aboot it?' asked Hamish.

'We're having a meeting on Friday night – all the skippers, aye, and anyone else who's interested.'

'Whereaboots?'

'In the County Hotel. Seven thirty, on the dot. We would have had it at McGinty's, but the way things have been, half the boys are barred until they can pay off their tick.'

'There's loyalty for you,' remarked Hamish. 'The McGinty sisters have nae shame – when you think o' the money that gets spent in there by the fishing community.'

'I know fine. This crisis wae the herring, it's the kind o'

thing that tears communities apart, and no mistake. Aye, an'
forbye that, the McGinties sell the cheapest dram in the toon.'

'They dae that,' Hamish agreed, 'but fae very small glasses.'

II

The function room of the County Hotel was thick with
smoke, as sweet blue pipe tobacco mixed with the bitter tang
of unfiltered cigarettes. A young waitress manoeuvred through
the crowd of fishermen bearing a tray of drams, which she
placed on the long table in the centre of the room, then fought
her way back through the throng of seafarers as they descended
on it like a pack of hyenas.

Sandy Hoynes took his seat at the head of the table. Since
he'd called the meeting, he reserved the right to chair
proceedings. By his side, his first mate Hamish took a sip of
his whisky and grimaced. 'I'm no' jeest sure whoot distillery
this came fae, but they've a lot tae learn aboot the art of making
a good dram, and no mistake. I've cleaned my kitchen floor
wae mair appetising fare.'

'Whoot dae you expect for two shillings a heid?' replied
Hoynes. 'In any case, we're no' here for the whisky.' He tapped
the side of his glass with the stem of his pipe, and soon the
room came to order. Though there were only thirty seats
around the table, as many again stood leaning on the backs of
chairs, looking expectantly at Hoynes.

'Can I make a point of order before we start?' said an old
man sporting a cavernous yellow Sou'wester despite being
indoors. Spare flesh hung from his throat beneath a sparse
grey beard, and His voice was rasping and weak, though his
dark eyes were keen.

'Aye, you can that, Johnny,' replied Hoynes with a sigh.

'I'm no' sure that you're the right man tae be chairing this august body of mariners. I'm the auldest skipper in the fleet, and as such the honour should be mine.'

'Well, if you're so old and wise, why didn't you call a meeting yourself?' piped up Hamish in defence of his shipmate.

'Och, Hamish, but you're a loyal wee dog, so you are. Your faither must be proud, looking down and seeing that you've replaced him wae Sandy Hoynes. The heavenly tears will be spilling doon his face, I've nae doubt. It's jeest a pity he couldna keep a hauld o' his own boat, then you'd be a skipper in your ain right noo.'

'Don't worry, Johnny,' intervened Hoynes. 'If he's looking tae replace his great-great-grandfaither, I'm certain sure he'll be at your door in jig time. Noo,' he changed the subject quickly, not giving the old man time to upset Hamish further, 'we all know whoot a perilous position we're in wae regards tae the fish – or lack o' them, mair accurately.' There was a murmur of agreement around the room. 'The question is: why is it happening, and whoot can we dae aboot it?'

'My mother says it's tae dae wae the telly and radio, and suchlike,' offered a tall, thin youth in a black pea jacket. 'She reckons the signals is fair going through the fish and sending them off in the wrong directions – you know, confusing the poor buggers.'

'Aye, aye. Noo, I can see that being a valid notion. If they're as confused as me when I listen tae thon pop music, I'm quite sure the buggers are driven tae distraction. But somehow, I canna think she has the right of it there, Wullie.'

'How no'?'

'Well, I've seen many things in my life – once you've been

45

at the mercy o' a German U-boat, the rest o' the world seems a gentler place – but I've yet tae see a fish showing any interest in the television. And even if they had, it's unlikely they'd get a decent signal doon there in the depths.'

Amidst the chuckles, Hamish said, 'You're right, Sandy. My poor mother gets nothing but interference, an' she's only at the top end o' the Glebe Row.'

Sandy Hoynes waited for the mirth to subside, then leaned forwards in his chair. 'The truth of it is, the wireless and television have been around for long enough noo and they've made nae difference tae oor catch o'er the years. There's something new, something different that's tae blame. Something oot o' the ordinary . . . no' natural.' He looked around the room to see if anyone would come up with the correct answer.

'Is it something tae dae with that daughter o' yours getting hitched?' asked Johnny, a gleam back in his eye. 'If you're asking me, there's naethin' natural aboot that.'

'You're lucky you're an old man, right enough, Johnny, or I'd jump o'er this table and give you the hiding o' your life,' replied Hoynes, his face beetroot. 'I'm telling you, her backside is hereditary, there's no' a thing she can dae aboot it.'

'Hereditary like a stately home, and no' much difference in size.' Johnny sat back in his seat and enjoyed the laughter.

A young man stood up. Beneath a mop of curly hair, his face was a mask of concern. 'I'm thinking it's something tae dae wae that plane, Sandy. If things go on the way they are, I'll have tae sell the boat – and whoot's going tae happen then? Mind, I've two young children and another on the way.' He looked around the roomful of fishermen. 'Do you no' all think the same? It's that bloody plane, and all the antics it goes through – thon banging and everything.'

'Well said, Paddy Meenan,' roared Hoynes. 'The very thing – the *only* thing it can be. We've never had bother like this before – no' even in the war, when there was all sorts o' craft, explosions and other goings-on. This plane, and that noise – well, it gies me the creeps. It's enough tae wake the deid.'

'That's likely how auld Johnny made it here the night,' said Hamish, relishing the opportunity to get back at the acid-tongued old fisherman.

Hoynes stood up. 'The question is, whoot are we going tae dae?'

'We could contact oor MP, Sandy,' said one of the fishermen.

'Och, that article. He's mair at hame doon in London than he is here. I canna mind the last time I saw him in Kinloch,' sniffed Hoynes.

'Whoot aboot the Fishery Office?' asked Paddy Meenan.

The room fell silent.

'Mind now, young Paddy,' said Hoynes, his tone serious. 'You give the Fishery Officer one chance and before you know it he'll be up at your house for tea, fair grilling you aboot nets and catches, and how much money's in your bank account, and whether you bought new underpants recently. The very Devil, they are. Much better they know nothing about it, and that's a fact. Agents o' the state they are – and the very worst kind.'

'Well, in that case, all we can do is go oot tae the airbase en masse and confront the buggers,' said Meenan. 'Tell them tae take their plane somewhere else.'

'Och, they'll no' listen,' said Hamish. 'Big company – even the French are involved, so I'm told. They'll nae mair listen tae us than fly in the air.'

47

'Mind you, Hamish, that's kind o' whoot we don't want them tae dae,' said Hoynes.

'No, we have tae be fly cute wae this one,' Hamish continued. 'The big thing these days is protest. Sure, they're never done marching doon in London. I even hear that women are burning their knickers oot o' protest.'

'For any's sake,' observed Johnny. 'Sheer desperation. Mind you, I can think o' a few lassies, who, if they decided tae set fire tae their undergarments, wid cause a fair conflagration.'

'They burn their brassieres, no' their knickers,' said Hoynes, eyeing Johnny vengefully.

'No, whoot we need is publicity,' persisted Hamish. 'If we march up and doon the Main Street, nae bugger'll ever hear aboot it – aye, no' even if we were tae burn oor oilskins. We need something tae attract the attention o' the papers an' that.'

'The pilots are nice blokes,' said Meenan.

'How do you know that?' asked Hoynes.

'Och, if the weather's rough – too much wind or rain – they canna fly. They head intae the Douglas Arms for a few drams. Ex-RAF pilots, good lads. No' slow tae put their hands in their pockets, neither.'

There was silence for a moment, then Hamish looked around the room with a smile. 'Wait a minute. In that case, I've an idea . . . And all we need's a right bad day.'

III

By the time the meeting was over, Hamish and Sandy had consumed more than their fair share of the two shillings a head whisky. They were lighting their pipes outside the hotel, looking absently down Main Street.

'You'll come a wee wander wae me o'er tae the hoose, Hamish. There's nae point in wasting a Saturday night, and I could dae wae a wee alliance against all these clucking women I've tae deal wae these days. Forbye, I've a fine bottle of malt on the go.'

'Where did you get that fae? I'll wager you didna buy it yoursel.'

'The new son-in-law to be, anxious tae please, if you know whoot I mean. Like him, it's fae Skye, but no' a bad drop for all that.'

'Could he no' have bought you a decent bottle fae one o' oor distilleries?'

'You know how it is. He's got tae be seen as being even-handed in his profession. If he was tae buy a bottle fae one, I daresay he'd have tae buy one fae the rest, tae. An expensive exercise, as you can imagine.'

'But mair whisky for you, Sandy.'

The old skipper thought for a moment or two, then smiled. 'You've got a keen mind, Hamish. I'm fair lucky tae have such a canny first mate, right enough. Would you look at that,' he said, momentarily distracted by a young woman in a mini-skirt crossing the road towards them.

'Any shorter and they'll no' need tae bother wae a skirt at all,' said Hamish, shaking his head.

'How ye, Hamish, Mr Hoynes,' shouted the young woman as she approached. 'A lovely evening.'

'Nice, right enough,' said Hamish. 'Is this you off on a wee night oot, Jenny?'

'I am that. Getting some practice in for your Maggie's big wedding, Mr Hoynes.'

'Well, I widna be setting my sights too high,' said Hoynes.

'I daresay we might manage a glass o' thon Babycham and that. Of course, you canna beat the fish and chips they dae up here for functions. I must say, the County have done us proud.'

'I'll have the chips, but I canna have the fish.' Jenny was standing in front of them now, playing with a strand of her blonde hair.

'Why ever not?' enquired Hamish.

'I'm a vegetarian noo. I started a week past on Thursday. It's all the rage doon in London.'

'Och, they say all sorts doon in London. They telt me I'd never had it so good a few years ago, but the bank manager didna seem tae agree.' Hoynes took a contemplative puff of his pipe. 'Anyhow, fish isna meat, so you'll be fine.'

'Dae you think no'?' Jenny's face brightened. 'I must admit, I'm no' enjoying my dinners jeest noo. No' much tae look forward tae when you're having cauliflower cheese and vegetable broth every night.'

'No' dae much for your wind, neither,' observed Hoynes.

'If folk were meant tae eat plants and naethin' else, then how come they made a Sunday roast so tasty? If I was you, Jenny, I'd put a' that nonsense oot o' my mind and go and get yoursel' a pie fae Blue's. You'll be needin' tae keep your strength up if you're courting. Who's the lucky boy, anyhow?' asked Hamish.

'Here he is coming up the street noo,' she replied. 'No stranger tae the pair o' yous, anyway, I'm thinking.'

Sure enough, a slim young man in a suit that looked at least a size too big for him was making his way up Main Street towards them, clutching a small bunch of flowers.

'Skipper, Hamish,' said Peter, his face flushing. 'I hope your meeting went well.'

'You sly young dog, Peter,' said Hoynes. 'But did you no' keep your romancing close to your chest.'

Peter shifted awkwardly from foot to foot. 'Oh, this is oor first date, isn't it, Jenny?' He smiled bashfully at the young woman who nodded and threaded her arm through his.

'And if we don't get a move on, we'll miss the film, Peter.'

'Aye, you're right. I'll see you bright and early on Monday morning, skipper,' said Peter as Jenny dragged him down the street.

'Aye, see you're in good fettle, tae. Bright-eyed and bushy-tailed, young man,' said Hoynes. 'And tell your faither we're asking for him, Jenny.'

They watched as the pair walked arm-in-arm down Main Street.

'There's no justice, Hamish.'

'No, you're right there – none at all.'

'How a miserable bugger like Watson the Fishery Officer can produce a bonnie wee lassie like that, I'll never know. If Maggie was as ship-shape in the beam as young Jenny, we'd have been rid o' her years ago.'

'But then you might have a boy like Peter for your future son-in-law, not a police sergeant, Sandy.'

'You've the right of it again, Hamish. Auld heid on young shoulders, right enough. Come on, you, and let's get a dram o' this poison fae Skye.'

'I daresay I'll manage tae force one doon, skipper,' replied Hamish with a grin.

IV

Hoynes lived in a neat, two-storey, semi-detached council house on the outskirts of Kinloch. Despite the time of year, there was a crackling fire in the grate; on the mantelpiece sat an ornamental ship's wheel flanked by old black-and-white photographs and a pair of brass candlesticks. The three-piece suite was old but comfortable, and as Hoynes went to fetch the whisky Hamish felt his eyelids grow heavy. A small television in the corner of the room flickered silently to nobody in particular.

'I don't know why they insist on leaving that thing on when there's nobody in the room. Instead o' turning the sound down, why dae they no' jeest turn it off,' complained Hoynes, brandishing a bottle in his large right hand. 'I'm fair crippled wae they electric bills. In the winter you can see this hoose fae miles aboot – lit up like the Ardnamurchan lighthoose, it is – every light in the place on. Aye, and us all sitting in here by the fire. Fair profligate they women are.'

'A waste o' electricity,' muttered Hamish, looking absently at the television screen, where Andy Stewart was busy mouthing the words to a song they couldn't hear.

Hoynes switched off the set, then slid open the glass door of the display cabinet which sat next to the television. 'Since you're no' jeest anybody, you can have your dram oot o' a crystal glass.'

'What's the racket upstairs, Sandy?'

'Aye, you wid think there was a herd o' baby elephants up there, no' jeest the wife and daughter. They're having the show o' presents next week, so they're busy getting the hoose ready.'

'Surely folk won't be parading aboot in your bedroom?'

'That's where you're wrong. The bloody presents are tae be in oor bedroom – three nights o' it. I'm going tae sleep on the boat. I canna be footered wae all this upheaval.'

Marjorie Hoynes looked on as her daughter admired herself in the wardrobe mirror. Maggie had chosen a plain white wedding gown. At thirty-five, she was far too old to be flouncing about in a fancy big meringue.

'We'll maybe get a shawl for you, Maggie.'

'A shawl? It's July, Mother. I'm already worried that I'll melt.'

'Och, sure you know a good shawl can hide a multitude o' things,' said Marjorie, her eyes drifting to the back of the dress again.

'You mean it'll hide my rear end.'

'Now, I never said such a thing. A shawl would complete the outfit. You could drape it o'er your shoulders, like so . . .' Marjorie mimed the action.

'And then I could drape it further over my big backside.'

'No, no, not at all. That's not what I meant. I could knit one – there's still time.'

'Aye, and you can maybe knit me a bikini for my honeymoon while you're at it.'

Marjorie thought for a moment or two. 'I widna recommend bathing in a knitted swimming costume, dear. The wool would just get waterlogged, and . . .'

'And then Duncan would get a right good look at my arse.'

'Och, there's no reasoning with you, Maggie. You're just as stubborn as your faither.' She folded her arms and looked away from her daughter.

'What's that I'm hearing?' said Maggie eventually.

Her mother cocked her head. 'It's your faither doonstairs. He must be back fae his meeting.'

'I bet he's guzzling that good bottle of whisky my Duncan brought him last week . . . I can hear another voice too.'

The women both looked into space and listened more intently.

'That's Hamish,' confirmed Marjorie. 'Ye canna mistake the drawl. If you ask him nicely he'll likely tell you if you'll have a boy or a lassie when the time comes. He's got the sight, the same as his faither and grandfaither afore him.'

'Well, that's the end of the whisky, then. I was hoping Faither would keep it for raising a toast at the reception.'

'Maggie Hoynes! When have you ever known a bottle o' whisky last mair than a few days in this hoose? It's like sitting a monkey doon in front of a banana tree and expecting it tae take a look and say, "Och, I'll just leave them until next week". Your faither lacks willpower when it comes tae a dram, and that's a fact.'

'Would you say they're whispering?'

The Hoynes women strained to hear the muffled conversation coming up through the floorboards.

'They've definitely lowered their voices – and that's never a good sign. Aye, an' maist unusual tae when they've had a few drinks.'

'They'll be planning something devilish for my Duncan's stag night,' said Maggie, slipping out of her wedding dress. 'I warned Faither aboot it. Duncan can't be seen to be up to any high jinks, not with him being the police sergeant.'

'Dae you mind whoot they did tae poor Johnny Souter? Och, it was a sin.'

'Well, if they think they're going to set Duncan adrift on a raft in the Atlantic, they can think again. The poor bugger nearly got washed all the way to Donegal.'

'An' him dressed as the Queen Mother, tae.'

Maggie pulled a housecoat over her shoulders. 'I'm going to have a wee look at what's going on. I'll soon put that pair's gas at a peep. Duncan's got a position in society to think about.

They'll not be plotting their wicked schemes on my fiancé.' She tiptoed out of the room.

Marjorie picked up her daughter's dress and looked it up and down. I better get those knitting needles oot, she thought to herself.

'So, have you got it, Sandy? Once an adequate sufficiency has been consumed, we'll suggest taking the session elsewhere.'

'Tae Geordie McCallum's bothy, am I right?'

'A hell o' a trip, but Geordie will lend us his Land Rover. It's damn near the only way tae get there along they auld tracks.'

'Agreed.'

'It's easy for a man tae disappear for a long while away oot there. Especially wae a good cargo o' booze aboard. When they're merry, we can make oor excuses and head back tae Kinloch. When they don't turn up for work the next day, there will be a right stink. We can take advantage o' the publicity tae draw attention tae oor plight wae the fish.'

'And nobody can accuse us o' kidnap, or the like. They came along willingly, and could've left at any time. Well, Hamish, it's genius. Pure genius, man. If you hadna been a fisherman, you'd have made a fine master criminal, and no mistake. They'll have a job on their hands making it back fae Geordie's on foot, and no mistake.'

'Aye, we'll sort that plane, Sandy.'

The pair chuckled and clinked glasses to toast their scheme.

On the stairwell, Maggie shook her head. If they thought they were getting her Duncan pissed and on a plane, they could think again.

V

Sergeant Duncan Grant sat behind his desk in Kinloch Police Office, the black Bakelite telephone receiver clamped to his right ear. He was conscious of the fact that it was late on a Saturday evening, and he should be out checking all was well in Kinloch's many pubs, but the Chief Constable of Argyll Constabulary was on the phone, so that would have to wait.

'Yes, sir,' soothed Grant in his soft Highland lilt. 'But you know how it is in these wee places. They see that kind of thing as their birthright.'

'Birthright be damned,' replied Chief Constable Semple. 'This illicit trade in clear whisky has to stop, and stop now. I've had my opposite number in Ayrshire on the phone twice this week about it. They're taking lemonade bottles full of the stuff across there from distilleries in Kinloch. Bloody fishermen. It's modern-day smuggling – nothing more, nothing less.'

It was true that a certain amount of newly distilled spirit made its way out of the distillery of its birth and into glasses across the town, but that was the way it had always been in communities where the distilling of whisky was entrenched. Indeed, workers were given a quarter bottle of 'the clear stuff' twice a day, as part of their contract of employment. This clear spirit, too young to be called whisky, was like the oil that lubricated the industry – as far as Duncan Grant was concerned, anyway.

Despite his feelings on the matter, he had to act. 'So, what do you suggest, sir?'

'I suggest you catch the buggers, Sergeant. I've spoken to Customs and Excise, and they're sending a special investigator down to Kinloch. Let me see, yes, a collector named Marshall. I want you to work hand-in-glove with him and his men.'

'Yes, sir. Of course. I'll make it a priority.'

'And I don't need to tell you who the main culprits are. Every stillman in Kinloch has false pockets, with these . . . these devices.'

'Dookers, sir.'

'Dookers?'

'That's what you call them. Usually a bottle, tied at the neck to a piece of string. They dunk them in the casks and fill them up, screw on the cap, and away you go – down the leg of the dungarees, and off home.'

'You seem remarkably well informed, Sergeant,' replied Semple with a sniff.

'Well, sir, it's common practice. I'm sure the distillery owners turn a blind eye. A perk of the job, I always thought.'

'Not any more it's not. We're a kick in the arse away from the seventies – we can't have this lawlessness going on. It's theft, no other word for it. Now these damn fishermen are exporting the stuff all over the west coast! Well, not with *my* force on the case. Have you got that, Grant?'

'Yes, sir, absolutely.' Grant could hear the Chief Constable breathing heavily on the other end of the line.

'I hear you're to be married, Sergeant Grant.'

'Yes, sir. A week on Friday, actually.'

'And to the daughter of Sandy Hoynes, I believe.'

'Yes, sir. Mr Hoynes is to be my new father-in-law,' replied Grant with a grimace, suspecting more was to be made of this.

'I was his lieutenant in the RNR during the war, you know. On minesweepers.'

'Oh, I didn't know that, sir. I'll tell him you were asking for him,' said Grant, considerably encouraged by the fact that his boss knew Maggie's father so well.

'Oh yes. He was made a petty officer because he knew the coast so well.' Semple let out a long, slow breath. 'But I tell you this, Grant. A more devious, ingenious, scurrilous mind I have yet to encounter – especially when it came to insubordination and whisky.' He paused. 'Now you're at the very heart of the family, you'll be well placed to keep an eye on things. This transportation of illicit spirit is just the type of caper I would expect from Hoynes, especially since the fishing has been so bad this year.'

'Sir, you surely don't expect me to spy on my in-laws?' protested Grant.

'That, Sergeant, is *exactly* what I expect you to do.'

The summer light was fading into starlight as Peter and Jenny stood at the front gate of the neat little cottage by the shore of the loch. The views across Kinloch and to the hills beyond reflected the mood as the couple took in the scene, hand in hand. Over on the pier, Peter could see a cart being loaded with provisions from a steam puffer. The whinny of the impatient horse at its head carried on the still night air.

'Did you like the film, Jenny?'

'Aye, I did. It wisna the maist romantic effort, but I enjoyed it.' She looked up at him and smiled.

'Who would've thought *The Charge of the Light Brigade* would be so . . .' He held her gaze for a moment, their faces moving closer together, as she angled her lips up towards his. They were about to kiss when the front door of the cottage swung open and a beam of electric light illuminated the garden and the young couple at the gate.

'That will be enough of that!' thundered Watson. 'Where have you been, Jenny? It's nearly half past ten.'

'Oh, Dad. It's nineteen sixty-eight, not eighteen sixty-eight. We went to the pictures and then walked back.'

'Well, you couldn't have been walking very fast. You should've had my daughter back here as soon as the film was finished, Peter,' he scolded the young man.

'S-sorry,' Peter stammered in reply. 'I didn't mean to upset you, Mr Watson.'

'Oh, don't be scared of him, Peter,' said Jenny, letting go of her beau's hand and opening the gate. 'Give as good as you get – I do.'

'Just get yourself indoors, young lady,' said Watson. 'I want to have a wee chat with Peter.'

Jenny stopped in front of her father and glared at him. 'Don't you be nasty to him,' she muttered under her breath.

'Get inside!' shouted Watson. 'This minute! While you're under my roof, you'll follow my rules.' He watched his daughter stomp up the path and into the house, then winced as she slammed the door.

Watson walked to the gate, where Peter waited, trembling slightly now that the sun had faded and the night air had cooled. The smell of the sea, cut grass and flowers was heady as the dusk turned into night under a full moon.

'Now, Peter,' said Watson, remaining on the other side of the gate, his voice almost friendly. 'How are you enjoying life with Sandy Hoynes?'

'Oh, fine, Mr Watson. He's a good skipper – fair instructing me in the ways o' the sea an' that,' replied Peter, hoping to sound as though he was making the best of his new career.

'Aye, well, that's commendable. Just commendable, indeed.' Watson paused. 'You'll be asking my Jenny out on another date?'

'Well, I'd like to – if she wants to go.'

'Or if I give her permission.'

'Yes, sorry . . .' mumbled Peter, gulping as he did so.

'I want you and me to be friends too, Peter.' Watson smiled.

'Aye, me tae.' Peter smiled back. Things were going better than he'd expected.

'And would you agree that friends help each other, Peter?'

'Aye, aye, I wid, Mr Watson.'

The Fishery Officer stared silently at the moon for a few moments. 'Glad to hear it. So, with that friendship in mind, here's what I want you to do for me . . .'

VI

'Well, would you look at that. An octopus. You don't see many o' them in these waters, eh, Hamish?'

'No, that you don't. It'll fetch a pretty penny fae auld Keacheran. They tell me he sends exotic stuff like that to Glasgow, and it ends up on the best tables in London.'

'Poor recompense for the lack o' herring.'

'Och, but at least we caught something, Sandy.'

The *Girl Maggie* was sitting on a gentle swell south-east of the Isle of Arran. The day had been milky warm – even out at sea. They had fallen upon a small shoal of herring and picked up other bits and pieces, including the unfortunate octopus, in a catch that would have seemed on the slim side only a few months ago, but was now enough to raise spirits on the vessel.

'Whoot are you up tae, Peter?' asked Hamish. 'We've no' had a peep oot o' you all day.'

'Nothing, jeest taking notes,' muttered the young fisherman.

'Notes on whoot?' asked Hoynes.

'Och, you know, places we fish and where we get the best

60

chances o' a catch. I've tae go tae college in Glesca for a whiles in November, so this is the kind o' stuff they're after. Jeest tae make sure you're learning on the job.'

'A college for the fishing – whootever next', remarked Hamish. 'They'll be sending nurses tae university before you know it.'

'You'll likely need letters after your name tae empty the bins, the way things are going', added Hoynes. 'Still, at least you've got something tae write doon the day, so that's a bonus for us all.'

'Can you tell me the weight o' they fish, skipper?'

'My, you're the keen one, right enough, Peter. If you hang on until we get back, you can take the weight from the scales on the pier. It's good tae see a young man so involved in learning his trade.' Hoynes smiled and sent a puff of pipe smoke heavenward.

'The weather's tae break on Wednesday. Did you hear it on the wireless there?' said Hamish.

The two older men exchanged a glance.

'Well, that will be as good a day as any,' said Hoynes.

'A good day for what?' enquired Peter, sensing there was something afoot.

'Och, ne'er you mind. Jeest you keep your nose in that jotter. And while you're at it, you can leave oot any mention o' that octopus. I'm sure me and Keacheran can dae a wee sale on the side wae that creature,' said Hoynes, rubbing his hands.

'A sale on the side? What's that when it's at home?'

'That's fae the advanced course they'll likely no' teach you at college, Peter. Time enough for you tae learn that. Whoot do you say, Hamish?'

'As the bard would say himsel', there are more things in heaven, earth and fishing boats than are dreamt o' in your philosophy,' replied Hamish.

'My, but was he no' a clever one, thon Shakespeare. Though I'd nae idea he'd been at the fishing,' said Hoynes with a wink.

As his crewmates laughed to themselves, Peter carefully jotted down the word 'octopus' at the back of his jotter, alongside the date and time.

Duncan and Maggie were strolling along Kinloch's esplanade. It had been a hot day at the police office, with the narrow gaps under the crumbling old sash windows letting in little of the scant breeze. The evening was mercifully cooler, and Duncan was enjoying being out in the fresh air, the waft of Maggie's perfume adding a pleasing note to the tang of the sea.

'Not long now, love,' he said, glancing at his intended.

'No,' said Maggie. 'Just the show of presents to get through. And then there's your stag night . . .'

'A few drinks with your father, Hamish and some of the boys – I wouldn't exactly call it a stag night, Maggie.'

She stopped and looked up at him, holding both of his hands in hers. 'You don't know what they're like, Duncan. It's a kind of tradition here – amongst the fishermen – when one of their own gets hitched. Oh, they have a bit of a carry-on, all together.'

'I'm not one of their own, though. Don't worry, they'll not get up to any high jinks with me.' He smiled reassuringly.

'That's what they all say.' Maggie was chewing her lip. 'They shaved off Norrie Maclean's eyebrows. He looked like something out of a waxworks on his wedding day. And big Tommy McMichael nearly missed his big day altogether.'

'How?'

'They tied him to a lamppost – he was there all night, and it set off his pleurisy. He looked like a ghost in front of the minister. They had to have oxygen on standby. Poor wee Sheena was bawling all through the service.'

'Maggie, trust me. Nothing like that's going to happen to me. I'm more than a match for your father and his cronies. In any case, there'll be a squad of my men there, so relax.'

She looked away. Across the loch the throaty putter of the Gardiner diesel engine heralded the arrival of her father's boat as it made its way into harbour. 'There's the old bugger there,' she said.

'Oh aye. And trailing some gulls – they must have a decent catch for once.'

'They're up to something, Duncan.' She grabbed his hands again. 'Something to do with a plane. I wouldn't be surprised if you ended up on Islay, or maybe even darkest Africa. That lot are capable of anything!'

'What do you mean, a plane?'

'Just that. I heard Hamish and my father on Saturday night. They were plotting something, no doubt about it. I know them better than you, remember.'

'I'm sure it's nothing,' said Duncan. Then he remembered his conversation with Semple. 'Surely they're not sending the stuff out by plane,' he said out loud before realising it.

'What are you on about?'

'Nothing, nothing at all. Just thinking about a case. It was when you mentioned a plane.' He stared across the loch. Sure enough, there was Sandy Hoynes at the prow of the *Girl Maggie*, puffs of pipe smoke billowing out behind him.

VII

As it turned out, the following Wednesday was exactly as

forecast. Rain pelted Kinloch, aided and abetted by a strong westerly gale, which kept mariners and aviators alike away from their toil.

Sandy Hoynes was standing beside Hamish and a slightly built man with a squint at the bar of the Douglas Arms. The hostelry was busy, with a fair number of land-bound fishermen taking advantage of the day off to enjoy a dram or two.

'No' a sign o' they pilots, Hamish. Isn't it jeest typical – the way oor luck's been playing o'er the last while, and no mistake.'

'Och, Sandy, but you're a right pessimist. I telt you, I had that dream last night – we'll meet them today, right here. There's nae doubt aboot it.'

'Fortunately I have faith in your prescience, Hamish. But I could still do wae another wee sensation – jeest tae keep the spirits up. Is it no' your round, Geordie?'

The man with the squint turned; he appeared to take in both Hoynes and Hamish at the same time before reaching into his pocket. 'Is it no' enough you're commandeering my wee bothy and my Land Rover? You want me tae buy drinks, tae.'

'We've filled her up wae diesel, Geordie. Aye, and this wee scheme will be an advantage tae you as well. You've caught less than us o'er the last few weeks,' noted Hamish.

'I don't deny it. If I hadna kept they sheep an' that oot at Glen Brackie, I don't know how we'd have made ends meet.'

'It's a hell o' a trek, mind,' said Hoynes. 'I'm no' sure I'd want tae dae that every day, especially efter a hard day at sea. Off tae look efter sheep and the like. You've got a big heart, Geordie.'

'You know fine I widna manage it mysel'. Beth does a lot o' that – unless the weather's the way it is today. She doesn't like running the risk o' the Piper's Pass in heavy rain.'

'The Piper's Pass is as safe as hooses. I canna mind the last time there was a landslide,' said Hamish.

'Easy for you tae say. Her grandfaither was crushed under it in nineteen forty-seven. Every time there's any heavy rain, she'll no' go anywhere near it. Jeest as well we're on this mission the day. I'd have tae have gone oot in any event.'

'Ten miles o' rough tracks, then a pile o' auld sheep for company. As I say, you've got a big heart, Geordie.'

Geordie paid for the drinks and sighed. 'It's no' all bad. The wee bothy is cosy enough once you get the fire set. Everything you need. I've even got a wireless, so it's no' much different fae being in the wheelhoose. I get a brew goin', get a bite on the wee stove, and sit back. Not a soul tae bother you, herself back in the toon, the gas lamps flickering wae the firelight – it's fair relaxing.'

'No' if the Piper's Pass comes doon on your heid,' remarked Hamish, taking the first sip of his fresh dram.

'It's happened once since I had the place – well, since I've been married tae Beth, it coming fae her family.'

'Was that in fifty-six, Geordie?' asked Hoynes.

'Aye, it was that. Fortunately, it was Davy, Beth's brother who'd gone oot. We'd had tae put in at Sanda, if you mind. Hellish weather, all together. Beth widna consider it, so he stepped intae the breach.'

'An' him busy at the bank all day, tae,' said Hamish.

'But the crofting's still in his blood. Mark you, he hasna offered since.'

'Are you surprised?' said Hoynes. 'Was he no' stranded for near a week?'

'He was that. It was the worst week o' gales anyone can remember. We managed tae get the lifeboat intae the wee bay at Caribeg and got him hame. He'd been eating limpets, the poor bugger. Near lost the will tae live.'

'At least it didna fall on his heid,' said Hamish.

'No, but he didna miss it by much. Maybe aboot half an hour. He heard the roar as the hillside collapsed, mind. Aye, and the piper, tae.'

'That's jeest an auld wife's tale,' scoffed Hoynes. 'It was likely the wind whistling through the eaves o' that bothy o' yours.'

'Indeed it was not,' said Geordie indignantly. 'He even named the tune – "The Flooers O' The Forest". You can ask him to this day.'

The three of them stood in silence, contemplating the plight of the stranded man. Their musings were interrupted when the door burst open to reveal two men, rain running off their slate-grey raincoats in rivulets.

'A pint of your very best, landlord!' shouted the taller of the two, as they shrugged off their soaking garments. 'And a drink for the bar, while you're at it,' he added, spreading his coat over a radiator.

Amidst the clamour of orders, Hoynes winked at Hamish. 'No' slow wae a dram, right enough. The game's on, my freens.'

Watson the Fishery Officer and Marshall, the stony-faced Collector from Her Majesty's Customs and Excise, sat opposite Sergeant Grant in Kinloch Police Office.

'My information is that it's to be today. Whatever they're up to, that is,' said Watson. 'We have to strike while the iron's hot, Duncan. I know this is difficult for you, under the circumstances, but the law is the law, and I'm sure you're more than aware of the seriousness of all this.'

'Difficult – why so?' queried Marshall.

'The sergeant here has a personal connection to Mr Hoynes ... sir,' replied Watson obsequiously.

'The fact that I'm just about to marry Sandy Hoynes' daughter makes absolutely no difference, Mr Watson. If a crime is being committed, my duty is clear. I'll not flinch from it,' said Grant.

'And it better had remain that way, Sergeant,' replied Marshall. 'There's a lot of interest in this case at Customs House in Glasgow. Make no mistake, *everyone* is taking this smuggling issue very seriously indeed. Careers may depend upon it. I hope I make myself clear?' He raised his eyebrows for emphasis.

'You needn't worry about me,' replied Watson. 'I've been after Sandy Hoynes for a long time. I've never been able to pin anything on him – slippery as an eel – but we've got him this time. Dealing in octopuses now, would you believe.'

'I'm less worried about the creatures of the deep and more about other matters,' said Marshall.

Watson stood. 'I have it on *very* good authority that Hoynes and his sidekick are meeting with someone today. A plot is on the go. This very afternoon.

'They are currently holed up in the Douglas Arms. I have one of my officers making discreet observations, as you requested, Mr Marshall. But I need to know more.'

'If our information is correct, they are meeting people with access to a plane. We can only assume that this is with a view to transporting Plain British Spirit out of bond, illicitly, to another destination. We already know that this stuff has made its way to Ayrshire.' Marshall looked the policeman in the eye. 'This is where it ends.'

Grant thought for a moment or two. Did he suspect that his prospective father-in-law may not exactly adhere to the rulebook when it came to fishing? Yes. Did he think he was smuggling large quantities of illegal booze? No. He thought about Maggie, the wedding, and just how difficult this was likely to make their nuptials. He had no choice. 'Of course, my resources are at your disposal. I've already talked to my chief constable about this, so Argyll Constabulary is ready to participate in any way you see fit.'

'Excellent, Sergeant,' replied Marshall, a gleam in his eye. 'Now all we have to do is watch and wait.'

Hoynes and his first mate, followed by Geordie, sidled up to the bar and introduced themselves to the pilots.

'They tell me you both served in the war. I'm privileged to say I did myself,' said Hoynes, his chest swelling.

'I was in Spits, but Bertie here was part of the lumbering squad.' He winked at his colleague.

'Lumbering, Ralph? Remember the parable of the tortoise and the hare, my friend,' joked Bertie. 'All very well for you chaps looping the loop and showing off with victory rolls. When it came to beating Jerry in his own backyard it was left to us.'

'*Touché.*'

'But things must be very different noo,' remarked Hamish. 'I mean that great beast you're flying jeest noo – can you imagine whoot they Nazis wid have done wae such a contraption?'

'Doesn't bear thinking about. If Jerry had managed to get a march on us with jet fighters – and they damn nearly did – the war would have had a very different outcome,' said Ralph, suddenly looking very serious.

Hoynes puffed at his pipe thoughtfully. 'I'm a seafarer, as you know. Served wae the RNR as a petty officer. I'm no' much good when it comes tae science, an' that.'

'Spit it out, Sandy,' said Bertie. 'Another dram?'

'Och, I don't mind if I do. Very kind, very kind, indeed.'

'Me too,' said Hamish, raising his glass.

As Bertie got the drinks in, Hoynes addressed Ralph. 'I was wondering how come that aircraft of yours makes such a bloody racket?'

'No magic to it. As we go past the sound barrier – the speed at which sound can travel – that barrier breaks on the nose of the crate. That's putting it simply, of course. It's a wonderful piece of engineering.'

'It would be mair wonderful if they could shut it up a wee bit,' observed Hamish.

The little group of drinkers savoured the first sips of their whisky before the conversation resumed.

'So how long wid it take you to get to New York?' asked Geordie. 'I've got a cousin there I would love tae visit one day.'

'From here? Oh, if we were going full tilt and given a decent wind we could be there in four hours,' said Bertie.

'Four hours tae New York?' spluttered Hoynes. 'It takes six hoors on the bus tae get tae Glesca!'

'They'll never fly it that fast with passengers, mind you,' Bertie continued. 'But our job is to test it to the limit.'

'There'll come a day when folk will be stayin' here in Kinloch an' working in America, or even Australia. It's all mapped oot, if you care tae think aboot it,' said Hamish.

'You boys must be remarkable pilots, right enough.' Hoynes tapped his pipe out in a glass ashtray. 'I'm thinking there won't be very many of you about?'

'With supersonic experience? I should say not,' replied Ralph. 'A dozen, maybe fifteen.'

'Are they all oot at the base at Machrie?'

'No, not at all. I meant in the whole world. We're a rare breed, aren't we, Bertie?'

'That we are.'

Hamish looked at Hoynes and winked. Rare breeds like these would be sadly missed – even if it was only for a short while. Time enough to attract the world's attention to the plight of Kinloch's herring fishermen.

VIII

The three women sat in the Hoynes' living room, nursing cups of tea. The fuller figures of Marjorie and Maggie bookended a birdlike woman, with a tiny face and hair scraped back in a scraggy bun.

'He canna hauld his drink. The least wee tipple an' he's singing like a bird,' griped Geordie McCallum's wife Beth. 'You jeest have tae be careful how you go aboot getting any sense oot o' him.'

'If they think they're going to spirit my Duncan off they can think again. That's not going to happen.' Maggie lifted her chin and stared from one woman to the other. 'He's finishing early today, and we're going to get him a suit for the honeymoon.'

'You better hope he's no' finished already and doon the Douglas Arms wae that faither o' yours.' Beth shook her head to emphasise the seriousness of their predicament. 'They're taking someone tae oor wee bothy – who else could it be, Maggie? Aye, an' whoot's goin' tae happen afterwards?'

'And how can we stop them?' pondered Marjorie. 'I know my husband – he's like a dog wae a bone. He never gies up. If he sets his mind on something, he'll go hell for leather tae make it happen. As soon as I got him interested in fridges, there was no stoppin' him.'

'That was a good piece of logic, Marjorie. How on earth did you manage that?' asked Beth.

'Dead easy. I jeest telt him a' the money we'd lose whoot wae food going off in the pantry. Did he no' go oot and do something that very day. Ordered the contraption and everything.'

'He doesn't like it, though,' said Maggie. 'Swears blind it makes the cheese lose its flavour.'

'It doesna improve it any, right enough,' said Marjorie. 'I always put a wee dollop o' mustard in wae a cheese sauce. Try it, Beth, gies it a great flavour.'

'Mother, we're losing the thread here. Beth's not interested in making a cheese sauce, when her man's about to be caught up in the machinations of my father and his trusty assistant.'

'Well, whootever it is, they canna dae it waeoot a Land Rover. That's where oor Geordie comes in.'

'Is that no' it sittin' at the front gate, Beth?'

'No, that's the auld yin. I cut aboot in it maist o' the time. It's a wee bit temperamental, but I nurse her through. The only way tae get oot the road. Geordie bought yin for himsel'. It was only second-hand, but he wishes he'd no' bothered noo, whoot wae the fishing goin' tae the dogs. Mark you, it's always stinking o' fish.'

'So they think they're going to imprison my Duncan then send him goodness knows where. It's time to get down to the Douglas Arms and put a stop to it all.'

'Aye, but we'll have tae ca' canny, Maggie,' said her mother. 'Think, once we've caught them, we'll have them that guilty, they'll no' stray for weeks, right through the wedding and

71

beyond. We can put all this nonsense o' my Duncan's stag night behind us. Jeest gie them enough rope.'

'We need to keep a watching brief, Sergeant,' said Marshall the Customs Officer. 'I don't want us going off half-cocked and them getting off on some technicality.'

'I have Hoynes banged to rights with that octopus. But I agree, we need to bide our time. Just give them enough rope,' whispered Watson.

Grant, Marshall and Watson were in the back of a police van, staring across the road at the Douglas Arms through a gap between the front seats. Though it was July, lowering cloud and a downpour of rain darkened the scene.

'Could you not go and issue some parking tickets, Sergeant. I can see at least three candidates from here. It'll distract attention from the van,' muttered Marshall.

Grant ignored him. 'So, the plan is, when they move – if they move – we decamp into the Customs vehicle and follow them at a discreet distance. Is that agreed?'

'I'm up for it,' replied Watson, a gleam back in his eye.

'All we have to do is wait,' said Marshall. 'This will be a feather in all of our caps, gentlemen.'

Grant stared gloomily at the Douglas Arms. Arresting his father-in-law might improve his prospects for promotion, but it certainly wouldn't make for a good start to married life.

Stay in there and get drunk and prove this pair wrong, the police sergeant prayed to himself, just as the pub's front door swung open and the distinctive blue cloud of pipe tobacco wafted out onto the street and was carried away on the wind.

'There! Father's there!' exclaimed Maggie. She was at the mouth of the close opposite the Douglas Arms. 'Who's that with him? That's not Hamish.' Sure enough, a tall man with a neat haircut was shrugging on a grey raincoat in the pub doorway. He and Hoynes were laughing at something, both looking somewhat unsteady on their feet.

'Did you ever,' said Beth, peering over Maggie's shoulder. 'The pair o' them are three sheets tae the wind.'

As the three women, remaining hidden, looked on, more figures appeared in the doorway.

'There's Hamish. No show withoot Punch, right enough,' said Marjorie. The first mate was with another man in a gabardine raincoat, slightly stockier, but just as smart as the other stranger. 'Whoever their freens are, I don't like the look o' them. Is there no sign o' Duncan, Maggie?'

'No. I've not seen him yet.'

'Och, he's likely incapacitated in oor new Land Rover,' said Beth. 'Likely tied up, or drugged, so they can spirit him off, the poor soul.'

'Steady on, Beth. My man's no' a monster. I can see him fillin' big Duncan full o' whisky, but I don't think they'll get tae the druggin'-and-tyin'-up stage jeest tae make him compliant.'

'You've great faith, Mother,' said Maggie, clearly not convinced that her father wouldn't resort to such means.

A small man in a cap was last to leave the Douglas Arms. He was searching in the pockets of his shabby overcoat.

'And there's my Geordie. I don't know how many times I've telt him tae bin that bloody coat. No' fit tae grace a tattie-bogle.' Beth looked on as her husband produced something from his pocket. 'Aye, that's him found the keys noo.'

'I can't see any sign of your Land Rover, Beth,' said Maggie.

'They're fly buggers. They'll have it parked in the backyard o' the County, oot the way. My Geordie won't take too much drink if he's tae drive, but he widna pass wan o' they new breathalyser tests the polis is using noo. They'll have parked up oot o' sight.'

'In that case, we better get going. If they're parked at the County, they'll need to pass here. If we sit in the motor, up the Well Close, we can follow when we see them.' Maggie shook her head. 'If they've done anything to my Duncan . . .'

'Received, Constable,' said Grant into his radio. 'They're getting into a Land Rover in the car park of the County Hotel, five of them. We can identify Hoynes, Hamish and Geordie, but no idea who the other two are.'

'That'll be their contacts,' said Watson. 'Smooth-looking operators, if ever I saw them. Not from around here, at any rate. And certainly not fishermen.'

'We have to be careful not to be spotted,' said Marshall. 'Will you take the wheel, Sergeant? You know the area better than me.'

As Grant started the engine, a battered old Land Rover puttered past, turned right and headed up the Glebe Brae. 'That's our men,' said Grant. He waited for a few moments then followed.

IX

'Great idea, gentlemen,' said Bertie from the back of Geordie's Land Rover. 'We don't get to see much of the countryside.'

'I daresay it jeest flies past in a flash – and a bang,' said Hamish who was sitting in the back with the pilot.

'We can take the top off one of these.' Bertie fished around the inside pocket of his raincoat and produced a lemonade bottle.

'Is that what I think it is?'

'"The clearrr schtuff", as you call it,' replied Bertie, adopting a Scottish accent. 'I've grown quite fond of it. Blows your cares away, eh, Ralph?'

'It does, indeed,' replied his fellow pilot. He was squeezed in between Hoynes and Geordie, who was gripping the large steering wheel and squinting through the windscreen at the heavy rain. 'Reminds me a bit of that scrumpy we used to get in Somerset. You know, with the bits floating at the bottom. A couple of those and you were set for the evening, and no mistake.'

'Och, but it's fine you like a drink or two. The price of whisky in that Douglas Arms – damn near daylight robbery,' said Hoynes. 'Once we've got tae the bothy we'll make a right good night o' it. We've a few bottles of our own.'

'Hear, hear,' said Bertie. 'Time for a bit of a song, I reckon.' He cleared his throat then launched into 'One man went to mow, went to mow a meadow'. Everyone joined in, apart from Geordie, who shook his head and concentrated on the wet road.

'That's not oor Geordie's Land Rover,' said Beth. 'He's got a crack in his rear light, and there's no sign o' anything like that. Anyway, it's too new.'

'Maybe he got it fixed,' suggested Maggie.

'No, nor fixed. We're following the wrong folk!'

'But they're going the right way, Beth,' said Marjorie. 'Surely that's a good sign.'

'They'll be accomplices, Mother. You better stay back a bit, Beth. You'll just make them suspicious. I tell you, this is getting murkier and murkier by the minute.'

As the rain got heavier, and the wind gusted to gale force, the three-vehicle convoy travelled on. About seven miles outside Kinloch, Geordie turned his vehicle onto a single track road marked 'Glen Brackie'. The engine strained as it took the steep hill.

'Heading well into the hinterland, are we not?' said Ralph, taking the bottle from his lips.

'It'll be well worth the wait, you'll see,' said Hoynes, a broad grin spread across his flushed face. 'Och, I'm fair enjoying oor wee jaunt, right enough.' He took a swig of whisky from the bottle in his hand. 'Whoot song will we murder noo?'

'Wid you mind no' murdering anything,' replied Geordie. 'I've tae keep my wits aboot me. This road's mair like a burn.'

Steep hills rose on either side of them, shimmering in the sheets of rain pushed along by the wailing wind. The sky was a dark grey, and seemed to hang over the landscape in heavy curtains.

'You wouldna think it wiz July,' said Hamish. 'It reminds me o' a story my faither used tae tell me when I was a boy.'

'Is it the one aboot the Raglin shepherd and his horse?' asked Hoynes, his voice slurring. 'If so, I know it off by heart.'

'We don't, though,' piped up Bertie. 'Come on, Hamish. It'll break up the journey. The speed we're going we'll be lucky to get where we're going by Christmas.'

'I'm goin' as fast as these conditions will allow. If you'll note, there's great drops either side o' us. We're heading onto the Piper's Pass.'

'And that's jeest where my story begins,' said Hamish. 'The Raglan shepherd – och, a way back in the last century – was comin' back fae an evening in Kinloch. It was a summer night – no' like this one – warm, great big sky, a beautiful day.'

'Aye, it's certainly no' like this one,' muttered Geordie, his windscreen wipers at full tilt.

'Anyhow,' said Hamish, frowning at his story being interrupted. 'The Raglan fella wisna worried in the slightest. He had a wee cottage jeest past the Piper's Pass, an' his horse – Jessie wiz her name – knew the road that well that the only reason he'd tae hauld the reins was so he'd stay on board, so tae speak.

'Everything was going jeest dandy, but then they came upon the Piper's Pass. Jessie fair whinnied, though she'd been there a hunner times afore.' Hamish's voice lowered to a whisper. 'The Raglan shepherd didna take any notice. He wisna a very sensitive man when he was sober, an' wae the drink he could be wile an' ignorant.'

'I'm sure you've never telt me that bit before, Hamish,' said Hoynes.

'Being here's fair making the story come tae mind mair vividly, skipper. Noo, if you don't mind . . .' He cleared his throat. 'He was near nodding off – the whisky bottle near copin' oot o' his grip – when he heard it. Distantly at first, then quite clear . . .'

'Was it Geordie's windscreen wipers?' joked Hoynes. 'They're screechin' fit tae burst here.' The driver scowled at Hoynes.

Hamish soldiered on. 'The pipes make the hair on the neck o' any Scotsman worthy o' the name stand up at the best o' times, but this pibroch . . . man, it was fair ethereal. The tune echoed off the hills, in and oot. And then . . . *he saw it*!'

Ralph jumped in surprise.

'Whoot did he see?' asked Geordie, despite himself.

'A figure swathed in tartan – in a philibeg no less – walking calmly doon the steepest part o' the pass, pipes slung o'er the shoulder, the tune fair deafening him.'

'And what happened then?' gulped Bertie he took a glug of the clear stuff from the lemonade bottle.

'Well, Jessie had seen enough. She reared up, and, of course, her normally being a cuddy o' sublime temperament, the Raglan shepherd wisna ready for such an event,' said Hamish. 'He coped off the back o' her and landed wae a crack on the groond.'

'I'm guessin' he didna spill his whisky, though,' remarked Hoynes dryly.

'Ne'er a drop. Aye, an' he was fair glad o' it, tae. Jessie jeest bolted – ran back doon the pass, her mane fleein' oot behind her like the hair o' a wraith, leaving the Raglan shepherd pinned tae the groond; the fall having fair incapacitated him. He could see the figure blawing at the pipes advancing on him in a steady, relentless march . . .'

'Bloody awkward position to be in,' said Ralph.

'Och, there was naethin' else for it,' Hamish continued. 'He took a right good charge o' his whisky and shouted tae the piper: "You, you've frightened my guid cuddy and left me here no' able tae move. Dae your worst, for you can hardly better the damage you've done tae me already."'

'Aye, he was brave, right enough,' said Hoynes, raising an eyebrow.

'The pipes stopped. Jeest stopped deid. The piper, though, kept on coming.' Hamish drew in a deep breath. 'It was only then that the Raglan shepherd got *really* feart . . .'

'He wisna too canny, then, if it took him a' that while tae

realise things wisna goin' very well,' said Geordie, his face a mask of concentration as he drove up and into the pass proper.

Hamish ignored the driver. 'The piper wiz standing above him. The Raglan fella jeest screwed up his eyes, no' at all anxious tae see whoot wiz in front o' him. It was then he heard it – a voice, a familiar voice.'

'Was it Jessie the horse?' asked Hoynes.

'No, nor Jessie. It was the voice o' his mother . . .'

'No' much o' a story that, Hamish,' said Geordie. 'My mother could get a passable tune oot the pipes. She didna go for the full philibeg costume, right enough, but when it came tae her interpretation o' "Major MacLeod Leavin' Harris", there were few better.' He started to hum the tune.

'Aye, but there was one difference. The Raglan shepherd was a man in his sixties. He'd lost his mother many years before – tae consumption, no less.'

'Och, this jeest gets better and better,' said Hoynes.

'What did she say to him?' asked Bertie.

'She stood there, a' white an' ghostly under the tartan, an' looked him right in the eye. "You'll mind taking they few coins off the mantelshelf," she said, a' matter-o'-fact, like. The shepherd jeest nodded his heid – sheepishly, whoot wae the profession he wiz in, an a'. "Aye, weel," said she, "that wiz the rent money for the factor, as you well knew. It's time tae make amends. If you're to be spared, every year, on this day, you'll pay the rents o' some poor soul in need. The day you don't is the day you'll die." And wae that she jeest vanished, pipes an' all.'

'And did he dae whoot he wiz telt, Hamish?' asked Geordie.

'Aye, he did that. Every year for ten years until he was a bent old man and could work no more, he saved his coin an' paid the dues o' some poor unfortunate soul. He forswore the whisky an' the baccy in order tae be able tae manage it.' Hamish looked at the floor of the vehicle and shook his head.

'And whoot aboot Jessie the horse?' asked Hoynes.

'I'm no' right sure o' whoot happened tae her. But the story's no' finished.'

'Carry on, Hamish,' insisted Ralph.

'This was the days afore the dole an' that kind o' thing. The Raglan shepherd had had tae gie up his toil. He wiz in fine fettle, though. Sitting one night wae one o' his freens enjoying his hospitality.'

'I thought he'd gied up the whisky.' Hoynes snorted.

'He'd gied up buying it himsel', so he could keep his word tae the ghost o' his mother. But he wisna beyond accepting a dram when it wiz offered,' said Hamish with a sniff. 'Suddenly, oot o' nowhere, there came the sound o' the pipes. "Oh!" shouts the Raglan fella. "I've nae money tae pay the debts o' some poor soul. I canna toil any mair. You have to forgive me." But no, the pipes jeest got louder an' louder. The Raglan shepherd sat bolt upright in his chair, his eyes jeest staring . . .'

'And then?' urged Ralph.

'That was it, he jeest died on the spot. But the real issue is: do you want tae know how I know how it went?' Not waiting for a reply, he carried on. 'The man – his freen sittin' wae him – was none other than my auld great-grandfaither. Hamish, too, as it turns oot.'

'You've no' gied them the moral o' the story,' said Hoynes.

'Right enough, neither I have. The moral is this: the piper comes for you and you alone. He, she, it is the moral compass o' oor souls. The piper is different for everybody. For the Raglan shepherd it wiz his ain mother, but who will it be for you?'

As the windscreen wipers screeched and the engine

complained, the looming hills shrank the world until the grey sky was all but obscured. They had entered the Piper's Pass.

X

'Looks as though we're heading for the edge of the bloody world,' said Marshall, as he wiped the steamed-up windscreen with the back of his hand. 'I hope you know where we're going?'

'Just about on the Piper's Pass,' Grant replied. 'I've been here a couple of times, but that's all. Do you have any idea what they're doing here, Mr Watson?'

'Aye, I have that. Geordie McCallum has a croft jeest a bit further on. Keeps some sheep, chickens and the like, grows neeps and cabbages. He's got a lobster boat, too, down in the bay. I'll tell you this, you couldn't find a more isolated spot on the whole peninsula to be up to no good, and that's a fact.'

Marshall grinned. 'Looks as though we've struck lucky here. This could well be their base of operations. I wouldn't be surprised if those two strangers were prospective clients come to sample the wares before they buy. This is just what we were after.'

Sergeant Grant said nothing as they drove on between the steep hills. He watched a swollen burn charge into a culvert below the road, a riot of white froth and peat-stained water. He'd heard stories about the Piper's Pass, and though he wasn't a particularly superstitious man, a shiver ran down his back, making him flinch at the wheel. He'd been dubious about Hoynes' involvement in an alleged smuggling operation, but he had to concede that something wasn't right.

'Can you hear that?' said Marshall, his head cocked to one side. Despite the rain, he cracked open the passenger window.

'Will you close that!' shouted Watson from the back. 'I'm getting soaked here.'

'Who would be playing bagpipes in this weather?' Marshall frowned.

Looking in his rear-view mirror, Grant caught a look of apprehension cross Watson's face. 'I never heard a thing,' he said nervously.

Marshall persisted. 'I know the skirl of the pipes when I hear them.'

They carried on along the narrow pass in silence.

All of a sudden the road dipped. They were heading into a broad valley now, the single-track road snaking into the distance under the glowering sky.

'Nearly there,' said Geordie. 'Jeest a few hundred yards now.' Between a gap in the hills, the grey waters of the North Channel were visible.

'I widna be happy being oot on the ocean the night,' said Hoynes, spotting the red corrugated-iron roof of Geordie's bothy in the distance.

'We'll be fine once we get a fire going,' said Hamish.

Geordie slowed the vehicle and turned onto a rough path, at the end of which sat a small stone building, abutted on both sides by small wooden structures – barns would have been too grand a name for them.

'Right, gentlemen,' he said, pulling up outside the bothy. 'Here we are, a home fae home.'

Rather unsteadily, the passengers got out of the vehicle and waited, shivering, while the small man pushed open the door. In the gloom he made his way to a windowsill upon which sat an oil lantern. After fiddling in his pocket for a lighter, he managed to put flame to the wick, and soon the cottage was bathed in a pale, flickering light.

'It's a bit gloomy whoot wae these tiny windows. If you give me a couple o' minutes, I'll get the other lanterns lit and put a match tae the fire. We'll be fair toasty in no time.'

'I see you've peat in the fire already, Geordie,' noted Hoynes.

'Aye, I always leave it set – even in the summer. You canna beat a peat fire.'

'It's just like *Brigadoon*,' said Ralph excitedly, making himself comfortable on an old couch. 'Exactly what the doctor ordered. We've been up in Scotland for months now, and all we've seen is the inside of the plane and the barracks.'

'And the Douglas Arms,' said Bertie.

With another two lanterns lit, Geordie busied himself lighting the fire with scrunched-up pieces of old newspaper. The heavy rain beat a tattoo on the iron roof. The bothy appeared to be a one-room affair, with various old chairs and the couch gathered around the fireplace. In a corner of the room a flimsy-looking camp bed was covered by a grey blanket, while on the other side of the dwelling sat an old pot-bellied stove and a tiny basin.

'No' much in the way of home comforts,' observed Hamish. 'Where's the cludgie?'

'Och, I jeest pee in thon bucket while I'm here. But if it's the secondary function you need to oblige, there's a dry closet oot the back. It can be a bit breezy in the wind, mind – I keep meaning tae get that hole in the wall fixed,' said Geordie as he got to his feet and lit his pipe.

'Damn near the Savoy, my bonnie lads,' said Hoynes, producing two bottles of whisky from a duffel bag. 'Here, I'll put on the wireless.'

Amidst a crackle and a high-pitched whine, the sound of twanging guitars backing a distinctive baritone could be heard. The five men listened in silence for a while, as drams were handed round in chipped mugs. The fire began to smoulder.

'Whoot on earth is that racket?' asked Hamish, his face screwed up.

'That's the Rolling Stones,' replied Bertie. 'My boy plays them all the time on a little Dansette record player his mother was stupid enough to buy him.'

'The Rolling Stones, eh?' said Hoynes, sounding as though the words were something new to him.

'As far as I'm concerned, they can jeest keep rolling – as far away as possible,' said Hamish. 'For me, you canna beat Jimmy Shand. Have a fiddle aboot wae that wireless and get us some proper music on, skipper, before thon wailing drives me mad.'

'Och, you're no' like a young man at all, Hamish. You should be up there gyratin' aboot like these young folk I see wae Pete Murray every Saturday on the television. If I was young you widna be able tae keep me back. There wiz nae such thing as the permissive society when I wiz a young buck. And it's still no' arrived in my hoose tae this day,' Hoynes observed, somewhat ruefully.

'Can't you get no satisfaction then, mate,' said Ralph, making his fellow pilot guffaw. The three fishermen were bemused. 'Oh, never mind,' he said with a smile.

'Wait the noo,' said Geordie. 'There's another Land Rover at the road end. Who the hell can be oot on a night like this?'

'They'll see us, Sergeant Grant,' said Marshall, a note of panic in his voice.

'Aye, well, they'll have to sometime,' replied Grant, turning the vehicle onto the track that led down towards Geordie's bothy.

'What if they're disposing of the evidence?'

'That would be a neat trick,' chortled Watson. 'There's no such thing as plumbing away out here.'

'Is that a crown on the side?' asked Hamish, peering through the tiny window, Hoynes at his side.

'It's no' the Fishery Officer, is it?' said Hoynes, his nose pressed to the glass.

'Whoot would it matter if it was, Sandy? There's no' a fish tae be had in the place.'

'I've got a couple o' tins o' sardines in the press thonder,' said Geordie.

'Och, you widna put anything past that Watson,' replied Hoynes. 'He'd likely find an excuse tae impound them, no matter that they're fae Spain and got tinned before the auld king died.'

'Are you worried aboot oor freen wae the eight legs, skipper?'

'Wait,' said Hoynes, relief in his voice. 'Is that no' oor Duncan?'

'Aye, but look who he's wae,' groaned Hamish in dismay.

Sure enough, Duncan Grant, Iain Watson the Fishery Officer, and a smartly-dressed man whom neither of them knew were out of the Land Rover and making their way to the front door.

'Turning into quite a party,' quipped Ralph. 'The more the merrier, I say.'

'Gie me another gulp o' that whisky, Hamish. I don't like the look o' this at all,' said Hoynes as three businesslike knocks sounded at the door.

'Sandy, Hamish, Geordie, open up!' shouted Grant. 'We need to have a word with you.'

'Och, I knew fine I should have got that light fixed on the motor. I've been meaning tae dae it for ages,' moaned Geordie.

'They widna come all this way tae pull you up aboot a tail-light, Geordie. Oor Duncan's straight as a dye, but even he's no' that keen,' said Hoynes.

'An' how wid he bring Watson wae him?' said Hamish.

'I'd better open the door,' said Geordie. 'We'll soon find oot.'

'Just stay here for a minute, Beth,' said Maggie. 'Look, they're all away into the cottage now. My poor Duncan all unsuspecting, likely, not realising he's about to be spirited out of the country to bugger knows where.'

'And there's thon snake, Watson,' said her mother. 'Your faither won't be happy at the sight o' him hoving intae view. The Piper's Pass was fair busy the night, an' no mistake.'

The women looked on as the door closed behind the three new arrivals. 'I canna think Iain Watson wid be part o' any caper,' said Beth. 'I mean, I don't think I've ever seen him smile – that poor wife o' his has got a terrible life. She must be fair miserable sitting in that cottage while he plots tae bring doon another decent fisherman trying tae make a living.'

'Well, one thing's for sure,' said Marjorie. 'We'll not learn anything sitting away back here. We'll park up behind these whin bushes, Beth. Then we can sneak over and surprise them before they get a chance to overpower my Duncan.'

'Overpower's a wee bit strong, dear. This is your faither and Hamish we're talking aboot. The last thing they overpowered wiz a fish or two – aye, an' no' that recently, neither.' Marjorie pursed her lips.

'And forbye that, we'll get drenched,' declared Beth.

'It's all for the greater good. Come on. It's taken me long enough to find a husband. I'll be damned if he's whisked off to the Levant before I get a ring on his finger.'

'Och, jeest your faither a' o'er,' said Marjorie.

'Where the hell's the Levant?' asked Beth as, pulling her raincoat over her head, Maggie jumped out of the Land Rover and into the rain.

XI

'Well, well, a pretty parcel of rogues here,' said Watson, a look of triumph on his face.

'You there!' shouted Marshall. 'Put that bottle down – it's evidence from now on.'

'You what, mate?' slurred Ralph, taking the lemonade bottle from his lips. 'I paid for this fair and square. If you want some, go and buy your own.'

Marshall reached into the pocket of his coat and removed an ID card. 'Alistair Marshall, Senior Collector, Her Majesty's Customs and Excise. That spirit you're drinking is stolen – from both the distillery and the Revenue. You, all of you, are breaking the law, and I'll make sure you'll pay for your crimes.'

'For goodness sake, son, whoot's this all aboot?' remonstrated Hoynes.

'I'm sorry, Sandy. We had information that you were shifting cases of the clear stuff. I had my doubts, but here we are.'

'Don't be ridiculous, man,' said Hamish. 'We're jeest having a wee dram. That stuff doesn't even belong to us. Does it, boys?' He addressed his question to the airmen, who now looked thoroughly perplexed by the whole situation.

'And then there's the matter of an octopus,' said Watson. 'Not declared in the catch, but I have proof positive that you profited from it, Sandy Hoynes.'

Hoynes looked sidelong at Hamish. 'Noo, come on, men. Let's sit doon and talk aboot this like civilised folk. I've no' seen a bottle o' the clear stuff since Adam was a wean, and that octopus was a squid. We jeest slung it back intae the sea, didn't we, Hamish?'

'Aye, we did that, Sandy. And in any event, Iain Watson, I'd like to know how you got to hear aboot such a small event. Aye, and manage tae blow it oot o' all proportion, tae.'

Watson held his ground. 'It was an octopus! I have a witness!'

'Sergeant, I want you to arrest these men on suspicion of smuggling,' said Marshall. 'I'll take the evidence we need.' He made a lunge for Ralph's bottle, just as the door swung open and Maggie rushed to the side of her fiancé.

'The first one to try to get my Duncan onto a plane will have to get past me first!'

'Maggie?' said Hamish.

'Marjory?' shouted Hoynes.

'Beth?' said Geordie.

'What on earth is going on here?' enquired Grant.

'Haven't the foggiest, mate,' said Bertie, looking on as his friend Ralph wrestled determinedly with the Customs Officer over the bottle of illicit spirits. 'One thing's for sure, you Scotch know how to throw a party.'

Before anyone else could speak, a low rumble interrupted the pounding rain. In a few heartbeats, the ground began to shake.

'Whoot that?' yelled Hoynes, as everyone froze.

'It's the Piper's Pass,' cried Geordie. 'It's a bloody landslide!'

Hoynes raced outside. Sure enough, he could see a great sheet of earth sliding down the mountainside like warm icing off a cake. Hamish and Duncan Grant were right behind him.

'Well, that's us stuck here for a while,' said Hamish. 'Did it no' take them the best part o' a week to clear this the last time?'

'It did that,' confirmed Hoynes.

'Father! Duncan!' shouted Maggie, poking her head out of the front door. 'You better come quick. The Customs man is out cold.'

Marshall was lying on his back on the stone floor, his eyes closed. A small pool of blood was congealing under his head.

'For any's sake,' screamed Marjorie. 'I think he's deid.'

Grant leaned over the injured man and checked the pulse in his neck. 'His heart's beating, but he's out cold. We'll have to try and stem the flow of blood. What on earth happened?'

'I was just trying to stop him whipping my bottle,' replied Ralph sheepishly. 'I stood up, and he went flying onto the floor. Must've cracked his head when he landed. Will he be all right?'

Beth turned on her heel, yanked the sheet from the camp bed and ripped a narrow strip. 'I'll use this as a bandage. At least it should stop the blood.' As Grant held up the unconscious man's head, she wound the impromptu bandage around his skull and tied it gently with a knot at the back.

'Dae you mind Erchie Boyd, Sandy?' asked Hamish. 'He fell o'er in Main Street one Hogmanay. Never recovered. He was deid afore the second o' January dawned.'

'Oh, you're a ray of sunshine, Hamish,' snapped Maggie, her hand on her fiancé's shoulder as he cradled Marshall's head in his lap. 'I'm sure he's just knocked out – he'll likely be fine in a minute or two.'

'I'm not so sure, Maggie,' said Grant. 'We have to get him help.'

Watson the Fishery Officer looked at Ralph in disgust. 'I don't know what schemes you've been cooking up with Hoynes here but you'll spend the rest of your days behind bars if this man dies. And him a representative of Her Majesty, too. I wouldn't be surprised if they brought back the gallows for this. Do your duty, Duncan.'

'Wait a bloody minute,' said Ralph indignantly. 'He attacked me, remember.'

'He was doing his job protecting the Revenue. Crooks like you have no place in a quiet, law-abiding community like ours. Sandy, you're for the high-jump as well, bringing such desperados to Kinloch. You'll likely swing too.'

'Iain, will you be quiet,' demanded Grant. 'We need to get this man some medical help. We'll take a look at the pass and see if there's any way through.'

'I wouldna be holdin' oot too much faith in that,' said Geordie. 'You've seen yoursel' how narrow the roadway is – a few boulders are enough tae make it impassable.'

'Nonetheless,' said Grant. 'Two of you can take one of the cars and have a look.'

'I'll go,' volunteered Hoynes. 'I canna bear seeing this poor wretch lying there. If there's any chance o' a way through, I'll get back here pronto, and we'll carry the gentleman aboard.'

'I'll come wae you, skipper,' said Hamish.

'No, no, no. You're not making a break for it as easy as that,' said Watson. 'If there's anyone going with Professor Moriarty here, it's me. You'll not escape my clutches, Sandy Hoynes.'

'Whoever's going, go now!' Grant urged. 'If there's no way through the pass, we'll have to think of something else.'

Reluctantly, Hoynes made his way out of the bothy with Watson in tow. 'And no fancy business, either,' said the Fishery Officer. 'I'll not be more than an arm's length from you at any time.'

Hoynes pulled his cap down over his forehead in an attempt to shelter from the rain. 'Do you know something, Iain Watson? I think you're as mad as a March hare.' He ducked into the driver's side of Geordie's vehicle. Soon the pair were making their way steadily back up towards the Piper's Pass.

Hamish, looking down at Marshall, shook his head. 'I knew I should've paid attention tae that nightmare I had the other night.'

'What nightmare?' asked Marjorie, biting her lip at the sight of her husband leaving with Watson.

'The Walls o' Jericho were tumbling doon. Folk were fair scattering everywhere – a dreadful sight, a' the gither.'

'Right,' said Maggie. 'I daresay it wasn't a trumpeter that brought the stones down. Would it be a piper, by any chance?'

'See you, Maggie,' replied Hamish. 'I've always thought you had the sight. Now I'm sure. You've got it bang on.'

'Jeest a pity you hadna the sight tae see how this wee caper wid end in such tragedy, Hamish,' said Geordie. 'I'd be at hame having a right good snooze noo, if I'd no' been foolish enough to join in wae your little plot.'

'I think it's time I knew just what's going on, Hamish.' Grant looked up at the fisherman.

'Scheme? What's all this?' said Bertie. 'What scheme?'

Hamish lit his pipe. 'Well, now, you see, when there's nae fish, there's nae joy in the world, and that's a fact.'

Geordie shrugged. 'If they two canna find a route out the pass – and they'll no' – we'll have tae take the Customs man on my lobster boat.'

'Roon' the Mull in this weather? You'll never make it,' wailed Beth.

'We canna jeest let him bleed tae death. No, nor turn intae a vegetable, because of his injuries.'

'And what about my wedding? Just tell me that,' said Maggie. 'I could strangle you, Hamish.'

The fisherman took a puff of his pipe and stared enigmatically at the ceiling. 'Do you know, I think we're aboot tae dae something quite exceptional.' A blue cloud of smoke wafted above his head as the rain continued to batter off the roof.

XII

The rain began to ease as Hoynes pulled up the Land Rover near a pile of slick mud and boulders that now blocked the roadway onto the Piper's Pass. He shook his head and sighed. 'Naebody's gettin' through this in a hurry.'

'It's still passable on foot,' said Watson sharply.

'Only a fool would attempt that, Iain. And whoot good wid it do? This Marshall fella wid still be lying spark oot on Geordie's floor, stuck behind this accumulation.'

'But it would raise the alarm. They could arrange for one of the helicopters to airlift him out. I know fine it would suit you to string this out as long as you can so that you can devise some way out of the mess you're in. Well, I'm here to tell you, it'll not work. I'll make sure you answer for your crimes, Sandy Hoynes.'

Hoynes looked at the Fishery Officer and scratched his head. 'You know, Iain, I've known for a very long time that you've had it in for me. Aye, an' I think I know fine why.'

'It's not hard to work it out. You stole that boat from under his nose. Fair cheated him. By rights, I should be a skipper, not . . .' He left the rest unsaid.

'I bought the *Girl Maggie* fair and square fae your faither. I liked the man. It's no' my fault he snuggled up tae John Barleycorn that much he couldna be bothered gettin' oot o' his bed tae take up arms against the fish.'

'But you took advantage of it, and forced him to sell at a knockdown price. You were his first mate, and you fleeced the man who taught you everything!'

'Man, oh man, but you're so wrong. I can see this has been eatin' away at you for near thirty-five years. Nae wonder you scrutinise my catch so closely. But you don't have the right o' it, Iain. Not only was your faither tight tae go oot on a wave, he didna lift a finger tae help wae the upkeep o' the vessel. Och, we tried oor best tae keep her in fettle, but it was jury-rigged at best. I gave your faither too much money, and that's the truth of it. It cost me a small fortune tae make her seaworthy again, and you know it.'

'Just enough money to make sure he lasted long enough to die of a broken heart.'

'Your arse, a broken heart. Though it pains me tae speak ill o' the deid, aye, an' my auld skipper, he died starin' oot the bottom o' a whisky bottle. You know it fine yoursel'.'

Watson stared belligerently at the fisherman. 'And you changed her name. Called her after your wee girl, Maggie. Do you know that ended up making you the laughing stock of the fleet?'

'How so?' asked Hoynes, temporarily thrown.

'She's a neat wee craft, but she's always been broad in the beam – just how your Maggie turned out.' Watson laughed harshly.

'I've said it once and I'll say it again: it's a family thing. All the women on her mother's side o' the family have big arses . . . Eh, where are you going?'

The Fishery Officer slammed the passenger door of the Land Rover and began picking his way through the debris left by the landslide.

Winding his window down, Hoynes shouted, 'Don't be daft, Iain. Get back in here. We'll take Marshall tae Kinloch in Geordie's lobster boat.'

'I'd rather take my chances up here on the pass than navigate the Mull with you at the helm, Sandy.' He stormed off, tripping over a small boulder, but managed to keep his feet. 'The McKinnons' farm is just on the other side, and they're good folk – unlike you.'

The fisherman watched him clamber over a large boulder, and soon he was out of sight. 'You're a braver man than I gied you credit for, Iain Watson. Who wid have thought you'd bear a grudge a' these years. I hope you don't hear the skirl o' the pipes before you get tae safety – or a boulder doesn't land on your heid,' he said to himself. He turned the vehicle round and headed back to the bothy.

Marshall mumbled incoherently as Hamish and Grant carried him out of the back of the Land Rover and down the beach towards a small stone jetty where Geordie's lobster boat was moored. Though the rain had eased off, the sea was still angry, whipped into white-horse waves by the strong wind.

It took the help of the two airmen as well as Hoynes, Hamish, Grant and Geordie to manhandle the injured man aboard the small vessel safely, as the three women looked on anxiously.

'Are you sure about this, Sandy?' asked Grant, a worried look on his face.

'As sure as I can be. Your man here's lost a lot o' blood. I learned in the RNR never tae take a blow tae the heid lightly. In any event, between me, Hamish and Geordie, we've damn near a hunner years o' seafaring under oor belts. If we canna get him tae the Cottage Hospital in Kinloch, who can?'

'I'd be happier coming, too,' Grant replied.

'Oh no, you're not! You're staying with me!' yelled Maggie. 'It's bad enough losing my father in a mission of mercy, without waving a hearty goodbye to my intended.'

'See, there's an example o' loyalty for you, skipper,' said Hamish. 'Jeest typical o' the wimmen, tae. Fair calculated that you've done your bit bringing her up, and noo that there's somebody else tae take the strain, you're expendable.'

'Just you make sure he's not expendable, Hamish,' said Maggie.

'Och, you wid think we were heading intae Corryvreckan the way you're all lamenting oor early deaths. A couple o' hours and we'll be sitting wae a dram, fair getting warmed up,' remarked Hoynes. 'I'd like tae take you all, but as you can see, there's precious little room aboard as it is, whoot wae this Exciseman floppin' aboot the deck, an' all.'

'You've made the right decision, skipper,' said Hamish. 'I canna see your pair making it aboard. Beth, nae bother, there's hardly a picking on her . . .' He stopped when he caught Hoynes' eye. 'Och, I'm jeest meaning they're fine figures o' wimmen,' he continued, with a cough.

'We'll send a bigger vessel back for you. Wish us luck,' shouted Hoynes, as Geordie fired up the boat's diesel engine in a flurry of smoke and clatter. Slowly, against the swell, they made their way out to sea, leaving Grant, the airmen and the three women on the shore.

'I can see us having the wedding here, Duncan,' groaned Maggie, as she watched the small boat set sail.

'Your father knows what he's doing. He'll be fine,' he replied confidently, biting his lip all the same.

Iain Watson was making better progress than he'd hoped for. He was already more than halfway down the Piper's Pass. The highest section had been the worst. He'd had to climb over a pile of slippery rocks and mud on his hands and knees, but now he was at the other side, the obstacles he faced were of an altogether less challenging nature. The rain had stopped completely now, and he felt a wave of confidence that, if he was being honest, had been utterly absent when he parted from Hoynes.

'Push on, Iain,' he told himself. 'Just a little while and the MacKinnon farm will be in sight.'

As he uttered those words, his foot caught on a boulder. He fell forwards, landing on his side and winding himself badly. As he sat up, trying to get his breath back, he heard a distant sound. It was barely discernible at first, but after a few seconds it rang clearly, echoing around the high hills that hemmed him into the pass.

'You've banged your head, you daftie,' he muttered, pulling himself to his feet. 'There's nothing there – it's all in the mind.' But as he took a few faltering steps, something made him look up.

There, on a small rise up ahead, stood a figure standing stock-still.

'Bugger me,' he gasped. 'It can't be . . .'

XIII

Out at sea, the swell was greater than the fishermen had expected. Though they were trying to stay as close to the coast as possible, an offshore wind, combined with an ebb tide was proving too much for the tiny engine of Geordie's lobster boat, meaning their progress was slow: three lurches to the side, one forward.

'If we carry on like this, we'll be taking Marshall tae the hospital in Newfoundland, Geordie,' said Hamish, as an unexpected wave sent a shower of seawater into his face and extinguished his pipe with a gentle hiss.

'This old girl's jeest designed tae go oot in the bay and collect creels. She's no' an ocean-going liner. Once we're roon' the Mull, the conditions should improve.'

They had wrapped Marshall in woollen blankets taken from the bothy, under which he mumbled and moaned. His bandage was now stained a deep red.

'This fella's still bleeding, though it's no' as bad as it was,' said Hoynes. He had put on an oilskin jacket and a Sou'wester he had found under a bench seat on the boat. The garments stank, but at least he wasn't getting soaked by the spray like Hamish, who was cursing as he frantically tried to relight his pipe.

'There's the Cat Rock,' shouted Geordie. 'Once we've weathered that, it's plain sailing.'

The little boat was caught by a wave, cresting the top of the swell and then plummeting down into the trough it had

97

created. There was a sharp clunk, then what sounded like a dry piece of wood being broken in two.

'I hope that's no' whoot I think it is,' shouted Hoynes.

'It's the bloody rudder,' said Geordie. 'Look at this.' He spun the boat's wheel, to no effect.

'I'm betting there's no radio aboard this craft, neither,' said Hamish.

Geordie shrugged. 'I told you I jeest potter about in the bay. There's never been the need for a radio. If you lift the lid on that chest, you'll find a flare or two.'

Hamish did as he was asked, and the bright orange flare rent the dark sky above them as they drifted out to sea like a cork in a bath.

'We should be thankful for small mercies,' remarked Hoynes. 'At least we're not being driven ontae the Mull.'

'But the Barrel rocks are no' that far off,' countered Hamish. 'And if we're lucky enough tae avoid them, we'll no miss the coast o' County Antrim.'

'My, but you're the cheery one, Hamish. Every craft within ten miles o' here will have seen that flare. I'd be surprised if the Ballycastle lifeboat isn't preparing tae make way, as we speak.' His words were lost as a wave crashed over the vessel, drenching all aboard.

'Well, they better get here quick,' shouted Geordie, 'or we'll be having oor supper wae Davy Jones.'

'The next time I'm foolish enough tae listen tae one o' your schemes, Hamish, be sure tae gie me a skelp in the chops an' tell me tae brighten up,' said Hoynes, huddling down beside the recumbent figure of Marshall.

'Och, you can hardly blame me! How was I tae know the forces o' nature an' the state were going tae unite against us?'

'Aye, well, they sure have. Not only are we in the midst o' one o' the worst seasons for fish that anyone can remember, we've been accused o' smuggling whisky, almost killed an officer o' the Crown, and now we're in danger o' sinking.'

'No tae mention that octopus,' said Hamish. 'I should've known that landing a creature like thon wid mean bad luck.'

'Bad luck's something we've a sufficiency of, that's for sure,' said Hoynes, as the boat plummeted into another trough. 'Time tae start sayin' oor prayers, I reckon.'

'I started saying mine as soon as the polis, the Excise man, and the Fishery Officer came knocking at the door,' confessed Geordie.

'Wait!' shouted Hoynes as they were propelled back up by the swell. 'There's a vessel on the horizon. Quick, Hamish, launch another one o' they flares.'

Jackie MacKinnon was about to tuck into a plate of lamb chops and mashed potatoes when an insistent knocking sounded on the farmhouse door.

'Jean,' he yelled to his wife, who was still in the kitchen, 'can you see who on earth's at the door at this time? I'm no' wanting tae eat cauld chops.'

He heard his wife making her way along the hall, grumbling as she went, and then the familiar creak as the old front door was tugged open.

A scream from his wife sent Mackinnon to his feet, cutlery crashing down on his plate with a clatter. 'What the . . . ?'

The door to the room was flung open, to reveal a wide-eyed man covered from head to toe in mud.

'Jackie, for the love o' all that's holy, you've got tae help me!'

It took MacKinnon a few moments to recognise Iain

Watson the Fishery Officer as the man who had just collapsed face down on the floor.

'If you're in disguise looking for an illicit catch, you'll no' find it here,' Jackie said, before resuming his place at the table and lifting his knife and fork. 'Jean, will you come and see tae this man afore these chops congeal.'

The vessel was huge and painted scarlet. Too big to be a fishing boat – even a trawler – it steamed towards them at a rate of knots that left the fishermen aboard the stricken lobster boat scratching their heads.

'I've seen some o' they big trawlers oot o' Hull and Grimsby, but they're like skiffs compared tae this monster,' said Hoynes.

'I widna be bothered if it was the *Queen Mary*,' said Hamish. 'They're getting us oot o' a pretty pickle, and no mistake. Whoot flag is that at her prow, I wonder. I can make oot that it's red, but that's jeest aboot all.'

'It's no' one o' they new boats oot o' Oban, is it?' asked Geordie.

'If it is, there'll no' be room for another vessel in the bay,' opined Hoynes. 'The Mull ferry wid look like a rowing boat moored next tae that. Aye, and as far as that flag goes, I recognise it only too well – it's the hammer and sickle.'

'You don't mean the Bolsheviks, dae you, skipper?' Hamish peered out to sea.

'There's no' been Bolsheviks since thon Lenin was at the helm. They're Communists noo, an' a brave band o' brothers they are, tae. We'd be well under the Nazi jackboot if it wisna for their heroics at Stalingrad, an' the like. They gave Adolf pause for thought,' concluded Hoynes fervently.

Geordie looked at the Russian boat and stroked the stubble

on his chin. 'I've got two questions. Will they take my vessel under tow, and if they do, whoot on earth will the salvage amount tae? I'll likely have tae get doon and ask the bank manager tae gie me roubles.'

'I widna worry aboot salvage or the like. These boys are a' aboot sharing and equality. Commendable stuff it is, tae,' said Hoynes.

'You're no' tellin' me you're a red under the bed, skipper,' said Hamish, a look of horror on his face. 'I never had you doon for anythin' o' the kind.'

'No, don't be daft. But I mind in the war, the boys fae they Russian convoys wid come back wae tales o' how the folk survived jeest by boiling the odd turnip and quaffing some snow. Hardy buggers – they'd have no time for Iain Watson or his like. And even less for this poor unfortunate doon here.' He glanced across at Marshall whose face had taken on an even more pallid hue.

The Russian vessel now towered above them.

Hamish stared up, open-mouthed. 'How are we going tae get up thonder? I hope I've no' got to scale one o' they rope ladders. I'm no' keen on heights. That's how I went tae sea in the first place – nice an' near the groon', if you know whoot I mean.'

Without warning, a door opened about halfway down the side of the craft and a head popped out. The man was wearing a black peaked cap above dark eyes and a darker beard. 'You will want rescue, no?' he shouted across the swell.

'Aye, rescue wid be jeest fine,' returned Hoynes.

'Ask him aboot salvage,' insisted Geordie.

'Aye, and if he says it's goin' tae be a thousand pounds, dae we jeest tell them tae sail on? I'm telling you, salvage will no' be a problem for these boys . . . Yes, we need rescue,' shouted Hoynes. 'Workers o' the world unite!' he added, for good measure.

Hamish took in the Russian boat with a jaundiced eye. 'She's big, but she's a trawler, right enough. Are you thinking the same as me, skipper?'

'That it might no' be thon plane and its booming that's frightened the fish, after all?'

'This beast could pull mair oot the water in a day than oor whole fleet, an' she's no ring-net vessel, neither. I'm betting she's got a sister somewhere oot tae sea.'

'We'll soon find oot, of that there is no doubt,' said Hoynes. 'For better, or for worse, Hamish. I hope they've got some Bolshevik baccy aboard. I left my new packet back at the bothy.'

XIV

Aboard the USS *Newark*

Captain Walter P Rumsfeld scanned the sea with an enormous pair of binoculars. A lookout on the old destroyer had spotted a flare near the Kintyre coast, and they were steaming in that general direction, ready to assist. Though his hair was iron grey now, being back in these waters off the coast of Scotland brought the dark-haired young lieutenant he'd been more than twenty years ago to mind.

Being on friendly exercise with the Royal Navy over the last two weeks was somehow like a pilgrimage, a nod to those days that now seemed so far off. The ragged convoys of merchantmen – easy prey for German U-boats – were under their care. The long, long hours searching the waves for any sign of a periscope. The fear, the joy, the exhilaration of being young – of being a seaborne warrior, of living life on the edge – had miraculously returned, as though the feelings had never been away.

He felt his fingertips tingle at the memory – almost forgot that he now operated in a very different world, one where the enemy came from further to the east.

But how could he forget? He, his crew, in this very warship, had shadowed the ships from the Soviet Union, stowed with their cargo of nuclear warheads, only a few years before as they neared Cuba. That was the last time he had felt the thrill he felt again now – of being on the edge as the world held its breath.

His eyes sparkled as his lieutenant spoke. 'Sir, we have a visual, fourteen degrees to starboard.'

Rumsfeld swivelled his binoculars in the general direction he'd been given. Though they were a few nautical miles distant, he could make out a tiny vessel, probably wooden in construction, dwarfed by a red ship many times its size.

'Lieutenant, confirm or deny, do we have the flag of the Soviets?'

'Yes, sir, we do.'

'Does that look like a fishing trawler to you?'

'Yes, sir. Roger that.'

Rumsfeld let the binoculars hang on his chest by their leather strap, and rubbed his hands in anticipation. 'Gentlemen, I need not remind you of the dual function of the Soviet fishing vessels.'

'Spy ships, sir,' piped up a young ensign behind him.

'Good, Palliser, very good.' He turned to the young man. 'And what are our standing orders?'

'To intercept and investigate such vessels, sir,' the young officer replied immediately.

'Correct.' He leaned over a speaking tube and spoke with a commanding tone. 'Helm, steer fourteen degrees to starboard – full steam ahead!'

'Sir, if I may make an observation?' asked his lieutenant tentatively.

'Ask away.'

'Sir, we are about to enter UK waters. I mean, do we have the mandate to intercept the Soviet vessel under these circumstances?'

'Mandate? Mandate, Lieutenant?' He gave the man a withering look. 'We are entering the waters of our closest ally. The country we fought for in World War Two. The country that, alongside the United States of America – our fine nation – saved the world from the tyranny of the oppressor.' He paused, looking into the distance. 'Did Dwight D Eisenhower ask for a mandate to defeat our enemies, to preserve our way of life? If JFK – may the Lord rest his soul – had asked us to enter Cuban waters to save our country from the horror of nuclear annihilation at the hands of the Soviets, would we have questioned his mandate?'

'No, sir,' came the reply, as USS *Newark*'s Lieutenant stood to attention, as though he was on parade.

'We are, and will always be the beacon of freedom. Mandate or no, full steam ahead!'

The warship turned and the bow wave rose at her side as she made her way towards the Russian vessel.

Hoynes sat in the Russian captain's spacious cabin, a large glass of vodka in his hand. He looked across at Hamish who was draining his glass. 'Well, if you're in peril at sea and in need of rescue, these are the very boys tae oblige, eh.'

'I've never been a fan o' this vodka stuff,' said Geordie. 'But this fair hits the spot tonight. Nectar, sheer nectar.'

'But whoot aboot oor fish?' lamented Hamish. 'Did you see the size o' they nets on the deck? You could scoop up half o' Kinloch in they bloody things.' He lowered his voice. 'It's nae wonder we've hardly landed a herring this year.'

'Och, but these boys are no' interested in plowtering aboot oor wee bit shoals, Hamish.' Hoynes puffed at his pipe, which emanated a cloud of deeper blue smoke than normal. He spluttered, eyes watering. 'The vodka might be like nectar, but the baccy fair tears your throat oot.'

'Dae you think oor wee silver freens jeest hang aboot the coast waiting for us tae entice them intae a net?' said Hamish sceptically. 'They're deep-sea creatures. They're no' going tae turn their noses up at a net jeest cos it's a Ruskie one.'

'Dae fish have noses?' asked Geordie, smacking his lips as he emptied his glass. 'I've never been o'er sure.'

'But you're being a right Jonah, Hamish,' said Hoynes. 'Here we are getting a five-star passage intae Kinloch, wae their doctor looking efter Marshall, an' us downing the tsar's best vodka, and you're still no' happy. Dae you no' think there's hunners o' boats oot in the broad Atlantic, and have been for years? No' jeest the Russians, neither.'

'Well, I've never seen them so close tae hame, and that's a fact. And forbye, I've a feeling o' impending doom – an' that's never a good thing.'

With that remark the cabin door swung open and the rotund figure of Captain Vladimir Pushkov strode into the cabin with two large bottles of vodka clasped in his meaty fists. 'Good for you, gentlemen,' the Russian seafarer boomed. 'I am thinking we are needing some more vodka.' He smiled beatifically as Geordie held out his glass. 'And your friend – this Marshall – he will be living very well. I am speaking to doctor. So, my friends, a tragedy no more. Let us have toast!' He unscrewed the top of one of the bottles and, one by one, poured the vodka so generously it spilled over the edge of each glass.

'Aye, here's tae you, Vladimir,' said Hoynes, clinking glasses with the Russian seafarer. 'And tae the brotherhood of the sea – *slainte*!'

'The brotherhood of the sea . . . Sandy.' He said the name tentatively. 'I am thinking your name is Alexander. Am I right?'

'Aye, you have the right o' it there,' confirmed Hoynes.

'So, in the tradition of Mother Russia, I will call you Alexei.' Pushkov drained his glass and reached once more for the bottle of vodka.

'You better watch your eye, *Alexei*,' said Hamish pointedly. 'You'll need tae work oot how we're going tae get everyone back fae Geordie's bothy when we get back tae Kinloch. You'll be in no condition tae organise a rescue the way you're downing that stuff.'

'Och, they'll send oot the lifeboat. But the way the swell is noo, and it no' being an emergency, it'll no' be until the morrow, I'm thinking.'

'Does that mean you'll be in charge o' the show o' presents?'

Hoynes stared at his first mate for a while, then burst out laughing. 'There'll be green snow an' yellow hailstones before there'll be any show o' presents at my hoose the night. Here's me jeest been rescued by the pride o' the Baltic fae a watery grave. No, no, no. I'm quite happy tae sink intae this vodka – especially efter the few hours we've had. Man, Hamish, but sometimes you're fair strait-laced.' Hoynes hiccupped loudly, making Pushkov roar with laughter.

A slight cough made everyone turn around. A man in an immaculate grey suit, white shirt and red tie stood framed in the doorway. His clothes, indeed, his whole demeanour couldn't have made him look less like a fisherman. He stared at each man in turn.

Quickly removing his cap and standing up, rather unsteadily, Pushkov addressed the man as 'Commissar'. There followed a flurry of Russian, which the fishermen from Kinloch could not understand but certainly got the gist of. It was obvious that, despite Pushkov being captain of the vessel, he was somehow in thrall to this individual.

'Which one of you is in charge?' the commissar barked.

'Him,' said Hamish and Geordie in unison, pointing at Hoynes. This man bore none of Pushkov's bonhomie.

'You are British, yes?'

'Of course I am,' replied Hoynes, his hiccups even more frequent now. 'Four years before the mast of Her Majesty's Royal Navy, tae.' He stood up and gave his interlocutor an exaggeratedly proud salute.

'I see. So you are soldier of capitalism.' The commissar looked at Pushkov, who was fiddling with his cap nervously, and more Russian spilled from his mouth like gunfire, then he turned on his heel and left the cabin, without the slightest gesture of farewell.

'He's a nasty piece o' work, is he no'?' remarked Hamish.

Pushkov poked his head round the door, to make sure his visitor was out of earshot. 'He is commissar. He makes sure we remain good Russians when temptations of the West placed in our way.'

'One o' Stalin's boys?' said Hoynes.

'No!' said Pushkov. 'Never mention Comrade Stalin. His memory . . . bad.' He shrugged, having failed to find the correct words to use in English. He leaned towards Hoynes and whispered, 'This man reports every move back to Moscow. He is eyes and ears of Politburo. You lucky such a man not in your country.'

'That's where you're wrong, Vladimir, my friend,' said Hoynes, patting the Russian gently on the back. 'You've obviously no' come across oor Fishery Officer, Iain Watson. He'd gie the KGB a run for their money any day.'

'That's if he's still in the land o' the living, and no' lyin' deid on the Piper's Pass,' said Hamish.

'Aye. Wae a bit o' luck . . .' Hoynes sat down heavily, held out his glass with a beaming smile and belched loudly. 'C'mon, Vladimir. Time we had another charge, comrade.'

XV

USS *Newark*

'Sir, we're gaining on them, but we'll have to slow down. The charts show rocks ahead.'

Rumsfeld thought for a few moments. 'Hand me the radio, Lieutenant . . . Chief, find me a frequency where I can speak to these Commies.'

The radio squeaked in protest as they searched for the Russian trawler's communication channel. 'Sir, I think we have it.'

'Soviet vessel. This is Captain Walter P Rumsfeld of USS *Newark*. Stop immediately.'

On the other end could be heard a babble of Russian.

'Stop your vessel immediately!' ordered Rumsfeld.

Again, some incomprehensible Russian . . . and the Russian trawler kept on sailing, regardless.

Captain Rumsfeld turned to his lieutenant. 'Prepare to send a warning shot over her bows.'

'But, sir, I have to remind you we're in UK waters. Shouldn't we inform the Royal Navy?'

'Are you questioning my orders? No? Well, fire that shot!'

'And here's tae Yuri Gagarin.' Hoynes raised his glass.

'And to your Winston Churchill,' Pushkov responded in return. 'But do not be telling my commissar, no?'

Each man downed a measure of vodka.

Just as Hamish was about to propose a toast to the international brotherhood of fishermen , a loud whine could be heard through the open porthole in the captain's cabin. It became louder – almost deafening – until it stopped for a few heartbeats, and there followed a massive explosion.

'Whoot on earth was that?' cried Geordie.

Hoynes blinked at him in surprise. 'It's a long time since I heard one o' them,' he said, his hiccups now gone.

'Heard whoot?' asked Hamish.

'That was a shell – a big one, tae. I do believe we're under attack, Vladimir. All hands on deck!' he shouted wildly before falling back in his chair.

'Quickly, my friends, let us get to the bridge,' said Pushkov, dropping his glass to the floor. 'What can this be?'

Hamish held a hand out to Hoynes to help his skipper up from his chair. 'I'm hoping they've no availed Iain Watson o' his ain gunboat.'

Shakily, the three Kinloch fishermen followed Captain Pushkov along the gangway and up a steep flight of steps.

On the bridge stood three agitated-looking sailors, dressed in dark blue jerseys and oilskin trousers. Alongside them was the commissar, still in his suit and tie. He looked at the new arrivals with disdain and addressed Pushkov sharply, standing almost on his toes as he glared into the burly captain's face.

'Things is no' looking good,' surmised Hamish. 'Who on earth can be firing on a fishing trawler? Aye, an' us jeest a few miles fae the toon.'

Pushkov made his way across to the Kinloch men, shaking his head. 'No crew here speak English. There have been messages. Surely Royal Navy would not fire on us?'

'No, I don't think so,' replied Hoynes. 'But I'm no' sure the Fishery Officer wouldn't.'

Amidst a shower of static, the radio burst back into life. 'This is USS *Newark*. Bring your vessel to a stop immediately, or we *will* fire.'

'How can this be? The American Navy? We're in British waters,' said Pushkov, grabbing the radio from a bewildered Russian fisherman.

The commissar spoke up, this time in English. 'I believe these men to be agents of the capitalist devil, America. You have been tricked, Captain Pushkov. This vessel must not fall into enemy hands. That is an order.'

'This is Vladimir Pushkov, captain of the *Kirov*. We are fishing vessel on mercy mission, heading for Kinloch. Please explain your actions!'

'Sir, they say they're on a rescue mission,' said USS *Newark*'s lieutenant.

'I'm not deaf, Lieutenant,' said Rumsfeld. 'I have given them an explicit order, with which I expect them to comply.

They are sailing in the sovereign waters of our ally. We shall not turn our backs on them and let these Commies spy with impunity. That, son, is no more a fishing vessel than I'm Abraham Lincoln.' He put the radio to his mouth. 'This is Captain Walter P Rumsfeld of USS *Newark*. You are in sovereign UK waters. I demand that you halt your vessel and let my men come aboard. This is non-negotiable.'

Pushkov listened to more orders from the commissar before replying, his face blanching above his black beard. 'You have no right to stop my vessel. This not your country. We continue to Kinloch. Mercy mission. Repeat. Mercy mission.'

Hamish looked at Hoynes who was stroking his chin. 'Aye, this is a fair pickle, right enough. We set oot the day tae try and draw attention tae the plight o' diminishing fish stocks and noo we're aboot tae light the touch paper for World War Three. And forbye that, we've likely been responsible for the death o' a Fishery Officer, as well as seriously injuring an officer of Her Majesty's Customs and Excise.'

'If these Yanks don't blow us oot the water, we'll hang for sure,' wailed Geordie. 'Whoot an end tae a life – deid and infamous for the destruction o' the planet. It wiz bad enough wae thon Cuban missile crisis. This'll tip the balance, for sure.'

Hoynes was about to reply when another deafening whine followed by an explosion and a huge plume of water indicated that the US Navy was not bluffing. 'You men are right pessimists,' he said, once the noise had cleared, and Pushkov and the commissar had retired to the other end of the bridge to finger-point and argue. 'This is just a wee misunderstanding – happens at sea all the time.'

'A wee misunderstanding!' replied Hamish incredulously. 'Oor backsides have near been blown four hunner feet in the air – an' wae the rest o' us no attached – an' you're calling it a wee misunderstanding!'

'Here, Vladimir,' said Hoynes, heading towards Pushkov and the commissar who were still arguing heatedly. 'I'm an ex-petty officer of the Royal Navy. Let me speak tae this American captain – jeest tae put him right, you understand.'

The commissar was about to object, but the big sea captain pushed him aside and addressed him in English. 'This is my vessel. I decide what happens now we are being attacked.' He called to his crewmate in Russian, who handed Hoynes the radio.

Hoynes grabbed the mouthpiece and cleared his throat. 'How ye getting on? I'm Alexander Hoynes, skipper o' the *Girl Maggie* fae the Kinloch fishing fleet. These brave sons o' the sea were good enough tae pull us oot o' a right tight spot a wee while ago. They're jeest taking us back tae Kinloch. Will yous stop firing, and you can follow us intae port an' we can sort this a' oot o'er a dram?' Almost as an afterthought, he added, 'Over' and clicked off. He winked at Hamish. 'My radio etiquette's a wee bit rusty, but they Yanks will get the message. Noo, where's my pipe?'

'They give us safe passage, Alexei?' asked Pushkov.

'Och, it'll no' be a bother. You jeest need tae talk tae them in their ain tongue. You Ruskies haven't got the English jeest so – like a native, you understand. Full steam ahead tae Kinloch, I'd say.'

'Who on earth was that?' said Captain Rumsfeld, frowning at the radio speaker on the bridge of USS *Newark*. 'Do you have any idea, Lieutenant?'

'Didn't sound like a Russian, sir. Possibly an Arab? Could

just be a delaying tactic, trying to make us believe there are other nationals aboard.'

'These Commies don't know when they're beat. It's Cuba all over again. Full steam ahead and to hell with the consequences. If they think they can fool a captain of the US Navy, they can think again.' He contemplated the Russian trawler in the distance. 'They have left us no choice. Prepare to fire on that vessel.'

XVI

'Sir, for the record, I must register my objection to the action you are about to take. We have no right to fire on a vessel in UK waters. Even if it is the Soviets, sir.'

Captain Rumsfeld eyed his lieutenant. 'Your concerns are noted. Now, remove yourself from duty and confine yourself to your cabin. Palliser, find the correct range for that Russian trawler and fire.'

'Yes, sir!' shouted the ensign enthusiastically, bending over his range finder.

Rumsfeld watched his lieutenant hurry from the bridge, then announced, 'I want you men here to remember this day. It's the day America took a stand. Took a stand against these Soviets, and in defence of our allies. We, the crew of this fine warship, have drawn a line in the sand. While we don't want to take the lives of those Russians, we have to stand up for freedom and our way of life. This day will go down in the history of the United States of America.'

Captain Pushkov looked at the warship through his binoculars and frowned. 'You are sure they understand message, Alexei? Guns moving...'

'Have nae worries on that score. They widna fire on an ex-Royal Navy sailor like mysel'. Man, they wid go doon in history as brutes – and likely cause one major diplomatic incident in the process. Nae doubt, Her Majesty wid get personally involved, knowing that one of her seafarers had been cruelly treated. Anyhow, I've enough on my plate, whoot wae weddings, nae fish in the sea and the like, tae take up arms against a superpower.'

Hamish eyed the grey warship with narrowed eyes. 'I've a wile bad feeling aboot this.'

Captain Rumsfeld was waiting for the trawler to rise to the top of the swell to give him the clearest possible target. He opened his mouth to give the order to fire, but before he could speak, he was interrupted.

'Sir, ten degrees to port, looks like a minesweeper. Royal Navy, sir.'

Rumsfeld hesitated for a second, the silent command still on his lips. Eventually, he let out a long and heartfelt sigh. 'Stand weapons down, Palliser.'

'Aye, aye, sir!'

As the Russian trawler docked at Kinloch's second pier, the harbour master rushed to the side of the vessel. 'Ahoy there! Dae you have a Sandy Hoynes aboard?'

'It's yoursel', Ritchie,' greeted Hoynes, leaning over the rail of the trawler. 'Wait the noo till I tell you whoot an exciting time we've been having.' Standing beside him, Hamish looked heavenward.

'Och, I know fine whoot's been happening. There's been a bit on the radio a' aboot it.' Ritchie Brown shook his head.

'Damn near an international incident oot in the Sound. Some yachtsman called it in tae the Coastguard. Warships firing guns, and all sorts. We'll have a' the newspapers here by teatime – aye, an' the television, tae, so I'm told.'

'Whoot a stramash. These good men were good enough tae rescue us fae the Mull. That's all there is tae it.'

'That's no' whoot I'm hearing,' said the harbour master. 'And on top o' that, that polisman Grant has gone missing, and Watson the Fishery Officer's up at the Cottage Hospital.'

'Oh, that's good news, right enough,' replied Hoynes, nodding at Hamish. 'He's a fine fella, that Watson. A wee bit highly strung, mind.'

'He's highly strung noo, by all accounts. Arrived at Jackie MacKinnon's farm at the Pass thonder, covered fae head tae toe in glaur. He's only spoken two words since.'

'Was one o' them "octopus", by any chance?' asked Hamish.

'No, nothing aboot octopuses – jeest "Sandy Hoynes". That's a' he keeps saying, over and over. "Sandy Hoynes".'

Hoynes stroked his chin. Hamish had an infuriating I-told-you-so look on his face, while Geordie's hands were shaking so much he was struggling to roll his cigarette. 'As I say, fair highly strung, the man.' He looked on as two brawny Russian seamen carried Marshall on a stretcher down the gangplank. 'Good luck tae you, Mr Marshall. I'm sure that heid o' yours will be jeest fine in a wee while. The ambulance is on its way.'

'All oor geese are comin' hame tae roost at the same time. And we've still no' arranged tae rescue them back at the bothy,' said Hamish.

'It's getting dark noo, Hamish. I'm sure they'll be fine till the morning.' Hoynes smiled. 'It's chickens, is it no'?'

'The lifeboat's away roon' the Mull. Tae your bothy,

Geordie. Watson telt MacKinnon there was a party of folk stranded there by a landslide at the Piper's Pass,' said the harbour master.

Hoynes thought for a moment. 'You know, Hamish, the weather's set fair the morrow. I think we should jeest have a wee nap on the boat, then get oot and get an early start tomorrow.'

'You mean hide fae Marjorie and Maggie.'

'Away ye go, nothing of the sort. We've got a hell o' a lot o' fishing tae catch up on.'

Hoynes and Hamish tried to settle down for the night aboard the *Girl Maggie*, but there was an unusual amount of activity in the harbour. At one point, Hamish swore that he could hear Marjorie asking about the whereabouts of her husband, but Hoynes said he was imagining things.

After a restless night, Hoynes shook Hamish out of his bunk, pointing to his watch. 'It's been light for half an hour. Time we got fired up and back oot tae the fishing. Young Peter will be here directly.'

The fishermen were readying the vessel for sea when they heard someone shouting from the pier above. 'Is anyone on board?' The voice was insistent.

Reluctantly, Hoynes poked his head out of the hatch and craned his neck up to the pier, shading his eyes against the early morning sun. 'Whoot can I do for you?'

'I'm Timothy Halley from the BBC in Glasgow. Are you Alexander Hoynes?'

'Eh . . . aye, I am that,' he replied. 'But I've no time tae talk to the press. I've a fishing boat tae skipper.'

'I hear you had rather an exciting time yesterday,' shouted Halley.

'Whoot's he sayin'?' asked Hamish from below, cleaning his teeth with an old wooden toothbrush.

'Och, I widna say it was that exciting. Jeest another day for those o' us that make oor living at sea.' Hoynes gestured to his shipmate to be quiet.

'But weren't you caught up in some incident between the Russians and the US Navy?'

'Like I said, nothing we're not used tae on the ocean. Blown oot o' all proportion, I'd say.'

'Nearly like oor backsides,' observed Hamish, spitting into a metal bucket.

'I really hope you can share your experience with our viewers, Mr Hoynes.'

'As I telt you, I've a vessel tae get ready for sea. Another time, perhaps. No' that there's anything tae talk aboot anyhow.'

'Oh, that's a pity, Alexander . . . may I call you that?'

'You can call me anythin' you want,' replied Hoynes.

'You can be sure everyone else will,' said Hamish, under his breath.

'I've been authorised to avail you of five pounds for your thoughts, Mr Hoynes.'

Hoynes tilted his head. 'Five pounds, did you say?'

'Yes, I have the money here.' Halley pulled a fiver from his pocket and waved it in the air. 'Look!'

'I daresay I could describe the hardship that was put before us yesterday,' said Hoynes, clearing his throat.

'Dae you think you're daein' the right thing, Sandy?'

'Wheesht, Hamish, there's a fiver at stake here, man.'

Five minutes later, the two fishermen were standing in the early morning sunshine on the pier, while a technician fussed around a huge television camera and Halley looked at his notes.

'So, Mr Hoynes. You're the skipper of a fishing boat here in Kinloch, am I right?'

'That's a fact,' replied Hoynes.

'Now, can you tell me what happened to you yesterday? You were rescued by a Russian trawler when out on a small lobster boat with some colleagues?'

'Yes, yes, we were. And damned grateful we were tae oor Russian freens. A valiant effort, I must say.'

'My information is that, before you reached the safety of Kinloch harbour, this trawler – your rescuers – was fired upon by an American naval vessel. Is this true?'

Hoynes paused, then turned his focus from the reporter to the camera, which he fixed with a beady eye. 'I'm no' jeest sure where you're getting a' this from. But whoot should be being addressed is the disappearance o' herring in these waters this summer.'

Halley tried to interject, but Hoynes raised his hand to silence him. 'You see, ladies and gentlemen, a plane's being tested in the skies o'er Kinloch ...'

XVII

The sun shone down on the wedding party as they made their way down the kirk's long drive and headed towards the town centre and the County Hotel reception.

Duncan Grant, resplendent in his best uniform, complete with white gloves, walked arm-in-arm with his new bride. It was a warm day, and Maggie appeared rather flushed, although whether this was because of the summer temperature or the long woollen shawl that was draped over her shoulders and down her back, it was hard to tell.

Next in line came Sandy Hoynes and Marjorie, alongside Grant's parents, who had arrived the day before by ferry then bus from the Isle of Skye. Marjorie beamed as she watched her only child walk in front of her with the handsome policeman at her side. 'She's right bonnie, is she no', Sandy?'

'Aye, bonnie, right enough,' he said, feeling naked out in public without his skipper's cap. He patted down his Brylcreemed hair, before searching in the pocket of his best suit for his pipe.

'Don't you dare light up that smelly thing,' said Marjorie with a scowl. 'You know fine Duncan's mother's allergic tae pipe smoke on account o' her asthma.'

'But we're outside, woman. I can understand a body no happy wae smoke at closed quarters in the hoose, but whoot's the problem when we're oot here in the fresh air?'

Marjorie fixed him with a stare, and the pipe remained in his pocket. 'You've done a rare job running up that shawl, right enough. Does the job very well,' remarked Hoynes.

'Be quiet, you!' his wife hissed. 'You've nae idea how much persuasion it took tae get her tae wear it in the first place. I'm surprised you noticed anything in the church, whoot wae they puppy-dog eyes you were making at Ina Blackstock.'

'Ina? Och, I didna even see her.'

'Aye, right. You should be payin' attention tae your daughter on her big day.'

'She'll no be worried noo, anyhow. Now that the ring's on her finger, she can let her arse grow, untrammelled. The way you did yoursel', my love.' Hoynes pursed his lips, missing the comfort of his pipe.

'See if this wisna the day it is, Alexander Hoynes, I'd belt you roon' the lug good and proper. I hope you brought your wallet. They'll be expecting tae get paid at the County.'

'They better serve up a better dram than they did the last time I was there.'

'Oh, I'm sure they'll see to it the local celebrity only gets the best,' said Marjorie. 'I don't know how many times I've been stopped in the street in the last week by folk telling me how brilliant my man was on the telly.'

'You've either got it, or you've no'. At any rate, they tell me that bloody plane's away at the end o' next week. That's the power o' the press for you. We'll maybe get back tae some kind o' normality at the fishin' noo.'

'We better, Sandy, or you an' me will be as poor as church mice, whoot wae this wedding an' a' . . .'

They wedding party turned onto to Main Street, and were soon heading into the County Hotel for the reception.

In the County Hotel, Hamish was savouring his first glass of whisky at the bar, when he was approached by two men. One was dressed in a red shirt with wide trousers and black boots; the other wore a smart dark uniform, adorned with brass buttons and gold braid. 'How ye daein'?' he said as they joined him. 'It's a fine day for a dram or two.'

'My friend, Hamish,' said Pushkov, enveloping the fisherman in a bear hug. 'I not recognise you with clothes you are wearing.' He patted the sleeve of Hamish's suit, a garment that had once belonged to his father, and was hopelessly old-fashioned, as well as being at least two sizes too big.

'I don't get the opportunity tae get dressed up much,' Hamish said, patting down the quiff that was now plastered to one side of his head. 'Och, but I fair enjoy it when I get the chance. And how are you faring, Captain?' he enquired, turning to the tall grey-haired man in uniform.

'I'm enjoying the company of a fellow sailor,' Captain Walter P Rumsfeld replied. 'In all these years, I've never met a Russian, but I have to say that Vladimir here is a good man. Here's to friendship.' Rumsfeld raised a small glass of whisky and clinked glasses with Hamish and Pushkov. 'Here's to friendship!'

'That's the way it should be. A' brothers under the skin,' remarked Hamish, his smile creasing his eyes. 'Here, I might even get another in.'

Hoynes watched his first mate with a smile. They'd had dinner and, as was the tradition, had heard speeches from the groom and best man – a fellow policeman with whom Duncan Grant was friendly. Now, as was tradition in Kinloch, the father of the bride would say a few words and propose a toast once everyone was a bit more relaxed, the tables had been cleared, and a few drinks had been consumed.

'Surely you're no' nervous,' said Geordie. 'A man that's addressed the nation on the television is surely no' worried aboot speaking tae his freens and family?'

'No, no, not at all. I'm jeest taking it a' in. Marjorie and I thought this day might never come.'

You weren't alone there, thought Geordie, as he watched the bride and groom circulate among their guests. 'She's a lovely bride, right enough. Tell me, whoot's happenin' aboot them bottles o' the clear stuff they pilots had. I hope they know it was nothing tae dae wae us?'

'A storm in a teacup. Oor Duncan gied them a warning – nae mair than a slap on the wrists. Sure, they'll be away hame next week, and probably no' think aboot the whole episode again.'

'No' so much thon Marshall. I'm amazed he didna press charges.'

'He knew fine where his bread was buttered,' said Hoynes, lighting his pipe. 'After all, he was the aggressor. He jumped on the man and tried tae get the bottle oot o' his hands. In any event, there's nae harm done. The man has a wee scar on his forehead – it'll jeest make him look mair rakish, like thon Germans wae the duelling scars.'

'Oh, here we go,' said Geordie, nudging Hoynes in the ribs, almost making him drop his pipe.

'Whoot on earth?'

Watson the Fishery Officer was making his way determinedly to their table.

'This doesna look good,' said Geordie.

'Jeest you keep your hand on your ha'penny and let me dae the talking,' whispered Hoynes as Watson stopped in front of them.

'Gentlemen,' he gushed. 'My, but you're looking like real gents in these suits.'

'You're no' looking too bad yoursel', Iain. Will you be having a dram wae us?' offered Hoynes.

'I have something to say,' declared Watson.

'Can you no' leave the man alone on his daughter's wedding day,' Geordie said accusingly.

'Now, now, Geordie, let the man speak.' Hoynes took a hefty swig of his whisky and looked squarely at the Fishery Officer. 'Spit it oot, man.'

'I'd just like to say I'm sorry,' said Watson, causing Geordie to choke on the pint of beer he was drinking.

'Sorry? Sorry for whoot?' asked Hoynes.

'I've learned the error of my ways.' Watson sighed. 'Up there on the Piper's Pass . . . I saw him.'

'Saw who? The piper?' asked Geordie, his eyes wide.

'Aye. There he was, blowing away at the pipes, a lovely pibroch, too.'

'Did you no' want tae run a mile?' said Hoynes.

'No, I did not.' Watson composed himself. 'You see, I recognised him.'

There was a brief silence. Geordie's mouth gaped, while Hoynes puffed furiously at his pipe.

'The piper was my father, my own father. Dead all these years, but there he was piping away, plain as day.'

'I didna know your faither played the pipes,' said Geordie.

'No, he didn't. But, man, he was playing a fair tune up there on the pass. That is, before he stopped.'

'Stopped? Whoot for?' asked Hoynes.

'He walked over to me and he said, "Iain, I'm fair affronted by you. For generations our family went to the fishing. Now you're the man responsible for making these men's lives a pure misery." Well, I didn't know what to say. I just stood there frozen to the marrow.'

'And was that it?' asked Hoynes.

'No, it was not. "Make amends," that's what he said. "Change your life and make amends." So, that's why I'm here. I want to apologise to you all. I've given up the job – I'm just working a month's notice, then I'm going to get a wee boat and I'm going to do the lobsters, or the like. A much more honest occupation than the one I've been toiling at these last few years.'

Hoynes was about to reply, when his wife tapped him on the shoulder. 'Come on, you. Less o' the gabbing. Get this speech o' yours done, so folk can relax and enjoy the night.'

Hoynes moved to the centre of the bar and tapped his glass with the stem of his pipe. 'The bride and groom, ladies an' gentlemen, if I could have your attention for a moment or two. My good lady tells me it's time I said my piece.'

'On yoursel', skipper,' shouted Hamish. 'And make it brief, mind.'

'I'm the proudest faither in the world today. My lovely daughter's found hersel' a good, well-doin' man.' He looked across at Maggie, who was beaming at him. 'You took your time – och, but no' tae the swiftest the victory an' a' that.' He saw Maggie's smile fade, then cleared his throat. 'No, no . . . We've folk here fae all pairts – Blaan, Machrie – aye, even Moscow an' the US of A.' He raised his glass to Pushkov and Rumsfeld. 'If this day – aye, an' recent days – reminds me o' one thing, it's this: we're at oor best when we stand together.' For this there was a smattering of applause. 'Now, as many of you know, the fishing's no' been whoot it was this year. Och, we've blamed planes and the like, but I've been thinking on it for a while. They tell me there's mair folk in the world than ever before. So, it stands tae reason that that'll mean mair folk eating fish. Noo, jeest because there's mair folk, it doesna follow there's mair fish . . .' There was a murmur of agreement. 'When I started on the boats, we used the ring nets – aye, a battle between the silver fellows and the men who were tryin' tae catch them – a battle, but a fair yin. Noo, och, they big trawlers – nae disrespect, Vladimir – and soon a' oor boats will be at the same thing.' There was silence in the hall. 'So, I suppose this is a message tae you, Duncan, my new son-in-law.' He raised his glass. 'O'er the course o' married life, you'll come up against the rocks mair than once – I know I've had my fair share o' rough water . . .' He looked over at Marjorie, who shook her head with a grin. 'But here's whoot I'm saying, Duncan. Bear in mind whoot I've jeest said. Be happy wae the catch you've got, for even if you're thinking there's mair fish in the sea, you're probably wrong.' At this, everyone applauded. 'Tae both o' you – my beautiful Maggie and big Duncan – here's tae you. The bride an' groom!'

Hoynes was about to sit down when he heard a voice. Coming towards him, looking rather unsteady on his feet, came Keacheran the fish merchant, clutching what looked like a jar. 'Sandy Hoynes, you've done Maggie proud – aye, and us all fine the night, wae a great spread and a few drams.' A cheer ensued. 'So, by way of thanks, I brought you the leg o' that octopus you were good enough tae sell me the other day. Knowing how fond I am o' the creatures, it was good of you. So I marinated a wee bit o' it, an' here you are!'

Iain Watson sat open-mouthed as Hamish shrugged and announced, 'Here's tae you, skipper! I telt you I'd a bad feeling aboot this.'

TWO ONE THREE

A Constable Jim Daley Short Story

I

Glasgow, March 1986

Police Constable Jim Daley smiled as he caught sight of his reflection in the window of the expensive clothing store. He had just finished his second stint at Tulliallan, the Scottish Police Training College, and his trim physique was testament to the rigorous fitness regime there.

He walked on, then paused for a few moments, gazing at the display in Curry's window. The latest VHS recorder took pride of place beside a Sony hi-fi system. He grinned; his sergeant, John Donald, had just spent a small fortune on a state-of-the-art Betamax unit, which already appeared to be obsolete. Serves him right, thought Daley, and moved on.

It was just after 5 a.m. As he scanned the shops and offices across the street, he passed his gloved hand over the plate-glass storefronts on his right. This way, he could check both sides of the road at the same time, ensuring that if any break-ins had occurred during the nightshift, they wouldn't go undiscovered. It was called Plate Glass Patrol, and his colleagues across Glasgow city centre were following the same routine.

When he'd first joined Strathclyde Police and embarked upon his basic training, he'd hoped to be sent to some of the more far-flung parts of the force area – the Cowal Peninsula, Ayrshire, even distant Argyll with its islands and county towns had been potential postings – but here he was in the city he'd grown up in, plodding down Sauchiehall Street in the grey dawn of a March morning. He was sanguine about this, though, and now of the opinion that he would learn more from the hard-bitten cops who worked the tough streets of

Scotland's largest city than from their despised country cousins.

A sudden noise made him stop in his tracks, and he averted his gaze from the shops across the street to the small lane immediately to his right, which ran between two office blocks. Steam was already rising from vents in the building as boilers were fired up in readiness for the arrival of the workforce. The lane was littered with the normal city detritus: fish-supper wrappings, empty beer cans, the green glass from a smashed bottle of tonic wine, blobs of white chewing gum, now stuck fast to the pavement, and scores of carelessly abandoned cigarette ends. He narrowly avoided standing on a used condom as he made his way up the lane to investigate.

There it was again, a cross between a mumble and a song, coming from a large refuse skip at the end of the lane. He took the heavy rubberised torch from the pocket of his flimsy uniform raincoat and flashed the beam towards the skip.

'Hey, you, ya bastard!' came a loud slurred voice as, from underneath mounds of cardboard and plastic bottles, a figure emerged. The man blinked in the beam of the torch. He was wearing what remained of a beige gabardine coat, torn and filthy, down which straggled a matted beard. His salt-and-pepper hair was long and tangled, almost dreadlocks, but Daley had encountered this man before, and knew that the hairstyle was merely the result of being left so long unwashed.

'Right, Dandy, come on. Time you had a wee trip up the road, eh? Get you cleaned up and a hot meal inside you,' said Daley, holding out his hand to help the man get out of the skip. He tried not to recoil at the stench as the tramp, holding his arm with a vice-like grip, vaulted clumsily onto the pavement, mumbling incoherent curses as he did.

'Dandy, man,' said Daley, screwing up his face, 'you're reeking. What were you drinking last night?'

The tramp looked at him through sad bloodshot eyes. 'Meths,' he growled. 'White sunshine for a cauld night.' He laughed hoarsely, revealing an array of rotting black and yellow teeth.

A number of tramps frequented Glasgow city centre, men ruined by drugs and drink, the product of fractured existences. The rumour was that Dandy – ironically named because he was anything but – had once been well-to-do, with a good job, and a middle-class life, but had given up when his wife took their daughter and ran off with another man. This, of course, could be true, but was more likely to be one of the many rumours that circulated among the city's finest. Whatever the reason, this unfortunate soul lived on the very periphery of life, in a sense neither dead nor alive: begging, finding shelter where he could, and spending most of his time anaesthetised from the misery of his existence with cheap wine or industrial-strength alcohol. He was arrested occasionally, not from fear of his being a danger to the public, merely as a duty of care. He would appear in front of a Justice of the Peace at the district court, be bound over to keep the peace, then a place would be found for him in one of Glasgow's homeless hostels, themselves remnants of the city's notorious Victorian slums. He would eat, get cleaned up and stay sober for a few days, then abscond, and the cycle of despair would begin all over again.

'Two one three to Alpha,' said Daley into the mouthpiece of his Motorola radio. 'Just found Dandy, need the van, over.' He gave his position to the crackly voice at the other end and escorted the tramp from the lane and onto the street to await transport back to Stewart Street Police Office. He held the sleeve of the tramp's filthy raincoat firmly, knowing that, despite his physical condition, the man was not beyond making a dash for freedom – if that's what he truly felt about his life on the street.

Dandy mumbled something and Daley leaned towards him. 'What is it? We're just waiting for the van. At least you'll get your breakfast.'

Dandy turned to look at him with what Daley thought was a smile. It wasn't, though. Before the young policeman could move, Dandy opened his mouth wide, as though about to yawn, then spewed copiously over himself and Daley's dark uniform.

PC James Daley, rooted to the spot for a few moments, looked down ruefully at the stinking green liquid that now dripped down his sleeve and lapel. He turned his head away and was sick on the pavement, just as the white Sherpa van drew up at his side.

II

Daley spent most of the morning trying to rid his uniform of the rancid smell of vomit, but to no avail. By lunchtime, he had given up, resolving to leave it at the dry cleaner at the first opportunity. He would have to wear his best uniform tonight. He looked at the clock and sighed, realising that he would have to get some sleep before going back on the nightshift at 11 p.m.

He shared a flat in Paisley's West End with two other young cops. It was far enough away from where they worked to afford some freedom for a group who hadn't long left their teenage years behind. For Daley, who had never lived anywhere apart from Glasgow, the tough, former cotton-manufacturing town seemed almost exotic. Paisley was famed for its rough pubs and its pretty women. It was upon the latter that the young constable mused as he made his way through the rows of shops, houses and high flats of the Townhead in Glasgow in the early hours of the next morning, his habitual beat.

By 2 a.m., he was ready for his refreshment break, but still had an hour to wait until he could return to the office to eat the sandwiches he'd made before reporting for duty. It was a weekday night, quiet as the grave, with most of the good citizens of Glasgow tucked up in bed ahead of another hard day at work. But not all.

His radio burst into life. 'Two one three, attend 18c Kennedy Path. A Mr Martin reporting a housebreaking, over.'

Daley acknowledged the call and made his way over to one of the multi-storey flats looming in the orange glow of the streetlights. As he approached the building he kept his wits about him, scanning the scene before him for someone – anyone – who appeared in the slightest suspicious. There was no one to be seen though, as he pulled open the heavy door and walked into the property, past walls daubed with the familiar graffiti identifying Glasgow street gangs. He pressed the button for the lift, noting that the plastic arrow pointing up had been burned, most likely by a cigarette lighter, and now a bare bulb was showing through the melted green plastic.

He coughed in disgust as he stepped into the lift, which stank of piss, though consoled himself that at least it was working and he didn't have to walk up eighteen flights of stairs. As Daley breathed through his mouth to avoid the stench, the lift juddered to a halt and the doors wheezed open.

The door to Flat C was brightly painted, and a garden gnome sporting a tiny fishing rod sat incongruously beside a thick hessian welcome mat. Despite the hour, Daley knocked loudly on the door. A glow appeared in the fanlight as someone shuffled along the hall.

'Mr Martin?' said Daley, as an elderly man in a maroon dressing gown opened the door. 'Constable Daley here. You reported a break-in?' He studied the front door, puzzled; it bore no signs of forced entry.

As though picking up on his thoughts, the man replied. 'Och no, no' my hoose. Doon the landing there, Flat G,' he said, pointing round the corner. 'I heard a commotion about an hour ago. Nothing unusual there, mind you.'

'Nothing unusual? What do you mean?'

'Lassie stays there . . . well, young woman, I should say. She has a lot of *friends*,' he continued, with an exaggerated wink.

'Sorry?'

'You know, *men* friends,' the old man said, looking into Daley's face for confirmation that he was getting the point, but noting that he wasn't. 'Aye, you're young, right enough. She's on the game,' he said, almost in a whisper. 'Folk coming and going all times of the day and night. Bloody disgrace, if you ask me. My poor wife's sick o' it. Mind you, she's a polite enough girl – always says good morning, that sort of thing, you know. Broken her faither's heart, I shouldnae wonder. Would break mine an' aw, seeing the state o' her.'

'The state of her?'

'Skin and bone, son. On the drugs. A strong wind would blow her away. Hell o' a way tae live, if you ask me.'

The man accompanied Daley along the corridor and around the corner to the woman's flat. One door stood in splendid isolation in an alcove, facing another which was boarded up and covered in graffiti. No garden gnome here. The door to Flat G had been forced open. Bright splintered wood showed through faded red paint, where the catch had been levered off, most likely with a jemmy. The brass screws of a Yale lock were scattered across the stone floor of the landing like small gold coins.

'They've done a number on it, right enough,' remarked Mr Martin. 'These bastard drug dealers, they'll no' stop at anything tae get their dosh.'

'How do you know it's the work of drug dealers, Mr Martin?' asked Daley, looking along the dim hallway of the flat.

'They're up here all the time looking for money. Scum o' the earth, as far as I'm concerned. If I was ten years younger, I tell you . . .' He left the sentence unfinished.

'I want you to go back to your flat, please, sir. If it's OK, I'll come in and take a statement from you in a few minutes. I need to check inside here, if you don't mind.'

As Daley watched the man padding away in his slippers, he radioed in the incident. 'I'm just going into the flat to take a look.' He could hear the controller making a call to his section sergeant. 'A-Alpha calls two ten, two ten – come in please, Sergeant Donald.' There was a pause, then the controller spoke again. 'Two ten attends in about twenty minutes from High Street, two one three.'

As Daley stepped gingerly through the open door and into the hallway, he pictured the look of disgust on his sergeant's face as he was forced to leave a comfortable doss – a bolthole from a chilly night where cups of tea could be made and cigarettes smoked – and venture out into the night at the behest of his young charge. But the feeling he had in the pit of his stomach concerned Daley more. He was relatively new to the police, but his instinct for something being wrong was already acute. He edged further into the flat.

To his right, he found the kitchen, illuminated by a single bare lightbulb at the end of a brown twisted flex. One cracked plate stood in a dish rack and a mug still half full of cold tea sat beside an old kettle. Daley felt his feet sticking to the grimy linoleum, which was stained with dropped food and spilled drink. The whole place smelled of decay. A cupboard door was lying open, but there was nothing inside apart from a single tin of tomato soup. Daley backed out of the room.

The next door he came to was closed. He pushed it with his boot and shone his torch inside. The bathroom contained a filthy toilet and a white enamel bath sporting a thick line of black scum. The wash-hand basin was spattered with what looked like dried blood. A single syringe lay on a glass shelf, together with a rubber tourniquet. A large beetle skittered across the floor at his feet.

There were only two doors left, sitting side by side across from the bathroom. Both were closed. Daley opened the furthest one, to find a large cupboard. Again, it was empty, save for an old doll's pram. His sister had had one just like it.

He took a deep breath as, with a gloved hand, he opened the last door. He shone his torch around the room. A wardrobe, with a cracked full-length mirror, stood beside a squat chest of drawers. A few clothes were scattered about the floor, mostly underwear. There were no pictures on the walls, no curtains on the window.

On a double bed lay the body of a young woman. A large plume of dark red blood was visible on the white sheet beneath her parted legs. Her skirt was scrunched around her thighs.

Daley felt his stomach churn as the light from his torch caught her lifeless staring eyes.

He reached for his radio.

Sergeant Donald looked down at the body. 'Another bloody junkie,' he observed, looking for somewhere to stub out his cigarette. 'What's its name?'

'*Her* name is Tracey Greene, Sergeant,' said Daley sharply. 'Shouldn't you maybe dispose of that fag outside? The forensic guys won't want to have to eliminate it from the inquiry.' As soon as he had uttered the words, he wished he hadn't. Forensic science was a relatively new discipline in the police force. It represented a great stride forward in the art of detection, but had yet to reveal its full potential.

Donald looked at the tall slim constable. 'If I need any fucking advice, son, I'll be sure to ask.' He stubbed out his cigarette on the windowsill and flicked the butt through the open window, where it spun eighteen floors to the ground. 'In the meantime, shut it.'

They awaited the arrival of the CID, who would take charge of the investigation, in an uncomfortable silence. Despite the position of the body, it was still too early to say how the young woman had died. Forensics would move her remains to the Glasgow Mortuary, where cause of death would be assessed. It was not yet obvious to Daley's barely trained eye.

'You getting a good eyeful?' sneered Donald.

'No, I was just trying to see if I could work out how she died,' Daley replied.

'You stick tae shoplifters and parking tickets, son. You don't have tae worry aboot this shit – probably never have to. A life on the beat for you, I'm guessing.'

'You never know,' replied Daley. He wanted to say more, but with only fifteen months' service behind him, disagreeing with his immediate superior would not make for the best career move. He had to pass his two-year probationary period, and this overweight man with the double chins and the wheeze could still make life very difficult for him. Sergeant John Donald was the kind of policeman they had been warned about in college. He was rude, arrogant and lazy. Daley wondered how he had ever risen to the rank of sergeant; he'd been told that Donald did his best to ingratiate himself with higher-ranking officers when off duty. The young cop himself had noted how Donald's behaviour changed when anyone with braid turned up. His rough working-class tones would be replaced by an accent altogether more refined; his habitual slouch transformed into a more upright, yet subservient, stance.

One of the older cops on Daley's shift had discovered that Donald had recently joined an expensive health club, of the type frequented by senior officers. No doubt the man they encountered there bore little relation to the uncouth specimen Daley saw before him in the dead girl's bedroom.

Donald broke wind loudly then looked at his watch. 'Right, bugger all else I can do here. CID'll be with you shortly. Try not to fuck it up, son, and don't be interfering with that poor lassie,' he said, making an obscene gesture.

Daley was relieved to watch him go, but he felt uneasy being left in the company of the corpse. He stared down at the girl's ravaged body. She probably wasn't much older than him, and already her life had reached its end. Daley thought about this predisposition towards melancholy he seemed to have. In the months since he'd joined up, he'd experienced things most other young men of his age would never witness.

All of the vices he confronted on the street seemed to be underpinned by two things: money and death. In an attempt to make sense of this, he'd started reading books by the great philosophers, but he'd soon given up when Nietzsche's theories left him profoundly depressed.

As he stared across the city from the bedroom window, he wondered how many more people's lives were on the brink. All seemed quiet, almost serene, but in the many streets below him, under the many roofs of the many buildings he could see, who really knew what was going on?

As he gazed down at the city, it was almost as though it was staring back into his soul. He was roused from his contemplation by a disturbance in the hall.

The bedroom door opened to reveal a tall, painfully thin man in a crumpled suit and light grey raincoat, accompanied by a young, harassed-looking colleague.

'Right, what have we got here, son?' asked Detective Chief Inspector Ian Burns.

III

Daley watched as the DCI took in the scene. The young DC took notes as his boss walked around the room, making comment only when he felt it necessary.

Burns knelt on the floor and pulled something from under the bed. He held up a plastic bag filled with condoms. 'Well, I think we can safely say that this poor lassie has been on the game to support her habit – heroin, no doubt. Possibly this new crack.'

'Do you think she's been murdered by dealers?' asked Daley, anxious to contribute something.

'No. Well, not the traditional way, anyhow. No knife to

the heart or baseball bat over the head here, son. I take it you never looked too closely up her skirt?'

'Eh, no,' said Daley, hoping he wasn't about to be the victim of yet another crude joke.

'Well, take a look and tell me what you see.'

Daley bent down, and forced himself to look between the victim's thighs. There was something sticking out from her groin, in the fold between her leg and her genitals. 'Is that a syringe, sir?'

'Yup. The usable veins collapse in the arm, and then the addict's forced to inject the drug anywhere else serviceable. Nice, eh? The question is: has her body just given up, or do we have another?' Burns gave his DC a knowing look.

'Another, sir?' queried Daley.

'In the last two weeks, two prostitutes have died from massive doses of heroin. The question till now has been why.'

'Suicide?'

'Aye, possible. We do see that from time to time, but three so close together – well, that's unusual. Also, these poor kids usually live from hit to hit. Why would they save up such a store of the drug just to end it all? The usual pattern would be of an addict doing away with themselves when they couldn't lay their hands on a fix. Paracetamol's a lot cheaper than H,' said Burns. 'And look at her lips – blue. Sure sign of poisoning.'

'What about the blood?' asked Daley.

'Massive haemorrhage caused by the overdose. Scenes of Crime should be here soon. But I think we have number three.'

'Oh shit,' said the DC.

'Oh shit, indeed, DC Scott. Bloody nasty.'

'Oh aye, well, I wisnae meaning that, exactly, sir,' he said awkwardly.

'What then?' asked Burns with a frown.

'I've just broken the end off my bloody pencil, sir,' said DC Brian Scott. 'If you pardon my French,' he added with a wink at Daley.

IV

When the Scenes of Crime Officers arrived, Daley and the detectives decamped to the landing. Burns lit a cigarette, but frowned at DC Scott when he went to do the same. 'You nearly choked me on the way here in that car of yours, Brian,' said Burns. 'Time you cut down a bit.'

'Aye, right, sir,' replied Scott, reluctantly placing the packet of cigarettes back in his pocket.

'How long have you been on this beat, constable?' Burns asked Daley.

'Just over a year, sir. I did my first few months with Constable Fraser in Two Section.'

'Who, Davy Fraser?'

'Yes, sir.'

'Bloody hell. Why on earth would they send impressionable young cops out with that booze bag? Must have been a bit of a culture shock after Tulliallan.'

'Oh, he was OK,' lied Daley.

'Aye, OK when he's sleeping,' remarked DC Scott, attacking the tip of his pencil with a blunt penknife.

'Right, fancy a bit of overtime?'

'Sure,' replied Daley, keen to get as many extra hours in as the next man.

'I want you to stay on until about eleven. Get yourself round the neighbourhood, see what you can find out about our tragic Miss Greene. You know the score: her habits, folk she hangs about with, anything. Start here in the flats, then hit the shops in the wee precinct. I'll clear it with your gaffer. Who is your gaffer, by the way?'

'Sergeant Donald, sir.'

'You've fairly lucked out there, my man,' commented Scott, admiring the sharp point of his pencil. 'Davy the booze hound and Donald the–'

'That's quite enough, DC Scott. You need to head back to the office and get the paperwork kicked off,' said Burns with a raised eyebrow. 'Right, we all know what we're doing so let's get on with it. I'm going up to Baird Street. The North dealt with the last victim. You and Daley can go back, have a break, and then get right into it.'

'No bother, sir. I've got it taped,' replied Scott. 'Eh, how are we to get back tae Stewart Street?'

'One foot in front of the other, Brian, one foot in front of the other,' said Burns, already walking towards the lift.

Daley couldn't help but smile at the young detective who was swearing under his breath.

As the two men walked back to the office, DC Scott regaled Daley with tales of life in the CID. 'Nane o' this standin' at windy street corners pish. I love it,' he said, then hesitated. 'It's a job, anyhow.'

'How long have you been in the CID?'

'Eight months. I'm fair enjoying it, though I can't see me reaching the dizzy heights o' old Burns, there.'

'What, DCI?'

'Aye, I don't think that's for the likes o' me. I just want a quiet time, dae my job, keep my heid doon, and stay out the rain.'

Daley smiled at Scott's vaulting ambition as the subject changed to that of football – the constant obsession of the Scottish male.

As they neared the office Scott stopped. 'Oh, here, we're having a night oot next week for auld Willie Finn. Since you've been seconded to the CID by the gaffer, why don't you come along?'

'OK, I will,' said Daley, suddenly wondering what Sergeant Donald would think of him being 'seconded' to the CID. He quite looked forward to his reaction.

Daley returned to the Townhead later and began asking people about Tracey Greene. His first port of call was the high flats in Kennedy Path where she'd lived and died. When he presented them with her photograph, taken from the flat, most people recognised her but that was about it. Yes, they thought she was a drug user; no, they didn't know if she worked, or how she spent her time; no, it wasn't a great surprise that she had met with a tragic end.

In Glasgow, addicts were all too often victims of violence. Theirs were lives lived on the edge, the yawning chasm of oblivion never far away. HIV was tearing through this community, and was now as feared as the many vicious gangsters and dealers who controlled the city's drug trade.

As Daley walked up to the next landing, he could see the police incident van drawing up in the car park below. He had made frustratingly little progress, but soon the regular CID would take over the door-to-door inquiries and no doubt Daley would be left to his normal beat duties.

He knocked on a door that bore the name 'G Hunter'. A middle-aged woman in a towelling dressing gown answered.

'Aye, what is it, son? I'm just off for a bath. I'm at work in less than an hour, so you better make it snappy.'

'I just wondered if you knew this woman? She lived on the eighteenth floor of this building,' asked Daley, showing her the picture of Tracey Greene.

'Aye, seen her aboot. Wee junkie, is she no'?'

Daley was about to ask her if she'd seen Greene with anyone else she could describe, when the woman turned in the doorway. 'Peter, get your arse oot here and talk tae the polis. My bath's getting cauld.' At this, a stout man with thinning hair and a potbelly appeared in the hall. His wife disappeared into the bathroom in a cloud of steam. Daley showed Mr Hunter the photograph.

'Aye, aye, I think I've seen her aboot, right enough,' said Hunter, barely looking at the picture. Daley noted that he seemed uneasy. 'What's she been up tae – drugs, no doubt?'

'Are you aware that she was a drug user?' asked Daley.

'No ... I mean ... you know ... she looks, eh, the type. I've spied her a few times aboot the flats an' that, know what I mean? She seems like too nice a lassie to be intae that shit. But looking at her ... well, you know what I mean.'

'So you've spoken to her, Mr Hunter?'

'Och, aye. You know, in the lift an' that. In the wee dairy doonstairs when I'm buying ma milk and the paper. Anyway, I take it she's in trouble if you are asking questions.'

'She was found dead in her flat last night. We have reason to believe she was murdered,' said Daley, waiting for a response from Hunter.

He got it. The man's face went white, then grey, and Daley was convinced that there were tears in his eyes. 'Oh, I'm sorry tae hear that,' he said hesitantly. 'This bloody place, eh? I mean what chance have these kids got?'

'Have you ever seen her with anyone? Boyfriend, family, anybody at all?'

Hunter shook his head and was about to reply when his wife's voice sounded from the bathroom. 'Peter, get me that wee wireless fae the kitchen, will you? I forgot tae bring it in wae me. And shut that bloody front door, I can feel the draught fae in here.'

'No, I've no' seen her wae anybody. Listen,' he said, jerking his thumb over his shoulder. 'I'll need tae go an' get my missus that radio. She who must be obeyed, eh.' He smiled weakly.

After Hunter had closed the door, Daley stood and noted their brief conversation in his notebook. There was something about the man's manner that convinced the young police officer he knew more than he was letting on. Daley scribbled 'Refer to DCI Burns' in his notebook, then carried on to the next flat.

It was almost half past ten when he knocked on the last door on the very top floor of the building. There was no response, so he jotted the flat's number in the No Reply column of his notebook. These addresses would have to be tried again.

He was frustrated, but not surprised by the poor response. This was a close community, where mistrust of the police was instilled at birth. The only real lead he'd had was from a young single mother who thought she'd seen Greene talking to a grey-haired middle-aged man in an overcoat, who she hadn't seen in the area before. Not much to go on.

It was time for him to finish his shift. He'd been on duty for twelve eventful hours and just wanted to get home to bed. He was walking past the row of shops in the small precinct across from Kennedy Path, when he saw two detectives interviewing a shopkeeper. He left them to it and went into the shop next door to buy a paper and a jar of coffee.

He was reading about Kenny Dalglish in the sports pages when he heard a voice. 'Excuse me, could I have a wee word?' Mr Hunter was hurrying towards him, his large belly wobbling over the waistband of his trousers.

'I'm sorry, I couldnae say much when you came to the door. The wife . . . you know how it is, son.' He shrugged his shoulders, looking embarrassed.

After paying for the coffee and the paper, Daley turned to Mr Hunter and, fishing for his notebook in the pocket of his tunic, asked him what he knew.

'The lassie Tracey . . . I . . . I used tae see her, like,' said Hunter, shuffling from foot to foot. 'Eh, can we go outside a minute?'

'Do you mean you paid her for sex?' said Daley quietly, aware of Hunter's discomfort, as they stood outside the shop.

'Aye, aye, I suppose if you put it like that, that's just what I did,' he sighed. 'I liked her, though, you know. She was nice – kind, if you know what I mean. It couldn't have been very nice for a young lassie like that tae . . . well, tae dae what she did with me. She never made me feel awkward aboot it, mind.'

'Did you visit her flat?'

'At the end, aye, I did.'

'What do you mean, "at the end"?'

'Well, I first met her somewhere else. I didn't know her fae Adam, then.'

'What, a brothel?'

'A sauna, son. Here, take this,' he said, pulling a business card from his pocket.

Daley took it from him and looked at it: *Cool Winds*

Sauna, Clyde Street. You'll be glad you came. The card was luminous pink in colour and showed a silhouette of a naked woman under a palm tree.

'I know what you're thinking, son. I'm no pervert, mind. I've been married for near thirty years. The magic's well and truly gone, if you know what I mean. She'd rather watch *Coronation Street* and go tae the bingo wae her mates than . . . well, you know.' Hunter's face went bright red.

'So this is where you first met Tracey Greene, at this sauna in Clyde Street?'

'Aye. We got talking, and she was nice. Maist o' the lassies just want tae get it over wae and don't say anything, but she was different. Made you feel as though you weren't just a dirty auld man. I couldn't believe it when I found oot she lived up the stairs in my ain block o' flats.'

'So that's when you started visiting her at home?'

'Naw, that's no' how it happened. She left the sauna. Some guy was givin' her hassle.'

'One of her bosses?'

'I'm not too sure. A punter, I think. Big payer, tae. He used tae knock her aboot a bit. Sometimes I'd go an' see her and she'd have a black eye, or bruises on her back. Made me feel sick.'

'Didn't the folk in the sauna look after her?'

'Och, they were mair bothered aboot the money than aboot how she was being treated. The guy paid mair for it – tae knock her aboot a bit. That's how she quit, so she said.'

Daley looked at the business card. 'You'll have to talk to the CID, Mr Hunter. This could be really important.'

'I thought you were going to say that,' he replied, head down, looking at the pavement. 'I suppose the wife was always going tae find oot somehow. I cannae just let the lassie doon, though. I want them tae catch whoever, well, whoever killed her.'

'Listen, I'll tell the chief inspector about you, and your circumstances. I'm sure something can be arranged for you to speak to him privately.'

'You mean go behind the wife's back?'

'I think you've been doing that already,' said Daley. 'In any case, what happens in your marriage is none of our business. I'm just glad you've come forward, Mr Hunter. Thank you. I'll be in touch.'

As Daley walked back to Stewart Street he reflected on what he'd just said to the man. He wasn't in a position to judge the morality of the situation. Was Hunter, a fat middle-aged man stuck in a loveless marriage, wrong to seek out the company of prostitutes? Certainly, it would have been much easier for him to keep quiet on the subject of Tracey Greene, but he'd chosen to seek out Daley to tell him what he knew.

Daley realised more each day that life was rarely black and white. As a police officer, he dealt with all its many shades. It was, he surmised, just the way things were.

V

As Daley made his way into the CID Suite at Stewart Street Police Office he could hear the intermittent percussion of typewriter keys, punctuated by swearing. DC Brian Scott was sitting behind a desk, his tongue sticking out. Beside him on the table was a bottle of Tipp-Ex. On the floor lay several balls of crumpled foolscap.

'Hi, Brian,' said Daley. 'Just finishing up. I've got something that DCI Burns might be interested in.'

'Oh aye,' replied Scott absently. 'I don't suppose you know too much aboot these bloody things,' he continued, making a derisive gesture towards the typewriter.

'What's up?'

'These tabs, or whatever they're called. I cannae get my heid round them at all. One minute the writing starts here, the next o'er here. Burns wants me tae have these notes typed up for the nightshift. Says the typing pool upstairs are too busy . . . aye, too busy gossiping and reading magazines, if you ask me.'

'Here, give me a shot,' said Daley. Scott happily vacated his chair, and Daley began repositioning the paper and fiddling with parts of the typewriter Scott hadn't realised existed. 'There,' said Daley, after a few moments. 'You should be able to type it up now with these tabs.'

'Impressive,' observed Scott. 'Where the hell did you learn that? We never got typing at the school I went tae . . . occasionally.'

'Don't ask,' replied Daley. 'My old dear used to take in typing to make a bit of extra cash. She was a secretary before she married the old man. Smart, too. Of course, he thinks the woman's place is in the home.'

'Och, my faither's the same. Mind you, my mother could've had three jobs and he wouldn't have had a clue. He spends mair time in the pub than I dae working in here.'

The office door opened, and DCI Burns flung his raincoat onto a hook, then lit a cigarette. 'Right, Daley, what did you get for me?'

'Well, a couple of things of interest, sir. One especially so, I think.' He handed the Cool Winds Sauna business card to the detective and told him about Hunter and his involvement with Tracey Greene. He also mentioned the young woman who had seen Greene with a middle-aged man with grey hair.

'Well done, son,' said Burns, taking a long draw of his cigarette, filling the room with pungent blue smoke. Daley noticed Scott looking on enviously. 'It's been a busy night and we're short on manpower, so I want you to help me out, Constable Daley. You don't look as though you're quite ready for your bed yet.'

Daley's knee-jerk response was to say that he was tired and had to go back on nightshift later, but he stopped the words in his mouth. When he'd joined up, his aim had been to find a berth in the CID after his probationary period was over. It would be stupid to turn down the opportunity of working with them now.

'Yes, sir, no problem,' he said. 'Tonight's my last nightshift anyhow. I'm on re-roster rest days, so I'm fine.'

'OK, I want you and Miss Moneypenny here to get yourselves down to that sauna. I want to know everything there is to know about this lassie and her clients.' He turned to Scott. 'Don't be frightened to heavy them, Brian. Got it?'

'Yes, sir,' replied Scott, leaving Daley wondering what exactly 'heavying them' might consist of.

'When you're done there, get down to the mortuary. Crichton's doing me a favour later with an early PM on Greene. I want to see if there's a material connection between her and the other two girls.'

The two young policemen were about to leave when Burns spoke again. 'Daley, I hope you've got some civvies to hand. One look at a uniform, and these bastards in the sauna will shut up shop or do a runner. Get yourself changed. You keep him right, Brian.'

Luckily, Daley kept jeans, a sweatshirt and a pair of trainers in his locker, just in case he went out straight after work. He accepted Scott's offer of a cigarette as they drove down Hope Street in an unmarked Vauxhall Cavalier, past a huge billboard advertising a gig in the city by new wave band Sigue Sigue Sputnik.

'First time on the cloth?' asked Scott.

'Yes,' replied Daley. 'It's quite strange being in my own clothes but still on duty.'

'Don't worry, you'll get used to it ... Oh, would you look at that,' Scott continued, eyeing an attractive blonde woman who was crossing the road in front of them.

'Aren't you married?' asked Daley.

'Aye, but there's nae harm in having a wee look now and again, is there? A'right, darling,' he shouted from the open window.

Something told Jim Daley that DC Scott was not overly burdened by concerns over Force Standing Orders. He smiled and shook his head. There was something disarming about the young detective.

'You fae the toon?' asked Scott.

'Yup, South Side. You?'

'East End, my friend.'

'Not many cops from the East End.'

'Naw, maist o' the lads I went tae school with are working for the other side, if you know what I mean.'

'Isn't that hard for you?'

'Aye, sometimes. I don't go oot wae my schoolfriends for a drink very often. But on the bright side, I can always catch up wae them at Barlinnie, where they a' end up eventually.'

'Don't you get a hard time?'

'No, no' really. As long as I don't grass them up, we're fine.'

'But that's your job, isn't it?'

'Let's just say that the situation hasn't come up yet. I know fine it will, but hey, what's the point o' worrying aboot something that hasn't happened? If I'm honest, I'm no' sure that me being in the CID has nothing tae dae with my background. Burns is a canny bugger – he knows the kind of folk I grew up with. Bit of inside knowledge goes a long way, eh?'

They turned onto Clyde Street, and drove alongside the great river that had made the city's fortunes. Daley looked at the river and the run-down warehouses and derelict buildings that flanked it. The council had promised to transform this city into a European cultural centre. Daley wondered if this would – could – ever happen.

The Cool Winds Sauna was located at the end of a lane behind a discount carpet warehouse.

'Hey,' said Scott, 'this used tae be a Chinese restaurant. Me and the boys used tae come here and get pished when we were fifteen. Spend two quid on your dinner and a fiver getting oot your heid.'

'I take it the owners didn't bother?'

'Naw, why should they? They sold us cheap wine and cider at a huge mark-up, and we weren't any bother – knew where oor bread was buttered. Safe, tae – the cops check the pubs for underage drinkers, but they're no' bothered aboot a back-street Chinese. Funny seeing the place again.'

Daley smiled at the way Scott referred to 'the cops', as though he wasn't part of it all.

The sauna had blackened windows and heavy doors. Scott

tried them, but they were firmly locked. On his right, a white intercom was attached to the door frame.

'Anybody in?' shouted Scott, pressing the buzzer.

After a few seconds there was a muffled reply from someone for whom English was most certainly a second language. 'We no' open. Come back for jiggy later.'

Daley waited for Scott to announce his credentials, but he didn't. 'Aw, come on, mate. Our girlfriends are away shopping. We've only got an hour. We'll pay you good money.' He produced a twenty-pound note from his pocket and waved it at the CCTV camera above the door.

There was a pause for a few moments, then the clunk of heavy bolts being released, and the door swung open to reveal a swarthy man with dark curly hair and a thick moustache. He was wearing an open-necked shirt with a gold medallion nestling in his hairy chest.

'Fuck me, it's Graeme Souness,' said Scott.

'Too early,' said the man, in what Daley thought was either a Greek or Turkish accent. 'We only have the one lady. So you can have her same time, or one after one, OK? Money up front, mister,' he added, holding out his hand.

'We'll need to see her first,' replied Scott.

Reluctantly, the man opened the door and admitted them to the premises. They were led along a dark corridor, which opened out into a room with a reception desk. Pictures of naked women in various poses adorned the wall, and the lighting was low. A radio was playing somewhere in the back, and the air was heavy with cheap perfume.

'You pay half now, you see girl,' said the man, standing by the reception desk.

'No,' said Scott, brandishing his warrant card. 'You help

153

us, or I close this place down and you go tae prison, amigo.'
He was speaking loudly and slowly, as though this guaranteed
he would be understood.

Suddenly, the man's hand jerked behind the counter and
a short baseball bat swung through the air. Scott neatly side-
stepped the blow, and caught the man in the back with a rabbit
punch to the kidneys. As his attacker doubled over in pain,
Scott brought the man's chin down on his raised knee, and
the man fell to the floor whimpering.

'Now, you be a good boy and listen tae me. My friend here
is going tae show you a photograph of a lassie that used tae
work for you. I want tae know everything about her, you
understand?' he said menacingly, his face red and aggressive,
all sign of good humour gone. He hauled the brothel keeper
up, and propped him up against the reception desk.

'Right, Jimmy, tell the man aboot Tracey Greene.'

Daley hesitated for a moment. He had seen plenty of
violence in his short spell in the police – he'd been attacked
himself – but for some reason he was shocked by the casual
way Scott had subdued his victim. He remembered DCI
Burns' 'heavy him' comment.

'Do you know this woman?' asked Daley, showing him a
picture of Tracey Greene.

'No! I no' know this woman,' he replied.

Scott grabbed the baseball bat and ran it along a row of
drinking glasses on a shelf behind the reception, sending them
crashing to the floor. 'That's just for starters,' he said calmly.

'OK, OK! She Tracey, junkie. We fire her months ago.'

'And her clients?' asked Daley. 'We want to know about
her clients, especially the one who hurt her. Do you know
what I mean?'

'I thought you guys were Muslims,' said Scott, holding up a string of pink balls, each one slightly smaller than the next.

'I am Muslim,' replied the man.

'Oh, right, so yous dae the rosary, tae.'

'What is rosary? Those are Chinese balls, put them up ...'

'Enough!' exclaimed Daley. 'Tell me about the man who hurt Tracey Greene when she worked here.'

The brothel keeper sank to his knees, his head forward. 'I can no' tell you. I have family.' He began to cry.

Daley looked at Scott, who was sniffing at the pink ball necklace with a confused look on his face.

'Listen. No, you're right. I tell you what, Mr . . . What's your name?' asked Scott.

'Suleiman, my name is Jat Suleiman.'

'Right, Jat, here's the deal,' said Scott, placing the balls down on the counter. 'You don't need to say anything. I'll make sure policeman standing here at your door all night, OK? No business.'

'No! No, you don't understand. We have private client. They no' like me telling you these things.'

'Here's my card, Jat. Just you call when you want the policeman to go. Come on, Jim,' said Scott.

They left Jat Suleiman crying on the floor.

Daley blinked in the sunshine as they got back into the car. 'Do you think he'll come round?'

'Oh aye, he will eventually. A few hours wae nae punters 'cause a cop's standing at the front door will be enough for him tae come a-running.' He thought for a moment. 'Still, didnae think that mob used rosary beads.'

'Like he said, that's not what they were,' replied Daley.

'Hell of a funny-looking necklace, anyway.'

'No, not a necklace.' Daley pointed to his lap.

'What! You're kidding. Dae you really mean that?'

'Yup.'

'Mingers! I want tae go and wash my hands. I thought they smelled funny,' said Scott, a look of horror on his face. 'Dirty bastards.'

VI

Jim Daley was dreading the visit to the mortuary. His first time there had been during training, and for the young constable, it had been the hardest part of his induction into being a police officer. The place stank – the cloying stench of death. He remembered feeling the bile rise in his throat as a body was efficiently eviscerated by a pathologist. Around him, fellow trainees had made their excuses and left the room, or simply collapsed. He had been determined that he would carry on until the end. However, when a diseased liver, swollen, green and suppurating, was removed from the body, Daley couldn't take any more. He'd rushed from the room and been violently sick.

The moment the CID car drew up at the door of Glasgow City Mortuary he could feel his stomach lurch.

'I wonder if the gaffer's right?' said DC Scott, getting out of the Cavalier and lighting a cigarette. 'Hey, are you wanting one?' he added, offering the open packet to Daley.

'No, you're all right. This isn't my favourite part of the job, Brian.'

'Och aye, I know what you mean. I just let it go over my head. Just imagine it's a piece o' meat. That's the advice I got at the start – worked a treat. I tell you, though, if these lassies have been killed using the same MO, then we've got a serial killer on oor hands.'

'We'll soon find out,' said Daley, staring at the red-bricked building.

Scott inhaled the last of his cigarette, then stubbed it out on the pavement with the toe of his shoe. 'Aye, here goes, Jimmy,' he said, pushing the heavy glass door open. As he did so, the sickly-sweet smell of decay assaulted Daley's senses once more. He gritted his teeth and followed the detective.

A man smoking a pipe approached them. He was of average height with unruly dark hair receding at the temples and bushy sideburns that spoke of a style long out of fashion. He had a friendly face, and a slightly distracted manner.

'Ah, DC Scott, isn't it?' he said, sending a plume of blue pipe smoke into the fetid air. 'DCI Burns said you were on your way. And this young man is . . . ?'

'PC Daley, Mr Crichton,' replied Scott, gesturing towards his colleague. 'Aide tae CID, at the moment. Couldn't afford a suit.'

'Pleased to meet you, young man,' said Crichton, shaking Daley by the hand. 'Embarking on a career as a detective – most commendable. You'll have to get used to this place, I'm afraid.' He smiled warmly. 'Follow me, gents. I'll need to get scrubbed up.' He ushered the police officers into the examination room.

A body lay covered on a metal gurney, under an array of lights, similar to the set-up in an operating theatre. A mortuary assistant removed the cover, as the bright lights flickered into life over the corpse of Tracey Greene.

'I've done as DCI Burns asked,' said Crichton. 'Managed to get a bit ahead of myself, this morning, so I can show you what's what.'

Daley stared down at the remains of the young woman. She was skin and bone; her ribs were showing, breasts barely visible, and her hip bones looked as though they would pierce her flesh. It was easy to imagine the skeleton beneath. Her face was waxen, eyes staring into space. A thick dark gash, running from her chin to her genitals, had been cut, then resewn with thick black thread in a criss-cross pattern. It was the same pattern in which he laced up his football boots, Daley thought.

As he looked down on the scene, he felt his head swim. The woman looked even more pathetic lying here on the gurney, all dignity removed, under the glare of strangers, than she had lying in the spartan flat that had been her home.

'Now, can I draw your attention to the bruising here and here,' said Crichton. 'I know it's difficult to see, given the pallor of the corpse, but I would say she's been restrained somehow – perhaps handcuffed, or tied up. The trauma to her wrists and ankles match up, so restrained hand and foot,' he relayed in an even tone.

'She had sex – both vaginal and anal – in the few hours before death. I've taken samples of semen for analysis. Suffice it to say, though, that it looks as though she's been pretty badly treated – not just in the last moments of her life, but in the weeks, perhaps months, prior to her death. There is extensive, more mature bruising, and three of her ribs have been cracked in the recent past. She has two distinctive burns to her buttocks, probably caused by a cigarette, or more likely a cigar, given the circumference of the burn, being applied to the skin.'

'What about the cause of death?' asked Scott, casually placing a stick of chewing gum in his mouth, much to Daley's disgust.

'That's where it gets interesting,' said Crichton. 'Her veins have collapsed in the normal way, due to the misuse of intravenous injection – common enough. Ostensibly, it would appear as though she administered her last fix with an injection to the groin – we recovered the syringe DCI Burns spotted, which had been filled with a heroin-based solution – but it wasn't enough to kill her, in my view.'

'So how, then?' asked Scott, looking puzzled.

'Here.' Crichton lifted the dead woman's right arm. 'Look here, just below her armpit. Can you see a small discolouration?'

Scott leaned forward and peered at the corpse, still chewing enthusiastically. 'Aye, a wee purple bruise.'

'Yes. Exactly right, DC Scott. This is the mark of another injection of heroin. Because we have a bruise, we can be sure that it happened prior to death, but not long before.'

'So she injected herself with the drug twice. A suicide?' asked Daley.

'No. It couldn't be suicide. I've calculated the strength of the second injection into her groin by studying the remnant of the drug on the sides of the syringe. It was a hefty dose, but not enough to kill her. In any event, given the injection of the drug, only a few minutes before into a serviceable vein in her armpit, she couldn't possibly have retained the dexterity to administer the second dose.'

'So the injection into her groin was done by someone else?' asked Scott.

'Almost certainly. I've looked at the crime scene shots. It's obvious by the way her skirt was pulled up, and her right hand placed on her thigh, that we were expected to conclude that she had injected herself. However, the fatal injection to the groin was administered by someone else.'

'So, the same as the other two girls, Mr Crichton?' asked Scott.

'In a nutshell, yes.'

'There goes my weekend off,' said Scott ruefully.

'Indeed. And the collective weekends of many of your colleagues, I shouldn't wonder. We have a serial killer of prostitutes on the streets of our fine city,' opined the pathologist. 'Are you feeling all right, Constable Daley?'

Not waiting to reply, Daley rushed from the examination room, hand clamped over his mouth.

VII

During the short train journey to Paisley, Daley looked around the carriage. Two old men were swapping opinions about football; five teenage girls, all dressed in the same school uniform, giggled as they looked at a copy of *Smash Hits* with a picture of George Michael on the cover; and a young mother looked wearily out of the window, gently rocking a sleeping baby in her arms. A spotty youth was listening to a Walkman, doing his best to avoid any eye contact with his fellow passengers.

Daley had no idea what they had been doing prior to catching the train, but he was pretty sure that they hadn't been staring at an eviscerated dead girl on a metal gurney. He sniffed at his sleeve; the smell of death would be his close companion for the next few days. He knew that, no matter how much he showered, no matter how much deodorant he applied, or Jovan Musk Oil he plastered across his face, the smell would linger.

As he set his alarm for seven thirty, he knew he wouldn't need it. For Constable Jim Daley, sleep would not come. At six o'clock, he gave up, went to buy a fish supper, and got ready for the nightshift.

'A wee word in your ear,' growled Sergeant Donald, as Daley got ready to go on the beat after the muster.

He followed Donald into the sergeants' office, where his superior took a seat, the buttons of his uniform shirt straining to contain his gut. He stared at Daley with undisguised distaste.

'So, you're Burns' new rent boy, are you?' he said, reaching for a packet of Benson & Hedges on the table in front of him.

'Sir?' replied Daley, pretending he didn't know to what Donald was referring.

'You listen to me, you lanky bastard. Let me remind you, I had the pleasure of writing your probationary progress report the other day. I've not finished, mind, and I've discovered a couple of things that won't go down too well. In fact, could well put the skids under your *career*,' he sneered.

'I don't know what you mean, Sergeant.'

'I was signing books out in the darkest recesses of Two Section, the other night. Bumped into oor old pal Davy Fraser.' Donald drew deeply on his cigarette. 'Of course, he was well on. Had a good cargo of bevy aboard, as per.'

'What does that have to do with me?' asked Daley, his heart already in his mouth.

'Nice to see you've the decency tae go pale when you've been sprung, Daley. Aye, when I telt him I had nae choice but to put him on paper for the drink, he started blabbing. You know, the way he does when he's pished.'

Daley said nothing, fixed his gaze to the wall behind Donald. Like most new cops, his initiation onto the shift had been to take a glass or two of whisky when out on duty while the experienced officer was supposed to be showing him the ropes. He'd been unlucky enough to be assigned to Fraser, an officer notorious for his illicit boozing. Despite dire warnings of instant dismissal, young police officers still serving their two-year probationary period had no choice other than to accept the alcohol forced on them by their so-called mentors. The risk of being caught was infinitely preferable to the disapproval of colleagues, who would simply ostracise a young officer who didn't play the game, thereby reducing the chances of getting through probation unscathed.

'So you like a glass of whisky or two,' said Donald, the smile on his face one of triumph.

Daley did not reply, merely looked straight ahead, though his heart was now pounding in his chest. If Donald chose to pursue this, his police career would indeed be over.

'Och, you know me, Jim.' Donald stood up and walked over to his young charge. 'I'm no' the grassing type, I'm sure you'll agree.' The shorter of the two, his face was angled up, only inches away from Daley's, and the stench of stale booze was obvious at close quarters. 'Just you tell DCI Burns that you're not interested in becoming CID's little helper, and we'll forget all aboot it.'

Daley recoiled as flecks of Donald's spit landed on his face.

'If any bastard's going tae get a shot at CID from this shift, it's going tae be me. *Comprende*?'

There was silence between them for a few heartbeats, then Daley made the only reply he could. 'Yes, Sergeant.'

'Good,' said Donald in a brighter tone, as he returned to his desk. 'Now, get yourself out on the beat. You're late.'

As Daley turned to leave the office, the sergeant had the final word, the menace evident in his voice. 'Oh, and remember to be a good boy and stay off the whisky, won't you.'

Daley went over what Donald had said as he walked the beat. He was called to a domestic dispute in the Townhead, which fizzled out on his arrival. As was often the case, when Daley questioned the husband, clearly the worse for drink, his hitherto mute wife jumped to his defence, demanding that the constable leave them alone to sort out their own problems.

About an hour later, being the closest available officer, he was called from Killermont Street to respond to a code 26 in Sauchiehall Street – an alarm sounding in an office block. He waited in the cold for almost an hour for the fractious keyholder to arrive, then checked the building with him. There were no signs of anything untoward, and the incident was assigned to a system malfunction, the cause of many similar call-outs across the city every night.

As he walked back down Sauchiehall Street, his thoughts turned again to Donald. He didn't have a choice. Donald was twisted enough to follow through with his threat. Daley had enjoyed his brief time working with the CID – it was what he'd joined the police to do. Now, he would have to speak to DCI Burns and tell him that he couldn't take on extra duties. He cursed his luck, and the fact that, not only had he been unlucky enough to have Davy Fraser as a tutor cop, his section sergeant was one of the most venal men he'd ever met.

A knocking noise to his right attracted his attention. Across the road, up a set of broad stairs, a uniformed security guard was waving at him from behind the glass entrance doors of a multi-national oil company's office.

'How are you doing, son?' asked the security guard, through the now opened door. 'Could you do with a cup of tea? Quite chilly tonight, is it no'?'

Daley knew the man – an ex-traffic warden called Bobby – and was pleased to accept his invitation to get out of the cold for a while.

'While since I've seen you about here,' said Bobby, now sitting behind a large set of screens, showing black-and-white images from CCTV cameras around the building.

'Yeah, I've been up in the Townhead for the last few months. My new beat,' replied Daley. 'I was down on Plate Glass Patrol the other night, mind you.'

'Aye, no' many places to get out of the cold up there, I wouldn't think, son,' said Bobby, handing Daley a warming mug of tea poured from his Thermos.

As Daley sipped his tea, he noticed that the security man had a troubled look. 'Anything wrong, Bobby?'

'Well, something and nothing,' replied the older man. 'You'll remember that I'm involved with the Salvation Army? When I'm not toiling away in here, that is.'

Daley nodded. 'Glutton for punishment, Bobby. Don't you hand out soup at the bus station?'

'Aye, I do. Poor souls. I don't know how they survive, out in all weathers all year round. It's a bloody sin we've got homeless people on the streets in the eighties.' He took a gulp of tea. 'Since my dear wife buggered off down south with the kids, I've not got a lot else on – might as well try to do some good.'

'I see them every nightshift,' said Daley sadly.

'Can I ask you a question, son? You don't need to answer if you don't want to.'

'Fire away, Bobby. I'll give you an answer, if I can.'

'It's not just the down-and-outs we help when we're doing our soup runs. Some of the ladies of the night come and get some hot tea, or that, too.' He hesitated. 'It's just I heard that one of the lassies we see quite often was found dead.'

'Oh, what was her name?'

'A nice lassie, polite, well brought up, I thought. She wasn't like the others. She seemed out of place, somehow. Tracey. Tracey Greene she was called. I just wondered if what I'd heard was right.'

Daley sat forward in his chair. 'I shouldn't really tell you this, Bobby, but yes, you're right. She was found in her flat up in the Townhead,' he said, leaving out the fact that she had been murdered.

'Oh, I'm sad to hear that. Funny enough, I just saw her the other night. When I say "saw her", she was picked up on here,' he said, gesturing towards the screens.

'Oh, what was she doing? Just touting for business? This isn't where she usually worked.'

'No, she wasn't working. Well, I don't think so. Here, I can show you. We've got it recorded.' He reached under his desk and produced a large VHS tape, which he pushed into a video player in front of him. 'We usually erase the tapes to use again, but I kept this when I heard she was dead. I'm not sure why, really.'

A screen in front of Daley flickered into life. The image was black and white, but the resolution was as good as Daley had seen. It was obvious that the oil company spared no expense when it came to protecting their property. A painfully thin young woman in a short skirt was walking up the street towards the camera. She stopped, and it looked as though she was talking to a huddled figure on the kerb.

'That's definitely Tracey Greene,' said Daley.

'I can zoom in a wee bit,' said Bobby. 'You lose a wee bit of definition, but you can make out who she's talking to.'

The image on the screen enlarged slightly, became less sharp. Daley looked on, fascinated by this vision of the girl whose corpse he had just seen a few hours ago in the mortuary – alive, animated.

She opened her handbag, and appeared to hand something to the person crouching on the pavement.

'See,' said Bobby. 'Heart of gold, that lassie. She's giving him money.'

Daley stared at the screen. Tracey Greene had certainly taken something from her handbag. The pair appeared to be having a conversation, then after what could only have been a couple of minutes, the young woman stepped away, walking up the street and out of shot.

'Can you stop it there?' asked Daley.

When the security guard pressed a button to freeze the picture, it became obvious just who Tracey Greene had been talking to. The figure of Dandy, with his distinctive matted hair and long coat, was obvious, even on the blurred screen.

Daley lingered in the office toilet at the end of his shift. After a few minutes he walked across the corridor and peered out of the window which overlooked the staff car park. Sure enough, there was no sign of Sergeant Donald's battered old Ford Escort, so Daley retrieved the video tape from the pocket of his raincoat and went to the CID offices.

He was surprised to see DCI Burns already hard at work at his desk. Daley knocked on the open door, and Burns looked up from the document he was examining.

'Daley, what can I do you for?'

The young policeman handed Burns the tape and explained its significance.

'Excellent. Come with me and we'll take a look.' Burns led Daley through into the general CID office, where six detectives were busy. On the wall, three photographs were linked with red tape and spidery black writing. One of them was of Tracey

Greene. The incident board also bore images of the Cool Winds Sauna, Greene's flat, and a number of other locations Daley didn't recognise.

Burns called to a couple of detectives, who joined him and Daley at a large television. They watched the footage a few times, Burns rubbing his chin thoughtfully as he did so.

'Aye, that's Dandy, right enough. He's been knocking about the city centre for years.'

'Looks as though she's given him money, sir,' said Daley.

'If she has, it's the first time I've seen anything like it in nearly thirty years. But I suppose anything's possible. Junkie prostitutes don't usually make good philanthropists, but by all accounts she was a decent lassie, so you never know.'

'That footage was shot the day before she died, sir,' observed a young woman in a neat trouser suit.

'I lifted Dandy the next night, sir. He was sleeping in a skip off Sauchiehall Street, not far from that locus, in fact.'

'Aye, and you spewed your ringer, man,' shouted a voice from the back of the office. Brian Scott was hanging up his raincoat.

'And you're late,' rebuked DCI Burns.

'Yes, sorry, sir. My train didn't turn up.'

'Right, I want to speak to Dandy,' said Burns, ignoring Scott's excuse. 'You and Daley get out there and find him. Shouldn't be too hard, just look in the nearest doss house, or in that skip.'

Daley shifted uncomfortably. 'Sir, could I have a word?'

Burns looked at his watch and sighed. 'Yes, if you're quick. Come with me.' He led Daley back to his office. 'And, Brian, you get that coat back on – no time for your usual three mugs of tea.'

Daley shut the door behind him as Burns took a seat behind his desk.

'What's the problem, son?'

'I've had a bit of a run-in with Sergeant Donald, sir,' replied Daley uncomfortably. 'He's made it clear that he doesn't want me to do any more work with the CID.'

'And let me guess, he's threatening to bugger up your probationers' report, by way of leverage.'

'Yes, sir,' replied Daley, surprised by Burns' prescience. 'That's basically it. I–'

'Right, that's it. I won't be gainsaid by that prick. As from tomorrow, I want you to report here for duty. You're officially aide to CID, and I'll clear it with the boss today.'

'Sergeant Donald won't be happy, sir,' said Daley, fearing a reprisal from his shift sergeant.

'You're right about that, son. He most certainly won't be happy when I'm finished with him. Now, get changed and get out and find me Dandy. Welcome aboard, ADC Daley.'

VIII

The man admired himself in the bedroom mirror. He was in his late fifties now, but still had a square jaw, not the jowly folds of most men his age. He kept fit: ran, played squash and golf, and swam regularly. Though he enjoyed alcohol, he was careful to limit his consumption. Similarly, he restrained his appetite, eating no more than eighteen hundred calories a day. He liked a good cigar, but was careful not to inhale.

His grey hair was the only pointer to his true age. He liked it, though. It gave him gravitas, something he'd lacked in his twenties and thirties when he was taking control of the family haulage business from his ailing father. Though his parents had doubted his business acumen he'd expanded the company; he now had a fleet of some forty vehicles, as well as a burgeoning civil engineering company – his own creation. Sadly, his father was too long dead to apologise for his error of judgement in doubting him. He saw little of his mother, now that she was safely ensconced in an inexpensive retirement home, and had the sprawling family mansion on the leafy northern boundaries of the city to himself.

His father had been driven by demons: an almost overpowering desire to leave his poverty-stricken roots in Glasgow's East End behind him. His son had made sure those roots were now a very distant memory indeed.

But he had demons of his own.

He ran a finger over an eyebrow and stalked over to the chair where his overcoat – the best Savile Row could muster – was draped. He shrugged it on and checked that the keys to his Jaguar XJS were still in the pocket, along with his wallet.

He glanced over to the bed where a naked young woman lay motionless.

'You have a good day,' he said to her, as he turned on his heel and left the room.

She didn't reply. Her eyes stared blankly at the roughcast ceiling and into oblivion.

Try as they might, DC Scott and ADC Daley couldn't find any trace of Dandy. They made enquiries at every doss house in the city, then checked the hospitals – even the mortuary. It was as though the tramp had disappeared into thin air.

'Bugger this,' said Brian Scott. 'Yer man could be anywhere: in a derelict flat, on some poor bastard's couch, lying dead in a ditch. There's no telling where he is. We'll have tae go back and tell the gaffer we can't find him.'

Reluctantly, Daley had to agree, though he wasn't happy that his first official task in the CID had ended in failure.

Burns looked at them distractedly. 'Right, lads, I've put this out to the uniform shifts across the city. Somebody like Dandy is going to turn up sooner than later. I want you pair to sign off. Get some rest – you won't have the chance for much in the next few days, so take advantage.'

'Are we going for it, sir?' asked Scott.

'Aye, we are that, son. The ACC has put me in charge of this investigation, so I want this bastard caught pronto. I've only got eighteen months left until I retire. I don't want a series of dead prostitutes lying across the city to be my legacy. Get back tomorrow at eight sharp, and bring your toothbrushes.'

'Yes, sir,' said Daley and Scott, in unison.

'And wear a suit, Daley,' added Burns, then returned to his paperwork.

As they left the office, Scott sighed. 'The gaffer's got the bit between his teeth. Nae chance of any time off until we've cracked this.'

'Guess that's my rest days up the spout,' replied Daley.

'The joys of the CID, young fella. What are your plans now? I'm gasping for a pint.'

'I was going to go out for a while tonight. I suppose I better just forget that and get to my bed,' declared Daley gloomily.

'Bugger that. You'll soon learn in this game, Jim, unless you make hay while the sun shines, there's never any hay tae make. Where were you thinking of going?'

'Oh, just for a couple of beers, then to this club in Paisley. I've got my eye on a lassie. She's there every Wednesday night with her mates. They go for a few drinks after playing badminton, or something.' Daley looked into the distance.

'I'm yer man,' replied Scott. 'If I go hame noo, I'll end up having tae go roon my mother-in-law's for dinner, or some bloody thing. I'll just tell Ella we've had a recall tae duty. Any chance o' crashing on your couch, big man?' Scott thought for a minute. 'Badminton. Is that no' something tae dae wae horses?'

The club was loud and cavernous. Discreet lighting disguised the flaking paint, stained carpet and torn seats. Though the over-arching smells were of tobacco, alcohol and cheap scent, something musty with a hint of disinfectant underpinned it all. On the wall behind the DJ a depiction of the Eiffel Tower with the word 'Paris' flashing in the strobe lights.

Daley and Scott bought expensive bottled beer from the busy bar and then found a table as far away from the rabble as they could.

Daley had changed into his casual suit, a powder blue affair with pleated trousers and sleeves worn pushed up to the elbows. A white shirt, with a buttoned-down collar, left just enough room to display the knot of a thin burgundy tie, which matched his ankle boots. He'd gelled his hair to make it look more slick, in an attempt to appear less like an off-duty policeman.

Scott was still in his working suit; his only concession to going out on the town being to splash his face with water and then spray on some of Daley's Jovan Musk Oil, which he'd sniffed at warily.

'I smell like a poof, Jim,' he complained as they sat with their beers. 'And you need a bloody mortgage tae buy a drink in here. This cost me nearly a quid!' He examined the contents of the German beer bottle, his lip curled. 'Tastes like shit, tae.'

Daley looked around the room. There was no sign of the girl he'd been admiring on and off for about three months. Though he'd visited the club on his weekends off with his flatmates, he'd only ever seen her on a Wednesday night, so if he happened to be off duty on that day, it was here he would come.

As the latest single from Tears for Fears reverberated around the room, Scott drained his bottle and looked into it ruefully. 'You don't get much for your money, eh? No' much mair than a half pint in this bloody thing. On a Wednesday night in oor bit you get a pint o' heavy for forty-five pence. Here, dae you want one?' He offered Daley a cigarette. 'I'll away up and get another round in. Just as well we'll be hammering the overtime in the next few days,' he roared above the din.

Daley watched his new friend thread his way to the bar, as he drew on the cigarette. He couldn't explain why his heart was thudding in his chest; it just was. The prospect of seeing her again thrilled him in a way he knew would seem ridiculous to his companion. The last time he'd been here she'd smiled at him, but before he could muster the courage to go and talk to her, a tall young man in a trendy suit had intervened and dragged her onto the dance floor. Daley had then drank too much and seen her again only fleetingly as he was about to leave, though he was pleased to see she was still with her friends, and not with the man she had danced with earlier.

As the DJ put on a slow song, one by The Blue Nile about

love, loss and lights that shone, he saw her. She was with three other girls, making her way to the bar from the cloakroom. Dressed in an elegant black shift dress, her legs were long and tanned, her copper-coloured hair feathered and flecked with highlights. On her wrist, a gold bracelet caught the light and flashed in response.

'Bang goes another three hours' work,' said Scott, placing two bottles of beer on the table. 'What's wrong wae you, seen a ghost or something?' He followed Daley's eye-line and saw the girl. 'Ah, is that the lassie you've been on aboot? Aye, right enough, I wouldn't kick her oot o' bed tae get tae you, it has tae be said. Get that doon you and go and get her on the floor. Strike while the iron's hot, big man. It's the only way, I'm telling you.'

Before he knew it, buoyed by Scott's encouragement and the beer, Daley was walking over to her. Just as he neared the bar, she turned round and smiled. 'I hope you've plucked up the courage to ask me for a dance this week?' She laughed, her friends giggling in accompaniment.

Awkwardly, Daley asked the question, and the pair forced their way onto the floor, just as the opening bars of 'Every Breath You Take' by The Police rang out across Paris nightclub in Paisley.

How appropriate, thought Daley, as they held each other, swaying in time with the music on the crowded dance floor. Though hardly any words had passed between them, and he knew nothing about her, he already liked her. There was something about her – unlike any woman he'd ever met. He couldn't explain it to himself, never mind anyone else.

When the music stopped, she whispered into his ear, 'I'm Liz, by the way. What's your name?'

'Jim, Jim Daley,' he replied, gazing into her cornflower-blue eyes.

'Well, it's nice to meet you, Jim Daley. Do you mind if we join you and your friend for a drink?'

'Yes, sure,' spluttered Daley. 'We're over there.' He gestured to where Scott was sitting, still examining his beer bottle grimly.

'I know. I saw you on the way in.'

'Oh, right,' replied Daley with a beaming smile.

'Hey, don't get your hopes up, kiddo. I was just looking for a table. Yours was the best option – away from the racket.'

'Right.'

'Oh, dear, Jim Daley.' She laughed. 'But don't you have an expressive face. Not much chance of you being a good liar, I reckon . . . I'll go and get the girls.'

He watched her walk away: tall, straight-backed and graceful. Though he'd never talked to her before, he somehow wasn't surprised that she was well spoken; it just seemed to fit, somehow.

'I'm going oot wae you again, Jimmy boy,' slurred Scott as the girls they'd shared their table with for the last three hours headed en masse to the toilet. 'Quality, every one o' them. You don't get birds like that in my local.'

'No, I bet you don't,' replied Daley.

'See when you get her outside, don't let on you're in the polis.'

'I noticed you never mentioned it to them.'

'Nae wonder. Biggest turn-off on the planet, Jim. Especially for posh birds. No way Daddy's going tae let them have anything tae dae wae a cop. Naw, merchant bankers and playboy businessmen, is all they'll have their eye on.'

'You reckon? So what do you suggest?'

'You'll have tae make something up, Jim. You've been in court enough times since you joined up. If you can sell a tale tae the Sheriff, you can surely convince some wee lassie.'

'I don't want to start off by lying to her,' replied Daley seriously.

'Och, it's like thon John Lennon says, if you tell a lie often enough, it's just as though it was true.'

'That was Lenin,' said Daley.

'Aye, like I said. Clever boy, much mair aboot him than that McCartney bloke. Anyway, you'll be hoping the song's "Ticket To Ride", the night, and no danger.'

As it turned out, Liz and her friends lived in Bridge of Weir, an up-market village about ten miles away from Paisley. Daley walked her to the taxi rank, his arm around her waist. He could hear Scott, a few yards behind, telling her friends jokes and sending them into gales of laughter.

'I'm at uni,' Liz said, smiling up at him. 'What do you and your friend do?'

There it was: the question he'd been dreading. 'Oh.' Daley hesitated. 'Eh, he's in insurance.'

'And you?' She stopped, and was eyeing him curiously now.

'Me, oh . . . I'm a civil servant.' He was as happy with this deceit as he could be under the circumstances. Strictly speaking, he was a civil servant. He smiled at her shyly. 'Could I see you again?'

'Of course you'll see me again. We're out every Wednesday – bound to bump into you.'

'Oh, right,' said Daley, deflated.

'You're so cute, do you know that?' She giggled as she

rummaged about in her bag, removing a Filofax and a pen. 'Here's my number, dopey,' she said, tearing a page from it and handing it to him.

She looked into his eyes, then kissed him passionately on the lips.

For the first time in his life, Jim Daley was utterly smitten.

IX

'Just as well you had some o' that mouthwash, big man,' said Scott as they made the train journey to Glasgow the following morning. 'Policeman's friend, and no mistake. Here, dae you want a Polo?' He handed Daley one of his mints.

'Feeling rough, Brian?'

'I'm used tae it. Nothing a few cups o' tea and a bacon roll won't fix, buddy.'

They had hardly entered the CID office before Burns leaned his head around the door and summoned them with an index finger. He was holding a clear plastic evidence bag, containing a slim notebook.

'Right, lads, this was found in Tracey Greene's flat. I've had the forensic boys take a look at it. There's a few names and addresses, but mostly just initials, phone numbers and car number plates.'

'Why the car numbers?' asked Daley.

'That's what the lassie's on the street dae,' replied Scott. 'If they go off in a car, their mates take a note of the car reggie. Kind of security – in case they don't come back, or take a beating. A way of identifying the punter. The girls give us the number of the motor, then we catch the bastard.'

'Well, that's the theory, anyway,' said Burns. 'I want you

boys to find out all you can about anyone in this book. I want to know who they are and where they live. Oh, and you'll see there's been a page torn out. The lab boys looked at the marks made by the pen on the next page when she was writing it. Here.' Burns handed a note to Daley that read 'M. A571 WHT' in bold letters.

'Obviously, check that one out first.'

'I wonder why she tore the original page out?' asked Daley.

'That's what I want you to find out. You'll find most of these are just punters, but we need to eliminate them from the inquiry. And you never know...'

'Any sign o' Dandy, sir?' asked Scott.

'No. Not a thing. If she was just giving him money out of the kindness of her heart, I doubt we'd get much out of him, anyway–' Burns was about to add to this when he was interrupted by another officer.

'Sorry, sir, but it looks like we have another dead girl. Same MO, in one of the high flats in the Gorbals.'

Burns sighed. 'Right, you pair get on with it. I want to know who everyone in that address book is before close of play this afternoon.'

Scott and Daley decided to take half of Tracey Greene's address book each. Daley was responsible for A to M, while Scott was taking care of the rest.

'You better try the one fae forensics first,' said Scott, about to make a call of his own. 'I'll call these phone numbers and you hit the car registrations, then we'll swap and see where we get.'

Daley wandered through to the uniformed side of Stewart Street Police Office, where Three Shift were on duty. Having worked with them on overtime, he knew some of the officers.

The controller, Derek, sitting behind his desk in subdued light, welcomed him in hushed tones. 'Right, we'll go through them in between calls,' he said, gesturing to the desk, where the radio communications of every officer in the division were being monitored and dealt with, personnel being deployed and their calls being handled.

'Can we start with this one?' said Daley, handing him the note that read 'M. A571 WHT'.

Derek typed in the letters and digits, then raised one eyebrow. 'This number was checked by your mates on the nightshift last night.'

'Oh, who by?'

'Your friend and mine, Davy Fraser. Not often he calls in a reggie plate, eh?' Derek laughed. 'You can't see many cars from the back room of the Hurdy Gurdy, can you?' He waited for the details of the number to display on the screen in front of him. 'There you are – company car by the look of things, Murchieston Transport, registered at their Possil offices.'

Daley wondered if the 'M' on the note might stand for Murchieston. He then pondered as to why Davy Fraser had checked the number plate during the previous nightshift.

Slowly, they worked their way through the list, until Daley had the address corresponding to every car number plate in his half of Tracey Greene's address book. Most of the cars were registered to residential addresses, but some, like that on the torn-out page, were company cars.

Daley decided to take a punt. He looked up Davy Fraser's personal details, then called him at home. There was something about that page torn from the address book: why tear out just one, and, if so, what for? He could see the image of Tracey Greene talking to Dandy the tramp in his mind's eye. For some reason, his thoughts kept drifting back to the grainy video footage.

'Davy, sorry to bother you mate, it's Jim Daley.' There was a considerable amount of coughing on the other end of the line, accompanied by some distant oaths, no doubt directed at Fraser by his long-suffering wife, who had taken the call.

'Jimmy, what the hell are you doing calling me at this time? I was in court all morning off the nightshift. I've got a heid like a jackhammer, son.'

'Sorry, Davy. I just have a quick question. I'm helping the CID out on the Tracey Greene case.'

'Oh aye, I know fine. I had Sergeant Donald in my ear half the night about it last night. He's no' happy wae you, and that's putting it mildly.'

Daley felt his hackles rise. 'Oh, you and him having another one of your wee chats?' he said, remembering that it was Fraser who had told Donald that he'd been drinking on duty.

'Aye, well . . . so what dae you want, now you've woken me up? I've got tae get some shut-eye before I go back on tonight.'

'You ran a vehicle check last night, on an XJS, A571 WHT. What were the circumstances?'

'Oh, that,' said Fraser, pausing to cough again. 'Och, I just ran that to get an annoying bastard off my back. Some guy, said he'd been walking across High Street when that car nearly took him out. Apparently it was fair tanking along. I ran the vehicle check and told him we were on the case.'

'Which we're not.'

'You know yourself, Jimmy. His word against the driver, and all that . . . the guy was walking about fine, no' a scratch on him. No harm done in my book.'

'So he was there when you checked the details? He heard the response from the controller?'

'Aye, well, if he can understand oor controller, he would've heard it. How, what's the matter wae that?'

'Not really good procedure, is it?'

'Listen, son, when you're no' so fucking wet behind the ears, you come and tell me aboot procedure. Now, dae you need anything else? I need a drink o' water. My tongue's stuck tae my mooth.'

'Just quickly, Davy. This guy who reported the speeding car, what was he like?'

'Och, just run o' the mill. Aboot my height, short hair, dark, going grey. Clean-shaven. Kind of rough-looking, if you know what I mean.'

'How rough-looking? Meaning he'd been drinking?' asked Daley, wondering just how easy it would be for Fraser to have spotted, given he'd probably been drinking himself.

'No' rough like that, son. Sort of lived-in features, craggy, you know what I mean. Big bags under his eyes. Looked as though he'd no' slept for a week. Don't get me wrong, he was polite enough. Ancient suit, though – big lapels, like fae the seventies. Aye, and he could've done wae a trip tae the dentist.'

Daley ended the call, astonished by the amount of detail Fraser had been able to retain. He supposed that old habits died hard, and that having been a cop for years, despite his drinking, Fraser must have clung on to some of his training and experience.

He went back to the CID office just ahead of DCI Burns, who had a short stout man in an ill-fitting suit with him.

'Scott, Daley, in my office!' Burns shouted.

Burns was sitting behind his desk, lighting a cigarette, when the two young officers entered the room. The stout man introduced himself as Inspector Ward from the Serious Crimes Squad and squinted at Scott and Daley through thick glasses.

'Seems you've been treading on Inspector Ward's toes,' said Burns ominously.

Without giving them time to respond, Ward spoke up: 'The Cool Winds Sauna, lads. Tell me what happened.'

As Scott stumbled through a roughly accurate version of what had happened when he and Daley questioned Jat Suleiman, Ward scrutinised him.

'Well, thanks to you pair, they've shut up shop and buggered off. We've been keeping tabs on the place for months. Part of an ongoing investigation into money laundering, amongst other things. And there have also been two vehicle identification requests on a vehicle – A571 WHT – the last one within the last hour, authorised by a Constable Daley.'

'That's me, sir,' replied Daley.

'Well, I want you to stop,' said Ward, banging the table in front of him. 'If you jeopardise my investigation, you can wave bye-bye to a career in the police. Got it?'

'Oh, hang on,' said DCI Burns, getting to his feet. 'The boys were acting on my orders. Are you going to jeopardise my career?'

'No, sir, of course not. But this investigation is critical.'

'Does it have anything to do with Murchieston Transport?' asked Daley.

'And what if it does?' roared Ward, swinging round in his chair to face Daley.

Burns intervened. 'Tell me about Murchieston.'

'Listen, do we have to speak in front of the boys here, sir?'

'*Boys*! These boys, as you call them, are part of my murder investigation team, Inspector. In my book, that trumps your inquiries. Spit it out!' shouted Burns, his face turning red with anger.

'Allan Murchieston has had a lot of success lately. The business has grown from a few wagons to a fleet of lorries and a construction company. All I'm saying is, we don't think it's happened by purely legitimate means.'

'Is this guy running knocking shops on the side?' asked Scott.

'He's into lots of stuff. But that's all I'm saying.' Ward turned to Burns. 'I'm sure you understand the need for discretion, sir,' he said curtly.

After Ward left, Burns listened to what Daley had to say about the vehicle and the man who had reported it to Davy Fraser.

'So, what do you think, Daley?'

The young constable hesitated. 'Honestly? I don't know, sir.'

'Listen, Jim,' said Burns, leaning forward on his chair, 'the greatest asset any cop can have is instinct. Never try and ignore it – no matter how ridiculous it seems. That'll set you in good stead. Now, I'll ask again, what's your instinct?'

'I think Murchieston is involved with this, sir. Especially now we know about his connection to Cool Winds. It can't be a coincidence that he has clandestine dealings with the place and one of his company car registrations appears in Greene's address book.'

'Yes, logical enough, Daley, but by the same token, it doesn't make him a killer, either. We'll have to tread carefully with this one. I don't want the Squad on my back, as well as everything else. You and Brian go to Murchieston Transport, find out who drives that car, and we'll take it from there.'

'You're no' bad at this CID stuff, Jim,' said Scott as the pair headed out of the CID office. 'That was impressive, man. We'll get the motor and get up tae Possil and see what's what at Murchieston Transport.'

'Hang on a second, Brian,' replied Daley. 'I just want to have a word with the collater.'

Daley walked through to the uniformed section of the office and knocked on the door that read 'Constable C. Reid. Divisional Intelligence Officer'. Despite the official title, the man who kept the records of suspects, convicted criminals and those known to the police, was known as the Collater. It was his job to keep tabs on the criminals who inhabited the division's area. And Charlie Reid was good at his job.

'Yes, son, what can I do you for?' asked Reid with a welcoming smile. A thick-set man in his early fifties, he'd been injured on duty in the late 1970s, and since then had occupied the role of collater with some aplomb.

'What do you know about Dandy, Charlie?' asked Daley.

'You mean the jakey?' Reid replied.

'The very man.'

'Been on the streets since I was on the beat here, so that must be eighteen years ago. I'm buggered if I know how he's survived this long.'

'You know the stories about him – the gossip. Any truth in it?'

'Oh, you mean that he was once a professor, or something? Aye, I've heard that. I don't think that's right, but there's something in the back of my mind about him.' He passed his hand over his bald head. 'I tell you what, I'm in the middle of

183

something right now. Give me half an hour or so, and I'll dig out what I have on him and give you a shout.'

'Cheers, Charlie. I'm off out, but you can get me on the radio.'

Murchieston Transport was based on a ragged industrial estate in Possil that had seen better days. Behind a barbed-wire fence sat a row of low office buildings, which abutted a busy garage. A small team of mechanics were busy working to keep Murchieston's large fleet of lorries on the road. A grizzled Alsatian dog on a thick length of chain barked furiously as Scott and Daley got out of the unmarked police car and knocked on the door marked 'Reception'.

After a buzz, locks on the door clicked and Scott pushed the door open. A young blonde woman with heavy make-up sat at a desk staring at a typewriter, a scowl on her face.

'Can I help yous?' she asked, without lifting her gaze from what she was doing.

'It's lovely tae see you too,' said Scott sarcastically, brandishing his warrant card. 'Stewart Street CID. We're enquiring about one of your company cars.'

'Another yin?' she replied exasperatedly. 'There was a guy in just a wee while ago, asked the same thing. Is it A571 WHT, by any chance?'

Daley and Scott exchanged a glance. 'Aye, that's the number,' said Scott. 'Who was the other bloke?'

'Said he saw the driver drop money oot o' his wallet when he saw him gettin' oot the car yesterday. Twenty quid. I said he could leave it here, but the guy wanted tae hand it over in person. Likely lookin' for a reward.'

'And who drives the car?' asked Daley.

'The boss, Allan Murchieston.'

'Did you give this man Murchieston's address?'

'Aye, I did. I know he's worth a few bob, but naebody can go aboot the place chuckin' away twenty notes, can they? Trust me, considering the wages he pays in here, every penny's a prisoner.'

'What was this man like?' asked Daley.

'I dunno, just a guy. Older man, maybe in his fifties or that. Maybe aulder. Who knows when they get tae that bloody age. Here, if you hang on, I can get yous a look at him,' she said, gesturing to the small camera on the wall behind her.

She got up, revealing a tight black skirt, sheer black tights and white shoes with impossibly high heels.

'The view's improving a' the time,' observed Scott quietly as she bent over a video player, which sat under a small television. After rewinding the tape she stopped and turned to the policemen.

'There he's there. No' a very bonny sight – no' a patch on you, big yin,' she said, winking at Daley.

They squinted at the picture, which was nothing like the quality of the CCTV footage from the oil company.

'Mind if I move it on a bit?' asked Scott.

'Dae what you want, darlin'' she replied, edging towards Daley, who could feel his face going red.

Scott played the image backwards and forwards until the man's features were visible. Daley remembered Davy Fraser's description of the old-fashioned suit, the short hair going grey, and the craggy face.

'It's the same guy who got Davy to check the registration number last night, Brian. Definitely,' said Daley. He was about to say more when he heard his name on the radio.

'A-Alpha calls ADC Daley, come in ADC Daley, over.' He

acknowledged the call. 'Jim, could you give the collater a call as soon as possible, over?'

Daley asked the receptionist if he could use the office phone, and dialled Charlie Reid's internal number.

'Right, son, Dandy. Real name Kenneth Lister. Ex-marine. There was some truth in the stories, right enough. He was on duty on some naval destroyer, when he was told that his wife had been killed in a car accident. Had a wee lassie, too. She was in the car, but she escaped with minor injuries. Looks as though he just lost it afterwards. Within a year he'd been discharged, and the wee girl was staying with her mother's sister.'

'What was the girl's name?' asked Daley.

'Rebecca Lister,' replied Reid. He paused. 'But she changed her name. She was in all sorts of bother when she was a teenager, but I managed to pick her up. Used her middle name and her aunt's married name: Tracey Greene.'

Daley stared at the frozen image on the tiny screen. Every picture told a story, but the one from the CCTV in Sauchiehall Street had lied. The prostitute wasn't handing money to an old tramp; she was handing her father the identity of the man who was persecuting her – just in case.

'Brian, we need to get to Murchieston's house. Where does he live?' he shouted to the receptionist.

'Hold your horses, big boy. He stays in the wilds, up near Mugdock Park. Here,' she said, as she scribbled down the address and handed it to Daley.

He took one last look at the image on the screen. The man's hair was cut short, he was clean-shaven, wearing an old suit, and he looked sober. There was no doubt. Daley was looking at Dandy, Tracey Greene's father.

Allan Murchieston took the stairs from his basement gym two at a time. He'd finished his daily workout and was ready for a shower and a coffee.

He was lucky that he didn't have to spend a lot of time involved in the day-to-day running of his business interests. He had a handful of trusted managers who coped so much better than he would have with the boring grind of piloting his companies. He was free to take an overview, to spot money-making opportunities and to indulge his private passions.

He unzipped his blue tracksuit top, went to his front door, and scooped up the small pile of mail on the mat. He flicked through various bills, a letter from an old aunt, and an invitation to a business initiative run by the local council. Nothing of any interest.

He walked into the lounge and took in the view from the large bay window. Early spring sunshine dappled the leafy garden. In the distance, the hills were beginning to take on a healthy hue after the cold snowy winter as they glowered down at the few expensive homes that dotted the valley.

Lost in thought, his eye caught movement on the drive. Sure enough, a miserable-looking man in an ill-cut suit was plodding towards the house. Being rather out of the way, Murchieston was lucky not to receive many cold calls from sales people. However, this individual bore all the hallmarks of the type who would try to sell him double glazing, garden fencing or driveway paving. It was the weary but determined trudge, he supposed.

He was in no mood to converse with the pathetic man, so he made his way back to the front door, opened it, and stared down the long driveway. The man in the suit was nowhere to be seen.

He took a few steps down towards the garden, but still could see no one.

He was about to turn on his heel and go back into the house, when something hard hit him from behind. He bent double, pain shooting through his kidneys. As he was trying his best to regain his breath, another blow, this time to the head, sent him spiralling agonisingly into darkness.

'Hang on, Jimmy,' said Scott, as they left the broad streets of the city behind and drove along the winding country roads to the north of Glasgow. The Cavalier's engine whined in protest as Scott put his foot down to overtake a lumbering van, far too near a corner for Daley's comfort.

'Who taught you to drive, Brian? Evel Knievel?'

'Och, we used tae mess aboot in cars when we were kids, Jimmy,' he replied, skidding around a corner. 'This baby's got nearly eighty-brake horsepower, so we'll be there in no time.'

'We're looking for a sign for Red Knowe. The house is set off the road according to the girl in the office.'

'Don't you worry, got a couple of miles to go before we get near,' said Scott, sounding the horn and swearing volubly at a man driving a tractor and trailer that had brought them almost to a standstill. 'Take that bastard's number, Jim. I'll give him a tug on the way back. These buggers think they own the place!'

After a few more miles of driving on the edge, frequent cursing from Scott, and even more frequent prayers from Daley, they saw a large red-brick house at the end of a long driveway, through the trees.

'Any money that's Red Knowe,' said Daley, relieved to have reached their destination without dying in a mangled car wreck.

'Probably right, Jim. We'll see if there's any signpost,' replied Scott, appearing almost deflated that the breakneck ride to get to Murchieston's house was over.

Sure enough, a wooden sign at the end of the drive bore the name of the house. In a last automotive flourish, Scott propelled the car towards the house, scattering stone chips as the wheels sloughed to gain purchase. They skidded to a halt behind a red XJS bearing the registration A571 WHT.

Daley was first out of the car – relieved to be getting out at all – and loped up the front steps towards a large oak door, which was ajar.

'Any bets your man Dandy's here already,' said Scott under his breath.

They entered the house. To their right was a spacious lounge with bay windows. To their left, a dining room with adjacent kitchen, replete with granite counters and expensive appliances. A curving staircase swept up to the top two floors of the house, while beneath it a smaller spiral staircase led to what Daley assumed was a basement.

The police officers stood for a few seconds, but could hear nothing.

'You take a look at the cellar, big man,' said Scott. 'I'll get upstairs. All seems pretty quiet. If you find anything just gie me a shout.'

Daley made his way as quietly as possible down to the basement. Finding himself in a dimly lit corridor, he was faced by two wood-panelled doors. Cautiously, he opened the first, to reveal a large bathroom with a capacious shower, WC and wooden compartment marked with a brass plaque as the 'Steam Room'.

Silently, he closed it, and paused. Just before crossing the corridor, he heard thuds – quiet, repetitive – coming from behind the door opposite. He grasped the brass handle and eased it open.

He found himself in a fully equipped gymnasium, where, at the end of the room, a middle-aged man was struggling silently, at the end of a rope, tied to the top of a weights bench. His face was a livid purple, the only sound coming from his feet as they flailed against the apparatus.

'Brian, quick! He's in here!' shouted Daley at the top of his voice, hoping his colleague would hear him through the open door. He rushed over to the man he guessed was Murchieston, grabbed him by the legs and took the weight of the rope. Now that Daley had taken the strain, Murchieston began to wheeze, a wailing noise that came from his throat, as he desperately tried to force breath into his lungs, the noose still tight around his neck. He pulled desperately with both hands, but couldn't loosen it. His wheeze grew deeper and less frequent, as though his life was draining away.

Still holding Murchieston up with one arm, Daley tried to reach up with his free hand to release the noose, but he couldn't get purchase on the rope.

'Brian, for fuck's sake, get down here!' he shouted again.

At first, he was relieved when he heard footsteps behind him. Then, as a figure moved into his line of sight, he realised that it wasn't his fellow officer.

The man was dressed in a double-breasted pin-stripe suit with huge lapels. His hair was cut short, and he was clean-shaven. The only thing that marked him out as the man Daley had removed from the skip a few days before was his grimace: the teeth black, yellow and rotten.

'Let him go,' the intruder shouted, in a deep husky voice.

He was holding a ball-pen hammer in his left hand. 'Let him go, young fella,' he said again, brandishing the implement.

'Brian!' Daley called desperately, just as Dandy brought down the hammer with excruciating force against his left shoulder. Howling in pain, he tried to keep a hold of Murchieston, but felt his grip weaken. 'It doesn't have to be like this, Kenneth,' he gasped, miraculously remembering Dandy's real name and hoping it would somehow rouse him from this murderous rage. 'This man needs to face justice, not just for your daughter, but for the others he's killed and abused.'

For a second, Dandy stared at him open-mouthed.

'I know Tracey Greene was your daughter. I'm so sorry this has happened,' rasped Daley, as the deep whine of Murchieston's laboured breath became weaker and weaker. 'Let this man do the time in jail, not you. You're helping him to get away with this.'

For a moment, Daley thought he'd got through to him, as Dandy dropped the hammer and paused for a second.

He was wrong.

The man leapt towards him, caught the young policeman by the neck with a vice-like grip, and started to choke him.

Daley lost his purchase on Murchieston's legs as he felt himself lose consciousness. The room began to spin, and he saw sparks and flashes of light. It was his turn to struggle for breath.

Just as he was about to pass out, he felt Dandy's body jerk, and his grip around Daley's throat slackened. Almost automatically, still struggling to remain conscious, he forced Murchieston back up to take the strain from the rope that was suffocating him.

'Aye, and goodnight to you,' said Brian Scott as he subdued

Dandy with an arm lock, rolling him over, face down against the carpet, and handcuffing him. 'Hang on, Jimmy,' he said, producing something from his pocket and scaling the weightlifting apparatus.

A few seconds later, Murchieston fell heavily onto Daley. As he struggled with Murchieston's weight on top of him, Daley saw Scott working at the rope with a long-bladed knife. Finally, Scott pulled the rope from the victim's neck, and with the obstruction removed, the man began to draw deep howling breaths.

Daley got up, leaving Murchieston on the floor on his hands and knees, and immediately yelled in pain as he twisted his injured shoulder.

'No' a bad wee result,' said Scott, above the rasp of Murchieston's breathing and the curses from Dandy. 'You look like you took a dull yin, right enough. Och, but you'll be fine. A nice wee feather in your cap, Jimmy boy.'

'Where did you get the knife?' asked Daley, still grimacing in pain.

'Och, I'm forever forgetting that baton o' mine. I'm fae the East End, Jimmy – grabbed this fae the kitchen when I heard you shoutin'. The gaffer would call it reverting to type.'

In the distance, Daley could hear police sirens. The cavalry were on their way.

XI

'So you hurt your shoulder falling down stairs in your office?' asked Liz, staring at the man with his arm in a sling, sitting in the trendy wine bar in Paisley's New Street.

'Yeah, basically . . . yeah,' mumbled Daley.

192

'Oh, I'm sure that happens to civil servants all the time. Hazard of the job, no doubt.'

Her eyes sparkled with mischief, and Daley knew she didn't believe him. He was frantically trying to think up the best – the easiest way – to tell her what his real job was.

'I'm really glad about one thing, though,' she said with a bright smile.

'Oh, what's that?'

'That you're not a policeman. My father hates the police. He'd disown me if I had any truck with an officer of the law. Taboo, big boy.'

'Right,' said Daley, now in a quandary, looking around the room for inspiration.

'You're funny, Jim Daley. You're funny and gorgeous, and I think I like you a lot.'

'Thanks,' replied Daley, brightening up considerably.

'Anyway, when do you get that sling off and get yourself back on the beat?'

'Oh, should be fine in a couple of weeks, the Force doctor says I . . .' He stopped, realising what he'd said.

'Spoofer!' she exclaimed with a smile. 'Be sure your sins will find you out, my mother always says.'

'Mine too,' replied Daley sheepishly. 'If you want to go back home, I'll understand. I didn't want to lie to you. Brian said girls like you hate the police.'

'Girls like me?' she asked in mock surprise. 'Whatever do you mean?'

'Well, you know . . . well brought-up girls.'

'You mean posh bints, don't you, Jim?'

'Well, you know . . .'

She leant forward and held his hand. 'Do yourself a favour

and stop listening to Brian Scott. He's a lovely guy, but I don't think you want to follow his example.'

'How did you find out I was a policeman?'

'You mean, apart from the short hair and the military bearing?'

'Well, yes, kind of.'

'Brian Scott told my mate he was an inspector and you were his sergeant.'

'Really? That bas . . . that swine . . .' he said, quickly correcting himself.

'I wasn't joking about my dad, mind you.'

'No?'

'But who cares what he thinks. The man's a dinosaur. There's not a man on earth he thinks is suitable for his lovely daughter. Be prepared for a hard time in that department.'

'You mean you want to see me again?'

'Oh, I want to see a lot more of you, Jim Daley.' She winked at him. 'You're not left-handed, are you?'

'No, right-handed, actually. Why?'

'Aw, pity. If you were left-handed and your hand was out of commission all of this time, I'm sure it must have been *very hard*.'

'What?' Daley's throat was dry. He could hear his heart pounding in his ears. Could he be feeling slightly faint, even? 'My flat's not far from here, Liz,' he said hopefully.

'Good-oh.' Liz winked at him, a large grin spread across her face. 'But let's have another glass of wine first, eh? Chop, chop, Jimmy boy.'

SINGLE END

A DCI Daley Short Story

I

Glasgow, 1989

It wasn't the first time Detective Constable Brian Scott had been in Strathclyde Police's Pitt Street HQ – not by any means. Usually he would push open the smoked-glass doors and trudge over the expensive carpeting to attend a training course, or, more frequently than he'd have liked, the Complaints and Discipline Office where he was becoming a familiar face.

He reflected on his last visit as he sat outside the office of one DCI Thomas Dines of the Serious Crime Squad. He'd been at the football with his father and Uncle Ronnie when things had taken a turn for the worse and they had found themselves at the heart of a bar brawl with their fellow supporters, which was unusual.

Despite his protestations that he was a colleague in the CID, Scott was huckled into the back of the van with the rest of the miscreants. He'd spent a miserable few hours in custody until someone had realised that he was a police officer and arranged his release.

That had been almost a month ago, and he'd hoped the official warning administered by the discipline inspector was the end of the matter. Now that he was sitting at the door of one of the Crime Squad bosses, he wasn't so sure.

He heard a buzzer sound. The fragrant secretary he'd passed on his way in leaned her head round the corner.

'DCI Dines is ready for you now, DC Scott. Just tap the door and go in,' she said brightly, clearly without the same brick in her stomach he had in his. The Serious Crime Squad were well named – this really wasn't funny. It was the last thing he needed.

He gave the door a rap with his knuckles and pushed it open, just as a voice called 'come' in an authoritarian fashion. This was the one aspect of policing with which Brian Scott was least comfortable. In short, he struggled with authority. He'd tried really hard to fit in with the protocols, but, somehow, calling a person he had little or no respect for 'sir', stuck in his throat – and that was just one of his issues.

'DC Scott, A-Division CID, sir,' he announced, doing his best to stand to attention.

'Take a seat, Brian,' said Dines pleasantly, from behind a huge, well-polished desk. He was a neat man with short dark hair, a well-ironed shirt and a pair of half-moon glasses, over which he appraised his visitor.

Scott noticed the expensive Swiss watch and a tan that pointed to the fact he'd holidayed abroad recently. Maybe he was getting better at this detective stuff, he thought to himself.

'Give me a moment, will you?' Dines returned his attention to a document he was reading, licking his thumb and forefinger before turning the page.

Scott tried to look as nonchalant as possible, but his stomach had decided to make loud gurgling noises – gurgles that seemed to grow in volume the longer he sat there.

'IBS, Brian,' said Dines, removing his glasses and fixing Scott with his steely green eyes.

'Eh, sorry, sir,' muttered Scott, trying desperately to remember which aspect of police procedure the acronym IBS represented. The bloody job was full of them, and, despite himself, he couldn't bring this one to mind.

'Have you suffered for long? My wife's had trouble too, poor thing,' continued Dines.

DC Scott decided to take a stab at it. 'I didn't know your missus was in the job, sir.'

'Sorry?'

'I didn't know she was polis, so tae speak.' Scott's face was getting redder, and his stomach chose that very moment to let rip with an extraordinary noise.

'She's a dentist, actually. Whatever made you think that?'

'Och, eh, just when you said she was having trouble wae they IBS boys. Must be a term dentists use and a', then.'

'Irritable Bowel Syndrome, man – IBS! That stomach of yours sounds as though it's doing cartwheels. That's probably why.'

'Aye, right, right you are, sir,' replied Scott, wishing the ground would swallow him up. 'Just get a bit nervous here at HQ, sir, if you know what I mean.'

'Considering your record I'm surprised you haven't passed a stool by now, DC Scott.'

Scott desperately tried to remember if he'd passed any stools on the way in. He was about to reply in the negative – all he could remember were the low metal seats with the blue upholstery – when Dines interrupted his train of thought.

'Anyway, I want you to know that you are of great interest to me . . . to the squad, in fact.'

'I am? Oh, right, sir,' said Scott, waiting for the bit where he'd have to justify some buttock-clenching misdemeanour.

'Yes. You must have wondered why your entry into CID has been so smooth. You're sitting your inspector's exam for the third time, I hear.'

'Aye, I'm getting better each time, mind. Right foxy, they guys that set the questions.'

'Well, never mind that. Let's just say you have a very interesting background, don't you, Brian? Grew up with some of the country's most notorious gangsters, I believe – not least Frank MacDougall and the self-styled Godfather himself, James Machie.'

'Aye, aye, I did. I don't have nothing tae dae with them noo, sir, you understand,' replied Scott hurriedly, realising the implications of such associations.

Dines paused and put his glasses back on. He lifted a green file from his desk and opened it, reading it in silence for a few moments.

'Do you know, they tell me all these files we accumulate will soon be things of the past? What with this new computer system on the way, it's all change. I'll have a screen sitting on my desk here, where I can access anything I want at the touch of a button. All stored on a central database,' he mused as he flicked through more pages, skimming the content.

'I cannae see it myself, sir. You know machines – oor washing machine never works right. Flooded the whole flat the other day. Aye, and the guy doonstairs, he wasn't too happy aboot it. Before you know it, the bloody things will be on the bum, and you'll be left haulding yer ain —'

Before Scott could further embarrass himself, Dines put down the file and spoke again. 'We want you to reacquaint yourself with your old friends, Brian.'

'Who, big Frank and JayMac? No chance, gaffer. They know I'm in the cops – won't touch me wae a barge pole. Likely try and blow my heid aff.'

'Oh, I don't know. They'd come round if you gave them something.'

'Sorry, sir, how d'you mean? Gie them what, exactly?'

'Something that will help them, Brian. Information, perhaps.'

'What kind o' information?'

'The Machie organisation has five saunas in the city centre, so I'm reliably informed, and your colleagues at A-Division have a squad dedicated to cleaning that up. They've been tolerated as legalised brothels for too long, so the divisional commander tells me.'

'Aye, that's true. I'm no' on the squad, though.'

'But your friend DC Daley is, I think I'm right in saying?'

'Yes, sir, he is,' replied Scott, beginning to get the gist of what was going on.

'We want you to get information on these sauna raids – I don't care how – and when you've done that, make contact with one of Machie's gang. Who do you know best?'

'Frank MacDougall was oor neighbour for years. Stayed in the same single end. But why don't you just get this information from the divisional commander, sir?'

Dines pursed his lips. 'We've got a rotten apple somewhere, Brian. Or, at least, we think we have. Some bugger is feeding information to the underworld, particularly Machie's organisation. If this approach of yours looks less than authentic, with a suspicion that it's come from me, your friends will find out from their source.'

Scott looked doubtful. 'What if I don't fancy this, sir? I mean, it's a big ask.'

'You don't need to play ball, of course. But then again, neither do I.'

'Meaning?'

'Meaning whatever you think it might mean, Brian. Man with your record of indiscipline, well . . .' Dines left the threat unsaid.

Scott sighed. 'So they'll know aboot these sauna raids already, then.'

'No. That's tuppeny-ha'penny stuff. Much more sensitive information is being leaked by a corrupt officer. We want you to ingratiate yourself with them, gain their trust, then find out who this bastard is.'

'I'm telling you, sir. As long as I'm in the polis, they won't trust me. They hate me because I joined up.' Scott could vividly recall some of the threats made against him by the lads he had grown up with when he first donned the police uniform, though he preferred not to.

'Oh, that won't be a problem, Brian. You're about to lose your job.'

'I'm what?'

'Oh, don't worry, leave that bit to me. All part of the act, but only you and I will know that. The fewer people involved in this, the better. This is a deep cover operation, Brian. I've spent almost thirty years in this job and I'll be damned if some dodgy bastard is going to make me – make us all – look like low-life crooks on the take. You have no idea how much I want this bastard.'

As Scott emerged into the noise of the city to walk the short distance back to Stewart Street, he felt as though his heart was in his boots. He'd never wanted to be like his peers growing up: never able to relax, always waiting for that knock at the door that would lead them to years of incarceration, or worse, oblivion at the hands of a gang rival.

Now here he was, about to be thrust back amongst them, and only he and Dines knew why. He could see the logic of it all. However, it needed a strong, clever man to do this. A stronger, cleverer man than him.

The return journey to his place of work became a miserable trudge.

II

The CID room in Stewart Street Police Office was empty as Brian Scott slumped in the rickety swivel chair at his untidy desk.

He looked around. Everything was the way it always was: a girlie calendar on the wall; jackets and coats almost toppling a flimsy coat stand; the odd briefcase on the floor, belonging to those who didn't take their sandwiches to work in a bread wrapper like him; a cork notice board, complete with various photos of criminals beside yellow Post-It notes; desks – some messy like his, others with everything in order. In short, nothing had changed; but, in his private world, everything had become different – darker, much darker.

He picked up a copy of the *Daily Reporter*. A large photograph of Prime Minister Margaret Thatcher was emblazoned across it, complete with the bold headline 'NO TO POLL TAX SAY SCOTS!'

He put the paper down with a sigh. Politics was the last thing he wanted to read about, and he'd exhausted the sports pages earlier in an effort to take his mind off the predicament he found himself in.

He heard the door creak open, and was relieved to see the tall figure of his friend Jim Daley walk into the room.

'How did you get on, Bri?' asked Daley, his attention still focused on the folded newspaper he was reading as he sat down, Styrofoam cup of coffee in his other hand.

'Och, you know, same old, same old. The usual grief.' Scott

wasn't ready to spill the beans on what had just taken place – not even to Daley.

'Oh well, not as though it's something you're not used to, eh?'

'No, that's true.' Scott thought for a moment. 'You fancy a couple o' pints later, Jimmy? I'm right scunnered, could do wae a bevy or two.'

'I suppose so. Liz is at her yoga tonight, so no rush to get home.'

'Yoga? I thought he was a bear.'

'Very funny, Brian. You know she likes to keep active.'

'Aye, I can see that every morning you come in here wae they bags under your eyes, Jimmy.'

Before Daley could reply, the door swung open again, revealing the bar sergeant, his shirt sleeves rolled up neatly, the bottom of his tie tucked between the buttons of his shirt.

'Is this all there is?' he asked, scanning the room.

'Aye, Bertie. What mair could you want?' replied Scott.

'Right, in that case, the pair o' you can get down tae the multi-storey car park at Sauchiehall Street. Your gaffer's just off the blower. He'll be there as soon as he can. Been a body discovered in a car there. The forensic boys and the FMD are on their way from Pitt Street. Three shift have cordoned it off.'

With that, he headed off.

'Come on, Brian,' said Daley, shrugging on his jacket. 'Better get down there before the boss.'

Clicking his tongue, Scott followed in his friend's wake, and soon they were in an Austin Metro pool car, making their way down the hill towards Sauchiehall Street.

It was early October, but still warm, with a hazy dusk settling over the city. In a few weeks it would be pitch-black at this time of day, almost five o'clock in the afternoon.

Scott nodded to the old caretaker in his woolly Partick Thistle hat.

'What's up, Jackie?'

'Your friends are all on the second floor,' replied the caretaker in halting English. 'A cleaner, she find the body earlier. Car has been there since this morning, but I guess everyone thought the poor guy was asleeping, you know.'

Jackie was an institution at the car park. He'd been a Free Polish fighter pilot during the Second World War – a decorated one, at that. Though he made little of his bravery, generations of cops had enjoyed his yarns as they sat out many a long, cold winter night in his cosy office, where the kettle was always on the boil and a packet of biscuits was regularly on hand.

'Do we know him, Jackie?' asked Scott, acknowledging the fact that the old caretaker was on good terms with many of the ne'er-do-wells the police spent their lives trying to keep in order.

'There is something familiar, I think. But I cannot place him. Sorry, Brian.'

Daley and Scott took the stairs, and on reaching the landing on the second floor were met by a wan-looking cop, his hat tipped to the back of his head as he smoked a cigarette.

'Davy Fraser,' said Scott with a smile. 'Imagine finding you hanging aboot a stairwell wae a fag when there's real police work tae be done.'

'Huh, what would you know about real police work? You and the boy there are just out the wrapper. Get in there and get this moving so we can get back on the beat.'

'Back to that wee pub at the top o' Wilson Street, you mean,' replied Scott.

Fraser shook his head as he stubbed out his cigarette and let the two young detectives through the door and into the spacious floor of the car park.

Though it was full of vehicles, no civilians were to be seen, only a small group of police officers, some stationed by exits, making sure no members of the public accessed the second floor. Two cops were standing beside a beige saloon at the end of a long row of other vehicles. Water dripped from the floor above, forming puddles that reflected the neon lights. The echo of their footsteps accompanied them towards the car in which the body had been found.

'What have we got, Denny?' Daley asked of the young uniformed constable next to the Ford Granada.

'Take a look for yourself, Jim. Guy sitting in the front seat, looks as though he's fast asleep. It was the cleaner who saw the blood at his wrists, eventually.'

'The big sleep,' mused Scott, peering in through the driver's window at the corpse. He turned to Daley. 'I tell you something else, Jimmy. I know him, tae.'

'Who is it?' asked his colleague, craning his neck to see past Scott.

'Ian Provan, that's who it is. Ring any bells?'

'You mean *the* Ian Provan, as in Machie's accountant?'

'Yup, I sure do. I've known him since I was a wean, and that's Provan all right. Started off as a tally man, then got intae university. Always a smart bastard. No so smart noo, mind you.' Scott shivered.

The duty force MD arrived with the forensic team. The doors of the car were opened carefully with gloved hands, ensuring any fingerprint evidence was preserved. The doctor, who neither Daley nor Scott knew, leaned into the vehicle and placed his fingers on the deceased's neck, checking in vain for a pulse. He knelt down on his hands and knees to get closer to the corpse, then lifted one arm. There was a livid gash on the wrist. The doctor sniffed at the pool of congealed blood gathered in the footwell.

'What do you think, doctor? Suicide?' asked Daley.

The doctor stroked his neatly clipped salt-and-pepper beard, deep in thought, before he answered. 'On first sight, that's what you'd think. But, look at the wrists. Lots of bruising, and a distinct mark here.' He flashed a small torch at the dead man's wrist. 'Some kind of restraint, I reckon.'

'So you think someone has tied him up then cut his wrists?'

'Yes, something along those lines. I'd bet money that the other wrist will bear the same marks. This type of bruising would only take place before he was in his death throes, so it's murder, boys – pending further examination, of course.'

'What's that sticking out of his breast pocket?' asked Scott, indicating a sliver of white on the front of the dark suit the victim was wearing. He beckoned to a forensic officer. 'Gie me one o' they rubber gloves, will you?'

Scott pulled the single glove onto his right hand, then, with thumb and forefinger, gently removed a little white card from the breast pocket. Something was written in rough capital letters on it.

'It's a bereavement card,' noted Daley. 'Like one that would be sent with flowers to a funeral. What does it say, Brian?'

'Doc, shine your torch on here, buddy,' directed Scott.

'OFF-HIRED'. The message was plain and simple.

'There you have it, gents,' said Scott. 'In his line of work you don't get a P45 when you get fired.'

'Or a leaving do,' said Daley.

Despite the bustle in the car park, loud footsteps could now be heard in the cavernous cement structure. A middle-aged man of average height was walking purposefully in their direction.

'Right, what's this?' he slurred.

'Murder, sir,' said Scott without hesitation.

'You'll not mind if I don't take your word for that, DC Scott. I take it you're the FMD?' he said, turning to face the doctor.

'Yes. And for what it's worth, I agree with your detective. The blood's been drained from this man while he was restrained in some way. I don't think he died here – not enough of the red stuff. But I'm sure we'll ascertain more at the post-mortem.'

'Dae you recognise him, sir?' asked Scott.

DCI Raymond Sanderson drew himself to his full height and sighed. 'Aye, I recognise him all right. Ian Provan, the Magician. Could make your money disappear in the blink of an eye.'

'Obviously made some disappear in the wrong direction,' said Daley.

'Maybe so, but try proving it.' He looked at the funeral card in Scott's hand. 'This is no doubt the work of James Machie and his associates, but don't think for a second we'll be able to pin it on him.' Though Sanderson had stopped speaking, his mouth remained agape – the reason for his unfortunate nickname, 'Flycatcher'. That, and the fact that he seemed to catch little else. He'd inherited the role as head of A-Division CID from his old boss, but was nowhere near him in terms of efficacy as a detective.

'Surely we can get something on JayMac for this?' asked Daley, the frustration clear in his voice.

'You have no idea, son, do you?' replied Sanderson wearily. 'Machie is hidden behind a million alibis and a team of expensive lawyers. As slippery as an eel.'

'What now, sir?' asked Scott.

'You boys stay here and get this thing tidied up. The mortuary ambulance is on its way, and Traffic will take the car to Helen Street for the once-over. But don't expect miracles. This is what happens when you cross someone like James Machie. I need to be off. I'm having dinner with the ACC. I'll want your preliminary reports to the duty officer in the next hour. The Serious Crime Squad will likely be head and ears into this by that time,' he continued, addressing Daley and Scott. That said, he turned on his heel and stamped out of the car park.

'We'll never catch Machie and his like with people like him in charge of investigations, eh, Bri?' said Daley under his breath.

Brian Scott just shook his head, imagining the agonies Ian Provan must have suffered before his life drained away. Then, with a sickening lurch, he remembered the meeting he'd had at Pitt Street earlier that day.

'Right, everybody! Let's get this mess cleared up so I can get away for a pint.' Scott stalked off to join Davy Fraser for a cigarette on the landing, his face as dark as Daley had ever seen it.

III

The Press Bar was the haunt, not just of its eponymous profession, but also of police officers. These very different occupations seemed to gravitate towards one another all over the world, with an illicit to and fro of information commonplace. Officers of the law and journalists, both of whom encountered the worst humanity had to offer on a daily basis, instinctively created an unholy fraternity.

A thick tier of grey-blue cigarette smoke hovered over one and all in the crowded bar, like a false ceiling. Signed football jerseys vied for wall space with blown-up photographs of sportsmen and celebrities, and mirrors bearing the name of the brewers who produced them. A stout barman, assisted by a slim watchful girl, kept things moving, as customers came and went, many of them wearing civvy jackets over their police uniforms.

Scott forced his way through the throng at the bar with two pints of Tartan Special. Daley was sitting at a corner table the pair had been lucky enough to grab when they arrived. For Scott, at least, this was a relief; he didn't want his discussion with Daley being overheard – didn't really want to hear it himself, if truth be told.

Just as the young detective placed the beer on the table, an argument broke out at the bar as to whether or not the flickering TV in the corner should be showing the horse racing or the golf. As Scott sat down, it was soon apparent that the aficionados of the sport of kings had prevailed, as Peter O'Sullivan's voice rose frantically above the general hubbub, describing the dramatic end to a race.

'What's up with you, Bri?' asked Daley, loosening his tie for the first time that day. 'God, this bloody thing feels like a noose.'

'Maybe cos you're putting on a few pounds, amigo,' replied Scott, patting his own stomach, but nodding at Daley's. 'Fair wee kite you're getting there.'

'Good living. Married life's suiting me.' Daley smiled and took the first sip of his pint. 'You still haven't answered the question. Why are you looking like a wet weekend? And don't tell me it's because you're depressed at Sanderson's detection skills, we've known about them for a while. You've been moping about since you came back from Pitt Street.'

Scott rubbed his chin and contemplated his beer. 'Och, it's a sore yin, Jimmy. I'm in a right bind, to be honest.'

'Spill the beans, Bri. You know it'll go no further than me. I thought that carry-on with your uncle had been swept under the carpet?'

'Aye, but the buggers up at the Evil Empire have me by the short an' curlies, an' no mistake,' said Scott.

'Go on. You know I'll help if I can, mate.'

Scott sighed, fishing in his pocket for his cigarettes. 'Turns oot, one o' the gaffers – an' I'm talkin' big bosses here – likes a wee bit o' R an' R in some unusual places.' He placed a fag between his lips, cupped his hands, and lit up. He inhaled deeply. 'Here, sorry, do you want one, Jimmy?'

'What do you mean, in some "unusual places",' replied Daley, shaking his head at the offer of a cigarette.

Scott leaned forward conspiratorially. 'Need tae watch in here. Mair folk wae shorthand than in Mrs Pitman's hoose.' Scott lowered his voice further. 'Turns oot, this gaffer – he's a chief super in charge o' car parks or some fuckin' thing – anyway, turns oot he likes tae visit a sauna or two.'

'What? Is he mad? You know that's what I'm working on just now. The squad's about to go active – in the next few days, in fact.'

'Aye, tell me aboot it.' Scott took a long draw of his pint. 'Of course, since they cannae be seen tae ask for themselves, they want me tae get them some info on what's being raided and when, so this bugger keeps his nose clean. Got the sword o' bloody Danny Cleese o'er my heid, an' no error, Jimmy.'

Daley decided to let the sword reference go. 'So someone's putting you under pressure to find this out, using that bar fight as leverage?' He shook his head in disgust.

'Och, come on, Jimmy. You know fine how things work. There's mair crooks in uniform than oot on the streets. I just need tae find a way tae sort this, or I'll be back on the beat in Royston Hill for the next twenty-five years. Aye, or worse.'

'It's going no further than this gaffer, whoever he is, right?'

'Oh aye, they assured me aboot that. Said that if I find oot when the places he goes tae are going tae get the burn, they'll tip him the wink. Problem solved – easy peasy.'

Daley sighed, swirled his beer around in the glass. 'Do you know where he goes?'

'Eh, wait the noo,' said Scott, fishing around in his pocket. He brought out a crumpled piece of paper bearing a few lines of his untidy handwriting and handed it to Daley. 'This is the five here, Jimmy.'

Daley read the list, then eyed his friend, who stared back expectantly. The pair sat in silence, sipping their pints.

'There's only two of these on the cards at the moment, but they're both being raided on the first night of operations,' said Daley eventually.

'Which is?'

'Monday night.'

'Shit, I've nae time tae find oot aboot times or anything. This is Thursday. But it's a good start, Jimmy. I owe you one, big man.'

'They're both at nine p.m. . . . . These two, Bri,' said Daley,

212

pointing at two names on the list. 'They have to be synchronised in case word spreads. We're doing them in batches, between two and three weeks apart. The idea being, just as they think the danger is over and get back to business, we move in again.'

'Very clever. Jimmy, I don't know how to thank you for this.'

'You can bring a decent bottle of malt over on Saturday night.' Seeing Scott's puzzled look, he grinned. 'You're coming to us for "a light supper and drinks", as Liz calls it. Remember?'

'Oh aye, aye. I'd forgot a' aboot that. Don't know aboot the supper, but I'm intae the drinks part. Ella's agreed tae drive. She's no' much o' a boozer.'

'She wouldn't need to be with you about.'

'Aye, very funny. You can sink a few yourself, big man. That's how you're growing that belly. Here, I'll get another in, least I can do.' He stood, picking up the empty glasses from the table.

'This is going to be okay, Brian, yeah?' said Daley, fixing Scott with a serious stare.

'Don't worry, Jimmy. Just saved some fat auld gaffer fae making an arse o' himsel'. Nae bother.'

Scott walked to the bar with a heavy heart. He hated having to lie to his friend, but everything came at a price. His worst nightmares were those where he'd lost his job and was left back on the mean streets of the East End, struggling to make ends meet, spiralling further and further down to the dark place from which he'd come. A couple of brothels would escape justice – so what. He was much more unsure about what was going to come next. He pushed the thought from his mind.

He was joined at the bar by a young man, long-haired and fresh-faced, apart from dark brown rings around his eyes.

Dressed in a trendy, but cheap suit, his fingers were visibly stained with ink.

'Are you Brian Scott?'

'Who's asking?' replied Scott, recognising a reporter when he saw one.

'Sorry. I'm Ronnie Wiley. I write for the *Reporter*. I'm new. Someone said you might be interested in passing on a few bits and pieces, you know what I mean.' He winked knowingly and looked at Scott.

Scott returned his gaze. The kid was no more than five feet five in height, painfully thin, and he still bore the pimples of youth.

'And just who was this someone?'

'Come on, man. You know fine I can't reveal a source.'

'Aye, well, here's a message for you and your *source*.'

'What's that?'

'Fuck off!'

Scott shouted his order to the barman, who acknowledged it with a nod. When he looked back, Wiley was gone, engulfed by the throng of customers in the Press Bar.

IV

Scott said his goodbyes to Daley then watched him head for the train station and home. He'd made the excuse of staying on for a few more beers after he'd bought another packet of fags, but instead, once Daley had gone, he went quickly to Buchanan Street Bus Station.

It was a busy place, with late commuters scurrying to and from the many stances where buses in a variety of colourful liveries sat. Scott checked his watch and then made for a line of public telephones, each enveloped in a Perspex bubble, offering the user as much privacy as possible. As he'd been instructed, he waited for the third phone along to become available, then ducked into the bubble, taking an empty cigarette packet from his pocket as he did so.

He read the number, scrawled in his own handwriting across the back of the packet, took a deep breath, inserted a few coins, and listened. The call was answered. He sighed as his coins fell into the box.

'Hello.' The voice on the other end was distant, but still recognisable.

Scott hesitated before replying, screwing up his eyes and desperately trying to remember his instructions. 'Aye, how ye doin'? Eh, dangleberry here. I have the information . . . Over,' he added out of habit, then grimaced at his mistake.

'Sloe, *sloeberry*!' growled the voice, clearly irritated that Scott had forgotten his designated codename so quickly. 'But you've done well – quick work. Now, all you have to do is communicate this to one of our friends, and you're in.'

'Aye, easy peasy. How dae you suggest I achieve that?'

'Frank MacDougall is attending a function at the Western Winds pub on Sunday night – some post-Christening event. I don't need to tell you what happens at such occasions with your friends from the East End.'

'No, you don't,' replied Scott, remembering how much booze was sunk to wet every baby's head. 'So . . . I just go there and spill the beans? Sounds dead easy, but I guarantee that it won't be, sir.'

'Not *sir* – I'm the Grocer. Bugger me, don't you take anything in, Br–. Sloeberry?'

'Aye, aye, sorry aboot that. So what do you suggest?'

'Just get in there and reacquaint yourself with an old mate. It can't be that hard. Call me back on Monday from the same phone. You know the times to call, or have you forgotten that, too?'

'Aye, okay, will do . . . Grocer. Hey, what if . . . Hello?' All Scott heard in reply were a couple of bleeps and a long tone. 'Bastard,' he cursed under his breath, feeling more like a dangleberry than a sloeberry at that moment.

As they drove towards Bridge of Weir, Scott took in the scene: lush fields, trees, big houses, the odd farm, all framed by the hills beyond. Dusk was trying its best to become night as he looked at his wife Ella, her head thrust forward as she propelled their ancient Morris Marina along.

'I don't know how you can drive like that, Ella,' he said with a shake of his head. 'Your nose is near touching the windscreen. Who the hell taught you tae sit like that?'

'My faither. Aye, an' he's twice the man – and driver – you are, so back off, ba'heid.'

'Charming, I'm sure. Here, I hope you're no' going tae speak like that at Jimmy's?'

'Oh no,' replied Ella. 'It would never do for one tae make a fool of oneself wae her majesty aboot.'

'Och, she's no' that bad. Oor Jimmy dotes on her, you know fine.'

'She's a bonnie lassie, I'll gie her that, but she's young. I bet her folks weren't that keen when a cop turned up tae whisk away their pretty daughter.'

'Seems she has her faither roon her little finger. Gets what she wants.'

'Fae Jimmy, tae, Brian, fae what you tell me.'

216

'That's how marriage is meant tae be, Ella. You're no' meant tae scrab my eyes oot when I say I want tae watch the telly. No, nor turn your back on me when I'm after my congenial rights, neither.'

'Conjugal, Brian, the word is *conjugal*. An' I'm no' obliged tae make hay wae you – this is no' the Mayor o' Casterbridge, you know. I mind it fae the school.'

'It's Bridge o' Weir we're after, no' Casterbridge.'

The car soon swung into the village, and, recognising the pub in which he and Daley had enjoyed a few drinks when he'd helped the couple move in to their new home, Scott was able to direct Ella to the small, newly built private housing estate where Liz and Daley lived.

He tutted as Ella took her time parking the car and noticed a light go on in the window of the semi-detached house. The silhouette of Jim Daley was framed in the doorway.

Brian Scott had never eaten moussaka before. It was a bit like his mother's mince and tatties with a white sauce, but not quite as tasty. However, he'd really enjoyed the fizzy wine that Liz had induced her new husband to pour, and had soon built up the requisite appetite.

He ignored Ella's scowl as he reached over to the serving dish in the middle of the table and helped himself to another portion.

'Here, leave some for me, Bri,' said Daley with a smile.

'No, you go right ahead, Brian,' interjected Liz. 'I swear Jim's putting on weight, so he's on reduced calories.'

'Och, he's a big lad,' remarked Ella. 'Just growing intae yourself, aren't you, big man? Who wants tae be wed tae a skinnymalink?'

'Who wants to be married to a guy with a big beer gut?' retorted Liz. 'Mind you, it's fun helping him work it off.' She giggled, nudging her young husband in the ribs.

'Would yous cut that oot!' joked Scott. 'I'm trying tae eat this moose thing . . . bloody nice it is tae, dear,' he mumbled, mouth full, grinning at his hostess.

'Now, would you like a bit of dessert now, Ella, or would you like a tour? I think you'll like what we've done with the bathroom.'

'Aye, all right, dear. I'll take a wee look wae you. Gie me ideas for oor ain hoose . . . when we get one, that is.'

'I'm just waiting till I get my sergeant's promotion behind me, Ella,' said Scott. 'That'll gie us the security tae buy somewhere. I know renting's no' what you want, but I'm on it, woman!'

'To be fair, if it hadn't been for Liz's folks, we would never have been able to afford a place like this. Well, certainly not here,' said Daley, coming to his friend's aid.

'Your folks don't live far away, do they?' enquired Ella cordially.

'No, just up on the hill. Nice to have them close by, especially when Jim's on nights. It can get lonely, so I'm glad I can just nip up to mum and dad's and get spoiled.'

'Aye, I'm sure,' replied Ella, glancing at her husband who was draining another glass of prosecco.

'Come on, let's do the tour, Ella,' said Liz.

As the women climbed the stair, Daley looked at Scott. He was half cut, with dark shadows under his eyes, and he looked ragged somehow – in a way Daley hadn't seen before.

'Any mair o' this fizzy wine, Jimmy? I've never been much o' a wine fan, but this stuff is going doon a treat.'

'You're on form with the bevy tonight, right enough, Brian,' replied Daley, refilling his glass. 'Be careful though, that stuff can catch up on you. Think you're fine, then the room starts to spin. Happened to me one of the first times I went to Liz's parents. Her brother-in-law kept topping up my glass. I was gibbering before I knew it.'

'That's the accountant guy, Henderson, isn't it?'

'Yes, Mark. Bit of a prick. Still, you can't choose your family.'

'Oh, I widnae say you're doing too bad, Jimmy. Nice lass like Liz tae keep you warm at nights, this hoose – fair beats anything me an' Ella can manage.'

'It's not that easy, Brian, know what I mean?' Daley sighed and turned to look at a photograph of Liz's stern father on the mantelpiece.

'Oh aye, I know all aboot stuff coming at a price, Jimmy.' Scott's face sank.

'How are you getting on with . . . well, you know, what we talked about?'

'Getting there, getting there. I'll no' forget what you did, mind. Fair pulled me oot a hole,' said Scott, knowing that in reality the hole was still being dug.

'What's done's done, Brian. I've been in the job long enough now to know how things work. It's not ideal, but maybe it won't stay that way. Always new blood like us coming through the ranks. Until then we'll just have to be pragmatic.'

'No' all o' it good, by the way. The new blood, I mean.' Scott emptied his wine glass.

'What do you mean?'

'We're getting a new DS, didn't you hear?'

'No.'

'Bugger. I meant tae tell you yesterday. All this going on fair put it oot my mind.'

'Who is it? You know him – or her?'

'Oh aye, and you know *him* tae.'

Daley hesitated, then his expression changed. 'You're kidding, Brian.'

'Nope, he starts wae us next week.'

'But he got sent to Motherwell when he got out of uniform. What happened there?'

'Back by special request, so they say. One o' the bosses had got him marked oot for great things, apparently. Because o' his *special knowledge* o' the division.'

'We are talking about the same man, aren't we?'

'Oh yes. DC James Daley, meet DS John Donald. It'll just be like old times, eh, Jimmy?'

Daley felt his mood darken. Of all the cops in Strathclyde Police CID, the man he didn't want as his sergeant was one John Donald.

'Here, Jimmy, boy. Any chance o' another yin? An' dae me a favour, gie me a bigger tumbler, will you? These wee ones are gone before you know it.' He hiccupped as Daley went off to find a larger glass.

Ella Scott peered into the darkness and switched on the windscreen wipers, as they negotiated a narrow country road near the motorway junction in Paisley.

Her passenger was swaying in his seat, humming an old Sinatra song.

'Will you shut up and put on the wireless. I'm no' listening tae that cats' choir a' the way hame.'

'You cannae beat the King o' the Board – Auld Blue Eyes.

What's wrong wae your coupon anyway? You've got a face like a long weekend.'

'You mean, apart from the fact my husband's a soak, and I've got tae go back tae my council flat, after getting a tour roon the palace? Aye, apart fae that, nothing at all, Brian.'

'Aw, come on, darling. It might no' be much, but it's still hame.' He stifled a hiccup.

'The bog doesnae flush right, there's a leak in the fridge, and damp in oor bedroom. Hame, sweet hame, right enough.'

'You forgot aboot that smell in the lobby press.'

'Go ahead, cheer me up, why don't you? I'd kill for a dado like hers.' Ella shook her head.

'Really?' Scott studied his wife carefully, one eye closed to help him focus. 'I widnae thought she'd need something like that wae the big man aboot. You don't need tae use anything wae batteries tae get satisfaction . . . no . . . no' wae me on hand, Ella, and that's a fact.' He burped.

'Dado, as in dado rail, Brian.' She shook her head. 'Though the state you're in, I'll no' be troubled by any conjugal rights the night.'

Instead of a reply, her husband's head slipped gently down the passenger window. DC Brain Scott was fast asleep.

V

The Western Winds was a forbidding-looking pub in the middle of a row of boarded-up shops. Empty shells, their windows were either smashed in or bore the distinctive graffiti tags of Glasgow's street gangs.

The neighbourhood of the Gallowgate, doorway to the East End of the city, was run down. Many of the old tenements had been demolished, the scars left behind awaiting beautification by visionary town planners and architects. It reminded Scott of the old bombsites he used to play on as a child, decades after the war had ended.

Sure, Glasgow was changing for the better, but the tendrils of those changes had yet to wend their way to the environs of the Western Winds.

He lit a cigarette as he lingered across the road, eyeing the grimy pub. The sound of singing and laughter drifted into the street from its single window, a narrow barred affair set high up in the wall. Like many of the old pubs in the city, windows were frowned upon; the business of drinking – and whatever else went on under their roofs – was considered secret, not for prying eyes. The windows were there to help dispel the fug of cigarette smoke and allow just enough light in to enable the customers to, roughly, orient themselves as to the time of day.

Scott stubbed out his cigarette and took a deep breath. Reluctantly he crossed the street, hesitated for a second, then pushed open the heavy swing doors of the Western Winds.

The hot stench of booze and fags hit him like a baseball bat across the head. The hearty laughter of men and the more screeching variety that came from their womenfolk launched him straight back to his childhood and the many Christening knees-ups he'd attended. Despite the scene of conviviality and celebration, he felt as though he was caught in the undertow of a spring tide that might suck him back from all he'd become, back into the darkness of his past.

At a table at the very back of the bar, a large man tapped his companion on the shoulder and nodded towards the door. The seated man looked across the bar and slowly got to his feet.

Scott felt his mouth go dry. His heart was pumping in his chest as the pair made their way towards him. One man was well over six feet, with muscular shoulders and a bull neck; the other of average height like Scott himself, but with a coiled, wiry athletic quality. His dark hair was shorter on top than the back, where it hung down almost to the shoulders of his shiny blue suit. His eyes were pale blue, and pierced more and more through Scott the nearer he came.

When they were almost toe to toe, the smaller man stopped and held up his hand to halt the progress of his companion, a couple of paces behind. The music from the jukebox happened to fade away, and Scott felt as though he'd walked straight into the set of a bad Western. All eyes were now fixed on him. The gales of laughter and murmur of conversation had diminished to such a level that the chink of ice in a whisky glass sounded ear-splitting. Near him, a little girl, sensing tension in the air, began to cry before running towards the safety of her mother's lap.

The man with the mullet haircut took a step nearer. They were almost exactly the same height, and his eyes bored straight into those of the detective, who, despite himself, felt his right leg begin to shake.

'Well, well, looks like you chose the wrong pub tae slake your thirst, Scooty.' Though his lips curled into a smile, the man's eyes remained unflinching.

'Frank, eh, how you doin'?'

'Better than you'll be in just two minutes when I let big Gerry here loose on you, *ya pig bastard*!' Frank MacDougall's final words left everyone in no doubt as to what Brian Scott did for a living. Lips pursed and heads shook as this information was assimilated by the rest of the company.

'I need tae have a word wae you, Frank,' croaked Scott.

MacDougall turned to his companion. 'Take him through the back, Gerry.' Then, to the barman, he said, 'Gie us a bottle o' Whyte an' MacKay, Bobby. Least we can do for a last request.'

Scott felt powerful hands on his collar as he was dragged, stumbling, through the sea of hostile faces, along a short corridor and into a dark room, suddenly illuminated by a striplight that buzzed its way into life.

A long table sat in the middle of the room, with a few chairs around it. MacDougall took his seat at the head of the table as his companion Gerry pulled out a chair and pushed Scott onto it.

The nervous barman appeared at the door, bearing a tray on which sat one bottle of whisky and three small glasses.

MacDougall studied the detective for a moment or two, his face expressionless.

'You're a right lucky bastard, Brian. Right lucky and fucking stupid.'

'I-I need tae speak tae you, Frank. Something's . . . something's come up, you know.'

'See if big JayMac was here, you'd a'ready be floating doon the Clyde wae your bollocks for supper, know what I mean?'

'It's aboot your saunas in the toon centre,' blurted Scott, desperately trying to avoid any more speculation as to what James Machie would do – or have done to him – if he happened to be in the vicinity.

MacDougall reached for the whisky bottle and poured out two glasses.

'You've had enough, Gerry. Anyhow, away and take a look oot in the street, make sure nae mair o' Scooty's buddies have turned up tae help him pass on this *message*.'

Wordlessly, Gerry left, leaving the two old neighbours alone in the room, the only noise the restored hubbub of the bar down the corridor and the drone of the striplight.

For the first time MacDougall smiled warmly. 'Why did you come tae see me this way, Brian? For fuck's sake, it's no' as though the filth don't know where I am. It's good tae see you, buddy, even if you are a pig bastard.' He slid a glass of whisky down the table in Scott's direction. 'Drink that. You definitely need it, man. I thought you were going tae pish yoursel' oot there. Bad form turning up like this, Scooty, know what I mean?'

'I'm no' here, Frank, if *you* know what I mean. Things are no' going well for me in the cops. Bunch o' dodgy bastards,' said Scott, more at ease now he had a glass in his hand, but still watchful. The man sitting at the table was his old friend, yes, but he was also the under boss of Glasgow's most feared criminal gang, with a well-earned reputation for brutality and ruthlessness.

'Have you just realised that? Bugger me, Brian, I knew you were a daft bastard, but I never thought you were stupid. The polis have always been dodgy bastards. I know for a fact – cos I pay some o' them,' he said grinning.

'I just want oot. Och, they're aboot tae gie me the order o' the boot anyhow. Best I go before I'm pushed.' He hesitated. 'But I'll still need tae pay the bills, Frank.'

MacDougall looked at him levelly. 'So, you've just scored the winner for the 'Tic in the cup final, now you want tae put on a blue jersey – just like that. Aye, you're some man, Brian.'

'I can help yous oot. I know stuff. That's how I can tell you aboot they saunas. It's a peace offering, Frank.'

MacDougall took a gulp of his whisky, draining his glass,

and poured himself another dram, topping up Scott's glass once he'd finished. 'Do you know what it felt like, man?'

'What?'

'My auld mate – the guy I grew up wae – joining the pigs. I felt like you'd kicked me in the bollocks, Scooty.'

'Had tae dae something, didn't I?' Scott was desperate to say the right thing. He knew MacDougall wasn't just all about beatings and extortion. In another world, he'd have been heading up the corporate ladder – one of these yuppies he kept hearing about with their flash cars, model wives and piles of cash. But then, Scott considered, MacDougall had all that anyway, just didn't pay too much tax on it.

'So you joined up, and then what?'

'Bastards just used me. Knew I'd grown up wae you and JayMac. Thought I'd just rat yous oot. Which, you'll note, I didnae.'

'Well, at least that was one clever move, Scooty. We wouldn't want your Ella in widow's weeds now, would we?' He took out a packet of expensive Russian cigarettes and handed one to Scott. 'Ever tried these? Sobranie Black Russians. Slip doon a treat, man.'

Scott took the black cigarette with the gold tip and lit it tentatively. Sure enough, he couldn't feel the smoke drag into his lungs, but the buzz was keen.

'Tell you what, Scooty. You tell me aboot these saunas, then I'll see what I can dae for you. I'm making nae promises, mind. You'll know fine oor boy won't be well disposed towards you. That'll take some persuasion. But, let's go wae what we've got just noo.'

'Nae bother, Francis, man,' said Scott. He knocked back his whisky in one gulp. 'It's good tae be back hame,' he lied.

Ronnie Wiley was still half asleep. He'd spent the afternoon with his brother in the pub near his home in Shettleston and was still feeling the after-effects of the tonic wine he'd consumed.

The tip-off had come out of the blue, but from a reliable source. As a young journalist, he had to make his mark, or so he kept telling himself as he stood in the cold doorway of the boarded-up shop opposite the Western Winds.

He fiddled with the expensive camera and the heavy lens. This wasn't his speciality, but he was adept enough to capture a decent enough photograph. In any case, he was too junior to warrant the services of a duty photographer. This, he thought, was an advantage, in a way. This scoop would be his, and his alone.

He stamped his feet to keep warm and banish the fug of booze from his head, and moved back into the shadows.

VI

Scott awoke in a strange room. Strange, not only because he didn't recognise it, but because the walls, furniture and carpet were all black. Even the television was encased in black, not like the cheap wood effect he was used to.

He was lying on a large comfortable settee, still fully dressed, with a duvet flung over him. Shafts of light were peeping through a chink in the black curtains, so he got up and staggered towards the window.

He had little or no recollection of how he'd arrived in this black room. However, if his banging head and parched mouth were anything to go by, he at least had enjoyed himself the night before.

It was then that reality slowly dawned, and he remembered where he'd begun the evening.

He pulled back the curtains frantically and was mildly relieved to note the rear of a large Georgian mansion facing him across a well-tended garden. His presence in this obviously well-to-do neighbourhood puzzled him though, as he struggled to recall the events that had brought him here.

He looked at his watch: almost eight thirty. Shit, it was Monday morning, and wherever he was, he was going to be late for work.

It was then he heard movement from outside the room. The black door swung open to reveal a man in a red silk dressing gown, hair wet and slicked back, with a towel over his shoulders, fresh from his ablutions.

'Scooty, man. Mair like Sleeping Beauty, eh?' Frank MacDougall walked towards him across the thick pile of the black carpet. 'Hey, what dae you think o' my room? The wife says it's shite, but what does she know? I've always wanted a black room, and now I've got one.'

'Aye, Frank,' replied Scott, as fragmented memories of the night before began to piece themselves together. 'Original, very original.'

'A bit different tae what me and you was used tae, eh? Nae fungus growing oot the walls here, and no' sharing a toilet wae the rest o' the close neither. Happy days, man, happy days.'

'Glad tae see yours are much improved, bud. Dae you have anything tae drink? Coffee, I mean, I'm fair parched.'

MacDougall laughed and led Scott into a bright hallway. Red carpet and abstract paintings on the white walls. They reached an oak door which MacDougall pushed open to reveal an enormous kitchen: black tiled floor, pine fitted cabinets, an Aga and two Belfast sinks, deep enough to bath a toddler in.

He padded across the floor, filled a kettle and put it on to boil.

'Tried tae get you up the stairs tae one o' the bedrooms last night, but even big Gerry couldn't move you. Deid tae the world you were.'

'Big Gerry? Your mate, right?'

'Gerry Dowie, the hardest man ever fae Paisley.' MacDougall laughed. 'Good man tae have on your side, if you know what I mean.'

'Oh aye, I can imagine that, buddy.'

'Never knew you was such a fan o' the old Charlie, eh, Brian. You're certainly no' the average copper.'

In a flash of horror, Scott remembered being offered cocaine and, after much persuasion, snorting it, just to keep those in his company happy. No wonder he felt so terrible.

'Listen, Frank, I need tae get moving, you know. Got tae get tae work.'

'Why are you so bothered? No' as though you've much o' a future. Chill oot, man.'

'No, no, I've got tae play the game fir now. You know what I mean? It's no' over till it's over. I can be mair help tae you boys in the time I've left than sitting on my arse looking oot the window at hame,' Scott said, pleased with this conceit.

'Aye, right enough. Help yourself tae milk and sugar,' MacDougall said, pointing to two green jars on the marble worktop. 'I'll get changed and gie you a lift. Here, where dae you stay now, by the way?'

'Shettleston. Me and Ella have got a wee flat up in the scheme.'

'Aye, good for you. You must be proud,' MacDougall replied with a wink. 'See if my car gets scratched by your neighbours, you're for the bill. Cannae trust folk in they kind o' neighbourhoods, know what I mean?'

Scott poured himself some coffee, stirred in three sugars, and sighed. He would have to make his excuses at work. He couldn't phone Dines until the evening, as instructed.

Life was getting complicated.

Daley stopped in his tracks. Two figures were approaching Stewart Street Police Office from the opposite direction. Sanderson's rolling gait was familiar, but so was that of his companion, who stalked along straight-backed at his side.

John Donald was transformed. He appeared to have lost weight, his unruly dark hair was slicked back, and he was tanned. Pristine white shirt cuffs emerged from the sleeves of an expensive black suit.

Daley waited for the pair to enter the office, then followed them slowly.

His worst nightmare had actually come true. He would be forced to work with this man who loathed him. Indeed, as his detective sergeant, Donald would be his immediate boss. The officer who had tried to stop him getting into the CID was now in charge of his career.

Daley made his way dejectedly to the ground-floor CID offices and sat at his desk. He began to organise his day, making sure that the follow-up to the initial report about Provan's discovery was ready to go to the DCI. Without warning, the door to the general office almost swung off its hinges as Sanderson burst into the room, making Daley and the two other DCs jump.

'DC Scott, where the fuck is he?' shouted his superior, his mouth taking on its characteristic slack-jawed appearance once he'd asked the question. 'Daley, you'll know if anyone does. Why's he not at his desk?'

'Don't know, sir. I'm just in. Getting the follow-up to the Provan report to you, sir.'

'Well, you needn't worry too much about that. The Serious Crime Squad took on the case, as I expected. Get it to me in the next hour.'

Daley wasn't surprised by this information. He'd seen DCI Dines interviewed on TV at the weekend, so reasoned that A-Division CID had lost out again – not that the squad seemed to be having much more success in bringing the Machie family to book than they had. JayMac and his associates always seemed to be able to escape justice, no matter how obvious their involvement in one case or another appeared to be.

'As soon as Brian Scott gets in, send him directly to me, got it?' barked Sanderson.

As he turned to leave, Daley spotted a figure at his back. John Donald strolled into the CID office as his superior left. He was smiling broadly, holding a large manila envelope in his right hand.

He walked to Daley's desk and loomed over the young DC.

'Well, well. Hello, *Jim*,' he said with an insincere smile. 'Imagine me and you working together again. Just like old times.'

'Yes, I'm sure, Sergeant,' replied Daley, noting that not only had Donald gone through a physical transformation since his elevation to CID, his entire demeanour appeared different. Gone was the guttural Possil twang; replaced by the cultured tones of Glasgow's exclusive West End. It was clear that John Donald was a work in progress, although the sarcastic tone remained.

'Thought you might like a little look at these. Interesting how your buddy spends his weekends, eh?'

Donald removed four black-and-white images from the envelope and laid them on Daley's desk.

The first showed Scott emerging from a seedy-looking pub with the Machie family's second in command, Frank MacDougall. They were accompanied by another man – tall, heavily built – whose face Daley couldn't put a name to.

The second photograph showed them getting into a large BMW. Scott's head was flung back in laughter and he looked more than at home in the company of one of Glasgow's most notorious gangsters.

In the third image, the venue had changed. The three men were at a corner table in a club with two pretty young girls draped over MacDougall, who was leaning forward, having his cigarette lit by Brian Scott.

The fourth photograph was the most disturbing. It looked to have been blown up, so the image was fuzzier than the others. However, despite the loss of detail, what it depicted was clear. DC Brian Scott was bent over the table, snorting a line of white powder through a rolled-up bank note. MacDougall and the other man were laughing uproariously, as were the girls, one of whom was trying to kiss Scott on the cheek.

'I don't get it. What is this?' asked Daley in disbelief.

'I'm glad to see you've lost none of your detection skills, Jim,' said Donald with a sneer. 'That is a picture of your new best friend snorting coke with two of the biggest scumbags in the city – Frank MacDougall and Gerald Dowie.'

'I don't understand . . . where did you get this?'

Donald gave Daley a sickly smile. 'That's the best bit. The *Daily Reporter* was good enough to give us fair warning about these little gems. They're going in tomorrow's paper, which, as you know, hits the streets . . . oh, let me see' – he looked at his watch – 'in approximately eight hours, for the early editions.'

Daley stared at the photographs, his mind whirling. Shock was giving way to anger, as he remembered Scott asking him for information about the sauna raids. Yet he couldn't believe that the man he'd come to know so well would intentionally deceive him in such a way. But did he really know Brian Scott?

'I see the implications of all this are beginning to dawn on you, Jim. One of the first on the scene when Machie's accountant was discovered murdered, out for a bender on drink and drugs with his first lieutenant a couple of nights later.' Donald scooped up the photographs and placed them back in the envelope. He leaned in towards Daley, almost whispering in his ear. 'Poor bastard. Did you hear how they killed him?'

'No, how? I haven't seen the post-mortem yet. All we knew was that he'd lost a lot of blood.'

'Death by a thousand cuts – an old chestnut, but no less horrific. He had literally dozens of small wounds all over his body – and I mean *all* over. Whoever killed him knew what they were doing.'

'How so?'

'Managed to keep him alive for hours, letting him suffer. Made sure not to administer the *coup de grâce* until the very end. Our man Provan died in agony. Torture of the worst kind.' His face took on a look of mock regret. 'And the best bit is, don't think you'll come out of this all shiny and new. Guilt by association!' he spat into Daley's ear. 'They've known Machie had a source in the police for a long time. Looks like we've found him – well, the *Daily Reporter* has, at any rate.'

'Nobody's proved anything yet,' said the young DC defiantly.

Donald stood up straight, sliding his hand through his oily hair as he did so. 'The only way Scott will get off with this is if some inept bastard like you is left in charge of the investigation, and that's not going to happen.' He looked around the room. The other detectives were keeping their heads down, fully aware that trouble was brewing. 'Just what you need on a Monday morning, eh? Turn up for your work and get arrested as an accessory to murder.' Donald glared at Daley once more, turned on his heel and walked out of the door, whistling tunelessly.

Daley couldn't believe it. It had taken his old nemesis no time at all to get back to normal, no matter how much he had changed superficially.

What the hell was Brian up to?

He got to his feet and, without a word to his colleagues, left the room.

VII

Daley walked out of Stewart Street Police Office, through a car park adjacent to the nearby flats, and along to Cowcaddens Underground Station.

He was pleasantly surprised to find that the public phone in the vandalised phone box was still working. He thrust a coin into the machine and waited for a reply. Sure enough, after a few rings, Ella Scott's familiar voice sounded on the other end of the line.

'Hello, Ella. It's Jimmy. Is he there?'

He heard a quick intake of breath and then, 'Aye, he's here. Just here, mind you. Been oot a' night. I don't know what the hell's got intae him.' He heard her hand muffle the call as, none too politely, she called her husband to the phone.

'Aye, Jimmy. Sorry, I'm having a wee bit o' a domestic here . . .'

'Never mind that, Brian. What on earth were you up to last night?' Daley went on to tell his friend about the photographs, emphasising just what a serious predicament he was in. 'They're after you, Brian. Donald says that if you don't turn up for work they're going to issue a warrant for your arrest.'

'Donald? Oh great, I'd forgot aboot him. What do you think I should dae? I tell you, Jimmy, there's something no' right here . . . Shit, this could be it. No' just losing my job, but ending up in the big hoose!'

'Tell me what you've really been doing, Brian. This is serious now, and I'm not buying the superintendent-in-charge-of-car-parks story. I never really did.'

As Scott relented and described his deal with Dines, Daley's heart thudded faster in his chest.

'You should never have agreed to that, Brian. No senior officer has the right to put you under that kind of pressure. We've got representation from the Federation, you know.'

'Aye, and the wean's got a toy monkey that shouts "hello, mama" when you pull its tail. They're fuck all use, Jimmy, you know that. The only chance I've got is tae get a haud o' Dines and get him tae sort this oot. Once he lets the gaffers know what I was up tae last night, we'll be sorted.'

'No. Hang fire, Brian. Don't contact Dines.'

'Eh? He's the only bloke who knows what's really going on. Why should I no' gie him a bell tae get this fixed. I'm no' wanting huckled away.'

'They're making a connection between you and Provan.'

'What dae you mean?'

'Well, you and I were the first cops on the scene. Two nights

235

later, you're out snorting coke with one of the prime suspects. What got into you, Brian?'

'I was just playing the part, you know, getting their confidence. Just like Dines telt me tae dae.'

'Well, you've played the part that well you've now got a starring role right across the front page of the *Reporter*.' Daley bit his lip. 'Listen, is there anywhere you can go? Somewhere they'll not be able to find you, I mean.'

'Who'll not be able tae find me?'

'The police – us!'

'I could lie low at my wee mate's hoose. He lives a few streets away. Good bloke, me and him go right back, but he's no a great fan o' the cops, so nobody knows aboot him. Likes the pigeons.'

'Well, see if you can roost there,' said Daley lamely. 'What about Ella?'

'I'll get her tae go oot tae. It's no' as though she needs much persuasion normally.'

'Well, probably best you're both out the picture for a few hours. Another thing, phone in sick. It'll go to the uniforms at the bar office. I don't think this will have reached them yet. You can cover your back that way.'

'Good thinking, Jimmy. What aboot you? I've left you in a right pile o' the brown stuff. Sorry, mate.'

'I've got an idea, but I'll have to be quick. What's your friend's phone number? I'll give you a call later and let you know how I'm doing.'

He heard Scott cursing as he tried to remember the number. Eventually this process seemed to help him bring it to mind, and Daley memorised the digits.

'Get moving, Brian, and I'll speak to you soon.'

'Listen, buddy, I owe you . . . again. But don't get yourself intae any bother. I appreciate your help, but this is my mess. If nothing can be done, nothing can be done, and I'll have tae face the music and dae my best.'

Daley finished the call and jogged the short distance to Stewart Street, trying desperately to work out what was going on as he went. He didn't quite know why he'd told Scott not to contact Dines – just instinct, he supposed. After all, the man was in charge of Strathclyde's top investigation team. However, Daley had been in the police long enough to realise that, given the right circumstances, certain senior officers would happily sacrifice junior colleagues' careers in order to save their own.

It seemed to the young DC that, whatever Dines had planned to do with Scott, thanks to the intervention of the newspaper and the death of Provan, things had gone spectacularly wrong. He would be under pressure, and who knew where that could lead. He needed advice, badly. Thankfully, he knew just who to turn to.

Daley bounded back into the CID office just in time to bump into DCI Sanderson, who was leaving, his face puce.

'Where have you been?'

'Call of nature, sir.'

'Still no sign of Scott?'

'No, sir.'

'Right, get a pool car and get out to his house.'

'Yes, sir.'

'And if necessary, arrest him. If you won't, I'll send the local uniforms to do the job. Got it?'

As Daley drove out of the car park he couldn't believe his

luck. Sanderson had given him the perfect excuse to get out of the office, as well as some precious time.

He knew he had to use this time well.

Instead of driving towards the east of the city, where Scott lived, he headed north. He hadn't had time to make a call. As he sped along, he hoped beyond hope the man he was looking for was at home.

As Brian Scott trudged through the scheme, he marvelled at the way his wife could adapt to anything. Ella and her sisters were no strangers to the trials of life, much of which had consisted of making sure their father – normally a pleasant, hard-working man – couldn't find them when he was on a particularly vicious bender. Ella had complained bitterly, of course, but Scott had managed to persuade her to make herself scarce, though his ears were still ringing from the process. He'd kept the full reason for this subterfuge quiet; he wasn't sure if she was in any way reassured by him telling the partial truth that they were, temporarily, at least, in danger. He hadn't told her from whom.

He turned the collar of his leather jacket up against the rain that was starting to fall heavily. He was only a few streets away from his friend's house, so the weather was the least of his worries.

He shook his head, wondering why he'd been so stupid. A dark shadow of doubt crept in. Was he only in the police thanks to his background? Had something like this been on the cards from the start? Had his career to date merely been a preamble to bringing down the men he'd grown up with?

He resolved not to think about it; after all, for the time being, he could do nothing about it.

He was only a few houses away from his destination when he heard a car slow down behind him and then follow him at walking pace. He didn't turn round, hoping that it was a coincidence. But the voice he heard calling from the vehicle stopped him in his tracks and froze his heart.

'Brian Scott. Now, imagine bumping intae you here, eh?'

Scott looked over his shoulder. A large black Jaguar was at his back, a face leaning out from the passenger window. The man had short cropped hair, almost a skinhead. Though he was young – mid- to late twenties – he could have passed for someone much older. His features were sharp, and the slant of his high cheekbones gave him an almost Nordic appearance. Indeed, the Viking had been his first nickname, and he'd done his best to live up to the wanton brutality with which it was associated. However, he was known by a different nickname now: JayMac.

With a hooked finger, James Machie beckoned Scott to the limousine. 'Come here, son. Me and you have tae talk.'

VIII

Daley drove through small villages, past country pubs and garden centres, and finally to the stunning hills and lochs of the Trossachs, before he came to the small Stirlingshire village that was his destination.

He drove up the steep incline that was the main street and looked around, returning the wave of a little girl with wavy brown hair who smiled at him. This place was much more like Bridge of Weir, his new home, than the place he was supposed to be visiting. Expensive cars lined the clean, well-kept streets, and there was no sign of the graffiti or deprivation he associated with the East End of Glasgow.

He'd been here a few times. The man he was coming to see had been his first mentor, the man who had given him his big chance out of uniform. Though he'd been retired for a few months now, he was still required to give evidence in the odd case or two left over from his last days in the job. On these occasions, Daley had been more than happy to act as his chauffeur.

At the far end of the village, Daley parked his car outside the neat sandstone home of Ian Burns, former DCI at Stewart Street CID.

As he unhinged the red wrought-iron garden gate and then headed up the little stone path to the front door, Daley prayed that his old boss was at home. If anyone could help him with Scott's predicament, it was the man they'd known as Wyatt Earp. In his day, he'd been one of the country's most respected detectives.

Amanda Burns beamed a toothy smile at him as she opened the door. 'Jim, what a lovely surprise! How are you – and Liz? You'll be looking for my husband, I take it.'

'We're fine, thanks,' replied Daley. 'Sorry to just drop by like this. I hope you don't mind if I borrow your husband for a moment or two.'

'Be my guest. He'll be in his potting shed, as usual. His new hobby. Something had to replace the police, goodness knows.'

She invited Daley to follow her out to the garden. 'You'll find him just down there. See the trees? You can't miss it. He's even got a little stove in there now.'

Daley thanked Mrs Burns and made his way down the garden. Sure enough, under a large copper beech tree, already losing its leaves to autumn, sat a sizeable shed, not the tiny construction 'potting shed' had conjured up in his mind.

A little chimney belched out smoke, and, through a window, Daley could see movement from within.

The door swung open and the thin, stooped figure of Ian Burns appeared. A smile spread across his face as he caught sight of his young protégé. 'Jim Daley, how are you, son?'

'I'm fine, sir. And yourself?'

Burns chatted away as he showed Daley into the shed. Two old leather chairs huddled around a small pot-bellied stove, within which crackled some logs. Between the chairs, on an old crate, sat a half-read newspaper and a leather-bound Roberts radio, emitting the low tones of a Brahms piece. A green tin ashtray bearing the name of a brewery held a pile of cigarette ends that revealed Burns's penchant for smoking – heavily.

'Sit down, sit down,' he said, guiding Daley to one of the chairs. 'If you were wondering what retirement was all about, well, this is it.'

Daley looked around the shed. Though there were plant pots, unopened bags of fertiliser and various gardening tools, everything looked new and in pristine condition.

'She thinks I've caught the gardening bug,' said Burns, following Daley's eye line. 'The truth is, it's just an excuse to get out of the house. Buggered if I know what I'm going to tell her when there are no nice flowers or lettuces come the summer. But, never mind. Just can't stand feeling as though I'm underfoot all the time. In nearly forty years of marriage, I never realised how much time she spent bloody hoovering.'

'Sir,' said Daley, anxious to get to the point, 'I need some help. Brian and I both do.'

'Anything to do with tomorrow's *Reporter*, by any chance?'

'Yes, it is. How did you –'

'Still got some friends who keep me up to speed, Jim. And

241

drop the "sir". That was then, this is now . . . My name's Ian. So, looks like Brian's got himself into more bother. I'm buggered if I know why, but the boy's got a real talent for it.'

Daley went on to explain the situation, withholding nothing from Burns, a man whom he had great respect, even fondness, for.

Burns sat back and lit a cigarette, belatedly offering Daley one, which he accepted.

'Tommy Dines. Now there's a man with ambition, Jim. Talented investigator, mind you, but ambition is his master, not detection.'

'What do you mean, sir? Ian, sorry.'

'I mean that I suspected that Tommy Dines had been sailing close to the wind for a long time. It's one thing using criminals as sources, but there's a fine line. I think, in an effort to reach the heights, your man Dines has acquired some pretty dodgy pals – the kind of friends it's hard to say no to.'

'I've been wondering. Do you think there's a connection between Provan's death and the trouble Brian's in? It's a bit of a coincidence, and –'

'If I were a cynic, I'd say that Dines has got himself in too deep with Machie and his crew. Who better to take the fall than poor, hapless Brian, if the hunt is on for a bent cop? It would certainly cover Dines's back. There's clearly some kind of flux within Machie's organisation, and flux is dangerous, as Provan discovered to his cost. I taught you not to believe in coincidences, Jim, but it all seems rather neat. What's Sanderson saying to it all?'

'As far as he's concerned, Brian's public enemy number one.'

'Ridiculous. How that man ever got into the CID is a mystery. He'd make a lazy cop in the Court Branch blush.'

'I don't know what I can do to help Brian. It looks like he's going to take the fall for Dines.'

Burns drew on his cigarette and exhaled sharply, blowing three neat smoke rings, one after the other. 'Let me talk to some people. I know you told Brian to keep his head down, but it would be better if he reports back to Stewart Street. I'll have managed to have a word in a few ears by then.'

'Thank you, Ian. It's really appreciated.'

'Don't thank me yet, Jim. I haven't done anything, but fingers crossed, eh? And remember, the way things turn out in this job, more often than not, is a fair distance from the point you were aiming for – pragmatism is the word. It's the most frustrating, disappointing word in the English language. But, as a cop, it's the one word that will encapsulate your career like no other. Take it from one who knows,' he said with a shake of his head.

'I'll remember that.'

'Aye, see you do. In the meantime, get a hold of Brian and get him back to the ranch. He's in for an uncomfortable few hours, but hopefully the outcome will be favourable.'

As Daley drove away from Burns's house, he felt a glimmer of hope. He'd never known Burns promise something he didn't think he'd have a chance of achieving. He knew his old boss would do his utmost to help Brian. Burns still had influence, favours were owed to him, and because of this – and years of friendship with many still in the upper echelons of the job – he could still make things happen.

He reflected on Burns's lifestyle. There he was, whiling away the hours listening to the radio and doing the crossword, staying out of his wife's way, while men like Sanderson tried to do his job. What a waste, Daley thought.

As he gunned the car along the country roads, he tried to picture himself in forty-odd years' time. Was a shed in the garden all retirement had to offer?

The high-rise flats of Glasgow's skyline were soon visible, and he pulled in beside a phone box. He had the number of Scott's friend lodged in his memory. He dialled.

'Where are you taking me?'

Scott was in the back of Machie's limousine, squashed between the gangland boss's two heavies. Gerry Dowie was driving, but of Frank MacDougall there was no sign. They'd been on a tour of the city, with Dowie ducking into various businesses and then returning with thick envelopes. Now, they were on the motorway.

'We're off tae see a friend o' mine. We call him the Professor,' replied Machie.

'How so?'

'Cos he's fucking clever!' replied Machie, changing his tone and making Scott jump. 'See you and Frankie had a good wee night out, last night, eh?'

'Aye, great,' said Scott, regret obvious in his voice.

They were heading into the city centre. A poster proclaiming Tears for Fears' imminent concert flashed past.

'I like that mob. Good sounds, man,' said Machie, then went on to hum their latest hit maniacally.

They crossed the Clyde and turned right, into what had been the Glasgow Garden Festival site the year before. Despite promises that this place would be transformed into affordable housing – a new start for the city – it was already beginning to take on a neglected look. The firm who had bought acres of land beside the Clyde had hit financial trouble. Glasgow's less optimistic citizens saw the end of yet another false dawn, in this city that had once been second only to London in the British Empire.

The Jaguar crunched onto an area of rough land where an old warehouse, a remnant from the days of Glasgow's pre-eminence as a port, stood stark and black against the trees and gardens that had formed the festival setting.

At a nod from his boss, Dowie sounded the horn – three short blasts – and in a few moments the large double doors began to swing open.

It was dark inside, save for a patch of light at the far end of the warehouse. They drove towards it, past loops of white steel lying like stricken serpents on the concrete floor.

'Know what they are, Brian?' asked Machie.

'Nope.'

'That's what's left of the Coca-Cola Rollercoaster. Mind you had tae queue tae get on? No' looking so exciting now, eh?'

'Right. So, what's it doing here?'

'I'm just waiting tae find a buyer. I don't sell many soft drinks, but I shift a mountain o' coke. Ironic, eh, boys?' He laughed heartily at his own joke, joined by the two men sitting on either side of Scott.

The car pulled up in front of a small office, no doubt once occupied by the overseer or Excise Officer when the building was used for its original function. A man in dark clothing was leaning against the wall, his arms folded across his chest.

Everyone followed Machie out of the vehicle.

'This is my good friend, the Professor,' announced Machie, patting the smaller man on the shoulder. He was probably in his mid-thirties, had a bulbous nose and a pockmarked face. His red hair was receding, and he'd grown it long so he could pull it back in a ponytail. He smiled at Scott, his eyes large and bulging.

'Ugly bastard, eh?' remarked Machie, wiping the smile from the Professor's face. 'But he's a useful guy tae have aboot, let me tell you.'

'Why the Professor?' asked Scott.

'Oh, your man here was destined for big things. Studied medicine, was all set tae become a surgeon –'

'Before I discovered Charlie,' interrupted the Professor with a giggle, finishing Machie's sentence for him.

'Aye, and no' Charlie MacBride that used tae stay in your street, either, Brian,' assured Machie. 'But the NHS's loss was my gain. The Prof here has turned his hand to *other* aspects o' medicine.' He paused, then turned to Scott. 'You were the man who discovered that thieving bastard Provan, am I right?'

'Well, I was there, aye. What's that got tae dae with anything?' The tremor in Scott's voice was obvious.

'You see, there's nothing I hate mair than somebody who's stealing from me. Well, apart fae the bastards trying tae put me away in the big hoose, that is.'

'Don't know what you mean,' muttered Scott.

'Boys, get Brian a seat. He looks tired. Keeping bad company and stayin' up too late, that's your problem.' He squeezed Scott's cheeks, as an adult would with a child.

From behind him, Scott could hear a squeaking noise, like badly oiled wheels turning. In the gloom, he could see Machie's henchmen pushing something towards them on a trolley.

'You know, I've always been o' the opinion that everything you dae should mean something – you know, send a message,' said Machie, leaning into Scott's face. 'You were oot last night wae your old neighbour, drinking and snorting, eh? Like old times, *Scooty*.'

'Eh . . .'

'Only, I know what you're really up tae.' Without warning, he grabbed Scott by the throat. 'A wee birdy tells me you're using that stupid bastard I trust as my right-hand man tae get information on me and my wee business. Know what I mean?' His eyes flashed with hatred as his grip on Scott's throat tightened. 'Frankie boy runs the show now. I have the ideas, but he does the legwork. Suits me fine, normally, but he makes mistakes. Mistakes like you!'

Scott, beginning to panic, saw Dowie disappearing into the darkness. 'It's no' like that, big man.'

Suddenly, Machie released his grip, letting Scott draw his breath with a harsh wheeze. 'Anyway, nae point in me expending precious energy choking you. This is where the Prof comes in. Best thing is, me an' the boys can get a bit o' fun at the same time.'

Scott stared ahead, stomach churning. He felt himself being grabbed by both arms. What looked like a dentist's chair was sitting in front of him – a dentist's chair with arm and leg restraints.

'I wonder how long you'll last, eh? How many cuts did it take before that bastard Provan was offed?'

'Oh, nearly seventy,' said the Professor.

'See what I mean? That's oor man's expertise. He knows where tae cut you, just enough to gie you agony, but no' enough tae kill you. No' straight away, anyway.'

'The loss of blood kills you in the end, but by that time you'll be happy that it did,' said the Professor, a sickly smile plastered across his unappealing face. He was pulling on a green rubber apron, of the type Scott recognised from the City Mortuary.

'Wait a minute!' yelled Scott. 'You've got this all wrong!' He tried to struggle, but strong arms were pushing him towards the chair.

'Aye, I get it wrong regular, like,' replied Machie with a sanguine nod. 'But, see if I am? Well, you have my sincere apologies in advance, Brian.' He looked around. 'Hey, where's big Gerry?'

'Gone for a piss,' said one of the men manhandling Scott.

'Listen, JayMac, honestly, you don't want tae dae this. I –'

Without warning, Brian Scott's world turned to black.

IX

Daley arrived back at his desk in Stewart Street, surprised to find the CID office empty. The concern he felt for his colleague and friend drove off any questions as to where everyone was, though. He'd phoned Brian's friend at the house where he'd been supposed to be lying low. While the man on the other end of the line told him that Scott had indeed phoned to tell him he was on his way, he hadn't arrived.

'Likely in some pub somewhere, if I know Brian,' he'd offered unhelpfully.

Daley knew just how mercurial Scott could be, but a little voice in his head – his instinct – told him things weren't right. He paced the office, trying desperately to think of what to do next.

He heard voices, then the door to the CID office opened. DC Paul Gemmill was at the head of a knot of detectives who were talking animatedly amongst themselves.

'Where the hell have you been, Jim? You've missed all the action.'

'Sorry?' replied Daley, his mind still on Scott's predicament.

'Your big mate Brian's in major strife.'

'What do you mean? He's not the first cop who hasn't shown up for work after a session.'

'A session? Are you kidding? He's all over the papers. We've just seen advance copies of the *Reporter*. We were in getting a briefing from that DCI Dines, you know, from the Serious Crime Squad.'

Daley was now fully engaged in the conversation. 'What kind of briefing?'

'Shit, you really don't know, do you?' Gemmill took a chair beside Daley. 'Brian's been at the madam – playing for the other side, apparently.'

'Bollocks,' said Daley, feeling his hackles rise. 'Who's come out with that shit?'

'Dines himself. Apparently, information has been passed to Machie's mob for ages. Stuff that could only come from a cop. Dines says Brian Scott's the man.'

'Come on, Paul. You know Brian as well as I do. Do you really think he's on Machie's payroll?'

'You should see the paper. He's snorting Charlie with Frank MacDougall. I'm sorry, Jim, but it's looking pretty bad. Mind, he grew up with that team. He and Frank were best buddies when they were younger. They both lived in a single end, just a few streets away from Machie.'

'I live along the road from the Celtic goalie, but do you see me standing between the sticks?'

'DS Donald says he should never have been in the job in the first place. He's in charge of arresting him. They've got a warrant.'

Doubts began to edge into Daley's mind. What if he was wrong? What if his friend really was crooked? He thought about the information on the sauna raids Scott had managed to extract from him – the story about Dines.

Dines. He remembered Ian Burns's expression when he'd mentioned the name. One thing was for sure, somebody wasn't telling the truth.

'What else did Dines say?'

'Told us about the death of Provan, Machie's accountant. Poor bastard was tortured to death. Over sixty stab wounds all over his body. Someone with medical knowledge, they reckon. Kept him alive to torment him. Sick bastards! He had to rush off before he could finish the briefing. He looked pretty harassed, actually. Got an emergency call. No doubt off to deal with more of Brian's handiwork.'

Before Daley could reply, the phone on his desk rang. 'DC Daley,' he barked impatiently.

'Jim, it's someone asking for you . . . won't give their name,' said the cop on the front desk. 'He's on the line now. Sounds quite urgent.'

'Put him through.'

The phone went dead for a few seconds, then he could hear noise in the background, loud music.

'Hello, this is DC Daley. Can I help you?'

'Listen, and listen good,' said the gruff Glaswegian voice. 'Get yourselves tae the old tobacco warehouse doon at the Garden Festival site.'

'Who is this?'

'Don't ask questions, just dae what I say. If yous don't – and I mean, *right now* – Brian Scott will be as dead as Provan, know what I mean?'

The line went dead.

He'd been tipped off, but why, and by whom? It didn't matter. He had to act, and act quickly. Should he go to Sanderson and tell him about the call he'd just taken? He doubted that he'd be treated seriously, and even if he were, it would take Sanderson an age to do anything.

Daley jumped out of his chair and ran across Stewart Street's vestibule and into the control room. Two cops sat in front of a desk, wearing headphones, a screen with a map emblazoned across it in front of them in the subdued light.

'Two-one-two, two-one-two, attend a code twenty-six at number ten Kennedy Path. A Mr Johnstone, the reporter at the locus, over,' said Divisional Controller Sergeant Philip Mason in his calm voice. He waited for the reply then turned to Daley.

'Code twenty-one, Sergeant. Officer in need of assistance. The tobacco warehouse down on the old Garden Festival site. Know it?'

'Yes,' replied Mason. He turned back to the console in front of him, and with an urgency in his voice spoke into the microphone. 'All stations, all stations. Code twenty-one, I repeat, code twenty-one. The Wills' tobacco warehouse on the Garden Festival Site. Urgent assistance required.'

It was the call every police officer subconsciously listened out for as they went about their business. Two radio messages would stop you in your tracks: the one with your own shoulder number, and a code twenty-one. One of your own – a fellow officer – was in danger. Every cop in the division and beyond able to attend would now rush to the scene.

Daley could hear the first responses coming back loud and clear over the control-room speakers. Everything else would stop now, everyone focused on racing to the aid of a colleague.

Daley sprinted out to the backyard. Already, a handful of uniformed cops were piling into a van, some still pulling on their uniform jackets, disturbed from a rest break.

He clambered in behind them. Soon, with the siren wailing and blue lights flashing, they were making their way down Hope Street, dodging the Glasgow traffic.

Daley looked out of the rear window. Sure enough, a line of police vehicles, marked and unmarked, were behind them. He bit his lip and prayed they'd be there in time.

X

Scott screamed in pain as the knife was inserted just below his right shoulder blade. Through his pain, he could hear Machie and his henchmen laughing at his plight.

He was naked, strapped to the improvised dentist's chair, his vulnerable flesh exposed to the cruelties of the Professor's knife. This was the third wound he'd suffered, but each stab had been the worst pain he'd ever felt.

'See what I telt you!' shouted Machie. 'The man's a genius. Knows how tae gie you the agony, man.'

His tormentor's ugly red face appeared in front of Scott's. 'I'm making small incisions where muscles meet bone, Brian. Just tiny ones, mind you. Don't worry, you're not bleeding much right now. That'll come.'

'You're one sick bastard,' croaked Scott.

'Now, time we had a wee look below the waist,' the Professor said in a voice loud enough to send Machie into a paroxysm of laughter.

'Oh, boys, wait tae yous see this. Your man's going tae slice him where it hurts, noo!'

Scott was still reeling from the pain of the first cuts as he felt the Professor run his hand down his back, onto his buttocks. He drew in a deep breath, screwing up his eyes, waiting for the agony to begin all over again.

He never thought he'd pray to die, but now it seemed the only option.

Distantly, through the horror, he could hear something, something familiar.

The vehicle skidded on the dusty gravel outside the big warehouse. Daley could remember visiting the festival with Liz. When they had left the building it had stood as a reminder of Glasgow's past, where tobacco in various forms was shipped in, then back out, transformed into cigars, cigarettes and a multitude of other products. It and whisky had made the city and some of its citizens rich.

Now, despite everyone's best efforts, there seemed only to be decay.

He watched as two police officers battered in the big warehouse doors with a metal ram.

In seconds, still with their lights flashing, police vehicles poured into the warehouse.

When they stopped, Daley looked around, frantically. Uniformed police officers were pointing their torches into the gloom. For a second, Daley panicked. Did they have the wrong building?

Suddenly, from much further into the warehouse, came a shout: 'He's here! Quick!'

Daley rushed towards the voice, with a dozen other officers whose torches illuminated the scene.

There, strapped to the frame of a chair, was Detective

Constable Brian Scott, his body smeared in blood, head bowed.

'Brian!' shouted Daley, rushing to his friend's side.

The stricken man looked up, squinting into the torch light, and moved his lips.

'Brian, what is it? What are you trying to say?' urged Daley, fearing the worst. He leaned close into Scott's face to try and hear what he was saying.

'Have you got any fags on you, big man. I'm fair gasping here.'

XI

Daley, Scott and their guest, Ian Burns, were in the Press Bar. It was almost a week since Scott's ordeal, and Daley was pleased to see him looking more and more like his old self. Certainly, he looked the part now, gulping down a pint, with a cigarette burning in the ashtray.

'Aye, sir, so they heard the cavalry on the way – you know, the sirens and that – and got oot a wee door at the back o' the warehouse, and off.'

'But we think we've identified the torturer. Alan McDaid, failed medical student,' added Daley. 'He was studying at Glasgow Uni when he lost the plot with drugs.'

'And fell into the clutches of James Machie,' said Burns.

'Yes, exactly. There's a warrant out for his arrest, but no sign of him so far.'

'I doubt you'll see him again,' said Burns. 'You don't think Machie will risk a guy like that exposing him. No, I think our Mr McDaid will be lying in some unmarked grave somewhere, in much the same way Machie himself will hide behind a multitude of alibis. He'll have been miles away from the site when all this was going on, you'll see.'

They were silent for a moment, contemplating Burns's theory.

'Serves that Professor bastard right,' said Scott, breaking the spell. 'Here, what's this I hear aboot Dines?'

'DCI Dines has resigned. Family problems, apparently,' replied Burns, his face expressionless.

'Must have been bad for him to have sacrificed his precious career,' remarked Daley.

'Apparently a ledger appeared at Pitt Street – just out of the blue. Former property of the Magician, Provan.'

'Really?' said Daley

'Yes, so they say.' Burns sounded mysterious. 'Records of payments made to those in the thrall of James Machie. It made for very interesting reading, so I'm told.'

'Ya beauty,' exclaimed Scott. 'So they've got Dines banged tae rights, sir?'

'I wouldn't quite say that, Brian.' Burns smiled at Scott's quizzical expression. 'As I told Jim here, don't ever look for neat conclusions in this job – you won't get them. If you were the chief constable, would you really like it if the man you'd chosen personally to head up your elite investigative squad turned out to be a wrong 'un?'

Daley smiled wearily. 'Wonder how that came to light?'

'Oh, DC Daley, the world is a fascinating place.' Burns tapped his nose. His smile said, *I know, but you'll never know.*

'I see, sir. But he still gets off with it.'

'Oh, I wouldn't say that. Big drop in his pension – the end of a potentially glittering career.' Burns squinted at the bar. 'Is that John Donald?'

'Yes,' said Daley. 'DS Donald, now.'

'As I said to you, Jim, there are three types of cop you can be. The useless buggers who just see it as a way of paying the bills and have no ambition and even less sense. Then there's the good guys who see the whole thing as a calling – a service to keep people safe and keep the scum at bay.'

'What aboot the third?' asked Scott.

Burns stared absently at Donald, who was laughing obsequiously at the lame jokes of a DCI beside him at the bar.

'Oh, they just see the job as a means to an end. Yes, they'll work hard to get up the greasy pole, but not out of any desire to help anyone but themselves. Being in the police gets them where they want to go – nothing more.'

'And what happens when they get to the top?' asked Scott.

Burns returned Donald's wave as Daley looked on thoughtfully. 'Well, now, that's when the problems start.' He drained his glass and got to his feet. 'Right, boys, it's been a pleasure. But I've got to go now – off to book a holiday.'

'Where you off tae, sir?'

'Italy, next summer.'

'For the World Cup, sir?' asked Daley.

'Shh,' said Burns, holding his finger to his mouth. 'Mrs Burns doesn't know about that yet.' He smiled. 'And it's Ian, not "sir". How many times do I have to tell you?'

'Thank you, Ian – for all you've done, I mean,' said Daley sincerely.

The men said their goodbyes. Daley and Scott watched Burns leave the Press Bar, off to enjoy the rest of his retirement.

'Watch oot,' said Scott.

Daley looked up to see DS Donald making his way to their table.

'Well, well, if it isn't the Teflon team,' said Donald, with an unctuous smile.

'Meaning?' asked Daley.

'Meaning you're one pair of lucky bastards.' He tapped Scott on the shoulder. 'I know you're hand in glove with Machie and MacDougall. Don't think that little stage show fooled me. All done for effect, nothing else.'

'I tell you what,' said Scott. 'You're off duty, right?'

'Yes, and?'

'Well, here's what I'm saying. Why don't me an' you take a wee walk oot the back, while I kick you good-looking?'

Donald raised an eyebrow and turned to address Daley. 'And you, the hero of the hour, eh? I have you marked, James Daley, had you down from the start. Don't think for one minute you'll get any further than a DC. I don't care how much you suck up old Burns's arse. He's yesterday's man. The future's right here.' He thumped his forefinger into his chest.

'Aye, well, in that case, here's tae the past,' said Scott, raising his glass.

As they watched Donald thread his way back to the bar, Daley muttered under his breath, 'Who do you think phoned me, Brian?'

'Sorry?'

'You know, the day you were under the knife. Who tipped us the wink?'

'I'm buggered if I know,' said Scott with a shrug.

Daley looked at him for a few moments. 'It was Frank MacDougall, wasn't it?'

'How should I know? I'm just glad whoever it was did what they did, or I'd be like a teabag, the noo.'

Daley grinned at his friend. He supposed it was an answer

he'd never get. He suspected the boys from the single end would always stick together when push came to shove. Pragmatism: there was that word again.

'Here, you, away an' get the pints in. I've got a right thirst.'

Whatever horror he'd faced in the warehouse, Daley was glad to see that Brian Scott was back to his normal self.

ONE LAST DRAM BEFORE MIDNIGHT

A DCI Daley Short Story

I

Daley shuffled uncomfortably in his best uniform: shuffling, because, having spent most of his career in the CID, he found wearing it more like being in fancy dress; best, in that he'd finally been measured properly and it actually fitted him.

Yet again, he altered imperceptibly the trim of the braided hat that signified his rank of chief inspector as he watched Councillor Charlie Murray – relaxed and affable – chatting with a reporter. A cameraman nearby fiddled with his equipment, readying it for the interview with Kinloch's foremost politician.

Daley, for want of something better to do, gazed around the museum. The room was filled with paintings, stuffed birds, model fishing boats and flint tools; and even a full-size quern-stone that appeared as though it had been made the day before, rather than over three thousand years ago. Idly, he tried to imagine how the world would have been then. What did people wear? What did they eat? What were the crooks like?

One item caught his eye – a jet necklace that rested on a white silk cushion within a case of thick security glass. It was constructed of jet triangles, large and small, and the animal hide that had once threaded through each stone had been replaced by a thin gold chain. Daley counted fourteen pieces in all, glinting under the bright lights. He found it hard to fully grasp the antiquity of this beautiful piece of ancient jewellery.

The British Museum was about to take temporary possession of the necklace, which had been found at an ancient burial site in the hills above Kinloch in the late sixties. The piece – of global significance – had become a talisman for the population of the small town. It was an object that had aroused international interest and some avarice in museums and collectors worldwide. Only reluctantly had the community council agreed to its sabbatical in London, the decision having been forced upon them by the regional council, who promised to keep the town's little museum open on the strength of the funds raised by the loan of the necklace.

Many, though, were unhappy, aware of the long list of precious historical objects that had been removed to London 'on loan' from around Scotland only to be declared of such importance that, 'for safety and to benefit the entire nation', they were held there in perpetuity.

'Och, of course we'll be sad tae see it go,' said Councillor Charlie Murray to the reporter, who was recording their discussion on her phone. 'But we need tae keep the toon's museum open, and if lending oor necklace tae London for a few months does the job, then so be it.' Having delivered his statement, he smiled, happy with this credible display of political pragmatism.

'Right, we're good to go, Councillor,' said the reporter on receiving the thumbs up from her cameraman. 'We'll just go through what we've been talking about, so don't worry about repeating yourself. It's all new to the viewers.'

'I've been repeating myself for near sixty-five years,' replied Murray with a grin. 'I'll hardly be scunnered by it noo.'

'He can say that again,' piped up an irreverent voice by Daley's side. 'Here, Jimmy, get that doon you.' DS Brian Scott handed his superior a mug of coffee. 'The wee lassie in the office made it. I'm fair parched.'

'At least you don't have to stand here like Lord Nelson on the bridge, Brian. I feel ridiculous parading about like this,' replied Daley.

'Now, you know fine that you're oor leader. It would be a bad show if you was tae trap up in thon cheap Asda suit you're so attached to – especially on an occasion like this. I think you look right smart.'

'Bugger off, Brian.'

'There's thanks for you. I bring you a cup o' coffee, and a' I get is abuse. You should take a leaf oot o' Charlie Murray's book and get your public face on. You can rest assured they'll be watching up the road for any sign of weakness. I'm surprised they let you do this by yourself, to be honest. Count yoursel' lucky, exalted police chief, wae a uniform that you didnae need tae be sewn intae, to boot!'

'I don't think I can remember ever seeing you in uniform, Brian, come to think of it.'

'You know fine, Jimmy, they're no' that happy I'm in the polis at all. The last thing they want tae do is see me advertise the fact. You just cut the right figure – big, imposing, like.'

'Fat, you mean.'

'No, not fat – mair kind of grown intae your ain skin . . . like . . . like, och, you know what I'm trying tae say.'

'Like an elephant.'

'You're right hard on yoursel'. No, not like an elephant – like a ship in full sail. Graceful, like.'

Daley's mouth was forming the beginning of an expletive when a petite dark-haired woman appeared at his side.

'Excuse me, do you know where the toilets are?' she said with a vague smile, not quite focusing on the policeman. She was dressed in a well-cut white trouser suit, and possessed the kind of easy authority that comes with a good education, a hefty salary and seriously expensive jewellery.

'Sorry, no idea. Do you know, Brian?'

'Aye, just oot the door tae your left. I hope you've mair luck than me. When I was in earlier, it smelled as though the bloke who originally owned thon necklace was lying deid behind the cistern.' He wafted his hand in front of his face.

'Thank you,' she replied with a look of disgust.

'Well done, Brian. Another happy customer, eh? That's the woman from the British Museum.'

'She looks like Cleopatra, right enough. Hope she doesnae get bitten on the ass.'

'Bitten *by* an *asp* – a snake – not bitten on the ass.'

'Aye, right, Professor Daley. Anyway, I don't fancy being the snake that bit her on the arse. I wouldnae bet much on its chances. Her backside's likely solid flint.'

'You're a real good judge of character I'll give you that. She just asked the way to the toilet, Bri. What are you on about?'

'What are you worried aboot? She obviously thought you were a security guard, or one o' they commissionaires. Mind, they auld fellas wae the white caps that used tae let folk in and oot – ex-army, they were. It's the uniform that's doing it. Anyhow, I'll leave you tae it. Someone roon here has tae get some proper policing done. There's no saying what's happening on the mean streets o' Kinloch while you're swanking aboot in here, Jimmy. Enjoy your coffee.'

Scott left, taking time to nod to a few locals he knew in the room. As he opened the door to leave, Daley could hear what sounded like a chant coming from outside.

He followed Scott out of the museum and into the street where a small knot of locals were standing with makeshift placards shouting something indistinct.

Daley noticed Annie, the formidable manager of the County Hotel, in their midst.

'What's all this, Annie?' he asked, scanning the ragged group of protesters.

Mainly men and women of a certain age, they had stopped chanting at the sight of the police officer.

'We're jeest making sure that they folk fae London know fine that we're no' happy,' she replied. 'If they think they'll spirit off oor jet necklace never tae be seen again, they can think again. Is that no' right, folks?' she shouted. '*Whoot dae we want?*'

'*Tae keep oor necklace!*' came the muted response.

'*When dae we want it?*'

'*Noo!*'

'There you are, Mr Daley. That'll send them back doon south wae a flea in their ear, eh?'

Unsure as to the efficacy of this protest, Daley shrugged. 'Well,' he said addressing the crowd with mock gravitas, 'I don't want this to get out of hand. Remember, we've tear gas and riot gear up the road if this gets nasty.'

He realised that he'd gone too far when one old woman gasped and put her hand to her mouth in horror.

'I'm only joking, Mrs Duncan. I'm sure this will be a peaceful protest.'

'Tae be honest, we'd hoped for a few mair folk,' grumbled Annie. 'Auld Mr Hutcheson's got a right bad cold, and Beth Paterson's getting her in-grown toenail sorted the day. Aye, an' we've a few absentees efter the Douglas Arms played that team fae Tarbert in the darts league last night. Hell o' a night, fae whoot I hear. Widna be surprised if there wiz a lock-in on the go, neithers.' She gave Daley a sly look from the corner of her eye. 'Some folk jeest don't know how tae run an orderly public hoose.'

'Well, I better get back in. Just you lot behave,' said Daley, ignoring Annie's sideswipe at the opposition.

As he took the few steps back into the ornate sandstone building, the chant began again: '*Whoot dae we want . . .*'

II

Scott had his feet up on the desk reading the sports pages of his favourite tabloid when Sergeant Shaw arrived at his side, a strained look on his face.

'Don't tell me,' said Scott. '*The Queen*'s stranded on a sandbank oot in the sound and I've tae go an' save her in a boat that's leaking like a sieve, in the heaviest sea this century.'

'No, nothing of the kind.'

'So, no boats. Well, at least that makes a change.'

'I've got a gentleman – a Mr Thomas Marchmount – at the front office. Says he's about to be a victim of a theft.'

'Aboot tae be? That's a new one on me.'

'Best you come and take a look yourself, Brian.'

Scott followed Shaw through to the reception area, where sat a small man wearing a trilby hat above thick dark glasses. A Labrador with a shiny black coat was curled up at his feet, a long white stick propped up against the wall behind it.

'Mr Marchmount, here's one of our senior detectives to have a word with you – DS Scott.'

'I've heard of you, Mr Scott,' replied the old man with a smile. 'Brave chap, but a bit of a rebel, by all accounts.'

'You're well informed, Mr Marchmount,' replied Scott.

'Yes, well, I try to be. People think that because you've lost your sight, your mind has gone with it. I'm always anxious to make sure I disabuse them of that notion.' He was well spoken and self-assured.

'A friend of mine is blind,' said Scott. 'Got injured doon the pit when he was a boy. I swear he knows mair aboot the world than most folk.'

'I think many people with a disability try their best to compensate, one way or another. Now, Sergeant, can you help me? I want to report a theft.'

'A theft, you say. Now, when did this happen?'

'It's happening tomorrow, I believe.'

'Right. If you don't mind me saying, Mr Marchmount, that's quite unusual. Most folk come in and tell us they've been a victim of theft after stuff goes missing, no' before.'

'Let me explain, Sergeant Scott.'

'I'm all ears,' replied Scott, patting the guide dog.

'I taught history in the local school for almost forty years. Thankless task sometimes, but one does one's best.'

'Aye, I know that feeling well.'

'To cut a long story short, although I ended up as a history teacher, I studied archaeology at university. Back in those days, I'm sad to say, that fine discipline wasn't given the funding it deserved, so consequently many of us graduates were unable to find work and ended up teaching. Different now, I'm glad to say.' He paused, fished in his pocket for a hanky, and blew his nose loudly, making the dog flinch. 'There, there, boy, nothing to worry about,' he said, leaning down to stroke his companion.

'So, you taught history here, but your real love was archaeology, right?'

'Yes, that's right. To keep my hand in, I began looking at places of interest locally. It was then that I discovered the old Iron Age settlement in the hills above the town here.'

'Where they found this necklace everybody's talking aboot?'

'Precisely, Sergeant – in fact, it was me who found it.'

'Really? That's some achievement, Mr Marchmount. I'm sorry, I'd nae idea it was you. You must have been right chuffed wae yersel.'

'Yes, I was delighted. I could see in those days, and I'll never forget finding the first black triangle in the soil. I suspect I'll never experience such a thrill again.' He fell silent, reliving the moment in his mind. 'However, I'm not pleased by the eventual outcome, and that's why I'm here.'

'Go on.'

'Well, to cut a very long story short, having found the piece, I followed the rules and informed the Crown Office. Discoveries like that are property of the Crown, should the Queen desire them.'

'She didnae want it?'

'Indeed not, rather short-sighted, I might say. But, it was the late sixties, and if something didn't glitter like gold, it wasn't deemed to be of any value. Over the years, of course, they came to their senses and have since been coveting the object. Therein lies my objection.'

'Now the museum's letting it go doon tae London for a while?'

'Yes, absolutely because of that.'

'But surely that's their decision, Mr Marchmount?'

'Actually, no, it's not. When the Crown Office declared that they weren't interested in taking possession of the necklace, it became my property. It was found on common land, a rough hillside not belonging to anyone, so it was a case of finders-keepers, if you like. Mind you, I didn't want the responsibility of looking after something so precious so I loaned it to the local museum. I wanted the people of the area to have the benefit of being able to go and look at it.'

'Loaned?'

'Yes, *loaned*. I was quite emphatic about it at the time. I was going to bequeath it to the people of the town after my death, but until that day I retain ownership. I always had it in the back of my mind that something like this might happen again.'

'You mean they've wanted to take the necklace before?'

'Oh yes, Sergeant. I'm afraid we don't have a very good record in this country of remembering what artefacts belong to whom. Look at the Elgin Marbles. A disgrace, if you ask me. They sent us a replica in the seventies, you know. Oh, it was very well made and convincing, and obviously wrought by a real craftsman, but you couldn't feel it, feel the spirit, if you know what I mean. They blithely informed us that the replica would make a fine centrepiece in our little museum, while they displayed the original in London. I'm pleased to say our local politicians had more sense about them then. Wouldn't consider giving permission for it to be taken.'

'But you've given permission for this to go to London now – why?' asked Scott, puzzled by the old man's change of heart.

'That's just it. I've given no such permission. In fact, I was left to find out about the whole thing in the talking papers. The council didn't even afford me the courtesy of informing me directly.'

'That's bad form, is it no'?'

'Oh, I suppose they've come to think of it as their property over the years. Probably thought I was dead. But I'm not dead and I do not want that necklace to go to London, from where, I believe, it is unlikely to return.'

'And you've told the council about this?'

'Yes. I've written to them, tried to phone – even had my granddaughter send some of these email things – all to no avail.'

'What? They've never replied?'

'No, nothing at all. So that's why I'm here. As soon as that necklace leaves Kinloch Museum tomorrow, I want to report it as stolen.'

III

The bar at the County Hotel was unusually quiet as the patrons stared at the wall-mounted television beside the gantry. Councillor Murray was busy telling the world how much the jet necklace represented Kinloch and urging interested parties to pay a visit to the place where it was discovered once they'd seen it at the British Museum.

'Och, you'll be jeest as much enchanted by oor wee toon as you are by the artefact itself. For me, it's part o' oor culture – a link tae the fine men and women who were oor forebears here in Kintyre,' intoned Murray, beaming at the interviewer.

'Here,' said an old man sitting at a table near the bar. '*Oor forebears*, bugger a'. His family's fae Glasgow – his grandfaither came tae work at the pit oot at Machrie. He's no' fae the toon.'

'Come on, Bertie,' said Annie, polishing a pint tumbler vigorously. 'Charlie was born here, so was his faither.'

'Aye, but see if I'm born in a stable it doesna make me a horse, noo, does it?'

Annie sighed.

At their usual table, furthest away from the bar, Daley and Scott sat with Hamish, the old man puffing away on his unlit pipe. As the news moved on to another item, he removed his greasy Breton cap and scratched his balding head.

'Typical politician, that's whoot I say. They wid try tae make you agree that getting your left leg cut off was a positive advantage. I've nothing against Charlie personally, mind, but he doesna half talk a lot o' pish.'

'Not a fan of the necklace being moved down to London then, Hamish?' asked Daley.

'No, not in the slightest. In fact, I'm no' sure they shouldna jeest have left it in the ground where it belonged. After a', it was a burial site. I don't fancy some interfering bastard poking aboot in my grave in a few hunner years and taking my pipe away tae put on display in some museum.'

'How likely is that?' said Scott, before draining his glass of orange juice.

'Ye o' little faith. I'm quite sure my resting place will be the cause o' much interest tae one o' they archaeologists in the future. No' least the fact that I come fae an unbroken line o' Kinloch fishermen going back tae time immemorial. Och, I wouldna be surprised if thon jet necklace belonged tae one o' my ain family. Way back in time, mark you,' he added, just in case the detectives thought he didn't appreciate the age of the necklace.

'I can just see you parading aboot wae something like that,' said Scott. 'You'd have tae be careful you didn't lose it on a big night oot, if you know what I mean.' He winked at Daley.

'A' I'm saying is this: when your man the schoolteacher found that thing in nineteen sixty-eight . . .'

'Mr Marchmount, you mean?'

'Aye, Brian, the very man. It was the worst year at the fishing anyone could remember. Years ago, I'm talking aboot. There's nae fish left noo, everyone kens that.'

'How can you equate the discovery of the necklace with a thin time at the fishing, Hamish?'

'Well, it's like this, Mr Daley. The man that had that piece taken fae his own grave was likely a king or something. An' kings don't like being disturbed – no' in this world nor the next. You know fine that back in they days they maist likely lived on fish. They would have been the most important thing in their lives, saving them fae starvation, I don't doubt.'

'And?' asked Scott.

'Stands tae reason that the way this fisher-king would show his displeasure wid be tae make sure the fishing wiz fair buggered when they took his ain necklace oot o' his last resting place. You boys are fae the city – yous wouldna understand.'

'You told me that it was some supersonic plane that frightened the fish away,' remarked Scott.

'Indeed I did, but as you know fine well, the Lord moves in mysterious ways – as dae kings, I daresay.' Hamish planted his pipe back in his mouth, happy – whatever the contradictions – that his reasoning was sound.

'Well, whatever you say, auld Mr Marchmount's no' happy that they're taking the thing tae London.'

The noise level in the bar that had risen after Murray's appearance on television lowered again. As Daley looked up, he saw the same diminutive woman who'd spoken to him in the museum. She'd changed into another trouser suit, only this time in black, which made her look even more self-assured and authoritative. A tall young man carrying a briefcase stood behind her.

'A large G&T, please. What would you like, Hal?' she asked, turning to her companion.

'Wid you take a look at that?' said Hamish. 'Bold as brass. Fair rubbing oor faces in the dirt.'

'How do you know who that is?' asked Daley.

'You'd have tae be fair stupid not tae pick up on who's who in this place – mind, Mr Daley, it's Kinloch. A stranger sticks oot like a sore thumb, especially when she's jeest aboot tae make off wae your heritage.'

Daley watched the proceedings at the bar. As Annie served the new customers, several burly fishermen slid off their stools and occupied the two, hitherto vacant, tables. Spotting this, Daley frowned. He eased himself from his seat and made his way to the bar.

'DCI Jim Daley,' he said, holding out his large hand to the small woman. 'We spoke briefly in the museum this afternoon.'

'Oh, pleased to meet you. Kate Thornberry,' she said, gripping Daley's hand with surprising strength. 'I'm the deputy curator at the British Museum, but you probably know that. I'm sorry, I don't recall meeting you earlier.'

'I was in uniform,' replied Daley. 'Please, join us. Tables suddenly seem hard to come by in here.' He glared at one of the fishermen sitting with an implacable expression, arms folded across his chest.

Scott purloined a couple of chairs for their new drinking companions, and as they made themselves comfortable Hamish sucked at his pipe with renewed vigour.

'Thank you for offering us a perch, DCI Daley. The tables did appear to fill rather swiftly there,' she said wryly.

'I'm sure folk mean no real harm, Ms Thornberry. I think everyone's just a bit uptight about the necklace being taken so far away.'

'Please, Mr Daley, call me Kate. And this is Hal McKee, my man that does, so to speak,' she said, dark eyes sparkling.

Once the introductions were over, Hamish sat back in his chair and sighed, rolling what was left of his whisky in its small glass. 'I'm jeest wondering. Is this something you dae a lot? Travel roon the country hoovering up precious things fae wee communities like this one?'

Thornberry smiled. 'Well, I'm no stranger to plunder, if that's what you mean. I happen to believe that everyone deserves to have the chance to look at such a wonderful piece of history, not just the people who happen to live at the locality in which it was found.'

'Sound logic, I suppose,' said Daley. 'I think the problem here is that folk think the necklace is unlikely to be returned.'

'Just like they chessmen fae up north,' spluttered Hamish, dropping his pipe at the sheer injustice of it all.

'Oh dear,' said Thornberry with a sigh. 'Some artefacts are deemed so precious that their security is at risk in smaller provincial museums. The trade in looted historical items is at an all-time high. It's our job not just to showcase these wonderful things, but to keep them safe from the criminal fraternity.'

'There you have it!' shouted Hamish, standing up stiffly. 'Fae your ain mooth, tae. You've no more intention of letting us have the jet necklace back than flying through the air.'

'That's not what I said, Mr . . . sorry, I didn't catch your name.'

'A concerned local, that's whoot I'm called!'

'His name's Hamish,' said Scott wearily.

'Aye, that's jeest great. You've jeest blown my cover, Brian Scott.'

'A *concerned local* is hardly up there with Malcolm X, Hamish,' replied Scott. 'Anyway, everyone knows fine who everyone else is here. You said so yourself no' a few minutes ago. All Kate here would have tae dae would be run oot in the street and shout, "Who's that auld duffer wae the greasy cap?"'

and she'd be sure tae get your name, address an' even the maiden name of your great granny, I shouldnae wonder.'

'Och, I gie up. Time I was in my bunk,' said Hamish. Wishing the company a polite – if rather stiff – goodnight, he made his way out of the County Hotel, threading between the tables to a rousing cheer from the locals.

'I'm afraid I didn't handle that very well,' said Thornberry, draining her glass. 'I should've learned long ago just to go to my room and stay there when in the midst of awkward situations like this. But it's a pretty grim prospect after a hard day's work.'

'So feelings often run high when this type of thing happens?' asked Daley.

'Oh yes,' she said. 'Poor Hal here was lucky to escape with his manhood intact when we were down in Dorset a few months ago. We were taking an old piece of seventeenth-century pottery away to restore it. An old tankard – thick with nicotine it was – had been on display in this pub for three hundred years or thereabouts. Belonged to some highwayman or other. You'd have thought we were visiting every house and making off with the first-born. I don't know.' She took a deep breath and sighed.

'So the people of Kinloch have nothing to worry about?' asked Daley.

'No, almost certainly not,' Thornberry replied.

Daley and Scott exchanged knowing looks.

IV

The moon was hidden behind a fat cloud that discharged its cargo of rain over the still loch. Large drops pockmarked the treacle-black surface as the shower hissed its way from the island down the pier and then to the seafront, sending a protesting sandpiper into the air with a mournful wail. The rigging of a fishing boat creaked in the damp air as the vessel rose and fell gently on the low swell. Streetlamp reflections cast shimmering lines of light over the water as the rain drummed on the tarmac.

A black cat that had padded its way along the quay jumped nimbly onto a tumble of nets and floats, its sleek dark coat catching the pool of white light spilling from the lamp above the harbour master's office. Lazy waves broke on the pebbles of the low shore while, high above the sleeping town, a passenger jet's tiny lights flashed as it flew from distant Glasgow out over the measureless Atlantic, passengers and crew blissfully unaware of the lives, loves, hopes and fears of the population of the sleeping town far below.

It was the dark of night, just around three; the sky was an impenetrable velvet behind clouds that blotted out the light of billions of stars. This blackness would prevail until it was banished by the swirl of dawn.

The only human figure abroad was that of Chunky McArthur making his way to the bakery to start his shift in time to ensure Kinloch had its full quota of bread rolls. The rain made him huddle into his jacket and he flipped up the collar over his ears. His was a rhythmic, practised trudge, born of almost half a century of making this ten-minute walk between home and workplace.

He sent his glowing cigarette butt spinning into the loch, where it fizzled out in the water. This thoughtless act momentarily disturbed a swan bobbing in the lee of the pier, itself a dim white glow in the inky night. She tucked her head back under one huge white wing, reassured that no real danger presented itself.

All was quiet – or so it seemed.

The rain had turned the roof slates of the sandstone building dark and slippery. Despite this, a sure-footed figure darted noiselessly upwards, stopping only when it reached the ornamental bell tower at the apex.

Though slight in stature, this fleeting shape displayed admirable strength, shinning up a narrow roan pipe, then pulling something sharp and bright from the recesses of dark clothing.

In seconds, with a muffled thud, the shadowy figure slipped out of sight through the tight gap of the blue-glazed window that opened into the bowels of Kinloch's museum.

Constable Frank Harvey yawned. His car was stuffy, and the thick jacket in which he luxuriated felt more like his duvet at home, where right now his new wife slept soundly. His mind drifted as he thought wistfully of the scent and heat of her body. What he wouldn't give to be snuggling in at her back, he thought, loins suddenly astir.

'Two-forty, two-forty!' The tinny sharpness of the voice on the radio made him lurch from the dwam into which he had descended. The longing for his bed and carnal pleasure was replaced by a clearing of the throat, before he spoke into the radio on his lapel. 'Two-forty, go ahead, over.'

'Frankie, we're showing an internal alarm at the museum. Have you spotted anything, over?'

Harvey rubbed his forearm down the windscreen to clear the condensation. 'No, can't see a thing, the place is in darkness. Do you want me to go out and have a poke about, over?'

'Nah, negative to that. Just been in touch with the keyholder. She tells me that there's an intermittent fault on the system. Thought I'd get a heads-up from you, just in case, over.'

'Ah, Roger. Make sure the kettle's on, I'm due back in two hours, over.'

'Roger to that. Enjoy, over.'

Harvey yawned again and squinted once more out of the window. He convinced himself that the shadow he'd seen was nothing more than a streak of moisture making its way down the windscreen.

Why they'd bothered to place a car outside the museum now was beyond him. The building and its contents – including that necklace about which there was so much fuss – had remained secure for decades. In his opinion it was unlikely things would change now.

He must have dozed off, because again he was roused from dreams of tumbling about with his wife, this time by the jarring, persistent shriek of an alarm. Above the bolted front doors of the building, a red light flashed. The noise was now echoing among the neighbouring buildings and out over the loch.

'Two-forty to control, over.'

'Go ahead, over.'

'Another code two-six, the main alarm, I think. Contact the keyholder, she'll have to come out. I'm off to take a look, over.'

As he exited the police car, the chill of the night air hit Constable Harvey just before the heavy blow to his head that sent him spinning into unconsciousness.

Out on the loch, disturbed by the commotion, the swan flapped into the air, casting a spectral figure as she gained height over the town, heading for the high loch in the hills beside what had been the old Iron Age fort. There she would find peace; there, in the old place, she would be undisturbed.

V

Daley fumbled for the phone at his bedside. He was used to rude awakenings – all part of the job – but they still made his heart race.

He listened for a few moments and gave only a brief reply. After a short time spent in the cold bathroom and a struggle with a difficult zip, he was off into the cool morning air, taking deep breaths to clear his head of the sleepiness he had not yet fully shaken off.

The scene at Kinloch Police Office was verging on pandemonium. Some wise head had seen fit to inform the press, still gathered in the town, that the reason for their presence had just been spirited from its supposedly secure home and, worse still, from right under the nose of the constabulary.

Ignoring the questions, smartphones, cameras and microphones that were thrust in his face, Daley pushed his way into the CID suite and to his glass box from where he commanded the area. The light from the phone on his desk flashed red, indicating messages were ready to be listened to. A handful of yellow Post-It notes in the familiar hand of Sergeant Shaw adorned the blotter in front him. He removed a pair of reading glasses from the breast pocket of his jacket and peered at them one by one.

He was placing the notes in order of importance when Shaw pushed his way into the office, bearing a large cup of steaming coffee that was gratefully received by the detective.

'How's Harvey?' he asked, taking his first slurp of the brew.

'Just a little shaken, sir. He's at the hospital now, but I don't think here's anything to worry about. The bugger's got a thick enough skull to ensure that.'

'And the necklace is gone, am I right? I don't suppose he saw anything?'

'Yes, it was the only item touched. Nothing broken, nothing else moved – just the necklace.'

'Shit, I was hoping that this was just some daft prank – you know, the locals making their feelings known.'

'No such luck, it would appear. We've a team down there with some of the museum staff now. I heard from them a few minutes ago – all's well, apart from the necklace that is. We still don't know how they got in and out, mind you, sir.'

'We probably won't discover that until it gets light.' Daley sighed and shook his head. 'What a place this is. I think we can bet our last dollar that this isn't some opportunistic art theft. It's folk from the town making sure their necklace stays put.'

'That's not what Ms Thornberry thinks, sir.'

'Great, she's quick off the mark. I thought it would be my job to go and tell her what happened. What are her suspicions?'

'She's of the belief that all the media coverage surrounding the necklace has drawn it to the attention of the criminal fraternity – those who supply the black market of rich collectors. She reckons they knew a soft target when they saw one. Just off the phone, in fact. She asked to speak to you urgently.'

'Wonderful,' Daley replied wearily.

Sergeant Shaw handed him a file. 'Everything's in here, gaffer. From Harvey reporting that he'd been assaulted, up until the time I phoned you. Thornberry and the press didn't waste any time, but a local baker on the way to his work helped Harvey, so I suppose the grapevine did its job after that.'

'As always – nothing's safe here. Apart from the answer, that is.'

'Tell me about it.' Shaw raised his eyes. 'I better go and restore whatever calm I can, sir.'

As the desk sergeant slipped out of the door, Daley could hear raised voices from reception. He was just about to pick up the phone when it rang.

'Chief Superintendent Symington, sir.'

'Put her through,' replied Daley.

'Jim, good morning,' said Symington, her voice crackling via a poor mobile signal. 'We have a *situation*, I hear.'

'You could say that, ma'am. I've just got in. If you give me half an hour or so, I'll be able to brief you more thoroughly.'

'But this necklace has definitely been taken, yes?'

'So it would appear.'

Symington's next comments were lost by the signal that made her sound like an enraged Dalek. All Daley caught was 'Nightshift ACC's not bloody happy', before the connection failed.

He was about to dial her number to finish the conversation when his mobile pinged into life.

En route. Should be with you in a couple of hours.

The reason her mobile signal had been so poor was that she was already on the way to Kinloch. At least that'll take care of the press, thought Daley, looking for some light at the end of the tunnel. The facts were plain, though: with the media encamped on his doorstep, he'd dropped the ball. Daley chastised himself for being persuaded by the museum manager not to have a police presence in the library itself. Somehow, his instinct had told him all was not well – or soon wouldn't be – but he'd been convinced by the argument that, if officers were placed in the building, all the internal alarms would have to be disabled.

He shook his head.

In the darkness, a hand delved into the wooden box and lifted the artefact with a delicate touch. The man clicked on a small lamp and peered at the necklace through a magnifying glass. Still threaded on a gold chain, each piece looked almost identical; tactile, smooth to the touch, just as though this precious piece of jet jewellery had been crafted by a modern machine correct to the tiniest fraction, not by a pair of human hands thousands of years ago.

He thought about the craftsman who'd made the object; wondered what he – or she – was like. Where had they learned their craft? Who had taught them? Was this their own design, or was it made to a set pattern – perhaps one of many? Certainly, it was unique among artefacts from the period. Had this artist been rewarded for their labour, or had the hand that made this beautiful thing been forced into servitude, either by a ruthless warlord or a wicked master?

Perhaps the necklace was a simple item of devotion, a tribute to a long-forgotten deity? A precious thing of beauty then, the product of many hours of hard, exacting toil, given up to save a soul, or ensure a good harvest.

But it hadn't.

He stared again, entranced by the ancient object in his hands, its perfect darkness almost pulling him in. One thing was certain, it had power – an almost tangible potency that his modern mind was unable to comprehend.

'Fairer than the blackest gold,' he whispered to himself.

'This is a right balls-up,' quipped Scott, his mouth half full of bacon roll, as he and Daley drove the short distance to the museum.

The day had dawned bright, but large, dirty puddles at the roadsides glistened and bore testament to the heavy downpour during the night.

'I think balls-up is rather understating the case,' opined Daley. 'Symington will be at the office at any time. Apparently the nightshift ACC wasn't too happy, to say the least.'

'Bad luck wae a' they journalists here for the big handover, Jimmy. No' the best time tae make an arse o' things.' Scott nodded his head sagely then looked around for something on which to rub his greasy hands.

'Don't you dare use my upholstery,' cautioned Daley. 'And I love the way you do this.'

'What?'

'Shake your head like that when I'm in the shit.'

'Just showing my support, big man. Tough at the top, eh? Especially when precious relics go walkabout on your watch wae the world watching.'

'This from the man who's never seen the inside of the disciplinary office!'

'Nae need tae be like that. I'm the first tae admit that on occasion I've encountered certain difficulties along the way,' said Scott, wiping his mouth with a tiny scrap of tissue he'd found in his pocket.

'Certain difficulties! That's like saying the last war was a bit of a scrap.'

'Ach, I'm still here, am I no'? It's a' aboot the battle, no' the odd skirmish here and there.'

Eyebrows still raised, Daley found a parking space on the seafront opposite the museum and parked his SUV.

As the men exited the vehicle, Daley noticed two men in SOCO overalls making their way up the roof of the building, using an improvised rope-and-pulley system. The slates looked dark and slick, and the men were clearly taking their time about this short ascent.

'They'll no' get any joy up there if that's where the bugger entered the building,' remarked Scott. 'It was a right bleacher wae rain last night. Woke me up, in fact. There'll be nae prints tae be found outside after that.'

'Cheery McCheery, eh? Come on, Bri. Oh, by the way, you've got tomato sauce on your shirt.'

Daley left Scott wiping at the stain with the tiniest serviceable piece of the tissue he'd found and bounded across the road to the museum. He was pleasantly surprised to note that none of the ladies and gentlemen of the press were to be found hanging about outside. However, this pleasure evaporated as he walked straight into a scrum of journalists and cameramen in the foyer.

With Scott having caught up, both detectives pushed their way through, ignoring questions and flashing lights, before arriving at the double glass doors where two stout constables stood guard. As they held back the press, Daley and Scott made their way into the heart of the museum.

Two SOCOs were performing their tasks in and around the empty glass case that had once contained the necklace, now cordoned off by police tape. The manager, a gaunt, anguished-looking middle-aged man named Bennett, stood nearby, rubbing his hands nervously.

'DCI Daley, glad you could make it,' he said rather dismissively as they approached.

'What have we found so far, Mr Bennett?' asked Daley, trying his best to ignore the manager's condescending manner.

'Nobody's seen fit to tell me anything. I'm just the manager, of course. What business is it of mine?'

'The young woman, the keyholder from last night – it wasn't you, obviously,' said Daley.

'Oh, well done. No, it wasn't. One can't possibly be on call every night of the week. There are three of us who take it in turns. The keyholder last night was Tracy Robertson, my assistant. Though what she could have done to prevent this awful, awful theft is beyond me. Especially when one considers that the police officer stationed right outside could do nothing.'

'She shouldn't have led my officers to believe that the internal alarm that sounded at three in the morning was down to a systems fault, for starters. And, knowing this to be the case, you should definitely not have discouraged me from placing a couple of officers in the building overnight, in case they set off the internal alarms.'

'Knowing what to be the case?'

'Knowing that your alarm wisnae working,' said Scott, distinctly unimpressed by the manager's attempt to transfer as much blame as possible towards the police.

'I had no idea there was such a fault, I can assure you of that.'

'Really?' asked Daley. 'You're telling me that, as manager of this establishment – hardly the largest museum in the world – you had no idea that there was an intermittent fault in your alarm system?'

Bennett sniffed, raising his nose in the air. 'Correct. At no time did Miss Robertson, or anyone else come to that, inform me of an alarm malfunction. Of course, if they had, I'd have made sure that the problem was rectified.'

Daley stood for a moment, looking around. 'This Tracy Robertson, is she here?'

Bennett looked at his watch. 'No, not yet. She doesn't begin work until nine – it's only just before eight.'

'I don't need a time check,' barked Daley. 'Call her now and get her here as soon as possible.' He turned away to catch the SOCO supervisor, whom he'd spotted on the other side of the room.

Bennett shook his head. 'My goodness, is your boss always so rude?'

'Oh, that wisnae him being rude.'

'Really? I've a good mind to have a word with his superior regarding his high-handed attitude.'

Scott shook his head. 'I wouldnae do that if I was you.'

'And why not?'

'Because then he'll get *really* rude, and trust me, you don't need that.'

'Are you threatening me, officer?' said Bennett, taking one step back.

'Is that you off tae call this Miss Robertson? Just be a good chap and toddle along noo.'

'Toddle along? How dare you!'

Scott edged towards the museum curator. 'Let's get things crystal clear, okay?'

Bennett, being slowly backed up against a wall, gulped.

'On your watch, that necklace – priceless, so I hear – has gone walkaboot. Am I right?'

'Well, one could argue –'

'Never mind arguing, Mr Bennett.' Scott's face was now only inches from the curator. 'All my gaffer has tae dae is say, "Och, thon museum bloke widnae let me put constables in the museum on the night o' the robbery."'

'What?'

'Obviously, he widnae put it quite in they words. I'm using my ain terminology, if you like.'

'What else is he likely to say?' said Bennett, the perilous situation he found himself in dawning for the first time.

'Now, I cannae predict that.'

'Well, what would you say, given such circumstances?'

'I'd likely just say, get yoursel' tae f–'

'Brian!' shouted Daley. 'Come over here, would you?'

Turning to face his boss, Scott shouted back, 'Aye, gie me two seconds.'

When he turned back to finish his conversation with Bennett, he smiled, spotting the skinny little man scurrying into a room marked 'Private'.

'You cannae learn it a' in books,' he said quietly to himself as he walked across the room towards Daley, a smile of satisfaction on his face.

'Look at this, Brian,' said Daley, holding up a small cellophane evidence bag.

'What is it?'

It was made of white rubber, with a short spout sticking up from a bulbous body. 'SOCOs found it about half an hour ago, in the middle of the floor. Is that right, Sergeant Comyns?'

'Yes, sir. I spoke to the cleaner and she's sure it wasn't here last night. She says she'd definitely have found it when she was hoovering. It's a dark-coloured carpet, so not hard to believe her. It was the first thing we spotted when we began work on this side of the floor space.'

'How does that narrow it doon?' asked Scott. 'In fact, what the hell is it?'

'I'm no expert, Sergeant Scott, but I was involved in a case where a man had been abducted – oh, a while ago now.'

'Right, Sherlock, nae need tae keep me in suspense.'

'Well, we were desperately trying to prove the victim had been held in a certain premises. We couldn't find DNA, fibres – we were up against a brick wall, in fact.'

'And?' asked Scott, impatient to know why Daley had such a broad smile on his face.

'Well, we found an object like this – quite distinctive. It's a ferrule from the end of a walking stick, long and thin . . .'

'So what? Fae that you've deduced that it came aff a long thin stick. Where does that leave us here – are we lookin' for Gandalf the Grey?'

'The man we were searching for was blind. This is the rubber end of a typical white stick, used by those with visual impairment,' concluded Sergeant Comyns.

Scott thought for a few moments then his jaw dropped. 'You mean auld Mr Marchmount, Jimmy? Cannae be.'

'I don't know what it means,' said Daley with a shrug. 'But it's something.'

VII

Thomas Marchmount's house was neat and sparsely furnished, to ensure he had as few obstacles as possible to negotiate. He led the detectives into his lounge, guide dog padding dutifully by his side.

'Gentlemen, please take a seat.'

As Scott took his notebook from his pocket Daley looked around the room. There was a large crucifix above the seat in which Marchmount sat, and above the fireplace a framed black-and-white photograph of an attractive woman whose dark hair matched her smiling eyes.

'Fine-looking woman, Mr Marchmount – in the photograph, I mean.'

'Ah, yes, that's my late wife Carole. Everyone who comes into this room – and there aren't many these days – makes the same comment. I miss her every day.'

'I'm sad to hear that. How long have you been on your own?' asked Daley.

'Oh, for a very long time. She was killed in a car accident not long after that photograph was taken. Only twenty-three years old – far too young to die.'

'It is indeed,' said Daley, reflecting momentarily on a similar tragedy from his own past. 'Did you meet here in Kinloch?'

'No, we were at university together. She was originally from Fife. In fact, it was she who kept the archaeology going while I went into teaching. Carole was more passionate about the discipline than me, in many ways, certainly beyond the physical discoveries. She was interested in the people who had come before – felt a connection with them, almost.' He smiled to himself. 'In fact, had it not been for Carole, the jet necklace would never have been found.'

'I thought you discovered it,' said Scott.

'I did. But I was working on her theory about the old hill fort. She'd had a dream that there was something up there – quite extraordinary. I always said that she had a gift – second sight they call it. She often predicted things.' His head went down, and he produced a large white hanky from his trouser pocket which he blew into noisily. 'I'm sorry. Even after all these years, it still gets me. The night before she died she told me that she was scared – scared that something bad was going to happen. Try as she might, she couldn't shift the feeling. Of course, I told her not to be silly, that everything was fine. Sadly, I was wrong. The feeling of impending doom she had proved to be justified.' He turned in the direction of the fireplace. 'I'll always feel slightly guilty about handing the necklace over.'

'She wouldn't have approved?' asked Daley, slightly puzzled at such an attitude from an archaeologist.

'Carole was very particular about grave goods. She felt strongly that, although it was fine to open up a grave and catalogue, photograph, make a record of contents, in order to make sense of history, it was another thing entirely to remove items of devotion from such tombs. It wasn't an uncommon point of view in those days – a profound respect for the dead – no matter how long they'd been gone. Doesn't prevail now, of course.'

Daley stayed quiet for a few moments, leaving Thomas Marchmount with his thoughts. 'She was very beautiful,' he said eventually.

'I've had virtually no sight for over fifteen years, but in my mind I can still see every part of her face in that picture.'

Daley cleared his throat. 'I'm not sure if you're aware, Mr Marchmount, but there was a break-in at the museum last night. I'm afraid that –'

'Oh, I know what happened,' interrupted Marchmount. 'This is Kinloch, remember. My phone rang just after seven this morning. Seems the necklace was spirited away under the noses of your officers.'

'Yes, I'm rather sad to say that is the case. Though not perhaps in the way the gossips portray, I'm sure.'

'We've come across a wee piece o' evidence we'd like tae talk to you aboot,' said Scott.

'Which is?'

'Your walking cane, Mr Marchmount – can you hold it up please?'

'Whatever for?' he asked, as his hands searched for the long white stick, which he grabbed and held out before himself.

Noting that the white rubber ferrule was intact, Scott raised his eyes to Daley.

'What are you not telling me, officers?'

'Dae you have a spare – spare stick, I mean?' asked Scott.

'No, I don't. Just what is going on here?'

'I'll be upfront with you, Mr Marchmount,' said Daley. 'A rubber stopper – a ferrule – from a cane such as yours was found on the floor of the museum this morning. I know this sounds bizarre, but we have to investigate everything. I hope you understand.'

Marchmount remained silent for a few moments, then angled his head back and laughed heartily.

'What's so funny?' asked Scott.

'Surely you must see that yourselves. I mean, I'm nearly ninety per cent blind – an old man with one foot in the grave. Do you really think I have the capability to evade the scrutiny of your officers, break into a well-alarmed building, locate a precious artefact, then make my way back out again undetected? All of this with my guide dog!' He laughed again.

'Yes, I know how ridiculous this must seem, but I have to ask, Mr Marchmount. In fact, I have to ask you another few questions about last night.

'I wouldn't waste my time if I were you, Officer Daley.'

'It's my duty, sir.'

'Yes, yes, I'm sure it is. But, in this case, there's really no need. Milly, are you there?' he called as Daley and Scott stared at each other.

There was a sound of movement from above, then footsteps padding nimbly downstairs. The dog began to wag its tail when a tall, well-dressed elderly woman entered the room. She was straight-backed as she took a seat beside Marchmount on his couch with an enigmatic smile on her face.

'You see, officers, apart from the comical notion that I could break into any building, I have a sound alibi.'

'Who are you?' asked Scott, his mouth agape.

'*I* am Lady Millicent Campbell of Glen Saarn. And who might you be?' she asked.

'DS Brian Scott. Wait a minute . . .'

It was Daley's turn to interrupt proceedings. 'If you don't mind, Lady Campbell – and I'm duty-bound to ask this – did you spend the entirety of yesterday evening here with Mr Marchmount?'

'If you're tactfully trying to ask if I was here all night, the answer is yes, I was. I arrived for dinner at eight, then Thomas and I got down to business.'

Scott stared between Lady Campbell and Daley, his mouth almost forming a word, but never quite managing to complete the process.

'Do stop gaping, man,' she commanded. 'The sight of your tonsils at this time in the morning is hardly likely to aid the digestion of one's breakfast.'

Scott did as he was told and gave Daley a bewildered look.

'Ah, I see,' said the big detective, clearing his throat

awkwardly. 'What time did you both turn in, if you don't mind my asking?'

'The wee small hours, Mr Daley,' replied Lady Campbell. 'It was one of those nights where neither of us were quite satisfied – we just couldn't settle on a final position, if you like.'

'Lot tae be said for that Sanatogen,' said Scott under his breath, with a nod of bewildered admiration.

'Right . . . okay,' said Daley. 'You don't mind if we note this – not the details, of course.'

'Please let me unburden you of your embarrassment,' said Marchmount. 'Though it's true that Milly and I did get down to business after dinner, that business was working on a new presentation for the local Antiquarian Society's quarterly magazine. We both have a passion for history, but the flaming passions of youth have long since departed.'

'Speak for yourself, Thomas,' said Lady Campbell.

'We co-wrote the piece, then found it hard to agree on a conclusion to the article. This is a two-bedroom house, and we slept in separate beds, I can assure you,' said Marchmount.

'Yes, of course,' replied Daley hesitantly. 'I knew there would be a reasonable explanation.'

'My goodness, the younger generation have become such prudes. We're both consenting adults, and if Thomas here wanted to give me a good gallop round the paddock, it would hardly be a police matter.' She patted Marchmount on the hand. 'I burned my bra in sixty-seven, you know. Bloody liberating it was, too.'

'No, no, you get me wrong. I didn't mean to infer there was anything wrong with you doing that kind of thing . . . not that you are . . .'

'Quit while you're ahead,' said Marchmount. 'No offence

taken, I assure you. At the end of the day, I find the theft of the necklace as disturbing as you do. However, it's the kind of thing I've been worried about ever since the bloody British Museum drew attention to our little treasure. If you check through my correspondence with the council, you'll see that I voiced my fears as to the growing profile of the piece. It's the kind of thing that was bound to attract the wrong kind of interest.'

'In other words, never mind chasing old duffers like us, and get out there and find the damn thing!' exclaimed Lady Campbell.

'That was embarrassing,' said Daley as he and Scott returned to the SUV.

'Aye, no' half,' replied Scott thoughtfully. 'I wouldnae have thought that pair was intae diving, neithers.'

Daley cast him a quizzical look as he switched on the engine. 'Diving?'

'You know, this aquarium stuff. Aye, sometimes life's stranger than fiction,' he continued with a shake of his head.

Before Daley could elucidate, his phone rang. He took the call.

Scott looked at him enquiringly. 'What's the scoop, big man?'

'The scoop is, they've discovered the point of entry into the museum. It's up on that bell tower. Do you know where I mean?'

'Aye, that wood and glass thing that sticks up like a fancy chimney?'

'Yup. But that's not all. They've found prints.'

'Don't tell me it's auld Marchmount's, because if it is you're going back in there on your ain.'

'No, even better. Charlie Murray's dabs are all over it, apparently.'

They headed back to Kinloch Police Office, speechless.

VIII

Although Councillor Charlie Murray was Kinloch's most prominent local politician, aided by two of his sons and one grandson he still ran his joinery business from a small workshop on the far side of the loch.

Daley and Scott walked through an open space normally held secure by a roller-shutter door. They were faced by the usual paraphernalia, all part of the joiner's art: lathes, workbenches, saws of various shapes and sizes; a half-finished object that looked like part of the gable end of a wooden-framed house; hammers and chisels, wire brushes and grades of sandpaper, all hanging by hooks on a wall alongside drills, punches and nail guns. All of this was covered by a thin layer of pale dust, and the floor was coated with sawdust and curls of shaved wood that emanated a fresh, earthy smell.

No one appeared to be there, but then Scott made out a hunched figure sitting in a tiny glass-fronted office, under a metal stairwell. He chapped the window, and the familiar face of Charlie Murray stared back over reading glasses which perched on the tip of his broad nose. He was sitting behind an old-fashioned desktop computer.

'Gentlemen, how can I help you? They telt me we'd save the wages o' a secretary wae this bloody thing,' he said, gesturing towards the dusty computer. 'Whoot they didna say was that I'd spend half o' my week fighting wae the damn thing.'

'I'm with you there,' agreed Scott. 'A bloody curse, if ever there was one. They did away wae the typing pool in oor office just like that, leaving us poor cops tae wrestle the damn things intae submission. A great source of sadness for a' sorts o' reasons. Bloody computers, you can keep them.'

'If you Luddites have quite finished,' said Daley with a smile. 'We have a couple of questions, Charlie.' Daley came into contact with Murray regularly and liked the man. Despite occasional self-seeking, disingenuous political conduct, Daley recognised that the joiner cum councillor had achieved many good things on behalf of the remote community, and he admired him for it.

'The boys are all oot on jobs, which is jeest how I like it,' said Murray. 'I'm here holding the fort in the office maist o' the time nowadays. There's only so much exposure tae wind and weather a man can take, and I've seen my fair share o' it in fifty-odd years o' this game.'

'Do you remember we have a record of fingerprints after that incident with the van a few years ago, Charlie?' asked Daley.

'Aye, of course I dae. What a fuss o'er nothing that was. Near cost me my place on the council. Lucky I've got a good few friends in the chamber up in Lochgilphead who owed my a favour or two.'

'Did you no' drag a guy oot a van and drive off in it?' asked Scott.

'It was oor van! At least by rights it was. Thon McLeary bloke was payin' it up, and halfway through jeest forgot where his bank was. I was well within my rights,' he said indignantly.

'Still, you were charged with a breach of the peace,' said Daley, recalling the judgment of the temporary sheriff, who had handed down the minimum punishment available, short of acquitting Murray.

'A storm in a teacup – that bugger still owes me four hunner pounds, mind! Anyway, how come we're back at this auld chestnut?' he said, managing to calm down quickly, another knack of the politician.

'We took your prints as part of the investigation, if you remember – from the van?'

'Aye.'

'And they've been on file ever since.'

'A travesty of justice. Me, that's never been in bother wae the polis before or since that wee episode. Well, apart fae a wee bust-up at the dancing in the George Hall in nineteen seventy-eight. But, c'mon, we all make mistakes.'

'Well, you'll never guess,' said Scott. 'They same fingerprints have turned up again.'

'Eh?'

'We worked out how the thief who made off with the necklace entered the building, Charlie. It was up at the bell tower. The window was jemmied open,' said Daley.

'And don't tell me,' said Murray. 'My fingerprints were a' o'er the glass.'

'Is this a confession, Charlie?' asked Scott.

'No such thing! Of course I'm no' surprised that my fingerprints are on that window. It stands tae reason.'

'Enlighten us, why don't you?' said Scott.

'Must be aboot three months ago. I know I said tae you that I'm no' oot on the job very often these days, but I still keep my hand in, you know.' He brushed a layer of dust from the computer monitor unconsciously. 'You'll mind that wild storm we had a few months back. Whoot a wind that was, near hurricane force they telt me.'

'Yes,' said Daley.

'Well, it was strong enough tae blow the window o' that wee bell tower clean oot. Thon Bennett idiot called me at half eight at night wae a right panic on. My boys were oot in the pub and had been at the beer long enough tae ensure they weren't heading up any ladders. Bennett was feart that someone wid break in, or the wind and rain wid damage his precious collection. So, oot o' the goodness o' my heart, I went doon there wae ladders mysel' and fixed the window.'

'On your own?' asked Scott.

'No. I took young Hughie wae me, my grandson. He's jeest started his apprenticeship, but no' quite at the stage I wid trust him wae windowpanes at height. He's intae climbing mountains, but this is another thing entirely. Apart fae that, me an' him was the only bodies in the company that wisnae three sheets tae the wind. He held the ladder, and I went up and did the job. Man, there's nothing worse than putty for leaving big fingerprints on glass. But that wisna my problem. I got the window back in, an' that was that. It's their job tae clean it.'

'Must have been dangerous on the roof in that gale,' remarked Scott.

'I daresay it was. Let me tell you, Sergeant, my days of scaling roofs are well and truly over. I did the job fae inside the museum. So yous canna frame me wae stealing the bloody necklace.'

'We have to look at the evidence we have, Charlie,' said Daley.

'Well, if I was you, Chief Inspector, I wid make sure your questions remain within the bounds o' reality. If you'd asked Sandy Bennett, he'd have telt you how my fingerprints came tae be up there.'

Scott turned to Daley with a grimace. 'Reckon anyone asked Bennett?'

'I'll have to find out,' replied Daley wearily.

'I'm no' sayin' I'm blaming yous, mind. Canna be easy for the polis tae look like fools in front o' a' they buggers fae the papers an' TV. I'm sure I'd be fair mortified, mysel'. But yous canna go aroon framing honest working men for things like this, jeest tae get yoursel off the hook.'

Despite the circumstances, Daley saw a twinkle in Murray's eye.

'And take a look,' said Murray, holding his ample belly with both hands through his bib-and-brace dungarees. 'I'm no' sure any expert witness wid be willing tae testify tae the fact I'd make it through that wee window.' He grinned. 'Good luck to you, gents, but no cigar.'

IX

It was almost lunchtime when the detectives arrived back at Kinloch Police Office. As Daley made his way into the CID suite, he could see movement in his glass box – Chief Superintendent Symington.

She was sipping a mug of coffee, the remains of a supermarket sandwich in its plastic wrapper in front of her on Daley's desk. She greeted him warmly and then asked about this latest crisis.

'Well, certainly very annoying, ma'am, but I wouldn't say it's the worst thing I've had to face since arriving down here,' replied Daley, somewhat put out that Symington had seen fit to ensconce herself in his office.

'Try talking to the ACC. You would think we'd lost the

Crown Jewels. You know as well as I do, Jim, Police Scotland is under scrutiny, and anything high-profile like this is bound to ruffle feathers.'

'We're doing our best, but the investigation is at an early stage.'

'Oh, you're talking to me, not the press. I know where we are with the investigation. The bosses wanted me down here for two reasons. One, to deal with the press, and two, to run the shop so that you can give this your full attention. So, here I am.'

'You're taking temporary command, ma'am?'

'Jim, that sounds rather grand. I'm giving you the time and space to get things done. Nobody doubts your worth – quite the opposite. You're one of the best detectives we have. That's why the gaffers want you on the case with no distractions. And call me Carrie for goodness sake!'

Before Daley could reply, there was a knock at the door.

'Sir, ma'am,' said DC Potts. 'I think you should take a look at what we've just found on the CCTV from last night.'

Daley and Symington followed Potts to the general CID office.

'This was recorded at just after four this morning. As you can see, we have two figures, the larger which is carrying what looks like a white plastic bag of some description.'

Daley stared at the screen. 'Fast-forward, please.'

'I've checked. It's best we rewind a bit,' said Potts, doing just that. As the footage spooled back rapidly, a muddle of shapes and flashes of lights, Potts watched numbers on the screen scrolling back, then quickly pressed *pause*. 'This is the first we see of them, as they enter the system in the town centre. This is the entrance to Well Lane.'

It was clear that they were looking at a large male figure accompanied by a smaller female. He was wearing a beanie; she had the hood of her jacket up, almost covering her face from the angle of he camera. Slowly, frame by frame, she held her hand out, palm facing skywards. She turned slowly to the man and then reached to her hood with both hands and pulled it back.

'You see,' said Potts. 'She was obviously checking to see that the rain had stopped, so that she could divest herself of the hood.'

'Yes, I think we got that, Potts,' replied Symington impatiently.

'Now, look.' As Potts pointed at the screen, the woman's features were caught by the camera for the first time.

'Oh shit,' said Daley.

'Isn't that your friend – the woman from the County Hotel?' remarked Symington.

'Yes, yes, it is,' replied Daley. Suddenly he felt as though a great weight had been placed on his shoulders. 'And, if I'm not much mistaken, the guy with her is Hal, the man from the British Museum.'

'Really?' said Symington.

'Yes, really. I just don't understand it, though.'

'Understand what, Jim?'

'Well, the very fact that she's out here in the middle of the night with a man holding a big sack places her under suspicion. The fact that she's with the guy from the museum just doesn't make sense.'

'Why?'

'They're on opposite sides. She was outside the museum with a placard yesterday. There, they look like bosom buddies.

I mean, you don't go for a stroll with someone in the middle of the night if you hardly know them, especially when you're against what they're up to.'

'Well, this is a mystery,' said Symington. 'But don't worry about it. I'll hold the fort while you concentrate on this. Good luck, Jim.'

'I think I'll need it.'

'Oh, and keep me up to speed, will you? I have the ACC on the phone almost every hour. I better get into my working clothes and face the press.' She walked off, smiling at Scott who had just arrived in the CID suite and held the door open for her.

'What have I missed?' he asked, slurping coffee from a cardboard mug.

'Come on, we're off to the County.'

'Bit early, Jimmy. Mind, we've got a thief tae catch and a necklace tae find.'

'We have to speak to Annie,' said Daley, pointing at the screen where her features were still frozen.

'Oh shit,' was all Scott could say.

Annie was heading into the dining room of the County Hotel with an armful of steaming hot lunches when the detectives arrived.

'Jeest go in the bar, boys. I'll be with you once I've served these customers.'

Daley and Scott waited in silence for her return, and she eyed the pair with curiosity as she bustled back through the lobby.

'Is the door locked? How come yous are not standing at the bar?'

'Can we have a wee word in private, please, Annie?' said Daley.

'No, no' my uncle Johnnie!'

'Eh?' said Scott, looking around for Annie's relative.

'I mean, I know he's a good age – nearly ninety – but well, I jeest hoped he'd last tae Christmas. Oor Cissie's a'ready got him a present: one o' they big slippers. Dae you know the ones, boys? Jeest one big slipper you pit baith your feet in tae keep warm in the winter – baffy-type yins . . .'

'No, Annie, it's not about your uncle. Can we speak with you in the office?'

'Right, jeest come through,' she said, leading them into a small room behind the reception desk, which was a muddle of papers, room keys, old suitcases and pieces of discarded clothing. On the wall, a faded poster proclaimed, 'Welcome to the Kinloch Highland Games 1985'. A large group of people were standing in a sunny field watching a muscular athlete in a vest and kilt swinging a hammer round his head.

Though Scott recognised the sport, on inspection it was clear that the field and the people were not local. The details of date and time were scribbled in block capital letters in faded felt tip, in a white space at the bottom. Clearly, no expense had been spared advertising this event.

'Aye, great times they were, Brian. We used tae get a great crowd at the Highland Games. They keep sayin' they'll dae it again, but I don't think it'll work noo. Folks aren't happy unless they're glued to their phones. Nae time for good healthy pursuits like tossing the caber these days. Incidentally, oor uncle Johnnie was a fine tosser o' the caber in his day. It always ended up straight up and doon – jeest like it's meant to.'

As Scott raised an eyebrow at this comment, Daley took a seat on an old swivel chair, which groaned in protest.

'Oh, be careful, Mr Daley. That's my favourite chair. The miserable buggers that own the hotel won't replace it if . . .' Her voice tailed off at the sight of Daley's expression.

'Annie, what you were you doing at four this morning?'

'Noo, let me see,' she said, rubbing her chin, eyes suddenly furtive.

'Well, let me put it another way,' said Daley. 'What were you doing at four this morning, walking about the town – in the rain, mark you – with the gentleman from the British Museum?'

'Aye, right.' She sniffed. 'My, yous boys miss nothing, eh?'

'Just answer the man, Annie,' said Scott. 'We're no' messing aboot here. You know fine that necklace was half-inched fae the museum last night, so don't come across a' coy. And, since you were parading the streets just after the time we reckon it was taken, you're of major interest to the investigating officers. And that's me and the big man here. So, spill the beans, kid,' said Scott firmly.

'Is it a crime tae go for a walk noo? I wisnae aware that there was a curfew on the go. This place is getting mair like a polis state every day. Yous are fair carried away wae a' these powers. Cameras in the streets, phone taps, looking at oor emails an' that. I'm feart tae indulge in a bit o' harmless gossip in case some bobby turns up at the door an' harangues me aboot it. Even Chairman Mao wid baulk at the goings-on.'

Neither detective replied, both just staring at the County Hotel's manager with identical impassive expressions.

'If yous must know, when yous went away last night, the lassie fae London wisnae far behind you. Me and big Hal jeest got talking. He's a lovely big bloke.'

'Aye, half your age, tae,' observed Scott.

'Listen tae you. I hope that's no' the green-eyed monster talking? You a married man, tae.'

'Just get on with it, please, Annie,' said Daley.

'Right, anyhow. We gets talking, and he was telling me all about himself. Turns oot he's a right fascination for photography. Loves taking pictures o' places at dawn. He travels a' over the country and gets his kit oot.'

'I bet,' said Scott with a snort.

Ignoring him, she carried on. 'He asked me if I knew o' any interesting buildings that might look good at sunrise. Och well, yous know me – up wae the lark. So, I said I'd take him a quick tour roon before I got the breakfasts ready.'

'So what time did you return to the hotel?' asked Daley.

'Maybe half four, quarter tae five,' replied Annie. 'Breakfast is my domain, so I've got tae make sure I get the ovens on an' that. But yous know fine I dae the best breakfast in the toon.'

'So where did your little photographic jaunt take you?' asked Daley, stony-faced.

'Roon and aboot. I took him tae the Long Road Church – doon Well Lane, past the distillery. I left him tae it when he was heading doon tae the loch. He was keen tae get some snaps o' the fishing boats as the sun rose. Sensitive man, he is.'

'Despite the fact he's hell-bent on removing your precious necklace,' said Scott.

'Aye, well, it wid seem somebody's beaten him tae it, eh?'

'And you didn't see or hear anything suspicious at this time?' asked Daley, anxious to stick to the point.

'No' a soul aboot. Mind you, I got a wild fright when a big rat jumped oot at the Glebe fields. But big Hal shooed it away,' she replied dreamily.

'Okay, Annie,' said Daley, getting up stiffly from the swivel chair. 'That'll do for now. Sorry to say, because of the seriousness of the crime we're investigating, I'll need to check the CCTV and speak to your new friend in order to confirm what you've told us. But thanks for your time. I'll let you get back to your work.'

'I should think so, tae,' she replied, nose in the air. 'The very notion that I'm some master thief – jeest plain stupid. But I daresay yous have your jobs tae dae.'

As they walked out of the hotel Scott looked at Daley. 'So, big man, next stop the museum, I take it?'

'Yup. Let's see what the lovely Big Hal has to say for himself.'

As they walked down Main Street, Scott shook his head and sighed.

'What's up, Brian? Case getting to you?'

'Naw, nothing like that. Just surprised at what a flirt Annie is, Jimmy.'

'And you've never noticed before?'

'No, cannae say I have.'

Daley flung his head back and laughed uproariously, leaving Scott bemused at his side.

X

At the museum, only the large display case that once held the necklace was cordoned off by police tape. A SOCO was busy removing fibres from inside the case, in the hope that some tiny piece of forensic evidence would give the investigating team a lead. When Daley looked at him hopefully, the officer shook his hooded head and went back to his painstaking work.

As they made their way to the office Scott spotted the museum manager heading for the exit.

'Here, you, what's the rush? Is there a fire?' shouted Scott.

Bennett stopped in his tracks and sighed when he realised who'd asked him the question.

'If you must know, this is the first time today I've had the opportunity to get out for a bite to eat. If you wish something more from me, please accompany me to the Copper Kettle, where I will be replenishing myself. I feel quite faint, if you must know. I've got low blood sugar, so it's all hell to pay if I don't pay rigorous attention to my diet.'

'We're looking for Miss Thornberry and Mr McKee,' said Daley. 'Are they in the building, do you know?'

'They are very much in the building. Not very happy, and it would appear that they feel the blame for this fiasco lies squarely on my shoulders.' He coughed. 'Something I absolutely refute.'

'Did you get tae the bottom o' that alarm problem wae the Robertson lassie?' asked Scott.

'Yes, I did. As I mentioned earlier, it was an unfortunate mix-up. She thought I'd reported the malfunction – I, her. She's spoken to one of your detectives.'

'Mair than unfortunate, I'd say,' replied Scott.

'Please go for something to eat, Mr Bennett,' said Daley, anxious that this exchange of views should end. He had a nagging feeling at the back of his mind, that familiar little voice telling him that something wasn't right. He wasn't about to ignore it.

'Who stole your scone, Jimmy?'

'Och, nothing really, Bri. But doesn't it strike you that everything is just too neat? Everybody has the perfect alibi to explain away this and that – even Annie.'

'You seriously cannae think she pocketed the necklace?'

'No, I don't think that for a moment.' He stroked his chin, staring up at the bell tower.

'What now?'

'I just think it's strange. Look up there. If our thief entered the building via that forced window, how did he or she manage to get down here to ground level? And, even if they did manage this using some rope or other, how come our SOCO team here haven't found one shred of evidence to prove anybody even walked across this floor or got anywhere near the cabinet?'

'Aye, fair enough. Someone who knows what they were up tae, that's for sure,' replied Scott.

'Come on, Brian. You know how meticulous these guys are, what they have at their disposal now. I think it would be virtually impossible for anyone to access this place, then break into the cabinet without them being able to nail something.'

'Aye, but we know somebody forced the window. And what aboot the cop who got knocked on the heid? If you're trying tae blame some kind o' phantom, Jimmy, it's one wae a big stick.'

'Just ignore me, Brian. Let's get in and see what Big Hal's saying to it.'

'Big Hal, eh? Pin-up for female hotel staff everywhere, I daresay.'

'I'm worried about you,' said Daley with a smile.

Bennett's office was one flight up. When Daley and Scott arrived they found three people in the room. A pale, thin young woman was pouring tea from a pot into a mug held by Hal McKee. At a large desk – presumably Bennett's – Thornberry was typing furiously on an iPad.

'Well, well, the very thin blue line,' she said as the policemen entered the room. 'Any closer to finding our cat burglar?'

'We'd like to speak to Mr McKee, please,' said Daley, ignoring the barb.

'Over here,' said McKee, rather unnecessarily. 'Fire away – it's Hal, by the way.'

'Aye, we know a' aboot that,' said Scott under his breath.

'In private, please, sir,' added Daley.

They walked out into the corridor and found a nearby unoccupied office. Hal sat on the nearest chair, leaving Daley to usher Scott into the only remaining one. He perched gingerly against the edge of an old desk.

'You're lookin' tired, Hal,' said Scott.

'Oh, not especially. I don't tend to get much sleep when I'm away from home. You know how it is.'

'Aye, sure do,' replied Scott with a curl of his lip.

Daley gave his number two a glare and addressed the young man himself. 'So how do you like your job, Hal? Can't be easy, you know, travelling around the country removing much loved items from the bosom of communities.'

'Oh, it's not all about that. We often take historical objects to be assessed by experts in terms of their value, or just to restore or save them. You wouldn't believe the sheer amount of bits and bobs from our past at risk of being lost. Mostly, because people don't know how to take care of it, or they don't know what's there in the first place.'

'So you and your gaffer come along tae keep them right,' said Scott with a sniff.

'Something like that.'

Daley decided to stand, as the desk was making increasingly alarming noises. 'Did you get any decent images this morning?' he asked.

'Yes, I did. This is such a beautiful little place – the harbour was stunning as the sun came up this morning. It was the light through the mist and clouds – just glorious.'

'Would you mind if we took a little look at what you photographed?' asked Daley. 'We spoke to Annie from the County a short while ago. She confirmed that you were getting the guided tour.'

'Lovely woman.' Hal smiled while Scott glowered. 'My equipment's in my bag next door, give me two seconds.'

He left the room, returning quickly with the big white padded bag the detectives had seen on the CCTV footage. It contained various lenses, a small tripod, as well as a camera, all protected within their own little cases. He unzipped the camera case and removed the expensive-looking item with great care.

'Here we are, gentlemen. It's got a reasonably big screen, so you'll be able to see what I managed to get. I can blow the images up on a laptop if you want.'

Daley and Scott both rummaged in their pockets for reading glasses, then the three gathered around the camera as Hal flicked through some of the pictures he'd taken in the early hours of the morning. While Daley was visibly impressed, Scott remained tight-lipped.

'Love the distillery buildings. You've really captured something there,' said Daley.

'Thanks. I love the light at dawn, it's magical somehow. Ah, here we are, the shots from around the harbour.'

As Hal flicked through each image, Scott moved his face nearer to the screen. 'See this one, can you make the boat here a bit bigger?'

Hal zoomed in to a small boat at the pier. The figure on board was crystal clear in the hazy light.

'Hamish!' said Daley and Scott in unison.

XI

The old fisherman was sitting on a pile of tangled nets, puffing on a pipe. He had his trusty penknife out, and was busy trying to dislodge a piece of recalcitrant rope from a pink fluorescent buoy while clouds of blue pipe smoke billowed into the air.

'Well now, what can I do for you fine gentlemen?' he said as Daley and Scott approached.

'You were out on the go early this morning, Hamish,' said Daley.

'Aye, I was that. Time and tide wait for no man, as the Bard would have it. He was right, too. You'll be aware that some bugger's been thieving fae lobster creels? Och, but maybe yous are too immersed in finding oor necklace, jeest so they buggers fae London can whisk it away.'

'We're mounting a joint operation wae the Fishery Protection folk about they missing lobsters, as well you know,' said Scott.

'And no' one bugger brought tae justice, neithers. I've got tae be extra vigilant, noo. Up wae the lark and oot tae the creels. I've never met a criminal yet that got oot his bed early. Sure, that's how they turn tae crime in the first place. Jeest fair oot o' laziness. As it turns oot, I got a couple o' beauties this morning. So I'll no' run oot o' whisky for a few days, at least.' He smiled then licked his stubby forefinger, holding it in the air. 'The wind's on the change right enough. I widna be surprised if there was a squall on the way.'

'So I don't suppose you saw anything of note this morning before you put to sea, Hamish?' asked Daley.

'No, nothing at all oot o' the ordinary. All was quiet. Since there's hardly any boats left in the fleet, and maist o' them away oot for a day or two, there's nae bustle on the pier at all noo. Makes me sad, but there we are. One day the powers that be will make fishing illegal. The seas will be fair teeming wae fish and there'll be no' a soul tae get them oot the sea and ontae the plate. That's a fact, mark you – jeest you wait. They're no' going tae be happy until we're all eating insects. Insects, of all things!'

Daley looked out along the loch. Sure enough, dark clouds were gathering over the distant Isle of Arran. Hamish was right. Heavy weather was on the way.

'And like everybody else, you've no idea what happened at the museum last night, eh?' asked Scott.

'I don't concern mysel' with museums and a' that. I'm jeest fair scunnered that the necklace has gone, but this is the world we're in. If your creels aren't safe, what is there left? I sometimes wonder where it's a' going. You boys are facing an uphill struggle – like thon wee Dutch boy – you know, the one wae his finger in the dyke. There's jeest a big tidal wave o' crime and godlessness on the horizon that'll consume us all.' At that moment the wind gusted, sending litter scudding down the pier and capping the small waves in the loch with white.

'I'm not so sure,' said Daley. 'I think there are crimes and then there are *crimes*.'

'I'm sure I don't know whoot you mean,' said Hamish as he put his penknife back in the bib pocket of his greasy dungarees.

They said their farewells, and Hamish disappeared into a shed on the pier as the two policemen made their way back to their car.

As Daley switched on the engine, the wipers burst into life, sweeping large raindrops from the windscreen.

'What's this *crime* thing?' asked Scott, echoing Daley's comment to Hamish.

'As I said to you, it's all too neat. And there's something else.'

'What?'

'The way folk are behaving. One minute the whole town's up in arms that their precious necklace is being taken to London, worried they'll never see it again. The next – and you saw Hamish just now – it's just a shrug of the shoulders, and isn't the world an awful place.'

'I'm confused.'

'Me too,' said Daley.

As they drove up Main Street, Thornberry could be seen at the boot of her SUV, which was parked at the front door of the County Hotel. The redoubtable Hal, burdened by an armful of bags and suitcases, was helping her to pack the car.

Daley pulled up beside them and wound down his window. 'Off so soon?'

'What's there to stay for, DCI Daley?' she replied. 'In any case, we've got a job in Yorkshire, so we have to make tracks. That is, unless you've found the necklace.' She grinned knowingly.

A woman ran past Hal on the pavement, chasing a large green brolly that had been torn from her grip by a gust of wind.

'Safe journey. It looks like the weather's on the turn, so the quicker you get going, the better.'

Thornberry laughed. 'That's the feeling I've had since we came here.'

'That's small towns for you,' said Scott, leaning across Daley. 'Don't think we've no' had the same feelings fae time to time.'

'I'm sure. A case of when's a crime not a crime, I should imagine. It seems to me as though local justice still prevails here. Anyway, if you'll excuse us, this rain's getting heavier and we must get away.' She gave the policemen an inscrutable smile, slammed the boot shut and joined Hal in the car.

'Is it just me, or is everyone speaking in riddles?' asked Scott as they went through the gates of Kinloch Police Office. 'Mair o' this crime, *crime* business. She's as bad as you.'

'It's just your imagination, Bri,' replied Daley, deep in thought.

Jean McGinty gripped the collar of her coat as she strode along the promenade on the way back home. She'd just finished her job cleaning for a local doctor in his big house on the outskirts of the town, and she was anxious to get out of the rain and home. Her husband had promised to make dinner, and she hoped he'd also had the good sense to put the central heating back on. As well as the rain, there was a distinct chill in the air, as though winter was on its way, rather than giving way to summer.

As the rain soaked her, she wished she'd taken her employer's offer of a lift back home. However, her new walking-to-work regime had paid off. She'd lost almost two stones in weight, and she felt as fit as she'd done in years. She would get home, draw a bath and sink into its warmth as her husband prepared the evening meal.

Just as Jean passed the putting green, she noticed a large object on a bench. On closer examination, this item proved to be a leather bag – of the outsized variety favoured by some women who insist on taking half the contents of their homes with them wherever they go. It had clearly been there for some time; it looked sodden with the heavy rain.

She picked up the bag, pulling at the drawstring that held it closed. Wiping the rain from her eyes, she peered inside. At first, she thought the bag was empty. The lining was black, but seemed dry, despite the drenching. Then, she spotted something glistening as raindrops landed inside. She thrust her hand in, almost gasping when she felt the cold hard object at her fingertips.

Jean closed the bag, hefted it over her shoulder, and made not for her home on the other side of the loch, but into Kinloch's town centre and straight to the police office.

XII

Daley was slumped in the large chair within his glass box. Scott had gone to bring them some sustenance from the fish and chip shop.

Symington popped her head round the door. She was in full uniform and her braided hat and raincoat were soaked.

'You don't mind if I put my coat on your radiator, Jim? The one in my office seems to be on the blink.'

'Not at all,' replied Daley, helping her shrug off the dripping garment. 'How on earth are you so wet?'

'It's raining, Jim, or hadn't you noticed?'

'Yes, but – well, I mean, why were you out in it?'

'On the beat, DCI Daley,' she replied triumphantly. 'Despite getting soaked, I loved every minute of it. I used to love being out and about in the community when I first joined up. It's what policing's all about, getting to know those on your beat and showing the caring side of our work.'

Daley nodded at this, but remembering his experiences of life on the beat in Glasgow, he couldn't quite reconcile his time among shoplifters, drunks, brawling young men outside nightclubs and speeding motorists with Symington's halcyon view of policing. Times had changed, but not enough to persuade Jim Daley to don his uniform and take to the mean streets of Kinloch *à pied*.

'I see the museum staff have packed up and gone,' said Symington. 'The ACC's still fizzing about this. I reckon there may be trouble ahead.'

'I don't know what he wants us to do. Brian and I have been out all day following leads and we've come up with absolutely nothing. Same goes for the SOCO boys – not a thing – I mean not a single trace of forensic evidence.'

'And you think there's something strange about this, Jim?'

'It's not just that. We all know that perfect crimes don't exist. But this one seems damned close. That and the way everyone's behaving as though nothing's happened. You must've noticed when you were out and about. For a town that loves its past and cherishes this bloody necklace, they're doing a fine impersonation of folk who don't give a shit . . . ma'am.'

'Yes, I did detect an apathy of sorts. Odd. Of course I don't know the people here the way you do.'

There was a sharp knock as the door swung open to reveal Sergeant Shaw holding a large leather handbag from which water was dripping.

'Ma'am, sir, you'll really want to see this. Just been handed in.' He gave the bag to Daley, who examined it.

'Bit busy to deal with lost property. What's this all about?'

'Take a look inside, sir.'

Daley peered nervously into the bag. 'If there's a snake in here, you can . . .' He fell silent when he glimpsed the contents of the bag. There, lying on the black silk lining, was the jet necklace, glistening under the harsh office lights, the thin gold chain brighter still.

Daley looked up, mouth agape, and handed the bag to Symington.

'Here,' said a voice from the doorway. 'They'd no smoked sausage, so I got you a haggis supper, big man.' Scott stopped in his tracks when he saw the bemused looks of the three occupants of Daley's office. 'What's up? Don't tell me you're no' hungry any more.'

'Brian,' said Daley, 'you're not going to believe this.'

'So they've got the bag?' said the voice on the phone.

'Aye, they have that. The woman who cleans the hoose for Dr Wallace found it and took it straight tae the polis. I'm guessing there'll be mair than a few sighs o' relief up the brae.'

'And what about you? Are you ready to do the deed, or should we wait until this filthy weather has passed?'

There was a pause as the man holding the grubby phone thought for a few moments. 'Ach, well, now, you see, if we was talking aboot jeest any polisman, I'd say we could hold off. But, as you might have realised yourself, DCI Daley's far fae your average Joe when it comes tae detection. Despite the rain and gales, I think we have tae dae it the night.' He listened to the reply and replaced the receiver as a very large striped cat jumped on his shoulder, purring loudly.

'You, ya big bugger. Where have you been, eh?' Still with the cat on his shoulder, he made his way to an old chest of drawers and removed a wooden casket from the creaky drawer. As he forced it shut again, he resolved to oil the runners, a job he'd been meaning to do for more years than he could remember.

He sat down heavily in an old winged chair, then removed a tiny key from his pocket, which he used to open the casket. The cat miaowed as it looked down from his shoulder.

'Aye, nae wonder you've got something tae say. You'll no' see this every day in this hoose – no, nor many others, I fancy.'

The lid of the box creaked as he pushed it up.

There, arranged artfully on the red velvet lining, sat a black jet necklace, a thin gold chain holding it together.

'My, whoot a bonnie thing. Would you no' agree, Hamish?'

The big cat purred deeply, its green eyes flashing at the sight of the precious object.

Scott put the phone down with a sigh. 'Doesnae look as though your man Bennett is at his work, or at home, Jimmy.'

Daley thought for a few moments. 'Well, if we can't find him, we'll have to think of somewhere to keep this until tomorrow.'

'What about Thornberry?' asked Symington.

'Not my job to contact her, ma'am. Anyway, by this time they'll be well on their way to Yorkshire. If you want to inform the ACC, I'm sure he'll be more than happy to share the news.'

'You're right, of course, Jim,' she replied. 'After the fuss he's made about this, I'm sure he'll be more than happy we've come across it. What a stroke of luck. Anyone could have happened upon that bag.'

Scott eyed Daley as he nodded. 'I know that look. What's up, big man?'

'Oh, nothing really. We've got the necklace back. We can hand it to forensics, but I'm willing to gamble my pension on the lack of any firm evidence they'll find.'

'You're a pessimist, DCI Daley,' said Symington. 'These days they can work miracles.'

'Like they did in the local museum, ma'am?' Daley forced himself out of his chair. 'In the meantime, we better get this little treasure under lock and key. We don't want it going walkies again, not until we can leave it in the capable hands of Mr Bennett.'

'You're the boy for the sarcasm, Jimmy,' said Scott.

'Regardless, all's well that ends well. I'll go and let the ACC know he can come down off the ceiling.' With that, Symington left Daley's glass box with a spring in her step.

Scott looked at his old colleague and friend. 'Penny for them?'

'Just ignore me, Brian. Just ignore me.'

XIII

First, Daley tried the County Hotel. There was no sign of Annie, and nobody seemed to have any idea where she was. Then, having checked the Douglas Arms and a number of Kinloch's other hostelries, he failed to find Hamish.

On his way down to the old fisherman's cottage, he called Bennett's home number, then his mobile. No reply. Nor was there any response at Hamish's home, though he could see Hamish the cat eyeing him with deep mistrust through the yellowed net curtains as he knocked the door once more.

His last port of call was Thomas Marchmount's home. Having rattled the knocker at the door, to no avail, he soon realised, with the house in darkness, there was nobody at home. Just to make sure, however, he stepped across the floral border under the front window, being careful not to damage any plants, and stared through the rain-lashed window. Using his hand to shade the fading light of day, he could make out no movement from within.

Rather than seeking refuge from the elements in his car, he stood for a few moments at Marchmount's gate, head tilted towards the sky, letting the rain shower his face. He'd been here for long enough now. He knew these people. The population of Kinloch was tight-knit, but normally there was a chink he was able to exploit, a chance to break through the self-imposed purdah the community placed itself under when strangers threatened to uncover their secrets.

But not this time.

Or, maybe there was a different answer. Maybe some things were beyond the remit of the police. Things that would remain mysteries long after he, DCI Jim Daley – even Police Scotland – were long gone.

He shook his head with a rueful grin and made his way to his car. As he turned on the engine, he remembered Marchmount's words as reported in Scott's notebook: 'Certainly wrought by a craftsman, but with no spirit.'

DCI Jim Daley, his job done, headed for hearth and home.

The hillside was open to the elements, but still the little band of people gathered round in the dying light of day, the wind tearing at their thick coats and tugging at their hats as the rain lashed down. A pile of stones that had formed a small cairn was now being rebuilt over a disturbance in the soil. When the last stone was put in place, they looked at each other. Despite the miserable weather, everyone was smiling.

At a nod from the blind man, they made their way back down the hill, an old fisherman and a thick-set joiner taking each arm of the man with the white stick, as his dog plodded alongside.

At the front of the small group, two women – one with

forthright clipped tones, the other with the cheerful accent of a local – assailed a thin man with a nervous demeanour.

Lagging behind, a teenage lad stopped to look back at the mound of stones. He wondered how long it would be before the necklace would again see the light of day, and what the world would be like on that far-off day. Though he'd been lectured on the point, he knew in himself that they'd done the right thing. Order had been restored, and what had been taken had now been returned.

At a call from his grandfather, he turned and made his way back down the hill. What he'd seen was, indeed, finer than the blackest gold.

'Yous are all welcome back at mine!' shouted the joiner as they neared the foot of the hill.

'It's getting late,' observed the old fisherman mirthlessly, wringing rainwater from his hat.

'It's no' every day you gie the deid back whoot's rightfully theirs,' said the man, his arm around his grandson's shoulders.

'Och, I've a fine warm fire on the go,' said the fisherman. 'Aye, and you know fine, there's always time for one last dram before midnight.'

THE SILENT MAN

A DCI Daley Short Story

'*Come with me,*' the voice insists.

    He rolls onto one side, trying to shake the dream and go back to sleep.

    '*Come with me.*'

    He opens his eyes.

    '*Come with me.*'

It had been almost twelve hours since the silent man had gathered together his few belongings, made his bed, and prepared to leave the place he had called home for nearly five years. The security camera had caught him as he slipped out of the care home and into the cold dark of early morning, just as the first fat snowflakes began to fall. It was the day before Christmas Eve.

Now, thick snow clothed Kinloch in a smothering blanket, tinged orange under the glow of the street lamps. DCI Jim Daley stood at an arched window of the town hall, looking down at the scene from one floor up. The cold breath of last-minute shoppers billowed into the air and around the decorations and fairy lights that adorned the street and illuminated a bright path from each shop doorway. Festive cheer, warm and welcoming, was palpable; an enticement to one and all, as the good people of Kinloch prepared for Christmas Day.

Daley turned his attention away from thoughts of Christmas and back to the hall. Stark white striplights picked out faces etched with worry and fatigue. This was the impromptu incident room from where the search for John Sweeney had been coordinated for most of the day. Darkness had descended more than two hours ago and with it the realistic hope that the old man would be found alive; this, though, remained unspoken.

Sweeney's family – daughter, husband and their little boy – sat at a table. The daughter wrung her hands, face red and blotchy from the tears that had spilled down it all day, while her husband fussed over the six-year-old who was working busily with thick crayons, stopping occasionally to glance up at his mother with big sad blue eyes.

'Don't worry, Mummy,' he said, reaching his hand out to pat hers. 'Grampa will be out looking for Santa. He said he would ask him to get me a bike. He told me he would.'

'Calum,' scolded his father, 'what have we told you about this? Grampa doesn't speak. You know he doesn't. I want you to be a big boy for Mummy and be good, OK?'

'He speaks to me,' replied the little boy, nodding furiously to underline what he'd just said. 'He does!'

'Stop it, Calum! Just stop it!' shouted his mother. 'I'm fed up listening to you tell me what Grampa said to you. He doesn't say anything! He hasn't since you were a baby. You'll go to the bad place for telling tales. How many times have I got to tell you? Just . . . be quiet!'

Calum looked on as his mother buried her head in her hands and his father put his arm around her shoulder. He sighed and quietly went back to his drawing.

Daley was surprised at the boy's self-possession. Most children of his age would have burst into tears had they been at the sharp end of a tongue lashing from a distraught mother threatening hell and damnation. Calum, however, seemed unperturbed, resigned almost, as though he was no stranger to such outbursts.

A murmur of voices heralded movement at the table at the head of the room, where the rotund Fire and Rescue officer was getting stiffly to his feet.

'Ladies and gentlemen, I'm afraid to say that the weather is closing in again, and now that darkness has fallen we have to suspend full operations until the morning. If the snow stops, the Navy and Police helicopters will carry on their work with searchlights and heat-seeking devices overnight.' He paused and cleared his throat as the woman's sobs filled the hall. 'We'll gather here again tomorrow morning at five o'clock. Myself and Sergeant Shaw will coordinate efforts until midnight, followed by DS Scott and my deputy thereafter. Where is DS Scott, incidentally?' he asked, looking at Daley.

'Just taking a break,' replied Daley, knowing full well where DS Scott was.

As Daley walked into the vestibule of the County Hotel, he noticed that the tables and chairs where customers normally had coffee, cake and a gossip had been cleared, and the space transformed into a gaudy Santa's Grotto; all tinsel, fairy lights and crushed baking foil. A long line of children and bored-looking parents snaked towards a rather moth-eaten Santa, who leaned forward and spoke to a little boy in an accent definitely not from the North Pole.

'And whoot wid you like fir Christmas, young fella?' asked Santa in a very familiar voice. The child took a step backward, wary of the slanted eyes in the crinkled face, and the exceptionally unconvincing cotton-wool beard. Despite his disguise, Hamish wasn't hard to spot.

'Excuse me, Inspector Daley,' said a voice from behind. Andrew Duncan, John Sweeney's son-in-law, had Calum by the hand. 'Thank you so much for all your efforts today. I really appreciate it; we both do.' He tried to smile.

'I'm sorry we haven't turned anything up yet, Mr Duncan.

But don't worry,' said Daley, kneeling down stiffly on one knee to talk to the boy, who stared back at him, his face pale under a mop of red hair. 'We'll be out looking for your grampa first thing tomorrow.'

The little boy fished around in the pocket of his anorak. 'This is for you, Mr Policeman,' he said, handing Daley a piece of crumpled paper. 'Can you give it to Grampa when you find him? It's his special place. He told me.'

'Sorry, Inspector Daley, my son has a rather vivid imagination. As you know, my father-in-law hasn't spoken for a long time. Not since the death of my mother-in-law, before Calum was born, in fact. Partly because of his condition, they reckon.'

Daley nodded and turned his attention back to the boy. He smoothed out the crude drawing of what looked like a cliff above a little slash of yellow, presumably a beach, bordered by blue squiggles representing the sea. 'This is very good. What's that?' He pointed to a shape picked out in black crayon on the yellow beach.

'It's a cross. My grampa told me about it. There's a dead man buried there,' said Calum cheerfully. He grinned, showing a big gap in his front teeth.

'Noo, hold on, children,' shouted Santa, his voice muffled by cotton wool. 'We've got a special little boy wae us. Come on ower here, Calum, an' tell Santa whoot ye want for Christmas.' It was clear that Hamish, having spotted Calum and knowing the circumstances, was keen to make a fuss of him.

The red-haired boy made his way past the line of parents and children and stood in front of Father Christmas.

'Noo, whoot present wid ye most like, Calum?' said Hamish in a gentle voice, leaning down and taking the boy by the hand.

Calum looked back at his father. 'I wanted a bike . . . but I'd rather have Grampa back. Please, Santa?'

'It's a wean's drawing, Jim. I can't understand why you've been staring at it for the last hour,' said DS Brian Scott, taking a sip from his pint of ginger beer and lime and grimacing.

'You're just fed up that's not a pint of lager, Bri,' Daley replied. 'I don't know . . . there's something about it – about the boy. Just a feeling, I suppose.'

'You and your bloody feelings, Jim. They're not right this time. You know as well as I do there's no way that old man will survive out there tonight. Aye, and that's if he's not dead already.' Scott spoke quietly, anxious that the other customers in the County Hotel bar wouldn't overhear his understandable pessimism. 'It's been freezing or thereabouts for most of the day. Well below it, now. The man's no' in his right mind. Dementia's a terrible thing. You know the score, Jimmy.'

A red sleeve appeared in between the policemen as Santa placed a small glass of whisky on the table, then sat down heavily.

'I don't know whoot they pay Father Christmas, but whootever it is, he deserves every penny o' it,' declared Hamish. 'I'm fair frazzled efter dealing wae a' these weans.'

'It's your age, man,' said Scott. 'Why did you volunteer?'

'Och, my faither used tae dae it every year. I suppose it's a family tradition. Aye, and that little elf o'er there's quite handy wae a dram or two once it's all over,' replied Hamish, gesturing to Annie, who was in a short green dress and busy pouring drinks for her customers, most of whom were already brimming over with festive cheer. 'Whoot's that ye have, Mr Daley?'

'This?' Daley lifted the boy's picture from the table. 'Och, Calum drew it. Said it was the old man's special place.'

Hamish looked at the picture, took his pipe from his pocket and sucked at it, unlit. 'And is this supposed tae be a cross, by any chance?'

'Yes,' replied Daley, 'how did you know?'

'It's Sorn Bay, jeest along the coast fae Machrie. A sailor was washed up there in the First World War, and the locals buried him on the shingle and erected a cross in his memory. I recognised it straight away,' said Hamish with a self-satisfied smile.

'So, it's a real place? I thought it was just something the wee boy had made up. Hmm.'

'See what you've gone and done now,' said Scott. 'He's got that look in his eye again. It'll be another mad idea, that no doubt I'll be up to my ears with sometime soon.' He watched as Daley walked over to the bar to buy a round. 'Mind you, you'd be amazed how many times he's right.'

'There's somethin' else aboot Sorn Bay. I jeest canna bring it tae mind,' declared Hamish, scratching his head with the end of his unlit pipe.

She slept fitfully, her father's face in every dream. He never said a word, though; she wasn't sure if she could even remember what he sounded like. It seemed so long since she had heard him say her name.

Suddenly, she felt the hairs stand on the back of her neck and a tingle ripple down her spine – an ancient instinct that somebody, something was behind her, watching her. She heard her heart pound in her ears, but she could hear something else.

'Come with me. Come with me.' The voice was soft, no more than a whisper.

She held her breath, too frightened to move.

'Come with me. Come with me.'

Unable to restrain herself, Helen Duncan screamed, and screamed again at the top of her voice.

'Helen!' shouted her husband, who, now sitting straight up in the bed, turned to reach out and hold her in his arms. It was then he noticed something. Across the room a shadow moved, illuminated suddenly by a shaft of white light coming through a chink in the bedroom curtains.

'Has Calum walked in his sleep before, Mrs Duncan?' enquired Daley. They were back at the incident room in the town hall. It was seven in the morning, and the woman before him looked shattered. Her eyes were bleary and circled with dark shadows.

'Once or twice, but nothing like this. Usually he just gets up and starts crying on the landing and I take him back to bed,' she said. 'This time, he spoke. He just wouldn't wake up.'

'He was staring straight ahead, Mr Daley,' added Mr Duncan, 'just saying the same thing over and over again.'

'Which was?'

'Come with me,' she said quietly. 'Come with me.'

'He didn't remember anything about it this morning,' added Mr Duncan.

As Daley left the distraught couple, he spotted Hamish waving at him from the entrance to the hall.

'I knew I remembered something else aboot Sorn Bay,' he said breathlessly. 'It jeest came tae mind this morning when I woke up. I came straight ower tae tell you.'

'Tell me what?'

'When John Sweeney was a wean the family stayed at

Machrie. He had an older sister, Maggie, a wee red-haired lassie. He doted on her – they went everywhere together.'

Daley brought the older man a chair, and they both sat down. 'Take your time, Hamish.'

'Aye, well, naebody knew how it happened. But one day the two o' them were out, jeest playing, the way weans do. John came back home hysterical, no sign o' his sister. Their folks were up to high doh. The whole village was oot lookin' for the lassie.'

'Did they ever find her?'

'Aye, they did.' Hamish looked at the floor. 'That's jeest it, her body was found on the beach at Sorn Bay. They reckon she fell off the cliff, lookin' for bird's eggs. Poor wee thing, she wiz only nine. John wid be six at the time, the same age Calum is noo.'

'And why has no one mentioned this, Hamish?'

'Och, well, you know how things are. In wee places like this, when tragedy strikes we a' dae oor best tae move on. I know John wid never speak aboot it. I'm a bit older than him so I mind it happening – that's the only reason I know anything aboot it.'

'But even if he's gone back there, he'll never have survived the night,' said Daley.

'Aye, well, there's the thing. There's a wee hut up on the hillside. It wiz used by shepherds in the old days for shelter – if the weather closed in, ye understand. They tell me walkers use it noo. There's a wee stove, some wood likely. If John Sweeney's gone there – aye, and he'll know aboot it – he could have got through the night. Jeest a theory,' concluded Hamish.

The snow had stopped. The bright winter sun sparkled on the

white mantle that covered roofs, fields and roads. A large yellow helicopter soared into the air above Kinloch.

The naval pilot chatted to Daley via the headset as they flew over the town. Those coordinating the search had been sceptical when Daley had first mooted the idea of looking for John Sweeney at Sorn Bay. However, with all hopes of finding the man virtually dashed, and nothing else to go on, they had let the policeman follow his instinct.

He looked down as a flock of sheep, a dirty cream colour against the white snow, scattered as the helicopter passed overhead. They made heavy progress through the thick snow, leaving deep tracks in their wake.

'Inspector Daley, look!' exclaimed the pilot, his voice tinny through the headphones. 'There, smoke!'

Sure enough, a thin line of black smoke spiralled up from a little shack below them, plain against the white ground.

'I can see footprints in the snow,' shouted Daley. 'Can we land here?'

The pilot brought the helicopter gently to the ground, its downdraft scattering snow into the air in a thick flurry.

Daley, after being helped out of the aircraft, saw a small line of footprints that led away from the shack and over a small rise. He followed them, and on reaching the top caught his breath at the beauty of the scene before him. The vast Atlantic appeared almost motionless beneath sheer cliffs. And there, dwarfed under the huge sky, Daley could see a figure in the distance.

He crunched through the snow, which was almost up to his knees, soaking his trousers. 'Mr Sweeney!' he shouted, the echo sending gulls screaming into the clear air.

Closer now, Daley could see the man turn around, look at

him for a heartbeat, then step nearer the edge of the cliff, facing back out to sea.

'John, please! Come on, let's get you back into the warmth. We'll freeze out here.'

The old man took another step forward, now only a few inches from oblivion.

Daley struggled to think what to say to prevent John Sweeney taking his own life, when a small voice rang out behind him.

'Grampa, come with me!' shouted the little boy, out of the helicopter now, and wrapped up in a thick coat and hat, in his father's arms.

The old man didn't move, and for a moment Daley thought he was about to step over the edge of the cliff. But, slowly, he turned. Daley could see his jaws working as he opened and closed his mouth wordlessly, then shook his head.

'Grampa, please!' Calum wailed.

John Sweeney looked up again. 'Calum, my wee lad, you're so bonnie,' he said, as he sank to his knees in the deep snow.

The little boy had wriggled free of his father's grip and was doing his best to plunge towards them. His hat had fallen off in the snow and his hair seemed even more red against it. Daley scooped him up in his arms and took him across to his grandfather.

'Grampa,' said Calum, holding his hand out. 'I don't mind if Santa doesn't bring me a bike. Don't worry.'

Tears coursed down the old man's face as the little boy clung onto his grandfather.

'See, Daddy. Grampa does speak to me. I wasn't telling tales.' Calum beamed at his father.

Just as they were about to climb aboard the helicopter, John Sweeney stopped and turned to face the cliff once more.

'Maggie, I canna come with you, not now – one day, but not now.' He took a deep breath and hugged his grandson.

'Don't worry, Grampa,' said Calum, his face sincere. 'The girl with the red hair is waiting for you.'

Andrew Duncan looked, astonished, at the boy. 'He doesn't know anything about Maggie,' he said to the detective.

All Jim Daley could do was shrug his shoulders.

STRANGERS

A DCI Daley Short Story

I

A tumble of exhaust fumes billowed into the cold November air as the old red bus pulled into the stance on Kinloch's seafront. It was already dark, but the passengers could glimpse the shimmer of the loch and the looming island at its head under the twinkle of the town's lights and the bright full moon.

Miss Jane Steele peered through the car window, occasionally giving the wipers a turn to rid the screen of the ice that was forming on it. She'd have liked to sit with the engine idling and the heater on, but that was now taboo, certainly for council employees, so she cupped her hands together instead, blowing into them in an attempt to keep warm. Normally, she'd be picking up colleagues or clients from various parts of the peninsula, but tonight it was her job to transport a family to their new home in Kinloch. These were not her usual charges; these were people who had endured a long and hazardous journey from a war zone.

She could see them alighting from the bus now. Though she was cold and tired, she was pleased to be part of this, proud to be the social worker dedicated to helping these lost souls settle in the town.

'Look, Badr,' said Faiz. 'A big new moon. It is a good sign – your name!'

'Yes, my love, you're right,' she replied and tried to smile. 'If this is to be our home, we must make the best of all the good omens.'

The little girl she was carrying, no longer lulled into sleep by the motion of the bus, began to stir. 'Ayisha, my precious one, we are nearly home. Soon you will sleep in a bed of your own.' She kissed her daughter's forehead as the child stared in silence, her deep brown eyes taking in these strange new surroundings.

'Hasan, quickly now!' Faiz shouted to his five-year-old son, who had found a playmate on the journey – a local child of a similar age. Though they didn't share a common language, the two boys had amused themselves on the back seat of the half-empty bus, both sets of parents relieved that their respective offspring had something to take their minds off the long journey from Glasgow to Kinloch.

Hasan – accustomed to obeying his father immediately – turned and ran towards him, pausing for a heartbeat to wave shyly to his new friend.

'Good boy, Hasan. It is time for us to be taken to our new home. Come with me,' he said, taking the tousle-haired child by the hand.

Miss Steele wiped away the condensation on the car window with a glove and immediately spotted her new clients. She pushed open the car door and emerged, shivering, into the cold.

The woman was tiny, of slender frame, and wearing what looked like a man's sheepskin coat of a fashion long forgotten. Her hair was covered by a bright blue scarf which matched the colour of her leggings, tucked into black Ug boots whose seam had temporarily been repaired with silver duct tape. The woman was holding a child – a little girl, Steele thought, as she watched the foursome move to the rear of the bus to collect what luggage they had. The husband, who walked behind his wife, was tall, painfully thin and dressed in sand-coloured jeans above garish fluorescent trainers; he was huddled into a ski-jacket from which poked wisps of foam lining through holes in the sleeves. The little boy bringing up the rear looked adorable; all big eyes and purpose, striding out behind his father, he was also in tatty jeans, and a thick blue duffel coat, several sizes too big for him. It was clear that the Karim family had been the recipients of donated clothes that had seen better days and Miss Steele felt a twinge of pity.

'Mr Karim!' she shouted, chasing after her clients as quickly as her short legs would allow. 'Mr Karim!'

The man turned round, his mouth agape, a sudden look of fear etched across his features. For him, the sound of his name being called brought back terrifying memories. 'I am Faiz Karim,' he called back in halting English.

Miss Steele was panting by the time she caught up with the family. She took a few moments to catch her breath in the frosty air. 'I'm Jane Steele,' she said, holding out her hand, ' and I'm here to take you to your new home.' She saw the confused look on Faiz's face, so decided to say the whole thing all over again, this time much more slowly.

'I'm sorry, my husband's English is not good,' said the tiny figure of Badr Karim. 'I am so pleased you can help us. My husband has some money left and can pay you for your kindness.'

'Oh, goodness, no! Not necessary,' replied Miss Steele, unwittingly deploying her slow Foreigners' Voice, despite Mrs Karim's obvious fluency. 'Please, get your bags and come with me. I' – she pressed a palm to her chest – 'will drive' – the mimicking of steering a wheel – 'you to your new house.'

Badr Karim was not sure what made her smile most: the thought of being – at last – safe, or this rotund lady in the huge padded jacket's attempt at conveying the act of driving. Although she was shivering, for the first time in a very long time it was definitely through cold, not fear.

Soon the family were being led towards Miss Steele's car with the council logo on the side.

'Why do they stare, Father?' whispered Hasan, drawing his father's attention to the small knot of people standing nearby.

'We are new. They have come to greet us.' To indicate this to his son, and in an attempt to be polite, Faiz Karim waved hesitantly to the bemused onlookers.

'I'm telling you, Betty, no good'll come of it.'

'Och, they look like nice folk to me. Look, the man's waving at us, May.'

'He might be waving now, but he'll not be waving when he's marching down Main Street with a machine gun, blowing us all to Kingdom Come.'

Ignoring her companion, Betty returned Faiz's wave. 'And would you look at that wee boy, the poor wee creature. Not a picking on him – no, nor any of them.'

'Sure, they do that on purpose to get sympathy. I saw it on that American news channel the other night. It's all an act to pull at your heartstrings.' May looked on, her mouth curling in disgust.

'What American news channel? I just watch the BBC, me. *Reporting Scotland*, Jackie Bird. I've never heard her say anything of the kind.'

'Naw, of course you wouldn't. She's just a puppet for the government. That Boris Johnson likely writes down everything she's to say. It's the proper news from America that counts – they tell the punters how it really is, none of this propergander business.'

Betty eyed her friend dubiously. No matter what May said,

she thought this family looked lost and scared; and her heart went out to them.

'And another thing,' said May, watching the family load their pitifully few items into the council vehicle, 'they've hardly a stitch of clothing, nor anything else. You know fine who'll be paying for that – aye, me and you, that's who.'

'How exactly will *you* be paying, May O'Halloran? You've not worked since two thousand and five,' objected Betty indignantly.

'Is it my fault I did my arm in that time when I fell on the ice? It's all down to the doctors that don't know how to mend it. You know me, Betty. When it comes to work, I'm always first in the queue.'

'Aye, to get home! You were absolutely mortal drunk when you slipped on that ice. I was there, remember.' With that, Betty turned her attention firmly back to the visitors.

'They don't look very welcoming,' said Badr to her husband, eyeing the locals with some dismay.

'Nonsense, that lady just waved to me. Like everything, it will take time. But, you'll see, we'll soon make friends and feel at home here. You have such good English, Badr, it's me who should feel like a stranger.'

His wife raised an eyebrow and thanked Miss Steele as she helped strap Ayisha into the back seat.

Without warning, a large explosion rent the air, followed by a flurry of smaller bangs.

'Quick! Down, get down!' shouted Mr Karim, throwing himself and his son to the ground, the little boy whimpering.

Only when the noise stopped did he dare look up from the cold concrete upon which he now lay, sheltering his trembling son with his arm.

343

He was amazed. Who were these people? They stood still, despite the explosions. They hadn't budged an inch. Maybe it was true what he'd read about these Scottish folk: fearless warriors, a brave nation. As he picked up his son, Miss Steele rushed towards them, talking quickly and gesticulating. He didn't understand a word. All he wanted to do now was get into this car and to his new home before the bombs went off again. They had abandoned everything they owned, walked hundreds of miles, and endured the terror of the sea in a hopelessly overcrowded rubber boat, just to end up here. His heart sank in his chest.

'One thing's for sure, Betty. They're not too happy with Guy Fawkes night, and that's a fact.' May O'Halloran turned on her heel and headed off into the night to begin the rumours about the strangers from Libya who had come to stay in Kinloch.

II

DCI Jim Daley and DS Brian Scott walked along Hillcross Road, the main route through what had been a council estate, or 'scheme' as they were called locally. Most of the houses were now privately owned; the bright colours, double-glazing and extensions testament to the fact.

'This isnae like the scheme I grew up in,' said Scott. 'I'm reckoning none o' these folk have tae burn their doors because they cannae afford coal tae keep the hoose warm.'

'Thankfully, time's moved on, Bri . . . well, for most folk. I'm sure there's somebody burning their dining-room table to keep out the cold, even now.'

'They'll no' have tae eat their ain pet rabbit.' Scott grimaced. 'Eh?'

'My faither . . . we were a' sitting at the kitchen table. It was a Sunday. I was getting knocked intae this chicken. Right tasty it was – the best chicken I'd ever eaten. I says tae the auld yin, "Here, where did you get that chicken fae, Mum? It's lovely." She just looks at me, a' guilty like. "Och, it's no' chicken, son," says my faither. "It's rabbit. I'm afraid tae say Thumper had tae make the ultimate sacrifice tae put food in oor bellies. I'll get up the hill an' catch you a new pet soon." Wae that bombshell, he wiped his mooth and off tae the pub.'

'He was all heart, your father.'

'Aye. If he'd stayed oot the pub a wee bit mair we widnae have had tae eat the family pet. But there you are. I'm sure I've telt you that story before.'

'Yes, come to think of it, you have.' Daley stopped to take a piece of paper from his pocket. 'Thought so, this is the house here.'

In front of them was a semi-detached house. No expensive double-glazing or extension here; the house looked grey and unloved, with peeling, faded paint on the window frames and the front door, and a clump of vegetation sprouting from a gutter. Much the same as the house next door, Daley thought. That one was in the same state of dilapidation, apart from a pimped-up old hatchback sitting on a concrete-slabbed driveway that had once been the front garden and was easily accessed by a gaping hole in the hedge. The car was bright yellow, boasting a wide selection of go-fast stripes, stickers and other adornments. Loud music thumped from an open upstairs window.

'That's mair like it,' said Scott. 'This is the kind o' place I remember. Pure shite.'

Daley opened the rusted iron gate, and he and Scott made their way to number 76, their destination.

Daley knocked smartly on the door, causing small flecks of paint to fall onto the step in front of him. After a moment, the door opened a crack to reveal the gaunt face of a dark-haired man.

'I'm DCI Jim Daley from the local police.' He smiled as he flashed his warrant card. 'This is DS Brian Scott. Can we come in?'

Rather to his surprise, the man let out a yelp, and, instead of admitting them to the house, slammed the door shut.

'And hello to you, tae,' remarked Scott.

Daley was just about to try again when the door opened, wider this time. A petite woman in a headscarf who looked every bit as thin as the man they'd just encountered looked out at them.

'Can I help you? My husband says you are the police,' she said in perfect English.

'Yes. I'm DCI Jim Daley. I thought we'd pop by and say hello. I know how difficult things have been for you.'

'Oh, yes, yes, of course.' Mrs Karim stood back from the door to admit the policemen into the hallway.

She showed the two men to the spartan but tidy lounge and a grey sofa that had seen better days. It was bookended by two armchairs that looked equally tired. The blue carpet was threadbare. Under the window sat a battered, fold-down wooden table and a widescreen television, incongruous in the room amid a random collection of more personal items.

The man of the house eyed the policemen with an anxious expression while addressing his wife in rapid, strained tones. A little girl clung to his legs and peered at the visitors with wary eyes. When Daley leaned forward to speak to her, she quickly sought refuge behind her father.

'I'm sorry my husband didn't let you in immediately. Where we come from a visit from the police is something to be feared. Please, can I get you something to drink? We only have tea, but it is good.'

'Oh, don't go to any trouble. We're just here to introduce ourselves. I can understand how hard it must be to have travelled so far, and under such awful conditions. If there's anything we can do to help, just let us know.' Daley fished a business card from his pocket and handed it to Badr. 'You're safe here in Kinloch, I assure you.'

'Oh, thank you so much.' She relaxed and smiled. 'This is my husband, Faiz. Sorry that he doesn't have much English, but he is eager to learn.'

'That's not a problem, Mrs Karim. My Arabic isn't too great, either. Come to that, Brian's English isn't as good as yours. So, where did you learn?'

'Oh, my father was a teacher. He told us children that the world was changing and to get on in the future we would need to speak English well. I'm glad now that he did . . .' She looked momentarily tearful but composed herself.

'I'm sorry. I didn't mean to upset you.'

'Not at all. My father was assassinated before we left Libya. There is no rule of law any more, only evil men seeking what is good for them. I almost wish Colonel Gaddafi was back.' She paused as she saw the look of horror on her husband's face at the mention of the deposed leader. 'Sorry. He was a tyrant, of course, but at least we had order. We knew our boundaries. Now in our country we have no such boundaries – no one has. Instead of one tyrant there are hundreds, thousands.'

'Here, lassie, you don't need tae make excuses. We've had oor own tyrant here. I'm no' sure John Donald was any better than Gaddafi . . .' Scott stopped in his tracks, pulled up by a black look from his superior at the mention of their notorious old boss.

'What's your name?' asked Daley.

'I am Badr. I am pleased to meet you both.' She held out her hand. 'Everyone has been so kind. Miss Steele – from your council – she gave us this television and would take no money. This house is more than we could have hoped for. We have food, we have all we need, and we are safe.'

'I heard your husband got a fright when you arrived the other night.'

'Yes, we all did. We didn't know about your tradition of fireworks. When you hear explosions in our country it means only one thing.'

The little girl had appeared again from behind her father and was now holding his hand, sucking her thumb, staring at the detectives.

'And what's your name?' asked Daley.

'This is Ayisha. We hope that for her at least the memories of our past will fade and all she will know of life will be here.'

There was the sudden bang of a door and the sound of a wailing child. A little boy burst into the room and ran straight into his mother's arms, ignoring the visitors.

Daley watched as his mother whispered into his ear, her voice soft and soothing.

'What's up wae the wee one?' asked Scott.

'He was out playing in the back garden. The old man next door shouts a lot – so does the other man. Hasan will get used to it. Already in his short life he has faced much, much worse.'

The policemen stayed for a few more minutes chatting to the Karims before leaving them to their new home. They seemed like good parents, decent people, damaged by events beyond their control. Ultimately, after so much fear and uncertainty, they were just happy to have somewhere to call home.

'Hey, where are you going, Bri?' shouted Daley as he watched his colleague head up the path of the house next door.

'I'm going tae find oot why this guy thinks he's got the right tae make wee boys cry.' Scott knocked on the door loudly.

An old man finally appeared. He was thick-set, with a head of lank, greasy grey hair sticking up in tufts above a pock-marked face. Daley reckoned the man was in his late sixties, but it was hard to tell. One thing was for certain: he had the bulbous purple-veined nose of a heavy drinker. Rather than invite the officers in, he stood framed in the doorway, a disgruntled look on his face.

'I was just wondering when the polis was going tae make it next door. They've been here for days now. I want them oot!'

'Whit?' exclaimed Scott, staring at the man in disbelief. 'I'm here tae speak tae you. What's your name?'

'I'm Tam Arbuthnot, what's your name?'

'DS Brian Scott, and this is DCI Daley. Tell me, what did you say to the boy next door tae send him running tae his mother in floods o' tears?'

'Oh, I see. Instead o' checking them – these people – you're here tae harass me. Well, I'll tell you, I'm fae Kinloch an' proud o' it. Folk like that don't belong here and that's a fact. How would I now what made the wee boy cry? It was nothing I said tae him. He canna understand a word o' English anyway. Likely never conversed with a civilised man afore.'

Scott raised his eyebrows at the thought of what Arbuthnot might mean by 'civilised'. He noticed movement in the hallway.

'What's up, Papa?' A tall, heavily-built young man had

appeared behind Tam Arbuthnot. He was smoking a roll-up and had an unpleasant stain on his faded red T-shirt.

'The polis! Here tae warn me tae be nice tae they immigrants next door, Gordon.' He pointed a gnarled forefinger at Scott. 'Well, yous can go and dae something mair useful. Maybe look intae who they really are. I canna sleep in my bed thinking o' what might happen. We'll be in the front line if that bastard decides tae let loose.'

'You listen tae me,' said Scott. 'Another racist outburst like that and you'll be coming doon the station, got it? Just you leave the Karims be. I'll be keeping an eye on you. I hope I make myself clear.' He looked over the old man's shoulder. 'And I take it you're the one responsible for that racket up the stairs, young man?'

'Aye, it's called music – what o' it?' protested Gordon Arbuthnot with a sneer.

'I'm calling it breach o' the peace. Get you up an' turn it off before you take a wee trip doon the road.'

Scott turned on his heel, and then paused to look at the yellow hatchback before joining Daley on the street.

'She's fully taxed an' insured, so you needna bother checking,' shouted Gordon Arbuthnot.

'Don't you worry, son. I've a note o' your registration number – it's the first thing I'm going tae do when I get back tae work. Oh, and get that shirt o' yours in the wash – it's disgusting!'

Daley grinned as he walked briskly back down the street beside his sergeant. 'No holding back there, Bri.'

'Nah, why should I? I cannae stand these ignorant bastards. We'd the same thing in oor street when I was a boy when the McCutcheons moved intae number six.'

'McCutcheon? Doesn't sound very Arabic to me.'

'Naw, they wisnae Arabs – Roman Catholics. Half the street widnae speak tae them. Some bastard shat doon their chimney.'

'What? Really?'

'Aye, really. There they were sittin' watchin' the telly when a big toley landed sizzling on the coals. Dirty bastards, some folk . . . There was no mair proud a Protestant than my auld faither, but that was the last straw for him. He had the auld dear run roon to them wae a stew, quick smart.' Scott nodded at the memory, leaving Daley to ponder on just how much things had changed in the last forty years or so. He wondered how his mother would have reacted if his father had directed her to 'run roon with a stew' given those circumstances. He shook his head.

III

A few weeks later, Annie was busy hanging up the Christmas decorations under the scrutiny of a knot of regulars in the County Hotel bar.

'I'd move the tree a wee ways tae the left,' said Hamish, squinting one eye and wafting his hand in the proposed direction. 'An' is it no' time yous got a new fairy? That yin must be aulder than me – aye, an' she's no' wearing as well neither. She's been danglin' on top o' that tree longer than Nelson on his column.'

'Listen tae Kirsty Allsop here,' exclaimed Annie, descending gingerly from the rickety step-ladder. 'I think I'm right in saying that the décor in your hoose hasna changed since nineteen fifty-one. That fairy was new jeest a couple o' years ago. Come tae think o' it, it cost me o'er a fiver an' I've still no' had the money back yet.' Now on terra firma, she stepped back to appraise the Christmas tree which now stood in the corner of the bar. 'No' a bad job, even if I do say so mysel'.'

'Typical o' a woman,' declared Hamish. 'Fair self-satisfied. If some bloke had flung that tree up the way you've done he'd no' hear the end o' it until the next Christmas.'

Before Annie could argue back, the tall figure of DCI Jim Daley entered the bar, loosening his tie as he did so. 'Can I have a pint of heavy, please, Annie? I've a right drouth for some reason tonight.'

'Of course you can, Mr Daley. You're late on the go. No Brian, I see.'

'He's on a split shift. Busy on the computer last time I looked. You can imagine the bad language.'

'Och, there are some destined tae sit at computers and others mair o' a practical bent – like mysel',' said Hamish.

Daley paid for his pint and headed to the back of the bar to talk to the old man.

'That's a fine tree. I've not had the energy to put mine up yet … Not much point, really,' he added somewhat self-pityingly.

'So much for the spirit of Christmas,' said Annie, approaching the table with a red bucket.

'You've not got to the stage of serving Hamish his drink in a pail, have you? I mean, I know he likes a drink …' Daley couldn't help laughing at his own joke.

'Away wi' you! No, this is a collection for these poor souls that arrived here fae thon Libya. Whoot's their names?' asked Annie, shaking the bucket under Daley's nose.

'The Karims. A good family – I paid them a visit today, as a matter of fact. Lovely people; they've been through a lot.'

'Well, get your giving hand oot. I'm hoping we can get

enough money together tae buy the weans something half decent for their Christmas.'

'I'm no' convinced they'll be much up for Christmas,' observed Hamish.

'Whoot?'

'On account o' them being Muselmanns, an' that.'

'Muselmanns?' said Daley. 'I think that term went out with Churchill, Hamish. That's a lovely gesture, Annie. I'm sure they'll be very appreciative – even though they are Muslims, Hamish.'

'You'll find the folk fae the toon will take them tae their hearts, Mr Daley. That's the kind o' place Kinloch is, and that's a fact,' said Annie, watching as Daley slipped a twenty-pound note into the bucket. 'Very generous, I'm sure.' She bit her lip. 'A pity they'd tae move them in next tae auld Tam Arbuthnot, though.' She shook her head as she made her way back behind the bar to stow the collection bucket.

'This Arbuthnot guy, Hamish. Do you know him?'

'Know him? Aye, I'm sad tae say, I do. One o' the maist objectionable men you could meet. He's been the same since he was a boy. A complete scunner, and, fae whoot I hear, that big grandson o' his is no better.'

'So he lives with his grandfather?'

'Aye, he does that. His father used tae work doon at the shipyard. When it closed he got offered a job doon south. The boy wanted tae stay in the toon, so when his folks left he jeest stayed wae his auld grandfaither. Well matched, if you ask me. Young Gordon's always after money, and Tam's the meanest man I ever met. It's no jeest wae money – right mean-spirited, tae. Funnily enough I saw him a whiles ago. Came oot o' Jenny's bar taking three sides o' the street. Fair mortal he was.'

'So, a heavy drinker?'

'For him, a day no' getting blotto's like a holiday. Tae say he's got a fair swally is no' doing it justice at a.'

Scott switched off the computer with a huge sigh of relief. He eyed the machine with barely hidden malice.

'That's you off tae sleep. You cannae torture me any more the day, you bastard,' he said, addressing the computer as though it was his mortal enemy.

He looked at his watch – still more than two hours of his shift to go. It was a weekday night, with none of the bustle associated with Kinloch Police Office at the weekends. Though he'd finished typing up his reports, there were a few cases he could review prior to calling it a night.

So, with this in mind, he decided to head to the coffee machine in search of a strong brew that would help him stay awake until the end of his shift. He left his desk in the CID suite and headed out into the dimly lit corridor.

Just as the dark, steaming beverage was filling the cup, he heard raised voices coming from the direction of reception, one of which – the wailing voice of a woman – he thought he recognised.

Scott left the coffee cup on a windowsill and went in search of the commotion.

As he turned into the bar office, he was shocked to see two burly young uniformed policemen struggling with Faiz Karim. His wife was holding their daughter tightly in her arms as she screamed in protest at the treatment of her husband. Her son was clutching onto her long coat.

'What the hell's going on here?' shouted Scott above the din.

'Mr Scott, please, please, help us!' shouted Badr Karim, her daughter sobbing quietly over her shoulder. 'They are taking my husband. Please help!'

'Right!' shouted Scott, standing in front of the struggling Faiz Karim. 'You remember me from earlier, yes?' He looked into the man's eyes, noting that he had a nasty graze on his cheek.

At a few words in Arabic from his wife, Karim stopped struggling and looked at Scott with pleading eyes. 'I do not do this,' he screamed. 'I do not do this!'

With the help of the uniformed officers present, Scott managed to persuade the Karims to take a seat in one of the office's family rooms. The family huddled together on a sofa, Badr dabbing at her husband's bleeding face with a hanky as the children burrowed into his neck.

'Constable Potts, what's been going on?' enquired Scott, now that the situation had calmed.

'We were bringing Mr Karim in, Sergeant.'

'Arresting him? What on earth for?'

'Assault, Sergeant.'

'On who?' Scott looked unconvinced.

'His neighbour, a Mr Arbuthnot. He's been taken to the hospital, taken quite a bang on the head, Sergeant.'

'This is not true!' Badr Karim wailed again. 'My husband would never do such a thing. He would not harm anyone. We are peaceful people.'

'Come with me, son,' said Scott to Constable Potts, indicating that he follow him from the room. 'Mrs Karim, just try to keep calm. I'm sure we'll get to the bottom of this.' He showed Potts out of the room and then followed him, closing the door to the family room in his wake.

'What happened?'

'We got a report that there was a disturbance in the street outside seventy-four Hillcross Road. When myself and Constable Cameron got there, we found Mr Karim kneeling over Mr Arbuthnot. At the time, Arbuthnot was unconscious, but I could see he'd taken a heavy blow to the head. We detained Mr Karim, who, as you've seen, resisted arrest. There was a bit of a scuffle. Just as we managed to get the cuffs on him, his wife and children appeared. All hell broke loose, Sergeant.'

'So what evidence do you have, son?'

'Well, apart from the fact that we found Karim at the locus, kneeling over the injured man, we managed to get a brief statement from Mr Arbuthnot.'

'So, he regained consciousness?'

'Yes, Sergeant. He came to when the paramedics administered oxygen as he was being taken into the ambulance.'

'What did he say?'

'He confirmed that he had been assaulted by Karim.' The young constable shrugged his shoulders.

'Any witnesses?'

'No, we haven't got that far yet. But apart from the arrival of the rest of the Karim family, the street was empty. We have no number for the person who reported it – withheld.'

'Right, son, you've done what you had to do. Get back in there and keep things as calm as you can.'

As the young policeman did as he was asked, Scott reached into the inside pocket of his jacket, bringing out his mobile phone. He squinted at the screen, pressed it, then placed the device to his ear. 'Jim, it's me. If I was you I'd get up here as soon as you can. We've got what you might call a situation.'

IV

Daley stood by Tam Arbuthnot's bed in Kinloch hospital. The old man was drifting in and out of sleep, his head heavily bandaged, looking almost vulnerable without his glasses.

'Only a few moments, DCI Daley,' said the staff nurse. 'He's had a nasty dunt, plus he'll have to sleep off all the booze he's had. Not getting any younger, either. Honestly, the way some people behave.'

'How would you say his head injury happened? I can't see much under that bandage,' replied Daley.

'The doctor says it's some kind of blunt force trauma. We see it a lot – assaults, car accidents, falls – so it could be any of these things.'

'Yes, I know what you mean,' said Daley thoughtfully. He leaned over the man in the bed. 'Mr Arbuthnot, it's DCI Daley. We spoke earlier today. I'd like to know how this happened to you. Can you remember at all?'

Arbuthnot peered up at his visitor, trying to focus. He licked his parched lips and cleared his throat noisily.

'I telt they ambulance men whoot happened. Thon stranger hit me, plain an' simple. The Arab guy that's moved in next door.' Suddenly his eyes blazed, his gaze now firmly on the detective. 'Aye, an' I'm holding you responsible, tae. I telt you earlier the man was a danger, and now here's me – a pensioner, mark you – lying in hospital after being attacked. I'm thinking it's time you and they Arabs were moving on.' With that, his eyes fluttered and he seemed to fall asleep.

'That will be enough for now,' said the staff nurse.

'Quite enough,' replied Daley, shaking his head.

He thanked the nurse and made his way out of Kinloch

hospital. In the car park he pulled the phone from his pocket and pressed the screen a couple of times.

'Brian, anything new? I've a statement, of sorts, from Arbuthnot. As we thought, he has named Mr Karim as the attacker.'

'Right, Jimmy. Nothing new here. I've sent the weans hame wae that Miss Steele, the social worker. I've had tae keep Mrs Karim here wae her man – she's the only person who can speak tae him. The uniforms are doing the rounds of the doors up in Hillcross Road, but nae joy at the moment.'

Scott ended the call with Daley and leaned back in his chair. He'd been a detective for years – almost every kind of rogue imaginable had crossed his path at one time or other – and he was certain that Faiz Karim wasn't one of them.

'I've a Mrs O'Halloran at the front desk, Brian,' said Constable Potts. 'Wants to speak to you urgently.'

Scott introduced himself to May O'Halloran who was waiting at reception and took her into an interview room.

'We've quite a lot on tonight, ma'am. I'm afraid I can't spare you much time.'

'I don't need much time, Sergeant,' she replied abruptly. 'I live across the road from Tam Arbuthnot in Hillcross Road. I had some of your boys at the door about an hour ago, and I've just remembered something.'

'Oh, aye. What have you just remembered?' Scott could easily spot someone who had been wrestling with their conscience – it was a skill you learned early as a police officer.

'I'm ashamed to say I didn't tell your constable the whole truth earlier. I saw what happened to Tam and I want to make a statement.'

'Just you hang on while I get my notebook,' said Scott.

Daley knocked at the door of 74 Hillcross Road. When there was no reply, he knocked again, though much louder this time.

Eventually the officers could see a light going on through the dimpled glass of the front door. It swung open to reveal Gordon Arbuthnot standing in the hallway, naked to the waist, his ample belly flopping over the unseen waistband of a pair of dirty jeans.

'I hope yous are here tae tell me that bastard Karim has been charged wae attacking my poor grandfaither.'

'Can we come in?' asked Daley.

'Aye, sure, whootever.'

The detectives were shown through to the lounge. A grubby three-piece suite was arranged around an old gas fire, above which was an old-fashioned tiled mantelpiece flanked by two brass candlesticks. A few pictures hung on the wall, mostly black-and-white photographs. Daley recognised a young Tam Arbuthnot in one. Like the Karims' lounge, the room was poorly furnished, apart from a huge television that dominated one corner of the room. Unlike their neighbours', though, this room was filthy and untidy, with a huge, unidentifiable stain on the carpet and an overflowing ashtray on a low coffee table stained with multiple mug-rings.

'Right, say whoot yous have tae say. I've tae get doon tae the hospital.'

'Where were you at six-forty this evening, Gordon?' asked Daley.

'At a friend's place. How?'

'So you weren't here at home?'

'No. I was at Malky's hoose.'

'Good,' said Scott. 'Can you gie me Malky's number?'

'How? I don't want my friends getting hassle fae the polis. Whoot is this?'

'*This*,' Daley said, edging closer to the younger man, 'is the chance for you to tell the truth.'

'Aboot what?'

'Aboot what happened tae your grandfaither, that's what,' replied Scott.

'I don't know what yous are on aboot!'

'We have an eyewitness – saw everything.'

'Aye, right. Who's that? Another bloody stranger, I bet.' Gordon looked suddenly uncomfortable.

'At six-forty this evening, you were seen arriving at this house, just as your grandfather appeared from the other end of the street,' said Daley. 'Our witness tells us that some kind of argument ensued in the street – a heated one, by all accounts.'

'Nah, that's no' right. Yous are at it!'

'For whatever reason, you chose to push your elderly grandfather, who fell, hitting his head heavily on the pavement. He'd been drinking all afternoon, as you knew.'

'Aye, but here's the best bit,' said Scott, spitting out the words. 'Instead o' helping the man – your ain grandfaither – who's now unconscious in the street, you do something else.'

'This is shite!'

'You're right there. Shite's the very word I'd use. Instead o' helping your grandfaither, you go through his pocket for money – and find some, tae.'

'Naw! No way, man – yous canna frame me tae save that mob next door . . .' Gordon reached behind him, grabbed one of the candlesticks from the mantelpiece, and brandished it at the officers. 'Get oot my way, or I'm tellin' you, yous are getting this o'er the heid!'

As he tried to barge past Daley, Scott caught him with a rabbit punch to the top of his bulging stomach, sending him to the floor howling in pain and gasping for breath.

Daley and Scott looked on approvingly as Annie fussed over the guests in the dining room at the County Hotel. The Karim children stared around the room at the Christmas decorations, their eyes wide with curiosity. Mrs Karim held her husband's hand, looking into his eyes lovingly.

'What are people all about?' Daley said to no one in particular.

'Och, all's well that ends well, Mr Daley.' Hamish was at his shoulder. 'The toon's fair buzzin' wae the gossip. They tell me three folk jeest walked past auld Tam as he was lying on the pavement – aye, including the minister fae the Lochend Church.'

'I don't understand it. Why?' asked Daley.

'Because they a' thought he was drunk,' said Scott, handing Daley a large whisky. 'No' an unusual occurrence, so I'm told. Only Faiz Karim came tae his aid. And look where that nearly got him.'

'Do you know what his job was in Libya, Bri? Before everything kicked off, I mean,' said Daley.

'No, what?'

'A nurse. Saved a few lives on the journey here, by all accounts.'

'An' he comes here and gets arrested for helping a man lying in the street. Makes you wonder,' said Scott.

'Here, I'm jeest thinking,' said Hamish. 'Is it no' jeest the perfect parable fae the bible.'

'What are you on aboot, Hamish?' said Scott with a grin. 'Did you share a glass or two wae auld Arbuthnot earlier?'

They looked on as Annie served the family with big bowls of steaming lentil soup.

'Och, have you no religion at a', Sergeant Scott. "But a Samaritan, as he travelled took pity on him." Luke, chapter ten, if I'm no' much mistaken. Sure, man o' the cloth passed by on the other side o' the road that day, tae. Karim – he's a modern good Samaritan!'

'I hope people remember that,' said Daley.

'Don't you worry. Folk in Kinloch are no' all like Tam Arbuthnot, I'm pleased tae say – no, no' by a long chalk. You'll see, Mr Daley.'

Daley smiled. He had no doubt that Hamish was right, but he couldn't help thinking of the many for whom refuge in a place like Kinloch must seem like an impossible dream. Still, the Karims were, at last, safe.

Notes

Dalintober Moon

This short story was written to help the Dalintober Beach Regeneration Fund. My thanks and best wishes to James MacLean and the rest of the committee. Thanks, too, are due to Fraser McNair for the wonderful photograph on the eBook. To see more of Fraser's work go to www.jfmcnair.com. Special thanks to my old mate Eddie Mitchell, now in Adelaide, who prompted an idea to form in my muddled brain.

Empty Nets and Promises

I would like to thank my old friend Andrew Robertson, who comes from a family of Campbeltown fishermen. He kindly helped me to understand the background and feel of fishing in the sixties, based on the experiences and stories of his late father, himself the skipper of the Campbeltown fleet. He followed in those formidable footsteps, becoming a fisherman himself. Few of us can imagine the dangers and discomforts faced by these men in the course of their daily toil. Tragically, many lost, and still lose, their lives. I dedicate this story to those fishermen.

One of my earliest memories as a small child in the late sixties was catching a glimpse of Concorde, the supersonic passenger jet then being flight-tested in the skies above Kintyre. If you missed the sight of the aircraft, you couldn't fail to hear the loud sonic boom as it broke the sound barrier. In a way, this plane heralded the dawn of a new age in the decade that defined much of the modern world in which we now live. Though Concorde itself no longer flashes through our skies, new and faster ways to travel will continue to shrink our world.

The airbase at Machrihanish, then in the hands of the RAF, was the site chosen for this testing because of the length of its runway. Indeed, it is one of the reasons that Kintyre may yet find itself the location of the UK's spaceport – another massive leap forward.

Again, back in the late sixties, you would have found a busy fishing port at Campbeltown, with small wooden boats crowded in the space between the town's twin piers. Sadly, modern fishing methods, combined with almost inexplicable political interference, have led to a catastrophic decline in the numbers of fish in our seas, and the fishing fleet in Campbeltown, as elsewhere, now numbers only a handful of boats.

Andrew Robertson, the ex-Campbeltown fisherman mentioned above, looked back on this loss with much regret. He lamented the disappearance of the fair contest between fish and man, as larger vessels worked together trawling the sea, giving their quarry no chance of escape, or time to replenish.

Fishing became a massive industry in the eighties. Many of my former classmates made my eyes water with tales of the money they were making back then. It didn't last, and the connection between the fishermen of Kintyre and the sea, which lasted for hundreds, perhaps thousands of years, has almost been lost. Hopefully, as modern and better informed attitudes prevail, sustainable fishing will again become the norm.

I have tried to capture a fictional taste of a life at the fishing, which – almost as a by-product – spawned such wonderful yarns, songs and poetry. For a more factual account of these days, and long before, please seek out the works of Freddie Gillies and Angus Martin, both great chroniclers of times past in Kintyre.

Two One Three/Single End

As readers will note, the Glasgow (and indeed the police force) Daley finds himself in at the beginning of his career is very different to the newly minted Police Scotland in which he and Scott ply their trade in the novels. His fictional career happens to span times of great change in both policing and society.

The Glasgow of the mid-1980s to 1990s was a city in flux. The days of industrial pre-eminence were reaching their death throes as the dear green place sought a future. Looking at Glasgow now, with its state-of-the-art architecture, welcoming shops, galleries, museums, restaurants, pubs and clubs, it is hard to imagine the dark days of the recent past.

Likewise, the police service has changed: the old six-feet-tall 'heilan'' bobbies were replaced by graduates, with the support of the very latest policing techniques and paraphernalia.

Times change, but I think it's fair to say that a cop from 1980 would have more in common with their counterpart of 1880 than the officer taking his or her place in 2018. Ultimately, progress, regardless of how one views it, is inevitable.

One Last Dram Before Midnight/The Silent Man

There is indeed a necklace, crafted using Whitby jet, on display at Campbeltown's wonderful little museum. It's been around for four thousand years and was clearly made for a person of high status who lived within a society it is almost impossible for us to imagine.

That the material used to make this beautiful piece is from what is now North Yorkshire suggests that the ancient people of Kintyre were neither insular nor parochial and likely traded with folk from across these islands and, who knows, far beyond.

These days Campbeltown is still considered a remote destination, most often reached by the long and winding road from Glasgow. As I've mentioned before, it is strategically situated for good access by sea from all directions and the ferry from the Ayshire coast is a great development.

One thing is for sure: however you choose to travel there, like almost nowhere else remaining in Scotland, you can still feel that echo of the past. Do make time to sample it before the future finds this wonderful, unique corner of the world.

Acknowledgements

For a long time, it seemed as though the art of short-story writing had been forgotten – viewed as out of fashion and favoured by neither publishers nor readers. However, much in the industry has changed over the last ten years, or so. More people are reading, and there are most certainly many more writers.

We live in a demanding, time-hungry world. For those keen to consume a full story in a short space of time – before bed, or on the train, for example – this form provides the ideal solution. Indeed, writers are liberated to try something new, perhaps a new angle on a character or setting, even a new source of inspiration entirely.

Though the art of short-story writing isn't for every wordsmith, I must admit to really enjoying it. I'm delighted that my publisher Polygon has seen fit to present my collection to date in this anthology. The reader will find out more about the young Daley and Scott; more of Kinloch, past and present; and for those yet to discover the DCI Daley novels, a mouth-watering taster.

As always, a huge thanks to the people of Kintyre, who have embraced my outpourings with such kindness and enthusiasm. Also to Hugh Andrew and my indefatigable editor Alison Rae, who saw enough to give me a new career (another one). Thanks too to my formidably inspirational agent Anne Williams of KHLA in London. Dealing with me isn't always easy! Finally, to my family – Fiona, Rachel and Sian – who will absolutely agree with my previous assertion.

And to you, dear reader, go on, take the trip to Campbeltown. Many have already done so and, to a man and woman, those who have contacted me have loved it. I'm sure you will too!

D.A.M.
Gartocharn
September 2017

The DCI Daley thriller series

Whisky from Small Glasses

DCI Jim Daley is sent from the city to investigate a murder after the body of a woman is washed up on an idyllic beach on the west coast of Scotland. Far away from urban resources, he finds himself a stranger in a close-knit community.

Love, betrayal, fear and death stalk the small town as Daley investigates a case that becomes more deadly than he could possibly imagine, in this compelling novel infused with intrigue and dark humour.

The Last Witness

James Machie was a man with a genius for violence, his criminal empire spreading beyond Glasgow into the UK and mainland Europe. Fortunately, James Machie is dead, assassinated in the back of a prison ambulance following his trial and conviction. But now, five years later, he is apparently back from the grave, set on avenging himself on those who brought him down. Top of his list is his previous associate, Frank MacDougall, who, unbeknownst to DCI Jim Daley, is living under protection on his lochside patch, the small Scottish town of Kinloch. Daley knows that, having been the key to Machie's conviction, his old friend and colleague DS

Scott is almost as big a target. And nothing, not even death, has ever stood in James Machie's way . . .

Dark Suits and Sad Songs

When a senior Edinburgh civil servant spectacularly takes his own life in Kinloch harbour, DCI Jim Daley comes face to face with the murky world of politics. To add to his woes, two local drug dealers lie dead, ritually assassinated. It's clear that dark forces are at work in the town. With his boss under investigation, his marriage hanging by a thread, and his side-kick DS Scott wrestling with his own demons, Daley's world is in meltdown. When strange lights appear in the sky over Kinloch, it becomes clear that the townsfolk are not the only people at risk. The fate of nations is at stake. Jim Daley must face his worst fears as tragedy strikes. This is not just about a successful investigation, it's about survival.

The Rat Stone Serenade

It's December, and the Shannon family are heading to their clifftop mansion near Kinloch for their AGM. Shannon International is one of the world's biggest private companies, with tendrils reaching around the globe in computing, banking and mineral resourcing, and it has brought untold wealth and privilege to the family. However, a century ago, Archibald Shannon stole the land upon which he built their home – and his descendants have been cursed ever since.

When heavy snow cuts off Kintyre, DCI Jim Daley and DS Brian Scott are assigned to protect their illustrious visitors. But ghosts of the past are coming to haunt the Shannons. As the curse decrees, death is coming – but for whom and from what?

Well of the Winds

As World War Two nears its end, a man is stabbed to death on the Kinloch shoreline, in the shadow of the great warships in the harbour. Many years later, the postman on Gairsay, a tiny island off the coast of Kintyre, discovers that the Bremner family are missing from their farm. There's a pot on the stove and food on the table, but of the Bremners there is no sign.

When DCI Daley comes into possession of a journal written by his wartime predecessor in Kinloch, Inspector William Urquhart, he soon realises that the Isle of Gairsay has many secrets. Assisted by his indomitable deputy, DS Brian Scott, and new boss, Chief Superintendent Carrie Symington, Daley must solve a wartime murder to uncover the shocking events of the present.